The Vermilion Riddle

Dana Li

Mt Zion Ridge Press LLC

Mt Zion Ridge Press LLC
295 Gum Springs Rd, NW
Georgetown, TN 37366

https://www.mtzionridgepress.com

ISBN 13: 978-1-949564-97-6

Published in the United States of America
Publication Date: March 1, 2022
Copyright 2022 by Dana Li

Editor-In-Chief: Michelle Levigne
Executive Editor: Tamera Lynn Kraft

Cover art design by Tamera Lynn Kraft
 Cover Art Copyright by Mt Zion Ridge Press LLC © 2021

Dedication

For Mom and Dad. I stand on the shoulders of giants.

Acknowledgments

The Vermilion Riddle is a pipe dream that came true and I didn't make it happen alone. I want to thank my publisher, Mt. Zion Ridge Press. If not for them, this would be another overly long document, languishing on my hard drive. Michelle Levigne, my editor, helped me take *The Vermilion Riddle* from a story with potential to a story I could publish. Her enthusiasm for the world of Japha and its characters kept me going through the rounds of editing. Tamera Kraft took a chance on a first-time author, answered all my newbie questions, and worked patiently with me to create a beautiful cover.

Oluwasanya Awe diligently and expertly designed the map of Japha. He has a knack for taking my rambling requests and creating a beautiful product. I'm grateful for such a talented friend and designer.

I don't have a degree in English or creative writing. My best teachers in the craft were other authors, most whom I have never met, and some who are no longer with us. But the beauty of writing is that their lessons and stories outlive them. Thank you to C.S. Lewis, J.R.R. Tolkien, Jane Austen, Lois Lowry, Harper Lee, and Khaled Hosseini, among others. Your books inspired and shaped me.

I owe a debt to the wonderful Realm Makers community as well. They've introduced me to fun-loving, fantasy/science fiction nerds, pointed me toward publishing opportunities, and helped me form a critique group. Shout out to the Mithril Makers - Amy, Jennifer, Elissa and Jason - who have supported me on this journey.

Though I grew up as a quiet, shy bookworm, God blessed me with a rich community in my family and friends. My Mom and Dad have always had my back, even when they weren't sure about my writing dreams (no one in our family has done this!). But they have been my biggest supporters in all things. Kai, my fiancé, has let me suck him into my favorite fandoms and joined me in storytelling ventures. But best of all, he's taking me with him on a lifelong adventure, which I'm sure will be just as good as the ones in my favorite books.

More friends than I can list have been an important part of my life over the years. Veronica, Nichole, Carrie, Angie, Chewie, and Jennifer have been my dear sisters in Christ and confidantes for over a decade. They have been there for me in moments of joy and in trials, and I'm grateful I can celebrate this achievement with them. Fight on! I'm also incredibly thankful for my community at Creekside Bible Church. Thank you to my friends, mentors, and pastors who have walked alongside me these past few years. There are many of you, and I particularly want to thank the ladies who I've been privileged to share life with in small group, as well as my "pandemic crew." From summer picnics to arduous hikes, these friendships have made life sweet, even in turbulent times.

Finally, thank you to my readers. It's an investment of time and energy to pick up any book. I truly hope you enjoy the ride.

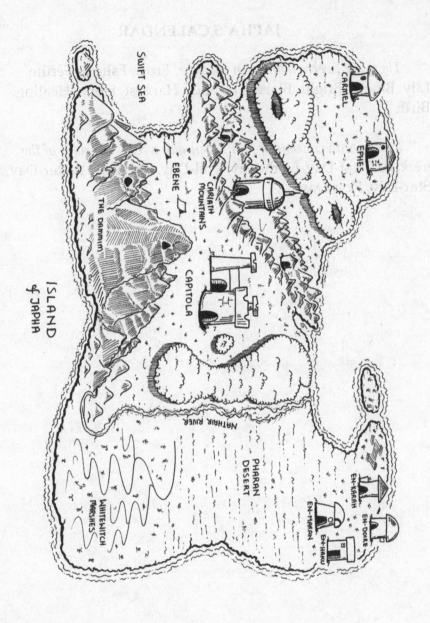

JAPHA'S CALENDAR

There are twelve months in the year: Frost, Fallow, Fertile, Lily, Bloom, Bright, Blaze, Thunder, Harvest, Hope, Healing, Birth

Each month consists of four seven-day weeks. The days of the week are: First-Day, Oath-Day, Toil-Day, Fire-Day, Water-Day, Star-Day, Rest-Day

PROLOGUE

Oath-breaker Camp, Island of Japha.
Month of Fallow: Second week, Toil-Day.

The bonfire sputtered and gasped as a constant *pitter-patter* of rain fell over the camp. A troop of men emerged out of the darkness with chopped wood, tossing it into the flames. A violent orange blaze shot upward with a loud hiss.

Benedict coiled the black cloak around himself, his sharp knuckles and angles stretching the fabric thin. The southern air pierced his skin with bitter cold. Their feeble tents around the fire flapped in the wind, and a brief, uncomfortable recollection of Cariath's fair climate crept into his mind. Cariath — just thirty-five leagues east of them, but it would never be home again.

He turned his gaze in that direction, where the faint glow of light behind the mountains illuminated their peaks. Before he could crush the mental image, Benedict pictured a hearty fire roaring on red-hot coals and the Marshals gathered for dinner around the marble table in his father's house. Outside, pinpricks of light sprang from the homes that dotted Cariath Valley. A silent ache cut through his breastbone.

"Fox!"

All the men recognized that tone of cold steel. Still, Benedict hated hearing his name wrung through the metal-clad voice.

"Nimrod," Benedict acknowledged, and rose to his feet.

The other man strode over from the direction of his tent. Even before he orchestrated the Oath-breaker mutiny, he bore an air of arrogant authority. Benedict wondered at how he had restrained himself under the thumb of the Guardians, and in particular, the Old Fox's rule, for years.

Nimrod stared hard at him, but Benedict returned his gaze. A glimmer of cynical amusement touched him. Did the man think an Oath-breaker, who forsook blood and kin, would cower beneath a frown?

Moments passed before Nimrod turned aside. He motioned to the tents. "Come in. I need a word with you." His tone was dispassionate.

Benedict trailed behind Nimrod. He passed a few men he knew vaguely, and they nodded at him. Hound, Nimrod's loyal watchdog, caught his eye and made a swift throat-slashing motion. He grimaced but ignored it. Nimrod was cruel, but he was also fair. He did not punish on whim, he showed no favoritism, and he gave his men their due. A merciless meritocracy — and the double-edged blade cut both ways.

He can fault me for nothing but my name.

Once inside, Nimrod motioned for him to take a seat. He paced the length of the tent with his hands clasped behind his back as Benedict watched him. He wore tightly laced knee-high boots and a black and gold leather vest. His square jaw and raven hair gave him a stern, almost handsome look.

"Of all the men who followed me, you surprised me most," he began. "You leave a wound on the name of your family."

"And the rest of you do not?"

"Not many of us bear the name of Fox." Nimrod paused in his step and locked gazes with him.

"Your concern for our honor is touching," Benedict returned, holding his stare.

Nimrod twisted his lips into a sharp smile. "You have always been bright, Benedict," he said half-mockingly. "So you must understand that I will have my doubts about whether we are of one accord, or you come with other motives."

As a spy for the Old Fox. Benedict heard his unspoken accusation.

He felt a trace of anxiety but maintained a stoic expression. Nimrod was testing him, and Benedict could sense the significance of this moment as the blood hummed in his ears. A strange recklessness began stirring inside him.

"The quandary of all great men," Benedict replied. "Climb too high, and you fear someone will dethrone you."

"Spare me your philosophy," he growled.

"This isn't philosophy. It's a preface. I have an offer to make you."

Nimrod gave him a death-glare. "Be cautious of your place, Fox. We are no longer Guardians here. You chose to follow me."

"I understand." Benedict nodded, but his trepidation dissolved as he felt a subtle change, like Nimrod's grasp of the upper hand was slipping. "Allow me to make a deduction. You believe you have three options, none of them favorable. You can either turn me away, but then you fear I could return home and inform the Guardians of your strategy. You can kill me, but you're short on soldiers and that would damage the men's respect for you. Or you can keep me in your army and live with the uncertainty of my true allegiance."

"You're treading thin ice," Nimrod muttered, tapping his foot. "What is your offer?"

"Make me your second-in-command."

Before he could react, Nimrod seized the brooch of Benedict's cloak and jerked him forward, so his face was inches away. "You must have a death wish," he growled, his expression livid.

Benedict did not move, but when he felt Nimrod relax slightly, he twisted himself out of his grip. He held out his hand to keep Nimrod from coming close, and laid his other hand on the hilt of his sword.

"My talents will be at your disposal. I would be unable to hide treason from you. And," Benedict paused for effect, "you are giving me a stake in this game that I would be loath to lose."

"Make a Fox my second, when I have men like Hound in my ranks?" he scoffed.

"If you prefer someone who knows how to tear out throats to someone who knows how to win the endgame," Benedict countered.

"*I* know how to win the endgame. I don't need another."

"Arrogance lost the war in Arieh's day. And there is no one this time to make a noble sacrifice if you fail."

Nimrod fell silent and paced the floor with his gaze intent on the ground. Benedict kept his hand on the sword hilt, but his heart soared in triumph—he knew he held the advantage now.

"You must swear me an oath," he said finally. "Swear me an oath of fealty."

Benedict let loose a harsh laugh. "Would that give you peace? I'm an Oath-breaker, Nimrod...just as you and all the men in this camp are. We broke faith with a tradition as old as time. Would you trust a pledge I make to you now?"

Nimrod growled, a guttural sound emitting from the base of his throat, but before he could speak, Benedict held up his hand and continued, "An oath will not hold me. It did not hold you—because you value something above honor."

"You never had any interest in power, Fox."

"I never said power is the thing I want most." Benedict felt the dull ache inside him again, snaking through his chest.

Nimrod raised a thin brow. "Retribution." A flicker of understanding entered his eyes as he appraised Benedict. "Only those who love too much seek vengeance." He paused, almost thoughtful. "And yet, it is a hot and bloody motive that is hard to exhaust."

His words pressed like a sharp knife on the ache in Benedict's chest. He hated that Nimrod could see through him, but he squashed the storm rising inside him. "Well, then?"

"I will accept your offer." Nimrod moved toward him so his face was inches away again. "But know that if you cross me, you can answer to the gods after I hew you to pieces."

A grim smile chiseled its way across his face. "Do not think the gods are on your side in this war, Nimrod."

Benedict turned away and strode out of the tent without a backward glance. A crowd of men huddled nearby, likely eavesdropping. They looked on him with renewed esteem and—perhaps—a hint of fear. He caught sight of Justin, his oldest friend, his face half-shadowed beside the fire. Benedict gave him a nod but marched straight to his tent and disappeared inside, collapsing on his thin cot.

Images of the Guardians filled his mind again, quickly drowning the euphoric high of besting Nimrod's politics. His thoughts wandered back to the day Justin arrived at Fox Manor's doorstep, wearing a lost orphan's look. That vulnerability vanished long ago, but whether he was warmed by the Old Fox's fatherly doting or hardened by Guardian training, Benedict could not say. He shook off the memory. Victory left only a sour aftertaste in his mouth and he fell into an uneasy slumber.

CHAPTER 1

Carmel, Island of Japha.
Month of Thunder: Third week, Oath-day.

Leah Edwards took a large sip of tea, feeling the heat swirl through her mouth and down her throat. She let out a jasmine-scented breath, watching the window before her table fog over unevenly. Outside, a bed of crisp autumn leaves covered the mossy ground and the skies were painted with gray clouds. Autumn always descended swiftly and without warning upon Carmel.

The loud clattering noises of pots in the kitchen jostled with the tones of a staccato piano piece downstairs. Leah caught a whiff of Mama's baked tilapia, a probable sign that a guest would be dining with the family.

"Shay, that high note was wrong." Mama's shrill voice sounded from the kitchen.

"I just learned this piece," Shay retorted, accompanied by a singular dissonant chord struck with fervor. Before Mama could speak again, she began a new melody.

Leah padded down the stairs and sat at the kitchen table, an unusual restlessness in her body. Mama, with her cream-colored apron about her waist, scurried around the kitchen with small bowls and frying pans. The living room space adjoining the kitchen was cluttered, barely fitting their two couches and upright piano. Books were scattered everywhere — most of them Leah's — to Mama's perpetual ire, and the coffee tables were worn with unruly scratch marks. Down a small corridor was the master bedroom, while Leah and her two sisters lived upstairs.

"Dinnertime," Mama called, balancing two large plates on the palms of her hands as she moved to the dining table. "Leah! How long have you been sitting here? Find Nyssa, quick, before the food goes cold."

Leah rose from her chair, but Shay skipped in and said, "Nyssa is dining at the Langfords'." She smiled, a mischievous glint in her brown eyes. "Mr. Langford has taken an extraordinary interest in our sister."

Leah thought a shadow of hurt passed over Mama's expression, but it came and went quickly, so she dismissed it as mere imagination.

"Well then, let us wish Nyssa well in earning his favor," their mother said with an almost forced cheeriness. "Your father will not be joining us either."

"Oh! But you made your best dish." Leah shot a puzzled look at Shay, who simply raised her shoulders and looked toward their mother. Baked

5

tilapia with saffron and paprika was her specialty.

"We don't need guests to enjoy ourselves, do we?" she replied stiffly. Without looking for a response, she settled into her seat and began spooning potatoes onto her plate.

Leah exchanged a bewildered look with Shay. Her appetite vanished, and she took only small portions from each dish. Her stomach churned as she swallowed the food, but she forced herself to chew vigorously to avoid the appearance of awkwardness. She unconsciously gripped her utensils tightly, leaving faint, red crease lines along her fingers.

Whenever their usually boisterous mother became reticent, something significant was amiss. One time, it was her disappointment at not being invited to a large dinner party in Carmel, and another time it was when an ardent suitor of Nyssa's disappeared from town without a trace, leaving only the wretched girl behind. Mrs. Edwards, a woman of high decorum, rarely lost her head in front of others, but her family knew she had a talent for remembering ancient grievances.

They ate in silence, and Mama made no remark even as Leah stacked the pale fish bones on her plate to make stick-like figures of men, a poor habit from childhood she never shook off. The silence was only broken by the clinks of silverware against dishes.

Shay, not nearly as able as Leah to bear uncomfortable silences, cut through the stillness. "Where is Papa?"

Mama paused in the middle of a mouthful. She swallowed, set her utensils down on the table, straightened her blouse, and looked Shay in the eye. "Your father is in town," she said primly. "He's settling some debts."

"Oh." Concern dawned on Shay's expression. "Are we having money trouble?"

Mama averted her gaze. A shiver ran down Leah's spine and curled around it. Mr. Edwards was known for his gambling problem and often his lack of social propriety—the complete opposite of his wife. Much of the livelihood he had saved from his youthful days was lost on card tables and risky investments. Yet, in spite of his weakness, Leah could never stay angry with her warm, doting father.

"Let us just say," Mama responded finally, "that we ought to be pleased if Nyssa captures Mr. Langford's heart. And if the two of you find suitors of your own quickly." Here, she raised an eyebrow at Leah, who was known to find the faults of every man her family took an interest in.

"Mama, are we losing the estate?" Leah's voice was quiet, and a few seconds passed before Shay registered her sister's query and swung her head around in shock.

"Of course not," Shay breathed. "How could you ask such a thing? This house has been the property of Edwards for generations."

Leah ignored her, and watched Mama, who was folding her handkerchief up precisely from edge to edge. A sigh escaped her lips.

6

"When I married your father, he was a kind soul with a large inheritance. For women in those times, the latter was sufficient and the former unlooked for. They married for security, not love. But your father — he loved me." Mama's gaze was fixed on the wooden table, but there was a faraway look in her brown eyes. "So what if he was a bit of a gambler?" Her voice wavered for a moment between weary and bitter, as if she could not decide which emotion dwarfed the other.

Shay's eyes were wide as she stared at their mother, but Leah simply looked out the window. Dusk was falling along with crimson-golden leaves.

Mama stood from her chair calmly, her gaze focused again and her hands steady. "I don't know about the estate. Your father will be home tonight to tell us the verdict." She stacked the dinner plates and carried them to the kitchen sink, her spongy slippers squeaking as they pressed against the hardwood.

~~~~~

The front door closed loudly, followed by Nyssa's high voice bleeding through the walls of the house. From her bedroom, Leah heard Shay's lithe and rapid footsteps traveling down the stairwell to greet their eldest sister. The two girls were close, though Leah thought their relationship was more one-sided than Shay perceived; Nyssa was loving but sometimes manipulative, a quality Leah was too keenly aware of in others, which often put her at odds with her sister.

Nyssa's words drifted up through Leah's closed door. "It was a darling place, and Mr. Langford and his family were charming."

Threads of inaudible conversation wove between the sisters before Leah heard Shay say, "We may lose the estate. Papa has been gambling."

"How will any of us be eligible after such a catastrophe?" Nyssa exclaimed. "He can't just ruin us like that."

Indignation rushed through Leah's veins. She turned off the gas lamp in her room and climbed between her cotton sheets. She rubbed her feet together to alleviate the chill and closed her eyes, wondering if her sisters measured all things by their profitability in attracting suitors. Despite her father's flaws, Leah remained stubbornly loyal to him, finding his weakness for money more easily forgivable than the inconstancies of the women in the family, with emotions and opinions that shifted like the shadows.

"His proposal will come swiftly," Shay was saying. "It's Leah and I who will be the greatest victims of this misfortune. No man of any prestige will look twice upon a woman disgraced and penniless."

"Don't make such grim prophecies, Shay. At the least, you will always be welcome in my home." Nyssa spoke lightly and with an air of detachment.

The conversation fell silent, and Leah heard footsteps on the stairwell, then past her door. She released a breath she hardly knew she was holding, as neither Nyssa nor Shay came to her room, leaving her alone with her thoughts.

Well, if I cannot marry a prestigious man, I will simply marry a good one, Leah thought. The loss did not seem like one, and the sting it had on Shay was lost on her.

CHAPTER 2

Leah awoke, bleary-eyed, to sunlight streaming mercilessly through her window, a strange contrast to the dreary weather of the day before. Burying her face in her pillow, she savored the sweet moments of drowsy stupor, but they were dashed to pieces as the recollection of yesterday's bleak dinner conversation charged into her mind like a wild stallion. Shaking the sleep from her eyes, Leah quickly rose from her bed, threw on a warm robe, and stumbled down the stairwell into the kitchen.

Mama was setting hard boiled eggs and slices of toast with honey onto the table, while Papa sat in his usual chair, reading the morning paper with his spectacles barely held up by the bridge of his nose. Leah could not perceive whether the silence between them was amiable or hostile as she pulled out a chair and took an egg from the porcelain plate.

"Good morning," Leah said, with forced cheerfulness.

Papa set the paper aside on the floor. "Good morning, Leah. Did you sleep well?"

"Yes, though it was bright awfully early." Leah gingerly tapped the egg against the table and turned it in a circle to crack the shell open.

"Jessie Lane sent word to you this morning, Leah," Mama called from inside the kitchen. "She wants to meet you at the park after breakfast for a morning stroll."

"I would be out of that house as often as I could too, if I lived with Mrs. Lane right now," Leah's father commented with a wink.

Leah felt a laugh rising in her throat and covered her mouth to keep from choking up egg yolk. All of Carmel had either seen or heard through first-hand witnesses of Mrs. Lane's frantic shopping trail, particularly winding through clothing and jewelry stores. Her eldest daughter, Laurel, Jessie's sister, was recently proposed to by the highly regarded Mr. Whitefield, and most of the town knew she was marrying up the social ladder. Mrs. Lane was intent on finding the perfect dress and decorations for Laurel's wedding, leading some to wonder wryly whether it was Mrs. Lane or her daughter who was getting married.

"Nonsense," Mama said as she stepped out from the kitchen, wiping her hands on her apron. "I overheard your father telling Mr. Lane what a fortunate man he was for having such a handsome wife."

"Common courtesy. Would you prefer I told him his wife was an eyesore?"

"A bit rude, but you'll hear no objection from me." Mama raised her eyebrows and sat down at the table.

Papa shared a secret smile with Leah, who felt her mood lighten considerably, as if a hefty burden were lifted from her shoulders. She loved listening to the playful banter between her parents, a tacit indication that the passing years had not snuffed out all flames of love and affection.

Loath to spoil the moment, Leah decided to skirt the subject of money and the estate. Instead, she swept the eggshell crumbs from the table and stood up. "I need to dress and meet Jessie. I'll be home by lunch hour."

Leah donned a simple white dress with a matching bonnet and left the house before either Nyssa or Shay awoke. The town was already bustling with people: horse-drawn carriages rolling down the roads, women huddled close together over tea on patios, and children chasing each other through the small shops and alleyways. Flurries of conversations filled the air, punctuated by the occasional high-pitched laugh or childish scream. The smell of freshly baked bread and sticky cakes wafted from nearby bakeries and filled Leah's nostrils.

She veered off the broad paths onto a beaten trail with unkempt moss and spidery branches. Pushing through the tangled shrubbery, Leah caught a glimpse of Jessie on a small bench in the open green fields ahead and called out to her.

The girl turned and sprang to her feet. "Leah!"

The two greeted each other with exuberance. Jessie squeezed Leah's arms tightly and said, "You look lovely today, and are just the sight these poor eyes needed. I was going to lose my wits at home."

"I thought they vanished long ago," Leah returned.

"You are right as usual." Jessie laughed, swatting her arm lightly. "Let's walk around the pond today."

Jessie was a slender young woman of twenty-four, Leah's age, with brown hair and blue-green eyes like the sea. Her lithe form and petite features drew men in hordes, yet the protective eye of her mother constantly guarded her. She was high-spirited but sweet, and often reminded Leah of Nyssa without the manipulation and cat-and-mouse games her sister was so proficient in employing.

"How is the future Mrs. Whitefield?" Leah raised an eyebrow comically.

"Wonderful, but it comes at an expense for the rest of us," Jessie sighed, "Mother can't stop running her mouth about Laurel and Mr. Whitefield to folk both in and out of the family. She's a complete embarrassment."

"She'll turn her attention to you next," she warned, then slanted her gaze toward her friend. "Though you have been very quiet on the subject of men."

"Because I'm perfectly sick of them. Mother would never hear of any suitors for me until Laurel was married and settled anyway." Jessie paused in her tracks and turned to grab Leah's arm. "But did you hear of the new gentleman in town?"

Leah shook her head and laughed, mirth twinkling in her dark eyes. "That, coming on the heels of saying you are sick of men!"

Jessie waved her hand. "Oh, Leah, you know I overstate sometimes. This man," she lowered her voice, "is purchasing Edenbridge. The haunted manor."

"That's only a legend." Yet Leah was still surprised by Jessie's revelation.

Edenbridge had had no occupants for decades, and the rumors around it grew more outrageous over the years. A few potential buyers had floated stories of ghostly encounters and hidden passageways. Leah felt certain most of it was hyperbole. After sitting empty for over twenty years, Edenbridge was considered public property, which meant the government of Carmel was its owner. Ever since King Amir appointed Governor Maris to oversee Carmel, the quality of public properties improved significantly as he regularly dispatched workers to maintain vacant residences.

"His name is Mr. Fox," Jessie paused, "and they say he's from Cariath."

Leah felt a thrill of disbelief. The only visitors Carmel received came from nearby villages like Ephes, and even those caused a stir in their insular town. The geography kept the outlying towns, like Carmel and Ephes, which bordered the Swift Sea, isolated from the other parts of Japha. Carmel's smalltown culture also meant families stayed there for generations. Rarely did anyone move to other parts of the island. And though they were near the harbor, the last few monarchs instituted an isolationist policy that limited travel to other nations.

Cariath was home to the Guardians, warriors who dedicated their lives to preserving the peace between men and faeries. None of them had visited Carmel in ages, and the passage of time almost dimmed them into myths. Amir's government dismissed them as nothing more than a religious sect, but Leah's history books indicated a previous era when Guardians were key political influencers.

"Sounds like a suitable match for a haunted manor," she said with a touch of sarcasm.

"Well, Mr. Fox certainly seems more flesh than ghost, what with ginger hair and dark eyes."

"You've seen him already?" Leah pictured a grim man dressed in black from head to toe, and it sent an icy shiver down her backbone. But the make-believe portrait fell out of her mind as a distant bluebird sang and she breathed in a lungful of the crisp, cold air. Dark mysteries and men did not visit Carmel, and if they did, they would certainly be shattered by the effervescent brightness of the town and its people.

"No, but that is how I've heard him described. You are late on the news." Jessie shook her finger half-mockingly, an impish smile on her face.

"You are too absurd sometimes."

"And you are too prudent. That is not all," Jessie added. "I heard he will throw a large party at his new manor and all the town is invited."

"You know how I feel about parties." Leah thrust her foot at a pinecone in her path, watching it fly then splash in the still pond.

"You can endure some discomfort for a chance at love. Since you have soundly rejected all current inhabitants of Carmel." She smiled, baring a strip of white teeth.

"So my hope now lies in a mysterious man out of myth?" she teased.

"Yes, that seems to fit you."

They both laughed, but Leah said wryly, "Love is only a dream in our world. Prospective mothers-in-law snatch men up faster than fresh fruit at the market."

"Such cynicism!" Jessie glowered at her with mock disbelief, taking her by the arm and steering them to a bench, an island in the grassy meadow. "Something is the matter with you, and we won't leave until you tell me." She crossed her arms, her lower lip protruding in a stubborn pout.

Leah grimaced. She kept her tone light, but her friend knew her too well. Dour thoughts of the fate of the Edwards estate broke across Leah's mind. As much as she tried to shake the subject from her mind, it clung to her like a leech, souring even the bright autumn day and the merry company of Jessie.

"It's nothing," Leah replied vaguely. "I simply don't love parties, and Mr. Fox sounds beyond my social reach, Cariath or not."

"Nonsense, you are from a respectable family and one of the most sensible ladies in all of Carmel," Jessie said loyally.

"If only fortune were as kind as you," she said before she could stop herself.

Jessie wrinkled her forehead and locked eyes with her, blue-green to brown. "Is it your father?"

"We may lose the estate." The words were blunt, startling even Leah as they escaped her mouth and cut through the air. She felt like she was bleeding somewhere.

Silence hung in the air for a moment, and then Jessie flung her arm around her shoulders. "Oh, Leah. I don't know what to say — but is it settled yet?"

She shook her head. "I couldn't bring myself to ask this morning. Nyssa and Shay will surely find out from Papa, and we will all know. God help us, I believe the whole town will know soon."

"Well, it will not change my opinion of you in the least, and if the people of Carmel have any sense, they would follow suit."

"Thank you." Leah mustered a smile, but Jessie's kind words did nothing for the cold pit in her stomach. She lost all desire to return home and hear the ruling on the estate.

Unfortunately, Jessie rose to her feet and pulled Leah up with her. "It's time we go back." Her expression livening, she added, "You must promise me you will come to the party Mr. Fox puts on, otherwise you will be leaving me treacherously alone."

"I will be there. I'm sure my family will see to it anyway," she promised reluctantly.

With that, the two women made their way through the park and back to the main roads of the town. They parted near the bakery shop, Jessie once again extracting her word that she would attend the gathering Mr. Fox would host. Leah then hurried back to the Edwards estate with the noonday sun beating down heavily on her, her footfalls feeling like lead in spite of her lightweight slipper-shoes.

~~~~~

All of the Edwards were lounging around the living room when Leah entered the house. Nyssa and Shay were reading a card, each gripping one side of it, animated expressions on their faces. Papa and Mama were leisurely eating cold-cut sandwiches with tea, talking in quiet tones.

"There are sandwiches in the kitchen for you," Mrs. Edwards called.

Leah untied her bonnet and hung it on the stairwell banister. She wiped her forehead and unwound her brown hair from the tight knot behind her head. As she made her way into the kitchen, Nyssa leapt from her seat and followed her.

"Leah! There's a new gentleman in town, and you won't believe what estate he just bought," her sister said, her indigo eyes glowing.

"Mr. Fox at Edenbridge, I assume?" Leah reached for a cold turkey and lettuce sandwich, suddenly ravenously hungry as her teeth sank into the meat.

Surprise crossed Nyssa's face. "How did you—oh, Jessie told you. Well, word is that he will throw a large housewarming party. You'll need to pick out your attire so I can ensure we will all be dressed properly to make an impression on Mr. Fox." She turned to leave, but Leah grabbed her hand.

"Nyssa, has Papa said anything of the estate?" she whispered.

A shadow fell across her sister's face as their eyes met. Leah's heart clenched and seemed to fly into her throat. She swallowed hard.

"We don't know yet. Father said the bank would inform us of the final decision. They will determine if they ought to collect the estate to make up for the money we could not put forward to the debts." Stone-faced, Nyssa spoke in a stoic tone. "We will receive word of their pronouncement by the end of the week."

"And if they do collect the estate..." Leah choked on the words.

"Papa located a small cottage on the outskirts of town that an acquaintance of his is selling. We would move there." Nyssa paused. "This is why it's all the more important we make a good impression at Edenbridge, where there will be many eligible bachelors, not least of all Mr. Fox. Mother wants us all married off before word of this spreads far."

13

Leah's trepidation transformed into disbelief. "How does she suppose that's plausible? If we lose the estate this week, word of it will be across town by the following nightfall."

Nyssa raised her shoulders and tossed her hair behind her, a semblance of her customary self returning. "Don't ask me what she's thinking. All I know is you will need to heighten your charm to extraordinary proportions to have a glimmer of a chance."

"When is the party, then?" Leah ignored the jab.

Her sister's expression grew more dubious. "It's later this week, on Star-Day."

Leah stared at her. "In three days? How will Edenbridge possibly be ready to host guests by then?"

Nyssa shrugged. "I heard the purchase went extraordinarily fast. Maris would be desperate to sell off that property for any price now, and it's his men's responsibility to have it fitted for Mr. Fox's arrival."

"Mr. Fox must be a hard bargainer."

"Or a fool to pick a place that people avoided like the plague for decades," she muttered. "But at this point, if he's a gentleman and not atrocious to look at, he will still be the most popular topic among the single ladies of Carmel."

Leah rolled her eyes. "Spare me."

CHAPTER 3

Oath-breaker Camp, Island of Japha.
Month of Thunder: Third week, Oath-day.

"It may be dangerous to spread our men so thin," Benedict said.

He looked across the trestle table to Nimrod, who was bent over the crinkled map of Japha. They were inside his command tent, the mid-day sunlight pouring in. The clang of metal-on-metal mingled with grunting echoed outside as men engaged in mock duels. Benedict itched to join them, already weary of debating strategy.

"That is not the greatest risk we have taken." Nimrod glanced up, a challenge glinting in his eyes. "We need all the keys."

Benedict held his gaze for a moment before looking back down at the map. His finger traced lightly over the path across the Nathair River to Whitewitch Marsh. It would be a treacherous journey. The Guardians avoided Whitewitch and rumors had long swirled around strange things that happened to travelers who braved its marshes. He knew this mission was critical—but Nimrod was also testing him.

"We don't need to go through Whitewitch." Benedict twisted his finger and sketched another route. "If we take the ship farther north on the river, we can cut through the Pharan Desert."

Nimrod shook his head immediately. "The longer you stay aboard the ship, the more opportunity for the Guardians to hunt you down. They *own* the river. But they fear the marshes, so, we must not."

Yet do you? Benedict read the question in his eyes. Nimrod was constantly challenging and pushing him, and it stretched him to the point of exhaustion at times. They were both brilliant tacticians, and he knew Nimrod would wring all the potential out of him and use it to advance their cause, but he would also appraise Benedict's allegiance at each step. Six months had passed since Nimrod christened him second-in-command, but he still did not trust Benedict. He doubted Nimrod ever would.

"There is wisdom in caution." He sighed, but decided to refrain from further protests. "The marshes it is, then. How many men?"

"Fifty. I have already chosen the soldiers." Nimrod handed him a scroll.

Benedict's face grew hot with indignation. "If this is my mission, I will choose the men I want," he retorted.

"You may inspect the names and propose any trades," he replied coolly. "I am taking the rest to Ebene."

Benedict unrolled the paper carelessly and scanned the list. By now, he recognized most of the names. Nimrod had put together a strange assortment of men—some were known to be categorically loyal to him, some were more detached, and some were closer to Benedict. He knew Nimrod feared the last group the most while he remained uncertain about Benedict himself. He ensured the list of names contained just enough allies to satisfy Benedict, but not enough for him to exert total influence to lead the expedition away from Nimrod's control.

"I will take it," he said, swiftly rolling up the scroll again. He had learned to pick his battles, and not every point was worth the clash.

"Excellent. Operate in stealth. You don't have many men to spare." There was a warning in his voice.

"I know how to value the lives of my men," Benedict snapped. *More than you do,* he thought.

Nimrod pulled a crumpled parchment sheet from his cloak and handed it to Benedict. "I made a copy. Study it when you can. We still need to decipher the fourth element."

"If there is one," Benedict muttered, smoothing the creases of the paper.

They had studied the document, taken from the library at Cariath, for hours. Legend said the first Oath-breakers, a group of rogue Guardians, sought to penetrate the Faerie realm, tempted by the power of enslaving immortals to their will. To guard against another revolt, the Guardians broke into four outposts, each one protecting a key to entering the Faerie world.

Benedict reread the riddle even though it was burnt into his memory.

To enter Faerie's blessed demesne
four secrets must be found:
the land unbound by time and space
opens only to the one who knows
the Light, the Song, and Mortal Gate.

Though faeries and Oath-breakers were rarely spoken of in Cariath, where the White Tiger Guardians resided, most of the men had heard whispers and rumors. The Light was supposed to be a lantern, hidden by the Cobalt Dragon Guardians in Ebene. The Song was a lyric or poem, protected by the Black Tortoise Guardians in En-doire. And the Mortal Gate—Benedict suspected his father and the Marshals of White Tiger guarded the knowledge of its location.

But they could not untangle the fourth element, if it existed. The Vermilion Falcon Guardians lived in the secluded Dammim Mountains, unheard from since the first Oath-breaker revolt.

Benedict folded the document into his garment. "I will ready the men and set out at dawn. If fortune finds me, I will send you a scout to report."

"If fortune does not find you, then use your wits and find it. Do not fail, Fox."

Benedict was accustomed to Nimrod's threats and they hardly affected him anymore. They were empty, meaningless words. Nimrod would not throw away talent of Benedict's echelon because of one failure.

Though to be fair, that was speculative, because he had not failed yet.

He strode out of Nimrod's tent without a response and was met by a sudden chill. A breeze swept up the bottom of his cloak until it billowed behind him and slipped off his shoulders. Benedict glanced up. The skies darkened into a hazy dusk, as time already began to set its course against him.

~~~~~

They were hidden only a few hundred feet from the edge of the Nathair River. A small ship docking station was straight ahead of them, and Benedict counted three medium-sized vessels roped to the wharf.

He signaled the men to drop down to their knees. In a flash, the entire contingent was on the ground. They were more efficient and capable than he expected, and there were no stragglers or weak links in the group. Nimrod was thorough and perceptive in his choice of men. While he distrusted Benedict, he had still given him a critical operation. Arguably, penetrating and robbing Black Tortoise was harder than Cobalt Dragon, which Nimrod chose for himself. The road to En-doire was more treacherous, and the Guardians there more alert and hostile.

Either he thinks I am more capable than him, or he cares less if I die, Benedict thought. *Probably the latter.*

He peered through the hedges that shielded them and waved Justin to his side. "What do you think?"

Justin, a fair-headed, lanky man took in the scene before them. He was one of Benedict's close friends from their Guardian days, and most knew he held little devotion to Nimrod or his cause. Many in the camp spoke ill of him, calling him Fox's dog, and gossip about his allegiances churned. Some men made it well known they thought Justin was still devoted to the Guardian way, but had broken away for Benedict's sake. Word of such rumors reached Benedict early in his career with Nimrod and he simply chose to ignore it. He appreciated Justin's friendship and would defend him in the camp if it came to that, but in the end, he cared little where Justin's loyalty lay.

They all knew Nimrod sought power, like the first Oath-breakers. The dream of subjugating the immortal realm to his will seized him. Benedict did not know the stories of all his followers, but he doubted they all signed on for the same agenda.

He never questioned Justin's motives, and his friend returned the favor.

"There can't be more than twenty men stationed here." Justin had keen eyes. "That would make sense, because it's far from Cariath."

Benedict furrowed his brow. "Twenty well-trained men can still do damage. I can't lose a single man here, this early on."

"You won't, if your gamble works."

Nimrod suggested this outpost on the river because it was weakly guarded and could be easily taken by force. But with the marshes and unknown dangers still ahead, Benedict wrestled to conceive a plan that did not involve fighting. Still, his best idea involved taking a risky chance.

"Will it work?" he asked uselessly.

"This is the sort of outpost manned by under-appreciated and barely graduated officers," Justin said nonchalantly. "I doubt they are too sharp."

"Lead the men out behind me. Make some noise so they are not suspicious of a covert attack, but not too much to alarm them."

Benedict sprang out of the copses and strode out to the wharf. He wore the White Tiger emblem, as did the rest of his party. Nimrod did not care much for uniforms, so many of his men had saved their Guardian garments. It proved most valuable in this mission — they could literally hide in plain sight.

Two men stood by the gates, and as Benedict approached, they threw their hands up in salute.

"Sir!" one of the two said in a strong, projecting voice. "We are Officers Jed and Birch at your service."

"Guardian Fox at yours." Benedict dipped his head slightly.

The two exchanged a look of astonishment, and Benedict released a silent breath. Though King Amir had sidelined the Guardians politically, they still enjoyed some celebrity, if only for the intrigue they inspired. The Fox family name still held repute among government officials.

"A privilege, sir. Forgive me for asking — the elder or the younger?" the one named Birch asked.

Benedict's lips curved into a half-smile. This would be simpler — perhaps even more *enjoyable* — than he thought. They could pin any fallout here squarely on August. The Foxes were known abroad for their unusual ginger hair, a rare trait among the Cariath natives. But without face-to-face encounters, few would know the difference between brothers.

"The elder."

Birch bowed. "How may we assist you?"

Benedict waved a hand at the hedges behind him. Footsteps and quiet chatter from his men grew louder. Perfect timing. He made a mental note to thank Justin later. He must have observed Benedict's conversation with the guards for cues on how it progressed.

"I have a scouting party with me, and our next destination is Whitewitch. We need a ship to cross the river."

Jed's face clouded over. "Whitewitch is unsafe. That's why no one

18

crosses the river from our post. You run straight into the marshes, unless you set course due north on the river."

"My men are well-trained. We are prepared to handle dangers on the road, and the Guardians need to understand the terrain."

Jed and Birch glanced at each other. Benedict saw a hint of doubt rise in their eyes, but he was not concerned. If they recognized him as a Fox, they were unlikely to contradict him. Though the Old Fox held no authority in Amir's regime, low-ranking officers would easily expect their family to maintain inside connections.

Justin and the rest of Benedict's men began filing in behind him. They were loosely organized into a line, with three or four men in each row. It made them appear fewer in number and not at all like a fighting army division. Benedict swelled with a sense of pride. This mission was proving easier than he had expected.

"Come in," Birch said, motioning for Benedict and his men to follow.

Benedict exchanged a quiet look of triumph with Justin, who simply nodded in return. They followed Jed and Birch through the gate onto the edge of the dock, where the two of them yelled for the others to prepare a ship. About a dozen men began to untie ropes and unfurl the sails of one vessel, the name *General* painted on the side, and enormous white sheets spun downward from the mast.

"Will you need any of us to accompany you?" Jed asked.

"No, we have experienced sailors with us." Benedict waved for his men to begin climbing aboard. "Sailors and experienced nautical men go onto the lower deck. Everyone else, find a lookout position near the edge or make yourself useful."

"If you really will go to the marshes," Birch began, casting a dubious look at him. "There is a dock due east of here on the other side. It's unmanned, so your men must tie up the ship."

Benedict dipped his head in acknowledgment. As they finished loosing the ship from the dock, he crossed the gangplank onto the ship. He waved gallantly at the men as they removed the bridge and the *General* floated free. They saluted him in return.

"Now you are just enjoying yourself." Justin leaned on the rail beside him.

"I need some amusement in this madness," Benedict muttered, turning toward the lower deck with Justin trailing behind him.

CHAPTER 4

Carmel, Island of Japha.
Month of Thunder: Third week, Star-Day.

As their carriage came to a halt in front of Edenbridge, Leah hardly recognized the large estate. A solitary home situated on a small hill above the town, it was widely regarded as a sinister place, particularly at nighttime. The Burns were the last family to live in the manor, and they became a local legend over the years. After Sarah Burns passed away in her bedroom, gossip circulated that neither she nor her family members were actually buried in the graveyard, though they had a headstone. Leah remembered asking her grandfather, Papa's father, about the story after she first heard it as a child. He had shushed her and gave a stern, closed-door talk to Papa. Despite her eavesdropping, Leah missed most of the conversation, but she knew Papa spoke much less about ghost stories, graveyard scandals, and Guardians to her until his father passed away.

Few had ventured inside the house since Sarah's death, and rumors of spooky sightings and cobwebbed closets permeated Carmel. Leah recalled years ago when her sisters, Jessie, and other children would tiptoe as close to the house as they dared—even touching the walls if they were particularly brave—and then flee as if all the devil's army had broken loose after them.

Tonight the manor was dressed in elegant glory. A cord of lights ran along both sides of the gravel pathway that led to the oak-wood doors, rid of all prior dust and grime and polished in a deep burgundy shade. Bright candles glowed behind the windows on both floors, illuminating the outlines of sturdy men and women in bouffant dresses.

A footman opened the door of the Edwards carriage and extended a white-gloved hand to assist each of the women. Papa had remained at home to await word on the estate. Leah rubbed her arms vigorously as she stepped outside, the chilly breeze of the autumn evening brushing past her.

Once they all clambered out of the carriage, Mama took Shay and Leah by the hands, with Nyssa standing by. "Girls, do your mother and yourselves a favor tonight. There are many, many eligible men here."

Shay was jittery with nervous energy. "Don't worry, Mama. I am the last woman in the world who wants to become an old maid."

Her mother patted her back and looked to Leah, who seemed unmoved. "Leah, promise me you will make some effort at least. For your mother."

"I won't refuse a dance if he's tolerable," Leah sighed.

"That is all I can hope for from you," Mama muttered. She herded her daughters toward the front door, and they made their way into the warmth of the house.

The floor was a dark wine-colored hardwood. A crystal chandelier hung above the curved stairwell, the light glancing off the beige walls surrounding it. Townspeople in formal attire milled about the first floor carrying wine glasses and thin appetizer plates, and Leah recognized some familiar faces. The scent of garlic potatoes and rotisserie chicken teased Leah's senses and awoke her appetite, so she meandered in the direction of the dining hall.

"Leah, we are going to the ballroom," Shay called, and Leah turned to see her and Nyssa moving up the stairwell. She nodded absently in response.

As Leah piled chicken, broccoli and potatoes high on her plate, she felt a tap on her shoulder and turned to see Jessie's face, her cheeks flushed and braided hair loosening at the sides.

"Thank heavens you came!" Jessie exclaimed. Leah set aside her plate to embrace her briefly.

"My conscience simply would not allow me to abandon you here," Leah said with a hint of jocular mockery in her voice.

Jessie swatted her arm lightly. "Don't scoff. You will be glad you came: the party has been marvelous and Mr. Fox has outdone himself. I wonder if all the parties in Cariath are like this."

Leah took a bite of the chicken, savoring the warm spices that ravished her mouth. "Marry him and find out," she teased.

"You are too much," Jessie cried. She glanced at the plate Leah held and began picking potato wedges off of it and demolishing them before she could protest. "I'm doing you a service," she mumbled, her mouth full, "because we need to go to the ballroom. I can't have you waste away here simply eating when there is a feast up there to devour." She winked, and Leah almost choked.

"You are unbelievable." She shook her head and then changed the subject. "Have you encountered Mr. Fox yet?"

"Encountered? Why, I have danced twice with him already." She looked as satisfied as a cat that had just lapped her milk.

"What was he like?" Leah's curiosity was piqued.

Jessie chewed slowly and her expression grew thoughtful. "He's very grave but not unkind. A man of few words, so it seems odd he threw such a grand party. I'm not certain how to describe him, Leah. He is a puzzle of sorts, a study in contradiction. Something you would enjoy."

"Sounds like terrible company."

"Well, they say a picture is worth a thousand words, so don't count on me for your knowledge of Mr. Fox." Jessie took the plate, set it on a passing servant's tray, and grabbed her hand, leading her to the stairs.

"Is he really from Cariath?"

"I heard it from his own mouth," Jessie said, as they reached the second floor.

The ballroom was the most splendid part of the mansion. It was brightly lit with paintings lining the pale walls. A grand piano sat angled in one corner. A petite young woman Leah recognized as Miss Lawrence played an upbeat piece. There were cushioned chairs along two sides of the room, and some folk were sitting and talking, but most of the people were paired off and dancing jubilantly, dresses of all colors twirling like pinwheels about the room.

Leah caught sight of Mr. Whitefield and Laurel—who looked more radiant than ever—dancing. Nyssa and Mr. Langford were together, and Shay was on the arm of a man Leah did not know. Her gaze swept across the room, searching for a man who might be Mr. Fox.

"There he is." Jessie's voice came over the commotion and Leah followed the finger she raised.

The first thing she noticed was his hair. The words Jessie spoke at the park earlier carried little exaggeration. Mr. Fox's hair was a strong ginger color: not too bright and carroty, which would have made him appear ridiculous, but rich and deep, with some coffee-colored roots. His nose was sharp and well-defined, and his thick brows a graceful arch above his eyes.

"He's handsome enough," Leah admitted, still watching him. Mr. Fox was dancing with a lady who appeared to be chattering on, but he simply maintained a polite but disinterested expression.

"A man who meets your standards!" Jessie exclaimed. "You must have a dance with him. I don't know when such a day will arrive again."

"Quit jesting," Leah said. "You know I'd fall below his standards." She spoke dispassionately, unwounded by what she considered the objective truth.

Before Jessie could protest, they were interrupted by the appearance of Mr. Whitefield and Laurel, who greeted them elatedly.

"Jessie, Mother wants to introduce us to some folk. It ought to only take a few minutes, but we must go downstairs," Laurel said.

Jessie sighed. "Mother has more acquaintances than is healthy," she muttered, but allowed Laurel to lead her out of the ballroom, leaving Mr. Whitefield with Leah.

"Since my lady has other matters to attend to, may I ask you for a dance, Miss Leah?" He bowed.

"Of course." Leah extended her hand and allowed him to lead her into the cluster of dancing couples. She heaved a quiet sigh of relief, silently thankful to escape the awkwardness of standing along the sidelines and risk Mama's disapproval, should she have seen her.

"Congratulations on your betrothal." Leah nearly shouted to be heard

23

over the din as they danced.

Mr. Whitefield smiled. "Thank you. Miss Lane and I are ecstatic." After a few moments of silence he added, "Have you had the opportunity to meet Mr. Fox yet?"

Leah shook her head. "Jessie pointed him out to me, but that's all."

"Then allow me the pleasure of introducing you."

Before she could respond, he led her out of the crowd to the other side of the ballroom. No longer dancing, Mr. Fox was engaged in conversation with another gentleman. When he noticed Mr. Whitefield and Leah approaching, he seemed to excuse himself and step toward them.

"Mr. Whitefield," he said, and the two shook hands. His voice was a rich tenor.

"Mr. Fox, I would like the pleasure of introducing you to Miss Leah Edwards." Mr. Whitefield swept his hand toward Leah. "She is a close friend of the Lanes."

Mr. Fox's gaze shifted to Leah, who felt uncomfortable under his piercing look. Something in the way his dark eyes fixed upon her made Leah feel exposed, but an indignant pride welled up in her as sudden inspiration, and she refused to be intimidated. She returned his gaze evenly.

After what seemed like long moments passed, he extended his hand to Leah. "Mr. August Fox at your service, Miss Leah. It's a pleasure to make your acquaintance."

"The pleasure is mine, Mr. Fox." She was pleased to hear her voice even and firm.

"I believe I have met your sisters, Miss Edwards and Miss Shay already."

"Yes, I am the youngest of the three."

Mr. Fox nodded slowly. He returned his attention to Mr. Whitefield and said, "Then if Mr. Whitefield will not object, I would ask Miss Leah for the next dance."

Mr. Whitefield held up his hands. "By all means, please do." He bowed to both of them before walking away.

Leah felt a heady, delicious thrill rush from her fingertips through the rest of her body as Mr. Fox took her hand and led her to the floor. Moments after, she rebuked herself mentally. There was no purpose in growing giddy over a man who would not look twice at her were it not for an introduction from another gentleman. She bit her lip unconsciously and quieted her thoughts, determined to be only cordial and nothing more.

Mr. Fox did not seem to mind her reticence as they danced. Instead, his expression turned grave and thoughtful, as if his mind were far afield. For a moment, Leah was tempted to interrupt his thoughts with some banal comment but decided against it, content to just observe him in silence. Jessie had not been mistaken in her scrutiny of him, as Leah felt he bore some great weight upon him—he carried himself with an air that struck her as one of the great men of old. Was he actually a Guardian? The notion seemed preposterous to her. What business would they have in Carmel now?

"You're quite different from your sisters." He broke the silence suddenly, startling Leah.

What a peculiar and presumptuous comment to make, especially to a new acquaintance, Leah thought. She looked at him oddly. "In what ways?" she queried.

"They are foaming with words to say." He paused. "You have been solemn in silence."

Leah felt a surge of resentment. "Well, I daresay you have been no different."

"It was no insult," he said, raising an eyebrow. "I don't believe in speaking unless there are words worth the effort."

Leah was not entirely appeased, and her diminished regard for Mr. Fox bred bold recklessness. "Then perhaps you should not have thrown a party. It's a social institution made to be filled with worthless speech."

"Quiet, but not without opinion," Mr. Fox surmised. "Perhaps I ought to say you're not like most *women*."

Chagrined by his assessment of her character, Leah merely held her tongue and gripped his hand more tightly. He did not flinch. She willed the music to finish playing so she could escape him, her earlier interest in him vanquished. Even his handsome features appeared blander in her eyes. But the music did not stop, and Leah inwardly cursed her misfortune, having fallen into Mr. Fox's hands for what must be the longest waltz written in the history of men. Yet he seemed to have sense enough to stop pushing the subject, falling silent as well.

As the music began to slow at last, Leah glanced around the ballroom, taking in the whole scene again. Some couples drifted off the dance floor, while others found new partners. Her gaze moved to the high-arched ceiling above the paintings. The room was certainly splendid, and beneath its bright lights and merrymaking, the old stories of Edenbridge seemed distant and absurd.

Leah blinked. For a moment, a strange shadow seemed to sprint across the walls...

"Are you feeling well?" Mr. Fox stared at her with what appeared to be faint concern.

She flushed, realizing her grip on his hand had tightened unconsciously. "Yes. I think I stared straight into the chandelier." She blinked again, surreptitiously looking at the wall overhead, but the shadow had vanished.

He nodded, accepting her explanation, as the final notes of the waltz played.

Leah felt uneasy parting with Mr. Fox — or anyone, for that matter — on disagreeable terms. "Do you plan to settle in Carmel, Mr. Fox?" she asked, with all the tone of civility she could muster.

A mild look of surprise crossed his expression, and Leah sensed a quiet satisfaction within herself for putting him off balance, if only in the slightest.

"No, in fact, I purchased Edenbridge as more of an investment. I may lease it or simply save it as a holiday retreat. My permanent residence is still in Cariath."

"We never receive visitors from Cariath. It's almost legend to us." She allowed the unspoken question to hang in the air.

He simply cocked his head. "Not all legends are divorced from reality."

The music ceased, and Mr. Fox opened his hand to release Leah, his gaze leveled on her the entire time. Refusing to be unnerved, she bowed to him and he returned the gesture. She vaguely noticed he held himself upright with impeccable posture.

Leah briefly wondered if she could walk off without a parting word to him, but after a fleeting struggle, wisdom outweighed impulse. "Welcome to Carmel, Mr. Fox, and I wish you a pleasant time here."

August Fox tilted his head toward her. "I'm sure it will be. Enjoy the rest of the party, Miss Leah." He paused, his mouth curving to form the slightest amused smile. "If you can."

He bowed once more and then melted away into the sea of people, leaving Leah with moist hands and burning cheeks as she recalled her petulant words.

~~~~~

It was late in the evening when Mama rounded up all the family in preparation for leaving Edenbridge. As they stepped outside, Leah could see her breath on the air, and she shivered as a cold draft blew through. The women huddled together, arm in arm, as the footman called their carriage over and held the door open for them.

"It was delightful!" Nyssa exclaimed through chattering teeth once they were all inside and the carriage was moving.

"You never would have thought the manor was rumored to be haunted. It was warm and cozier than many other homes we've been to," Shay added. "Mr. Fox outdid all expectations."

Leah remained silent for most of the journey, her mind still caught up in the bright ballroom and its new owner. He did not strike her as dishonest, but there was an air of mystery and grimness about him. Did the Guardians still dwell in Cariath? And why did he come to Carmel, to purchase Edenbridge no less? Did he know of the stories surrounding the estate? She thought of the shadows on the wall—more likely than anything, the excitement, lighting, and the ghost stories combined conjured up some trick on her eyes. But Leah could not help feeling a chill at the thought. It was only for a moment, but the shadows almost resembled a real scene, though nothing like the one in the ballroom of dancers and party-goers.

"He seems very reputable and wealthy," Mama was saying when Leah returned from her wayfaring thoughts. "I heard he owns an even larger estate in Cariath. Imagine that! I wonder what it's like among the Guardians."

"I thought the Guardians lived ascetically," Nyssa said.

"You are thinking of Papa's old books," their mother returned. "I'm sure they have changed with the times. Most religious sects do."

"Mr. Fox was very kindly disposed. He danced with nearly every lady he could," Shay said. "I even saw him dancing with Leah for the long waltz."

Mama brightened. "Is that so?"

Leah sighed. "Yes. Though I doubt either of us made a glowing impression on the other."

The carriage drew to a standstill in front of the Edwards estate. As they clambered out the door, Nyssa commented, "That's just something Leah would say."

"Then what did you think of him?" Mrs. Edwards asked.

As they hurried to open the door of the house, Leah tumbled her impression of August Fox around her mind. In all fairness, there was nothing ill she could accuse him of, yet something in his nature and interaction with her made Leah hesitate to compliment his character.

"I didn't like him," she said with finality.

CHAPTER 5

Papa was reading in the common area under a dim lamp when the women came into the house, shedding their large overcoats and woolen scarves. Leah rubbed her frozen hands together and looked toward her father tentatively, searching for any sign in his face or posture that indicated the arrival of the bank's decision. He was sitting with a slight slouch in his back as usual, looking down past the rim of his glasses at the book in his hands.

Nyssa, more forward and nimble, rushed to his side. "Is there news from the bank, Papa?"

He folded the corner of the page he was on and set the book aside, drawing in a heavy breath. He stroked Nyssa's hair absently. "I'm afraid it isn't good."

Leah felt like a knife turned in her heart. She watched numbly as Shay made a wailing sound and Mama ushered her to the stairwell, assisting her up the steps. Nyssa rose from her seat and followed them, not giving a second glance to Papa and brushing past Leah, who observed the scene before her in a dreamlike stupor. Her limbs felt inert and her feet were fastened tightly to the ground.

Papa stared down at his feet, unmoving, his eyes stormy. The lines around the edges of his face seemed more evident and Leah was keenly conscious of her father's age. A knot grew in the base of her throat.

"The cottage will be lovely too." The calmness of her tone astounded even Leah.

Papa smiled sadly at her and the wrinkles around his eyes became more pronounced. "You are too kind, Leah."

She forced herself to lift her feet and stumbled to the couch, sinking into the cushion beside him. He wound his arm around her back and she rested her head against his bony shoulder and closed her eyes. Some moments passed before Leah lifted herself off of him and picked up the book on the tableside.

"It's your copy of *Arieh and the Guardians*. I found it between the cushions," he said dryly as she fingered through the tattered pages. "An excellent story."

"Yes. Yes, it is." Leah opened to the first page and began reading.

She did not know how much time passed as she read the familiar soothing words, Papa looking over her shoulder, and her turning the page when he gave a nod. The dim lamp beside them flickered occasionally, so the black-inked words were sometimes clear, sometimes shadowed. The dull throb in her chest subsided as she lost herself in the old, wild world of men and faeries, where the stage was battlefields instead of ballrooms.

A warm drowsiness crept over Leah and her eyelids began to droop. Papa reached for a fleece blanket and spread it over her thin frame. He gently pried the book from her hands and stood up to allow her head to rest on the arm of the settee. Stooping down once more so his face was level with hers, he planted a light kiss on her forehead.

"I'm sorry," he rasped.

She reached out and grasped his hand in a vise-like grip. "Don't be." She swallowed the choking feeling in her throat mercilessly.

He stayed still as Leah straightened the blanket over her and shifted to lie on her back, staring into the white ceiling. She recalled when he would tell her a story before bedtime, a tale from times long gone or worlds never formed, and she would drift off to the steady rhythm of his voice. Back then, she had never noticed the fragility nestled beneath the strength of his tone.

"You have run me dry of tales to tell," he said, as if he had read her mind. There were times she vowed he could.

Her lips curved upward a little, her eyes closed. "That's all right. I'm half in the land of dreams already."

"Then I shall leave you and go there myself. Did you enjoy the party?"

"You know how I feel about parties, Papa." Even in her lethargy, thinly veiled sarcasm bled into her words.

He chuckled. "And did you like Mr. Fox?"

"Not particularly," Leah replied stoutly.

"Did he like you?" There was no surprise in his voice.

"Even less so, I believe."

Leah opened her eyes to see a roguish smile cross her father's face and she could not help but let loose a brief laugh. He kissed her again, this time on the cheek, and switched the lamp off. His sturdy footsteps grew distant and Leah let her heavy eyelids fall shut, allowing the yawning oblivion of sleep to consume her.

~~~~~

The Edwards home was quiet for days, each person engaged in separate activities until meal times, but even the talk at the table was diminished. Papa revealed the bank was giving them two months to move out of the estate, and since then, little conversation took place between any of them. Leah passed much of the time reading and drawing, reluctant to hear the complaints of Nyssa and Shay or the silence between her father and mother. She would catch Mama casting wounded looks at Papa across the dinner table that quashed her appetite.

Even Jessie did not call to ask after her opinion on Mr. Fox as Leah expected, but she assumed her friend was busy with plans for her sister's wedding. In the bustle of the party, they did not find a chance to meet and discuss Leah's impression of Edenbridge's new owner. She was secretly relieved, not keen on telling Jessie of both the family misfortune and the poor taste her encounter with Mr. Fox left in her mouth.

Nearly a week later, a message arrived that Mr. Langford and Mr. Fox were both passing by their estate that evening and asked to pay a visit. This snapped Mama out of her sulking and into a flurry of preparation. The scent of saffron and paprika wafted up to Leah in her room, and she listened to her sisters' happy chatter float up the stairs.

When the door knock came, the family was in proper form. The table was set, the ladies seated around it, and Papa received the visiting gentlemen and ushered them in.

Mama ruled the conversation for the better portion of the meal, receiving compliments on her cooking with delight, and attempting to highlight the superior qualities of her daughters to Mr. Langford and Mr. Fox. The former acknowledged her efforts with exuberance, particularly when she spoke of Nyssa, and the latter nodded politely but did little to encourage her.

Leah cringed inwardly at Mama's less-than-subtle statements, only mollified by the knowing, slightly mischievous looks Papa shared with her. She noticed Mr. Fox caught one of their silent exchanges across the table and looked down at her plate quickly.

"Tell us about home, August." Mr. Langford changed the subject after a lull in conversation. "I can't remember the last time we received visitors from Cariath."

"Yes! Do the Guardians still live there?" Shay interjected.

Mama shook her head at her. "Mr. Edwards indulged the girls in too many stories," she said apologetically.

To Leah's surprise, Mr. Fox offered a small smile to Papa.

"I'm glad to hear of that. I thought the Guardians might have vanished entirely from the consciousness of the seaside towns."

"What are they like?" Nyssa asked.

Mr. Fox was quiet for a moment. "Tales and years tend to make the common into legend. The Guardians are men, no different from the people of Carmel. They were ordained as peacekeepers between the Faerie and mortal realms. Cariath is one of their outposts. There are three other Guardian settlements scattered through Japha, in En-doire, Ebene, and the Dammim." He turned to Mr. Langford. "Life in Cariath is remarkably similar to Carmel, though perhaps marked with a greater sense of gravity. The conversations at parties, dare I say, are weightier." His gaze settled on Leah for a long heartbeat. She felt her face flush, but returned the look defiantly until he broke it off.

"Sounds rather dreary," Shay commented.

"Depends on your perspective," he returned simply.

"Many here see the Guardians as just another religious sect," Mr. Langford commented.

Something flashed in Mr. Fox's eyes. "It's safer for King Amir's government to paint the Guardians in that light. Conveniently, the conflicts that Guardians deal with become religious issues rather than political ones. Not every monarch of Japha has held that position."

"Do the Guardian settlements answer to the crown?" Papa asked.

"Not formally. In Cariath, the Guardians congregate in one part of the valley called the Bastion. They still answer to a Guardian Chief and their Marshals. The other actual towns around the Cariath region have a governor appointed by Amir."

"Isn't it dangerous if the Guardians have no accountability?" Shay asked.

"I daresay the Guardians hold themselves to a higher standard than Amir does with his officials," Mr. Fox returned dryly.

Leah noticed Mr. Langford and Nyssa exchanging looks across the table, but no one spoke. Debate over politics and religion were not favored topics at most dinner parties.

With a lull in the conversation, Mrs. Edwards scurried to bring dessert out to the table. The rich scent of chocolate mixed with tangy lemon drew further accolades.

"Do the Guardians still believe in Arieh?" Leah asked, as Mama doled out slices of the sticky bread.

Mr. Fox did not disguise his surprise. "You are well-versed in Guardian lore."

A brief, unholy rush of satisfaction went through Leah. Though offered with a hint of jest, his pointed remark about the parties at Cariath irked her, and she could not resist challenging his composed demeanor.

"I enjoy history and mythology." She caught Papa's eye again. "Something I inherited from my father."

"Well, Arieh is considered a mix of both: history and myth," he said. "Guardians are divided in thought about how many of the tales are true."

"A synopsis of Arieh, please?" Mr. Langford smiled good-naturedly as he cut into his lemon-chocolate bread. "Some of us are unschooled."

They looked to Mr. Fox, but he turned his gaze on Leah. "Would you?"

She knew the story well, but never told it in front of a Cariath native. Surely he would see any gaping holes or inaccuracies in her version.

Leah nodded reluctantly, recalling the text. "Long ago, men provoked the wrath of the faerie-kind by trying to penetrate the faerie, or immortal, realm. A tense treaty was established, stating that men and faeries would mind their own affairs, and the Guardians were created to keep the peace. But a group of rogue Guardians sought again to enter the immortal realm. They failed and were to be eternally imprisoned, but a noble Guardian — Arieh — offered himself as a substitute sacrifice.

"Faerie law dictated they accept his offer, and because he had done no wrong, they took him as one of their own, making him immortal. While some faeries continued to despise him for his human heritage, others followed him. The faerie world is supposed to be marked by cruelty, but he introduced mercy. They say he continues to watch over mortals today, and enlists his faerie followers to help him."

Silence fell over the table for a few moments. The Edwards all knew the story of Arieh to varying degrees already, though Papa and Leah were the most well-read. Mr. Fox wore an unreadable expression, as if her words pulled him into distant thought. Mr. Langford released a long breath.

"Sounds like mythology to my ears," he commented. "Most in Carmel believe in the immortal realm, but not that it intersects with our world."

Mr. Fox dipped his head. "The legend explains why our worlds have been sealed from one another. Beyond Cariath, in some of the wild lands, there are still occasional rogue faerie attacks from those that break through." A dark shadow fell over his face for a moment. "But no, the two do not intersect much."

"Then why do we need peacekeepers still?" Nyssa asked between forkfuls.

"Peace must be maintained, not just with the faerie-kind, but among men too," he said wryly. "Various cults have arisen where men worship faeries as gods. They've tried to open the doors to the immortal realm, desperate to bring faeries back in to rule over us. It falls upon the Guardians to stop them."

Shay blanched. "Sounds more like a job for soldiers."

"Well, Amir has neatly disengaged himself from religious conflicts, so he won't get involved," Leah noted. "Before the Faerie Wars, there was a time that Japha was unique as an island where mortals and faeries coexisted in peace. No other nation was like it. Even after the war, Guardians held prominent positions in the monarchy because they uniquely stood in the divide between the realms. Our government has tried to minimize that entire history."

Mama shot her a warning glance, but then smiled at their guests. "Leah is our resident historian."

Mr. Fox, however, looked at her searchingly. "That's a version of history many would deny today."

Leah shrugged. "History is nothing if not biased. But I do believe you can always find the thread of truth weaving through."

"You should consider settling in Carmel, Mr. Fox," Mama piped up, and Leah detected the gleam in her eye. "We are well-sheltered from chaos and danger here."

"I heard the manor I purchased has some notorious rumors associated with it." A touch of irony entered his voice.

Missing the subtle humor in his words, a fleeting look of mortification crossed Mama's face. She turned a pale beet shade, though no one but Leah seemed to notice. She choked down a laugh and felt a twinge of sympathy.

"Arieh will protect you," Leah interjected, addressing Mr. Fox and trying to rescue her mother from embarrassment. She cocked her head. "If you believe he is more history than myth, that is."

That drew an appreciative chuckle from Papa and Mr. Langford.

Mr. Fox turned to her. "Do you believe it?"

She glanced down at her bread, still untouched, before meeting his gaze again. "It's so absurd I think it must be true."

He raised a brow slightly, either intrigued or surprised, but did not respond.

The remainder of the evening passed with light conversation and pleasantries. While Leah felt her curiosity piqued over Mr. Fox's background and Cariath, her family and Mr. Langford were satisfied to move on to other topics, discussing local businesses and events. Nyssa and Shay chimed in excitedly to tell Mr. Fox more about life in Carmel.

Leah grew weary of the chatter and breathed a quiet sigh of relief when the gentlemen insisted on departing. Though they made no mention of the Edwards estate — Mama strictly instructed them to avoid the topic with the guests — the burden of it still weighed on her mind through dinner.

Still, spirits in the house were higher, even after Mr. Fox and Mr. Langford left. Mama cleared the plates from the table with a small spring in her step. Nyssa and Shay carried on their debate about social hierarchy in Carmel, a topic they had subjected Mr. Fox to for a criminal amount of time. Leah might have had greater pity on another gentlemen in a similar plight.

As she prepared to go upstairs for bed, Papa accosted her.

"I think you impressed him," he said, a quiet twinkle in his eye.

She nearly fell over herself. "Mr. Fox?"

"Well, I hope not Mr. Langford, for the sake of peace in this family." Papa laughed.

Leah shook her head, contemplating their enigmatic guest. "I don't think he's the sort to be impressed."

He shrugged. "Not easily, perhaps." He brushed a strand of hair from her face. "But you are formidable."

"I really would rather not be." She made a face, drawing another chuckle from him. He kissed her cheek and allowed her to ascend the stairs, her mind swirling with faeries and traitors, as her sisters' voices grew dim in the background.

CHAPTER 6

Whitewitch, Island of Japha.
Month of Thunder: Third week, Rest-Day.

A thick fog hovered above Whitewitch as Benedict and his men came off the *General*. On the Nathair River, the weather was fair, with a light wind and sparse clouds in a pale cerulean sky. The men's spirits had lifted considerably as they sailed smoothly across the water, and some had taken to games and gambling on deck during the journey. Yet Benedict was attuned to how the lightheartedness slowly dissipated as they approached the marshes.

When the Guardian youth exchanged ghostly stories around the campfire at Cariath, tales from Whitewitch were a favorite. Boys whispered about how the marshes were built on the backs of swamp monsters, ready to devour unwitting travelers. Or those who did survive a journey through the marshes emerged with no memory of themselves because of a faerie poison in the air.

Benedict recalled how the Old Fox dismissed all the stories as unfounded rumors, but he never sent an expedition of Guardians through Whitewitch either.

It was not quite evening yet, but the looming mist hid the sun. A grey, damp blanket spread across the eastern shore of the river, greeting them as soon as they disembarked. The banter and raucous noise aboard the ship diminished into hushed whispers and muttering.

Benedict pulled the hood on his cloak over his head. Moisture gathered stickily on his skin. The air reeked of a faint, sickly sweet odor and he wrinkled his nose in disgust. He suspected the scent blossomed from strange marsh weeds and plants growing in the area.

"Fox." A gravelly, harsh voice came from behind him.

"Yes?" Benedict did not turn around. He recognized Hound's tone and his mood soured even further.

"The men are asking why we are going through the marshes. We can sail farther up the river toward En-doire." He spoke with an arrogant swagger, as if he were intent on correcting Benedict's mistake.

"That's what I would do if Nimrod had not insisted otherwise," Benedict said, tight-lipped. He turned to face Hound, who towered over him. He had earned his name from his hulking size. "Would you like me to inform him that you are questioning his judgment?"

His words had the exact effect he intended. Hound flushed with anger, his face reddening, and he made a nasty, gurgling sound in his throat. He jabbed his large index finger at Benedict, the tip of his fingernail a hair's breadth away from his chest.

"We all know whose loyalties are sure, and whose are not," Hound breathed.

Benedict turned his lips up in a slight smirk, ignoring the bait. "Do you want a medal of honor?"

In a huff of fury, Hound spun around and melted into the group of men still huddled on the dock. He was soon surrounded by a circle of his devoted friends. Benedict had observed the subtle factions forming among his expedition party. Hound was at the head of one unofficial pack of men, while Justin and Benedict had their own faithful group. Some were detached from the rivalries, and a few were more reclusive, not appearing close to any in the party.

Justin appeared by Benedict's side. "What did he want?" he inquired calmly.

"Nothing." He waved his hand. "I think he's simply afraid of the marshes."

While Hound openly disliked Benedict, never having understood why Nimrod promoted him to second-in-command when his allegiance was doubtful, his attitude toward Justin was far more venomous. Justin did not even pretend to side with Nimrod's cause, yet remained in high standing in their ranks. Benedict knew if it were Hound's decision, Justin would be no more than a pig prepared for slaughter. Hound was bloodthirsty and bright, but Benedict was better, and Nimrod could not turn a blind eye to that.

"Are we going in now, then?"

"Yes, we want to make it through before night falls completely." Benedict clapped for attention and silence fell over the dock. "We need to move. It's approximately a three-hour trek from here to the northern tip of the marshes."

An uneasy murmur slithered through the group and some men shook their heads at one another furtively.

"If we have a problem," Benedict interrupted loudly, "please inform me." He gave a pointed look at the men, particularly Hound and his friends.

More silence, this time bloated with unspoken objections and complaints. He sighed and braced himself, tapping his foot impatiently as he waited.

"We all have heard some strange talk, about what happens in there." Ian, one of Hound's men, sounded nervous, and received a glare from Hound and a few others in his group.

Benedict nodded slowly. "Yes. I have heard the rumors as well. Unfortunately, Nimrod either does not believe them, or he does not care much for our lives." He paused, allowing the men a moment to wrestle with his statement.

"Your words become more seasoned with the taste of treason," Hound warned. A few murmurs of both agreement and protest came from the men.

"If truth is treason, then call me a traitor," Benedict returned, loosening a bitter laugh. "Nimrod cares little for lives. But he cares for this mission to succeed." He shrugged. "It doesn't matter. I will go through the marshes with those who will follow, but I don't lay the obligation on any who are afraid."

Justin leaned close to his ear. "Dangerous gamble. Hound and his men are itching to strike out on their own."

"Are they?" Benedict raised an eyebrow. "No, Hound would rather chafe under my command than be called a coward."

Whispers were still traveling through the groups of men, but he did not wait for them to make a decision. He motioned for Justin to start moving, and those most faithful to them—Kent, Meeker, Wills, and Gerard, he saw out of the corner of his eye—followed also. Stepping off the dock, they plunged headfirst into the fog.

Benedict had to stop and blink, his hand going to the sword at his side out of natural instinct. The white-grey vapor around him was heavy, and he was forced to take a moment for his vision to adjust. Slowly, the landscape came into a misty focus.

Whitewitch stretched out before him. It was a boggy, desolate place. A disgusting concoction of greenish-brown mud and swamp regions extended from the east to the west, with only a narrow pathway of solid ground snaking through. The fog hung a mere arm's length above the ground, keeping Benedict from seeing far into the distance. Even the men next to him were faint outlines, but for half their legs and boots.

"They say faerie witches made this fog, long ago," Wills commented. "That's why it never lifts."

"Cheery thought," Meeker replied dryly.

Benedict ignored them both. He tested the reliability of the pathway with one foot, stepping and prodding the ground. After a few seconds, he sprang lightly onto it and motioned for the men to follow.

"Shall we wait for the others?" Justin called.

"No." He drew his sword and pointed it directly in front of him as he broke into a rapid walk. "Those who are worthy will follow."

~~~~~

Benedict lost track of the time passing as he pressed relentlessly through the marshes. He kept a firm grip on his compass, checking it occasionally. There were no landmarks inside Whitewitch, but he calculated they would emerge in the right place as long as they pushed due northeast. The fog did not give way, but felt even thicker as they moved further inland, so it was impossible to tell how close they were to nightfall. He did not allow that to deter him, and did not break stride as they moved forward.

The men were silent during the journey, and Benedict would have thought most of his party had abandoned the mission, but for the dull slosh of footsteps behind him. He saw, dimly through the vapor, many had their swords drawn. It was a useless defense, he thought, though he did the same. There would be no Guardians or human foes hiding in this mist. If the old tales were true, the marshes hid things that a thousand swords would be futile against.

A scream pierced the air. Benedict froze for a moment before spinning around, dropping his compass into a pocket, and tightening both hands on his sword hilt. Someone bumped into his right shoulder and he started, but at a glance, found Justin beside him.

"What was that?" Benedict made sure his voice was free of fear.

Justin only shook his head. Frightened mutterings from the men grew. Benedict pushed through the ranks of men behind him until he heard Hound's voice in a quiet roar toward the back. Hurrying to the end of the line of men, he found Hound holding a terrified man by his brooch while others watched in silent apprehension.

"You could have awoken some—something!" Hound's face was livid with wild scribbles of terror and wrath.

The man at his mercy whimpered, shaking his head violently. "Please," he gasped. "I slipped, and I thought something grabbed my leg."

His boots and entire left leg were completely soaked in dark brown mud, and tangled vines hung off the bottom of his cloak. Benedict recognized him as Traven, one of the recluses in the party. Hound's friends were gathered near him, shooting glares at Traven, who had nobody to come to his defense.

"Tell me what happened here," Benedict rasped. "Be quick, unless you want us to be trapped in the marshes tonight."

"This man," Hound said, tightening his grip on Traven until he choked, "is going to get us all bloody murdered. He screamed like a woman, afraid to get his feet a little wet. Then held onto me like an infant."

The men around him tittered, but Benedict ignored them. "So what do you propose? We linger here and watch while you punish him as sport?"

Hound scowled at him. "I say we just drop him into the swamps and be rid of the fool."

"Bring him to me." Benedict waited as Hound half-dragged Traven and carelessly dropped him, so he stumbled at Benedict's feet. He did not get up, but kept his face pressed to the ground. "Traven, what happened?"

The man mumbled something inaudible. One of Hound's men kicked him hard in the shin, but Benedict held up his hand and gave him a warning glance.

"Speak up."

"My foot slipped. I thought something in the mud had me," he whispered shakily, lifting his face slightly. "I tried to grab something— anything—" He broke off and inclined his head toward his accuser.

Benedict cursed to himself. Of all the enmity he could earn, Traven had the misfortune of finding Hound's.

"You might have endangered our whole company," Benedict stated plainly, though he did not take on a severe tone.

There was a pause, before Traven said, "Leave me."

"Why?" Benedict frowned, irritated that the man would surrender so easily. Though, perhaps it would be more distasteful if he groveled for pity.

"I might do further damage."

"I don't abandon my men. If you will fight for me, I won't leave you."

Hound glared at Benedict from the huddle of men behind them. "Penchant for the faint of heart?" he mocked.

Benedict afforded him a brief glance. "Penchant for men of quality, actually, but seeing as Nimrod assigned you to our unit, he seems to ignore my preferences." That evoked some muffled titters, which quickly died as Hound swung a death-look to those around him.

"Well?" He returned to Traven. "We don't have a wealth of time."

A brief pause, before he replied, "I will fight for you."

There was a note of wonder in his tone. Though Benedict did not stop to ponder why, he had a fleeting idea. Public displays of weakness were shamed in Guardian culture but downright unforgivable in Nimrod's ranks. Benedict was not honor-bound to dismiss Traven, but his extension of kindness would appear as foreign as a garden bloom in Whitewitch.

He stooped and gripped Traven's hand, pulling the bedraggled man to his feet. Traven looked at him again, shock and confusion lining his face. Benedict dipped his head in acknowledgement, but maintained an emotionless expression.

Hound growled menacingly. "You want cowards in your army," he spat.

"I would choose admitted cowardice over counterfeit bravery." Benedict did not await Hound's reaction, but indicated Traven should follow him to the front of the line.

Justin was reorganizing the men at the head of the ranks as he and Traven approached. There was a question in his eyes, but Benedict shook his head. *Not now.* He did not have the energy to explain.

"We need to keep moving, and moving fast," was all he said. "Keep an eye on Traven."

Without further speech, they continued on the pathway through the marshes at a swift pace. Benedict's legs grew tired, but he refused to slow down. After the incident with Traven and Hound, he forced himself to be more alert to the surroundings, in the unlikely case that the commotion had roused someone—or something—nearby to their presence.

He breathed a silent sigh of relief when he glimpsed the end of the marshes and the fog thinning. Glorious dry ground was ahead. Benedict felt a rush of adrenaline and broke into a sprint. The air rushed by his ears, and he heard the men behind him give shouts of liberation as they saw what he did. With a constant, dull thudding against the ground the men raced after him, their spirits refreshed.

Some released a loud whoop as they collapsed onto solid land, and some even bent and kissed the ground. Benedict suppressed a snort as he watched these warriors act like children, but gave them a few moments of reprieve.

The sky was dark. They had passed out of the marshes not long after dusk descended. Though there was still a faint fog around them, the stars above were clear, bright dots wheeling across the open, black terrain. A faint, flickering light in the north was visible, and Benedict assumed that was En-doire.

"Let's go," he called. A few groans rolled across the ragtag-looking group of men. "Gird yourselves," he sighed in exasperation. "We will move a few hundred meters from the marshes and make camp."

Cheers arose from the men this time, and they followed Benedict northward. The land was vast and open, so he led them until they found a small woodland area of hedges and trees. Most of the land between Whitewitch and En-doire was uncharted, so Guardians who journeyed in the space between could only follow a basic compass and the movement of the sun. Benedict had traveled to En-doire only twice, and those times he crossed the Nathair River from Cariath, so the passage was shorter and easier.

"We will make camp here."

The men scattered through the area, laying down cloaks and weapons to claim a spot. Some gathered wood for fire. Benedict waited until most had settled before he placed his belongings at a distance from the group.

He lay on top of his cloak, and wrinkled his face in pain for a moment as his muscles protested. His legs ached from the nonstop trek through the marshes and the tension that had built up. Benedict closed his eyes and wished for sleep, but his mind was unwillingly drawn back to the scene with Hound and Traven. Was he moved by pity for the friendless man, spite for Hound, or both? What code of honor did he operate under now? His convictions were clear and sure when he left the Guardians. But they grew hazy, like the fog over Whitewitch, the more time he spent among the Oath-breakers.

Footsteps approached and a twig snapped. Opening his eyes, he expected to see Justin, but instead, Traven stood nearby. His cloak was tightly wrapped around him, and he was tapping his foot nervously.

"Traven." Benedict sat up.

"Sir." Traven glanced around uncertainly before refocusing on Benedict. "I didn't deserve your help. You showed me mercy."

He masked any reaction. "I taught Hound a lesson," he corrected.

"It's not what Nimrod would have done."

"I'm not Nimrod." But the words felt hollow. "Nimrod is after power. I simply want justice."

Traven appeared surprised. "Why did you leave the Guardians, then?" He flushed, likely realizing what a personal and potentially dangerous query that was.

"The faerie-kind have crimes to answer for." He watched the shadows and flames dancing above the campfire. "And the gods and Guardians alike are mute."

Silence fell over them, his words echoing like a challenge in the darkness. Benedict thought numbly of the faceless gods many of the Guardians believed in—gods who were supposed to be good and just, avengers of the downtrodden.

And yet, the sins of the faeries remained unanswered for. It made a mockery of the gods and the fools who waited on them.

"You are even more ambitious than Nimrod, then," Traven said. Benedict lifted his head to see a brief, small smile on his face. Before he left, he bowed. "I simply came to thank you. You have my loyalty."

He was about to lie back down when another shadow appeared on a tree in front of him. He turned, his muscles tensing and his mind wide awake and alert again. Justin stepped out of the darkness.

"You went a bit rogue today," Justin commented.

"That's rather an understatement when you're talking about an Oath-breaker," Benedict returned. "You weren't even there."

"More men were watching than you knew." He did not wait for an invitation before joining him on the ground, watching him intently. "So, you will mete out justice to the faeries?"

They had never broached this subject and Benedict felt a mixture of defensiveness and anger that Justin stepped over their unspoken truce. He knew it was irrational; moments ago, he spoke his mind more freely with Traven, whom he hardly knew, than he had with his closest companion.

"No one likes an eavesdropper."

"Have some mercy on this one," Justin returned lightly, though his tone held a somber undercurrent.

"I never asked your reasons either." He sat up and swept his hand over the camp, then lowered his voice. "I don't ask anyone here if they are in this sick game for Nimrod's dream—him, ruling the immortal realm? Stars, I hope only Hound is so mad." He blew out a breath. "You knew I was not here for that."

Justin met his gaze. "Yes. And though you never asked me, I thought you might guess my reasons too."

His stomach turned. He hardly allowed himself to think of what led Justin to the Oath-breakers. The possibilities were more agonizing than his own circumstances.

"I never asked, to protect us both," Benedict retorted, knowing it was a half-truth. "We are no longer Guardians, and this is a dangerous place for friends."

Guilt flitted through him briefly, but he quashed it. Justin may have extended an invitation to genuine conversation, but Benedict could not entertain the notion. He had fired a veiled warning shot across Justin's bow, but it was for his friend's sake too. They were no longer boyhood confidantes. They played on a precarious chessboard that rewarded cunning, not authenticity.

"Consider it forgotten." Justin's voice betrayed little emotion. Even before they left the Guardians, he had become increasingly harder to read.

Benedict nodded. "Good night."

Justin rose to his feet and rejoined Wills, Meeker, Gerard, and Kent near the fire. Traven was with them also, and they all laughed as Kent said something. A momentary loneliness enveloped him, but Benedict elbowed the feeling aside. He lay down on his side this time, facing the camp and firelight. Small sparks flitted upward from the flames and he watched them ascend, flickering, struggling, and then blinking out of existence, swallowed by the night.

CHAPTER 7

Carmel, Island of Japha.
Month of Thunder: Fourth week, First-Day.

Two days after the dinner with Mr. Fox and Mr. Langford, a knock on the door came at mid-afternoon. Leah was lying in bed reading, and the sound startled her, but she ignored it.

"Mr. Fox!" her mother exclaimed once the door opened.

Leah sat up straight in her bed. *Why in the heavens would Mr. Fox pay a visit, particularly without giving notice?* She tossed the sheets off of her and moved to her bedroom door, unable to resist the temptation to eavesdrop.

The voices quieted to inaudible tones for a moment, and then Mrs. Edwards called, "Leah! Mr. Fox would like to speak with you."

Bewildered, Leah moved to throw off her robe and put on a simple dress and large scarf. She ran a comb through her tangled hair, deftly pulling through the knots and smoothing it behind her back. Wild guesses of Mr. Fox's intentions for visiting sprinted through her mind, but all of them appeared terribly unlikely.

She made her way downstairs quickly and found her mother conversing with Mr. Fox at the front door. Mama paused mid-sentence as Leah appeared.

"Here she is," Mrs. Edwards announced unnecessarily, patting Leah on the back.

"Good day, Miss Leah." Mr. Fox bowed and extended his hand. Leah slowly stretched her own out and he grasped and shook it. He had a firm but not overbearing grip; his hand was callused but warm, and his touch momentarily brought her mind back to the ballroom at Edenbridge.

"Hello, Mr. Fox." While he glanced away, Leah flung a baffled look at her mother, who only shook her head vigorously and mouthed something she could not comprehend.

"Would you care to accompany me on a stroll?" He suddenly seemed awkward. "There are some — things I would like to discuss with you."

"I — suppose," Leah acquiesced dazedly. Caught off guard, she was all of a sudden unsure of what to do.

Mrs. Edwards swiftly handed her an overcoat and laid a pair of boots before her. Without a word, Leah slipped her arms into the coat and stepped into the boots. Her mother then opened the door and waved her out after Mr. Fox.

"Have a pleasant walk," she called, and before Leah could react, the door closed behind her.

Gathering her wits about her, Leah spun to face him. "What can I do for you, Mr. Fox?" she asked politely but with a slight edge in her voice.

"You don't have much of a taste for pleasantries, do you?" He raised an eyebrow. He tilted his head away from the house. "Show me the parks. At the least, your mother and sisters won't be watching you like a hawk there."

Grudgingly, Leah led him away from the estate and off the beaten path she had taken to meet Jessie days ago. They walked in silence for much of the trek, leaving her to observe Mr. Fox further. He had a long stride and locked his hands behind his back as he marched forward. Even the twigs crunched soundly as he crushed them beneath the heel of his boot. Her focus was divided though, as half her mind swam with furious speculations of what business he might have with her.

He seemed at ease with the stillness, but Leah grew increasingly nervous. She rubbed her hands against her sides to remove the perspiration and then clasped them together for warmth.

They stepped off the gravelly trail into the open grass plains. "You are wondering why I have come," he said with an air of certainty.

"You are quick in your judgments," Leah returned.

He held up his hands as if in surrender, but his stance did not show any sign of compromise. "I mean no disrespect. I tend to be forward in speaking. I apologize if you take offense."

Leah strode to a bench and sat with her arms crossed. "You are welcome to speak plainly." She fastened her gaze on him.

Mr. Fox paced back and forth in front of her, looking down at the grass. His mouth was moving quietly, as if he were conjuring up the right words, and Leah sensed a tenseness about him. Apprehension welled up in her belly as she waited and time limped on.

"Very well," he said suddenly. He stopped pacing and met her gaze, though this time the piercing quality of his eyes was less startling to her. "I have two things to say. First, what did you mean when you said the story of Arieh was so absurd you believed it?"

Her eyes widened, and she was taken aback. She had nearly forgotten that offhand comment—what made it so important he paid another visit to understand her? She thought for a moment.

"Stories that are too reasonable sound false. Like they were designed to begin and finish neatly. I don't think someone could have just imagined Arieh's legend out of nowhere."

"Because it's unreasonable?"

"Because it's too—" she struggled for the right word. "Ingenious. And I know the sorts of gods the Guardians believe in, just and merciless. But what Arieh did makes me think he knew the God I believe in, who extends mercy and forgiveness."

He nodded slowly, lost in thought, before his focus returned to her. "Ah, yes. Monotheism is popular these days under Amir's rule."

"I'm not monotheistic because King Amir favors it."

"I would never have thought that of you."

She frowned at his cryptic statement. "So, did you come all this way to discuss religion?"

"I was simply curious, so I asked."

"You go far out of your way to satisfy curiosity," she countered.

A glimmer of a smile crossed his face. "Well, I have come for another reason too." He paused and sucked in air through his nostrils. "I would ask to court you, but I cannot stay in Carmel long. My permanent home is still in Cariath…" He trailed off, and she detected the first trace of uncertainty.

Leah felt a thrill of shock. Papa thought she impressed Mr. Fox, but she sincerely thought the notion was nonsensical. She had witnessed enough women throwing themselves in front of him just at the Edenbridge party, while she could not recall a single flattering remark she made to him. She knew some Guardian lore, but what gentleman cared for that?

"So," she managed to prompt him, though her voice wobbled, "you came to say you cannot court me?"

Her attempt at humor fell flat, and his next words came in a rush. "I came to see if you would marry me."

Leah grabbed the seat of the bench as her vision staggered. "I'm not sure I heard you right—" Her voice sounded distant and feeble, and as it petered out, she became acutely aware of the silence.

"You heard me right." His voice sliced through the quiet like a dagger.

"You jest."

"You make me to be a cruel man, who would jest on such a matter with a woman."

Disbelief and denial flooded Leah's mind. She was still reeling from shock at his words, unable to grasp it in full. Yet almost immediately, she tasted fear, realizing she was caught in a thorny situation—regardless of why Mr. Fox requested her hand, sulfur and fire would have to rain down from the heavens before Mama would allow her to reject such a proposal.

She finally peered up into his dark eyes. He remained stoic, and whatever emotion he was experiencing, he concealed it well. He merely stood there, watching her and tapping his foot lightly on the grass.

Leah was at a loss for words. Finally, she managed, "Why?"

"I can't stay and court you, and I can't ask you to follow me to Cariath for a courtship, so—" He raised his shoulders, as if his conclusion was evident.

So…he found her so appealing he did not want to lose her? Or he desperately needed to marry for some unknown reason? Leah could not fathom how he might finish the sentence, and she did not have the wherewithal to ask.

"Why me?"

He appeared unmoved. "Who else should I ask?"

Angered by his casual tone, Leah had a sudden desire to hurl something sharp at him and awaken him to the dire circumstance he had placed her in. "You can't ask me to marry you, with no forewarning or even a prior friendship between us, and expect a response without giving an explanation."

He blew out a breath. "My father wishes me to marry. And from what I know of you, I believe we would be well-matched."

Well-matched?

Leah looked at him incredulously. Her thoughts crashed with a mixture of questions and insults. "Ask Shay! She's older than me. Or don't you know there are a dozen women in Carmel who would fall over themselves for you? What led you to choose — to choose the one person who isn't asking for this?" The words felt cruel coming out of her mouth, but Leah ignored it, riding on the tide of her antagonism towards him.

Mr. Fox did not seem to take offense. "I don't need empty affection. I don't have an easy life, nor does wealth always guarantee security." A hard edge entered his voice. "Consider that a compliment, Miss Leah."

Leah closed her eyes briefly, wishing with all her might that this was a nightmare, and she would wake up in her warm bed.

"Then answer me this." She fixed her gaze on him. "Are you a Guardian?"

Something flinched in his eyes. "Yes."

"Will my family be in danger, if I marry you?" She forced the words out.

"The Guardians are sidelined by Amir's government, and we face no threat from it." He paused. "If evil falls upon the Guardians from the immortal realm, then Carmel is no safer, regardless of your ties to me."

His words sent a sense of foreboding over her, quickly replaced by anguish over her immediate circumstance. Her initial, distasteful impression of Mr. Fox from the party had not dissipated, but her anxiety came less from the fact she disliked him than the fact that she did not know him.

It was not uncommon in Carmel for courtships to be short, or skipped entirely. Love marriages were the unusual ones, but Leah never imagined her story would unfold this way. Her earlier remark about the inauthenticity of too-reasonable tales drifted to mind, rife with irony.

She looked down at her lap. "I don't wish to marry yet, and marry you least of all," she said softly, more to herself than to him. She glanced back up at him, more distressed than resentful now. "You have put me in a difficult position, Mr. Fox."

He spread his hands. "I can be accused of being a hard man, but do not think me an evil one. You are perfectly within your rights to refuse."

46

"I can't," she whispered. She quieted for a moment, and then blurted out, "We're losing the estate! My mother will never allow me to reject such a proposal." Leah regretted the words once they were out of her mouth, and she looked up to see the surprise on his face. "You didn't know?"

Mr. Fox shook his head. "I'm sorry to hear that," he said, and she sensed a trace of sincerity in his tone.

Leah took a deep breath and exhaled, picturing her old life blowing away in the wind. As much as she hated this turn of events, she had known from the moment Mr. Fox proposed what she would do. Her duty to family prevailed against her unwillingness to accept him—as it prevailed against most things. Yet in her submission, she found an unlikely tranquility. She felt no real struggle over the decision. Her outward fighting spirit masked the white flag of surrender raised in her heart from the beginning.

"Will you tell my family what you are?"

"Do you want me to?" His question seemed sincere, free of guile.

The potential ramifications swirled through her mind. She did not even know what Guardian life entailed, but at the moment, did not care enough to find out.

"Only my father."

He nodded. "I will ask him for approval, of course."

A long pause settled between them. Mr. Fox seemed to wait for her to lead the conversation now, but Leah felt too numb to conjure up words. She rose to her feet and met his eyes, holding her trembling chin up.

"Then consider your proposal accepted."

CHAPTER 8

When the Edwards family overcame their initial disbelief at Leah's engagement, they sprang into a flurry of action to prepare for the upcoming nuptials. The stigma of losing the estate seemed almost forgotten. Mrs. Edwards was suddenly calling on Mrs. Lane every day to discuss wedding plans, shrewdly inserting boasts of her daughter's good fortune. Nyssa was even excited, and often brought up visiting Cariath with Mr. Langford once they married. Shay sulked silently around the house.

Mr. Edwards was initially quiet upon hearing the news, and Leah suspected he worried for her happiness. Yet once Mr. Fox visited him to ask permission formally, he seemed merry again, and Leah wondered what Mr. Fox had said to reassure him, if anything. How did he bring up his Guardian heritage and what did Papa make of it? Time passed in a headlong rush, and she barely had a private moment to speak with Papa.

Mr. Fox joined their family for dinner occasionally, and all the Edwards adored him. She was quietly thankful she spent little time with him alone, save for a few occasions when they discussed wedding details. Though pithy, their conversations were stilted and awkward, and Leah finally admitted it was more her fault than his, as she made little effort in civility toward him. A small part of her hoped beyond hope that he might change his mind and break off the engagement, but despite her minimal acquaintance with his character, Leah knew it was a vain thought.

On the day of the wedding, Leah awoke with fear gnawing at the pit of her stomach. Sudden panic seized her as she wondered what she was trading her familiar life in for. She wanted nothing more than to crawl beneath her covers and disappear, but before she could dwell on that any further, Nyssa burst through her door.

"Still not up—you will be late!" she exclaimed. "Hurry, I must help you get dressed and ready." She stepped to Leah's side and all but towed her out of the bed.

After a quick bath, Nyssa helped Leah put on the red gown Mama had bought for her. Elegant lace spun down both her arms while sheets of silk clung to her lithe body, opening in a large bloom near the soles of her feet. Working diligently, Nyssa pinned her dark hair on every side to keep it out of her face but flowing in layers behind her back.

"I feel ill." Leah finally broke the silence bluntly.

Nyssa continued to perfect her hair, undeterred. "It's normal to feel anxious on your wedding day."

Leah spun around while Nyssa had her hands in mid-air. Before she could protest, she grasped her sister by the arms. "I hardly know him," she breathed, wishing she could stem the flow of words from her mouth, but with her chest throbbing, she could not help but continue. "I don't know anything of his past, his life, his home. I'm marrying a stranger from a strange world. I can't, Nyssa, I—" She broke off, half-ashamed of her weakness but half-relieved the words spilled out so at least her sister knew.

Nyssa stared at her, unmoving, her eyes revealing nothing. Then in an uncharacteristic show of sympathy, she threw her arms around Leah's neck. Leah wrapped her arms around her sister's waist and they stood like that in silence.

"Oh, my little sister," Nyssa whispered. She ran her slender fingers through Leah's dark mane. Leah could not see her face, but her words sounded strangled.

"I'm a perfect coward," she said with fierce disgust. Her voice lowered. "But I can't help myself."

Nyssa loosened herself from their embrace and once again looked into her sad eyes. "You can be afraid and still be brave. You *are* brave. You were calm and kind to Papa more than anyone even with our losing the estate."

"This is different," Leah said, looking down at the floor.

"Leah," she began with an unusual sensitivity, "I know you agreed to this for the family. He's rich, and with pressure over the estate and our reputation…" She trailed off as Leah jerked her head up. "I know you're not after all those things. You're not like the other women. If only Mr. Fox had set his sights on Shay…but then, perhaps your difference is what won him over."

The corners of Leah's eyes grew damp. Her sister rarely spoke her heart. She pulled Nyssa back into an embrace to keep her from seeing the tears threatening to fall and wiped her face roughly with her sleeve. "Thank you," she whispered. With more of her customary tone she added, "I will miss you, even though you drive me mad sometimes. Now Shay and Mama and Papa will have to handle it all."

Nyssa swatted at her lightly and she leaped back. "I will miss you too, though I'm secretly glad because this means more space for me in the cottage."

"Until you marry Mr. Langford."

"Right. You know, if you really are so anxious, I might be amenable to trading husbands." She smiled and winked good-naturedly.

Leah shook her head. "Finish my hair, would you, or we really shall be late."

Her sister obediently returned to the pins in her dark locks and said, "We must make you look presentable, of course. Though Mr. Fox seems a stranger, he is certainly a handsome one."

They both giggled, and Leah felt the burden on her heart lifted for the moment and she breathed more easily.

The Edwards' carriage pulled up in front of Edenbridge and came to a creaking stop. They had decided upon a small ceremony there to the chagrin of Mrs. Edwards, who privately wished for an extravagant wedding. Only family and close friends were in attendance—the Edwards, Lanes, Whitefields, and Langfords. When Leah asked him, Mr. Fox said his mother had passed away and his father would be unable to join them, but would certainly throw them a celebration in Cariath when they returned.

Mr. Edwards, Mrs. Edwards, and all three girls clambered out and Mrs. Edwards herded them all through the front door. The wedding was to be held in the upper ballroom since it was the largest room of the estate. Leah found that an ironic twist of fate. As the rest of her family arrived upstairs first, Leah waited with her father at the foot of the stairs. He would lead her in at the prescribed time and give her hand in marriage to Mr. Fox.

A weary sense of detachment had overcome Leah. While there were still traces of fear and a wild dash of curiosity regarding her future life, she felt numb to the proceedings, as if her emotions were already drained and she had trained herself to merely walk through the motions.

"Leah." Papa's voice broke through her pondering. Startled, she turned to face him, wearing a questioning look. "Are you well?" he asked, tenderness in his tone.

"Nervous," she admitted. She paused to consider her next words. Finally, she said, "But I'm at peace with this." She did not wish to elaborate further, and hoped he would not question her more.

Mr. Edwards gave a nod. "He's a good man, Leah, though you might not know him well yet."

"How are you certain?" She bit her lip, afraid that her voice was too thick with acrimony.

If her father noticed the sourness of her tone, he did not comment. "I spoke with him for quite some time when he asked me for your hand." A crinkled smile spread across his features. "You must have been the only one of the family without her ear against the door while we were cloistered in my office."

Leah glanced at him hesitantly. "He told you what he is, right?"

He raised a brow. "A Guardian? Yes." Papa looked at her closely. "Does that worry you?"

She almost laughed. "I hardly know anything to judge whether or not it should."

"Even after all those books?" he countered, a twinkle in his eye. He grew more serious. "Don't let it worry you, then. I trust August."

She looked at him curiously. "Do you know something more about him?"

A strange look came into her father's eyes. She was not sure how to describe it, except that it seemed faraway and almost wistful.

"You will know far more of him than anyone, in time. The two shall become one, as the husband cleaves to his wife."

A tremble went through her body, and Leah realized her hands were shaking slightly. The numbness that was like a cloud over her seemed to be peeling away and a strange basket of emotions—apprehension, curiosity, even a thrill of adventure at her father's words—poured over her.

The grandfather clock chimed suddenly, and they both looked up, shaken out of their individual reveries. Leah looked at her father and he gave her a comforting smile before extending his elbow to her to grasp.

As she looped her arm through his, with his other hand he touched her chin, gently pushing her face up so their eyes met. "He may be hard at times, but he has a kind heart. Leah, I would not give up my daughter to a man less than that."

She squeezed his arm and returned a smile, warmth spreading in her bones. "I know, Papa."

~~~~~

The wedding was simple but lovely. The ballroom boasted rows of pew-like seats, and light pink flowers adorning the ends. A small altar stood in front of the pews. While most weddings took place at the Carmel chapel, August expressly did not want that. He said it was not due to disbelief in God—which was what Leah thought—but rather he did not want their marriage on official government records, which it would be if they conducted it in the church. Then, if Guardian relations with Amir's government soured, the Edwards might suffer from it indirectly.

While August confided his reasoning to Papa and Leah, they did not share it with the others. They told the rest of the family and guests that Cariath citizens often hosted weddings in their own manors. Besides, with the priest officiating and the presence of witnesses, it was no less legal.

The Edwards and family friends watched eagerly as Mr. Edwards led Leah up to the front where Mr. Fox waited. He was dressed in a proper black suit with a bowtie, his ginger hair slicked back stylishly. He wore a pleasant expression with a slight smile.

Leah murmured a silent prayer for strength as her father placed her hand in Mr. Fox's. The priest read the vows, and she was surprised each time she heard herself repeat after him, her voice astonishingly calm and steady. Mr. Fox was equally composed, and her nerves slowly unwound as they continued with the ceremony. When the vows were completed, he leaned in and they kissed lightly. She forced a smile as everyone applauded and they turned to face their audience.

Mr. Fox bent himself toward her and whispered, "They will lay out refreshments on the tables in the back and I have requested music for a short dance. That's all. Then you will be put out of this misery." Leah detected a hint of amusement in his voice.

As the attendees quieted, classical music swept across the ballroom.

People rose from their seats, some mingling, some walking toward the refreshments in the back, and a few waiting eagerly in the front to greet Mr. Fox and Leah. He offered her his hand to assist her down the step as she lifted the folds of her dress pooling at her feet.

To her surprise, he continued to grip her palm as they moved toward the others. She cast a quick glance in his direction, but he did not appear to take notice.

"Congratulations!" Jessie exclaimed, the first to rush forward. Mr. Fox smoothly released her hand so she could grasp Leah's arms and pull her into a tight embrace. She whispered into her ear, "I can't believe you won his heart so swiftly. You are the envy of the town, you know."

Leah could not help an eye roll. "I would not envy myself in the least."

Jessie pulled back and searched her face, a glimmer of sympathy streaking across the delight written in her expression. She glanced in the direction of Mr. Fox, who had moved away from them to greet the Whitefields. "You have always put a brave face on things. Be of some cheer, Leah. I think you will grow to be fond of him."

"I'm fond of my father. I'm fond of my sisters, of you," Leah retorted. "Fondness is no woman's dream in the great sport of romantic love." She exhaled. "But you know I will try. I can't despise my own husband."

"You are an admirable woman," she said sincerely. "Though, I don't imagine I would take it quite so hard if I had to marry Mr. Fox," she added playfully. "But in any case, I will make you a wager. Come back in one year and tell me you have learned to love him dearly."

Leah looked at her expectantly. "And what is the price on the wager?"

"Oh, nothing of monetary value. If you do love him, I will simply have the pleasure of being right and you will have the pleasure of being married to your great love."

"And if I do not?"

Jessie raised her shoulders. "It would be a sad loss for the both of us — so do try hard to avoid that."

Leah swatted her shoulder playfully and shook her head. "You are too much for me."

Jessie happily took her by the arm and paraded around the refreshments table, insisting on filling Leah's stomach as a means of celebration. Leah was not hungry in the least, and rather felt ragged and sick from all the pomp and attention she received. Every well-meaning soul greeted her with joy, and she learned to paste on a smile and graciously accept their felicitations while she desperately wished to be out of the ballroom and alone in her bedroom. Until she remembered with a sinking heart that her bedroom was no longer hers, and home was with Mr. Fox.

Home. She would not be here for long either — they would leave for Cariath soon. August had not given an express timeline, but she assumed that they would go once they settled into the rhythm of married life. Leah figured he had Guardian duties to attend to, though she had not asked for details. She would leave behind her family and all she had ever known for a different world. She would go with a new name, accompanied only by the stranger she now called husband. The thought of it was overwhelming, and she felt like a small bird in a tidal wave. There was no turning back now; the pieces were in place and the only path for her was forward into an unknown wilderness.

She had not admitted this to anyone, but a small part of her also felt a thrill of excitement—she was going to step out of her sheltered town into a world she only ever found inside Papa's books. It could be a nightmare, or a great adventure.

Leah did not know how much time had passed as she greeted family and friends, watching them mingle about the ballroom, some talking and some dancing merrily to the music. She felt like a distant observer, as if she were removed from the scene and watching an event in which she had no personal investment. It was an odd contrast with the reality, where she was the center of attention, the focus of the celebration, the reason for the gathering.

She had nearly forgotten about Mr. Fox, so wrapped up in her speculations about her future life that she did not think much of the man who would accompany her, until he appeared by her side again.

"Leah, we ought to give a quick speech, each of us. Then we can end the reception and send people home." His voice sounded tired.

Startled by his sudden presence, she stared at him for a moment, taking in what he said. She nodded slowly, briefly wondering at his weariness and if he actually disliked parties as much as she did. "You will need their attention."

He clapped his hands, a fluid and sharp motion. The room quieted and eyes turned toward them. Leah could not help but marvel somewhat at his commanding air, something she had never possessed. He, on the other hand, was a man people looked upon with deference despite his solemnity and reticence.

"We don't wish to keep you long," he began, "so Leah and I have a few words to share before we close this reception." She noted some smiles and eager faces, mostly from her family and Jessie. "I'm grateful to all of you for your kindness and friendship, though I have not been in Carmel long. I will think of this place fondly, and will visit often, both because it is the home of my wife and because it will be a delight to enjoy your company and the pleasures of this town. I look forward to my wedded life with Leah, and thank you all for joining our celebration as we are united." He spread his hands, indicating the end of his speech.

Polite applause resounded before they turned their gazes toward Leah. She swallowed hard, though her mouth was dry, grasping for the right words while part of her mind was distracted by how he called her his *wife*, a terribly short and understated word for so lofty and foreign a concept.

"Thank you for coming," she said, hoping no one noticed the slight wobble in her voice. She cleared her throat and breathed deeply. "You are the family and the friends I was raised with, the ones who taught me of life and love," she went on, her voice growing stronger. Leah looked intently at her audience—her father, her sisters, the Lanes, and more. "My heart is knit to Carmel and the people here. It will be hard to leave, but I carry you all with me wherever I go. Here's to a new journey I embark on with my—with my husband." She offered a weak smile. "I will always be here in spirit."

Leah hardly noticed the claps as she finished speaking, her palms damp with sweat and images of Carmel and her childhood spinning through her mind. She was shaken out of her reverie as she felt a warm hand against the small of her back, and looked up in surprise at Mr. Fox.

"Are you feeling unwell?"

She wondered if she imagined his look of concern.

"No. Just…thinking," she replied vaguely.

He nodded and did not press her further. "You're eloquent with words. I could use your help with speeches."

"Are those a Guardian tradition?"

"Dinner parties," he said by way of explanation. "My father enjoys hosting them and I am often left with the task of saying something that will tickle the ears of the guests."

"Well, you have the wrong woman for the undertaking. I'm no good with small talk and empty words."

"I learned that at our first meeting," he remarked dryly before changing the subject. "I will dismiss the party and we can retire. It's been a long day."

Leah numbly bade all the guests farewell as they departed the manor and the numbers dwindled. For a few brief moments, she recalled the strange shadows she had seen last time in the ballroom, but she had found nothing out of the ordinary during the day. Her family was the last to leave, and she embraced each of them tightly as they showered her with well wishes, even Shay, whose wounded pride seemed nearly healed. Her father gave her a small wink and smile, and she found more solace in that than most of the words spoken to her that day.

Soon enough, the estate was emptied of people and Leah felt a profound loneliness settle in the bowels of her spirit. The grandeur of Edenbridge felt alien to her, and the presence of her husband was no balm to her melancholy disposition.

CHAPTER 9

Pharan Desert, Island of Japha.
Month of Harvest: Second week, Fire-Day.

It was high noon, and the sun beat down ruthlessly on the earth. Benedict felt the ground warm his soles, even through his boots. They were moving eastward from the southern border of the Pharan Desert, just north of Whitewitch. It was about a twenty-day journey by foot, and unforgiving to the unprepared traveler with its limited water reservoirs and heat. They had been traveling for a fortnight already, and Benedict bitterly recalled a much easier trip by horseback when he traversed the terrain years ago.

The men around him were pouring water from canteens on their ruddy, crimson faces for relief. To their credit, no one complained in front of him. They knew the Pharan Desert, with its long stretch of red sand-dust, would meet them regardless of which path they took. Even White Tiger Guardians coming from Cariath needed to cross the Pharan to reach En-doire, which explained the decline in contact over the years.

Aimless chatter had diminished over the course of their journey. They were five days away from town, and most seemed weary from dehydration and hunger.

Benedict was less affected, mentally consumed with his mission. Mounting pressure grew in his mind during their trek. The Black Tortoise Guardians of En-doire were hawkish and suspicious, and he remembered vividly how the Old Fox last left on sour terms with Marcum, the Tortoise chief. The advantage of the cold relationship meant chances were slim that Marcum knew of Nimrod and the Oath-breakers, all of whom came from Cariath.

Yet Benedict could not stride in openly either, pretending to be an ally, for Marcum had no great love for the Foxes.

"We should rest," Justin said, interrupting his thoughts. "The men will not have the strength to fight if we continue."

Benedict shook his head. "I hope it won't come to fighting." He surveyed the surroundings quickly. They were nearing a sparse patch of cacti and shrubbery, but otherwise, the red desert still extended to the edge of his vision. "But we can rest. Let's make camp until sunset and avoid the heat."

As the soldiers pressed themselves against sparse shrubs for the shade of the meager foliage, Benedict motioned for Justin to follow him a slight distance away. He reached into his cloak and unfolded a crumpled piece of parchment.

"The clue?" Justin asked.

"The land unbound by time and space / opens only to the one who knows / the Light, the Song and Mortal Gate," he recited. Folding up the document again, Benedict glanced at him. "We *think* Black Tortoise guards the song. Have you ever heard otherwise?"

Surprised flashed across Justin's face but it vanished quickly. He took the paper from Benedict and skimmed it, his brow furrowed.

"We know the White Tigers guard the mortal gate. The Vermilion Falcon piece is a riddle, so unless we mixed it up with the Cobalt Dragon's lantern, Tortoise should have the song."

Benedict nodded. "Here is the other problem. We were Tigers and we know nothing about where or what exactly the mortal gate is. Only the Marshals do."

"So you think it might be the same with Black Tortoise." Justin caught his gaze, and Benedict saw a glint of unease in his eyes. "The men believe you know where to find the key."

"I'll figure it out," Benedict said, a defensive edge in his tone.

Justin handed the parchment back to him and fell silent for a moment, pacing back and forth. Benedict let out a sigh of frustration. Anxiety gnawed at the edges of his mind as they drew near to En-doire, and he had begun preparing for the most dangerous scenario—scattering his men inside the town to gather clues from townspeople about the riddle. But even that would prove fruitless if only an elite few knew about the key.

"Well," Justin began slowly, "even though we were never told about the mortal gate, you were able to hazard a guess about where it is, right?"

He raised a brow. "So?"

"Fox Manor?"

Benedict grimaced. He had tried hunting for it, years ago, when rumors first reached him that the White Tigers knew of the gate to the faerie world. He was certain it was hidden inside their home, one of the oldest establishments in Cariath and residence of Marshals throughout the ages. He had confided in Justin then, who joined him in furtive searches, but they never uncovered anything within the estate walls.

He crossed his arms, not wanting to dwell on those times, or think that Justin was remembering them either. "Your point?"

"A native of En-doire could give us a clue, even if they don't have definite knowledge."

"Fair enough. And do we just kidnap one?"

"Traven," Justin said.

"What?" Benedict looked at him in confusion, but he was already sprinting back to the main camp.

He returned with Traven trailing behind him hesitantly. Benedict aimed a half-irritated, half-questioning look at Justin. Traven was fast becoming part of their inner circle, but Benedict did not want him privy to all the details of the mission, particularly their sore dearth of information.

"Traven spent part of his Guardian years around En-doire," Justin explained swiftly.

Benedict straightened. "We never sent a contingent to En-doire." He winced internally at his use of *we*. His companions did not react, but he was sure it did not escape Justin's notice.

"I didn't go on Guardian business." Traven flushed. "My mother was from En-karah, one of the nearby settlements. When her father fell ill, I took a leave to stay with him."

"Does Nimrod know?"

"Nimrod? No, I—I doubt he even really knows who I am. Just a name in his ranks." He looked between the two men with a sense of bewilderment.

Benedict mulled over this new revelation. Among Guardian clans, Tiger and Tortoise experienced the most friction over the long years. He wondered if Traven had kept his mother's background quiet in Cariath, and he felt a strange tug of kinship.

Noting his silence, Justin picked up the conversation. "You know why we are going to En-doire."

"Yes, the song."

He said it so easily, so assuredly, Benedict felt a thrill of hope. "What do you know of it?"

Traven hesitated, scuffing his boot on the cracked ground. "It's difficult to separate the truth from myth. I thought you or Nimrod might have more knowledge." He paused, as if unsure whether he should offer his insight. "A common speculation, though, is that all of En-doire knows the song already."

"*What?*"

"They don't know they know it, of course," Traven clarified. "Music runs deep in the En-doiren culture, and ancient songs have been passed down through many generations. Some think that one of these is *the* song, the faerie key Tortoise protects, and the genius of hiding it is not in secrecy, but in openness. It's mixed in among all the old folk songs, perhaps combined to make new ones, and the original is lost in that sense."

The other two exchanged a long look. The earlier rush of hope began to sink like a stone in Benedict's heart. It might be speculation, but Traven's explanation carried a ring of truth. The keys would not all be hidden the same way, and a song could not be protected as a gate could. Better to hide it in plain sight, and allow time and changing tradition to cover its trail. He kept up a stoic expression for Traven's sake, but Justin would know the blow this information dealt to their mission.

"There was a verse my mother used to sing, though. She grew up in En-karah, but the Guardian culture of En-doire seeped into all the surrounding towns." Traven seemed distant in thought all of a sudden. "Maybe—" he trailed off.

Before either of them could prompt him, he began to sing in a rich but slightly off-key tenor:

> *O dream in a dream, what is truth?*
> *that stands from age to age.*
> *Though mortal empires rise and fall,*
> *the eternal realm remains.*

He glanced at them, his wiry frame and sheepish expression lending themselves to awkwardness again. "It seemed significant."

The melody and words threw Benedict headlong into the bright, vaulted-ceiling halls of Fox Manor. Mother would come in with a fresh spray of wildflowers and a quiet tune on her lips. Only when he came of age did he realize how unusual her gift was. Songs were not a tradition in Cariath, and the ones she sang seemed at once foreign and familiar, conjured up in an exotic place yet carving deep roots in their home.

He had never heard Traven's verse, but it echoed the same essence. Could the Old Fox have known Tortoise's key too, then?

Justin was speaking and watching Benedict out of the corner of his eye. He shook off the memory before the ache of it could reopen old wounds.

"Good instinct," Benedict interrupted brusquely. "But we need certainty, and we need the entire song."

"I was asking Traven if there might be a written record," Justin said. "They can't fail to preserve the original in some form."

Traven nodded. "If there is, it would be kept in—"

"—the Tortoise Treasury." Benedict shrugged as the other two jerked their heads toward him. "They keep all their valuables there, but Marcum boasts of its impenetrability."

"That's not a well-known fact," Traven said, thinly disguising the question in his voice.

A surge of renewed confidence rushed through Benedict at sight of a dim light ahead. They had a way forward now, and at the least, they did not need to walk into En-doire witless. He could not resist imagining Marcum's face once he learned of their success.

"Benedict has roots in En-doire too," Justin supplied, and then bit his lip, as if unsure of how much to say.

He waved away his friend's concern as his spirits lifted. "Yes, the Foxes are old friends of Marcum." A gleam entered his eye and his lips twitched into a smirk. "I know a scrap more than he would like."

They called for a full day's halt, spending the rest of the afternoon drawing up plans for their arrival in En-doire. Traven proved to be a valuable asset with his knowledge of routes, particularly leading into and away from the Treasury. Using wooden sticks and the thin layer of red sand-dust, they sketched crude maps and strategies on the desert floor.

By dinnertime, they possessed a rudimentary plan that Benedict thought would suffice. Dusk descended with glossy patches of pink and burnt orange in skies that gave way to rich mahogany. The evening breeze dissipated some of the warmth, but it also swept up desert dust onto their clothes and into their eyes. Earlier in their journey, the men would engage in mock duels at nighttime when the air cooled, but the long days of sun and sore feet took their toll. Most lay sprawled around the camp after supper, damp scarves wrapped around their faces.

"What a sight we are," Gerard said dryly.

He, Traven, Justin and Benedict still sat awake around their earlier sketches. They also wore scarves around their heads, against the red sand whirling like small, rebel storms around them.

"Good thing we have no plans to fight our way through the Tortoise," Justin noted.

Benedict was quiet, a nascent thought from earlier in the day finally taking in shape in his mind. He glanced at Traven. "You knew Nimrod sent us to find the song. The others all think we know where the key is. You knew it might be a fruitless expedition, but you said nothing."

He wished he could see the other man's face, obscured by the darkness and sand.

"Yes."

"Why?"

A gaping silence met him. Finally, Gerard cast a glance between the rest of the camp and Benedict and spoke up on the other's behalf.

"Why would he want the bastard to succeed?"

His whisper through the wind could not have reached anyone beyond their circle of four, but they thundered like war drums in Benedict's ears. Those were words of unconcealed sedition. Traven did not look at him, but Justin caught his eye.

"You knew not everyone signed up for Nimrod's agenda," he said in his typical, sensible tone, as if there was nothing earth-shaking in their conversation.

Unexpected fury stirred in Benedict's breastbone. "Listen," he hissed, clenching his fists, and waiting for each of them to turn and meet his glare. "Never say those words again." He jabbed his finger at Gerard. "I will not defend any of you if Nimrod accuses you of mutiny."

"Benedict—" Justin began.

"Be here for whatever reason you have. But I don't need to hear it."

Before any of them could respond, he rose to his feet, shook the dust off his clothes, and stalked away into the camp.

CHAPTER 10

Carmel, Island of Japha.
Month of Harvest: Second week, Fire-Day.

Mr. Fox—August, as Leah realized she should learn to think of him—gave her a brief tour of the manor after they changed into more comfortable clothing. It was nothing like the nightmarish picture she had of it as a child, with ghostly sounds and dusty corridors. The wine-colored hardwood floors were polished and spotless in the spacious kitchen and ballroom, while plush beige carpets covered most of the house. Every room was well lit, even the ones in secluded corners of the house.

A fair number of rooms in the manor were mostly bare. August had no servants with him—she learned he borrowed a few for the housewarming party—which was increasingly the norm in smaller households. But it was unusual to think he made the journey from Cariath to Carmel alone. Most middle-class families at least had a chauffeur or servant with them to go to Ephes or another seaside town.

"You ought to put in some more furniture, if only for decoration," Leah remarked.

"It would be unnecessary. No one lives in them, and even we won't be here for most the year."

He pointed out his room, which Leah noted was not much larger than any of the others, though it did hold a large bed and a desk populated with scattered books and papers. She wondered if he was a prolific reader, but she hesitated to ask.

August stopped at the room next to his and led Leah inside. There was a large bed with lilac print sheets and a petite nightstand beside it. The room was pretty, Leah thought, especially as the window faced west and a sliver of dusk light fell across the floor.

"I designed this room for you," he said, and she caught a hint of uncertainty in his voice. "Even though we will leave for Cariath, I thought you should have something of your own here still."

"Oh," Leah exclaimed and bit her lip. "I thought we would—since we're married—" She fumbled the words as her cheeks flushed with heat.

For the first time, he appeared equally uneasy and smoothed his hair back nervously, so ginger spikes peppered the top of his head. Leah braved a glance at his face, but his gaze was bent downward.

"You think of me as nearly a stranger still," he replied finally. "I didn't want to make you uncomfortable."

Leah stared at him for a moment, unsure of how to respond. A part of her was relieved, since she already disliked sharing a room with one of her sisters; she had struggled to imagine doing so intimately with a man, let alone one she hardly knew. While a fleeting sense of appreciation for his consideration flew through her, she felt a flash of humiliation, as if he were treating her as a child.

"*I* think of you as a stranger," she echoed. "And what of you? You think you know me?" She could not restrain the biting tone that infused her words.

"I don't," August said simply, and he looked exhausted. "I didn't mean to offend your pride. I believed the living situation to be preferable to both you and me, at least, until we know one another more."

"Fine." Leah felt a wave of shame at her small outburst, but her stubbornness kept her from apologizing.

They watched each other for a long moment: him, with a tired and otherwise unreadable expression, and her with the guarded look of an injured animal. Leah felt a prick against her conscience, accusing her of the vindictiveness she demonstrated around him, but she suppressed the guilt with her own charges against him for dragging her into an unwanted union.

"I will leave you to unpack," he said abruptly. "If you need anything, you can find me downstairs."

With that, August spun around and strode out of the room. Leah sank into her bed, watching the sun's last flare of glory before night spread its amethyst blanket over the skies. She closed her eyes to plug the onset of tears.

~~~~

Leah did not know how much time she passed staring out the window as the sky changed from fiery hues to a coal-colored darkness. The stars were clear, bright spots against the yawning black scroll that covered the heavens. As a child, she often looked upon them with wonder, curious what worlds lay beyond the reach of her sight. Nyssa and Shay had often scorned her imagination, seeing her dreams as nothing more than girlish fantasies she had yet to outgrow. Yet Leah had never become preoccupied with the things they enjoyed most—suitors and balls and town gossip—but found most pleasure in stories, particularly the ones her father wove in such detail that she could almost taste the air of other places and see the characters in all their flesh-and-blood glory.

Her mind slowly stepped through her favorite tales and allowed them to lull her into a cradle of drowsiness, a warm and sweet space to rest in. She pulled the lilac sheets over half her body and rested her head against the pillows. But as she was about to drift off into unconsciousness, a tap on the door startled Leah and shook her out of lethargy.

Warily, she slipped out of bed and peered through the doorway. August was nowhere in sight, perplexing her until she glanced down near her feet. A small tray bearing generous portions of wild rice and grilled salmon met her searching eyes. As if in response, Leah's stomach grumbled in a most unladylike manner, and she recalled she had hardly eaten all day, but for the few refreshments at the wedding reception.

She stooped to pick up the warm meal, the delicious aroma making her mouth water. Leah clambered back into bed with the food, eagerly consuming it with little regard to table manners, as no one was there to rebuke her.

After she was full, she piled the plates on her tray and made her way downstairs to the kitchen. She walked cautiously, unsure of where August would be, and not wanting an unwelcome surprise if he suddenly appeared. He was nowhere in sight, so she washed the plates in the sink, a knot of apprehension inside her chest. Her relief at avoiding an encounter with him was mingled with regret and discomfort. She hated being in a quarrel.

As Leah moved to leave the kitchen, she paused as she heard crisp footsteps on the stairwell. Her hands tightened and she drew in a deep breath. August appeared in the kitchen doorway, his ginger hair damp from a shower. He had donned loose-fitting clothes — though they were still black, making Leah wonder if he even owned other colors — and a mild but pleasant herbal scent touched her senses.

Silence hung in the air for a moment before they both opened their mouths.

"Thank you for dinner," Leah said, more stiffly than she liked.

"You didn't have to wash those," August said at the same time.

There was a pregnant pause where they stared at one another awkwardly, and Leah felt a small sense of satisfaction that he seemed as much at a loss of what to do as her. Suddenly, the idea that he was her husband struck her as preposterous all over again.

August finally broke the stillness. "I'm glad I've caught you. I just received a message from my father — I'm sorry, Leah, but we need to return to Cariath as soon as possible."

Sudden panic squashed her earlier indignation. "What? Why?"

He glanced down, his brows furrowed. "Do you know the Ebene region?"

"Yes, the grasslands. In the southern part of Japha."

August nodded. "The Guardians in different regions are not as well-connected as before, but we've heard troubling rumors from there. Some skirmishes or attacks."

"But how does that affect Cariath?"

"My father is worried that some are after ancient Guardian artifacts." He hesitated, seeming to mull over his words. "In the wrong hands, things could take a catastrophic turn."

Leah allowed the news to sink in, like a heavy stone inside her stomach.

She had imagined they would have at least a few weeks in Carmel—enough time to see her family settled into their new cottage, and still go for walks with Jessie and pour out her new marital woes.

Perhaps sensing her mood, August said, "I promise you won't be in any danger. The Bastion, which is what we call our part of Cariath Valley, is likely the safest place in Japha. Carmel might feel secure by nature of its geography, but the Bastion is protected by more than Guardians and mountains."

Leah detected a mystical implication in his words, but did not feel like probing. She simply shook her head. "I wasn't worried about that. When do we need to leave?" She steeled herself for his answer.

He was quiet for a moment. "Three days should be reasonable."

For a fleeting moment, Leah was tempted to propose that August return to Cariath himself, and she could remain with her family in Carmel. But duty and faith kept her lips sealed. She was raised with a strong sense of responsibility to family, and a high view of marriage as God-ordained. Whether she felt like it or not, August *was* her family now. When she took her vows, she had promised to walk with him, whatever the path ahead.

So she nodded. "Three days, then," she echoed. Her voice betrayed almost none of the emotion coursing through her.

August's eyes still looked troubled, but a small smiled touched his lips. "Thank you." Perhaps he guessed some of what she felt, even though she concealed it.

Leah tapped her foot nervously as he turned to leave. "Wait," she called, when he vanished behind the door. She stepped out of the kitchen to find him paused on the first step of the stairwell. "I ought to apologize." She wrestled the words out. "I spoke unfairly earlier."

He raised an eyebrow slightly and met her gaze. It recalled to Leah the intimidating and penetrating quality of his eyes she observed upon their first meeting in the ballroom.

"Forget it. It was inconsequential." He waved his hand.

A rush of frustration spilled through her. "That's all you have to say?"

His eyes grew hard. "I don't know what to say to please you. I attempt to consider your feelings and earn your anger. Now I accept your apology and find that's not enough?"

"I'm not as difficult as you make me sound," Leah returned.

"You were concise and I simply responded in an equal manner."

She ground her teeth and clenched her hands, trying to douse the fire that burned below her heart. "I'm concise, but I speak truthfully."

His posture appeared to relax and his eyes softened faintly. "I understand. I suppose—where I come from, I'm unused to such direct apologies," he admitted, his tone an odd mixture of embarrassment and sternness still. "You caught me off guard."

A wave of sadness swept over Leah and she stared at him for a

66

moment. She was terribly homesick all of a sudden. She felt trapped, like a hapless fish caught in a net, flailing about for something secure to cling to in this strange place.

"All right," she acknowledged tiredly. She broke her gaze from his face and strode to the stairwell, her shoulder brushing August's as she passed him. As much as she refused to admit it, Leah half-expected — half-hoped nearly — that he would stop her and express further contrition, but he made no movement or sound. Pushing aside her disappointment, she reached the second floor and marched to her room without a backward glance.

~~~~~

Leah passed the next two days restlessly, spending much of the time in her room. She occasionally wandered about the manor in an effort to explore the building that her childhood self once held in such awe and terror. Occasionally, she thought she awoke to echoes of conversations in the empty house, or she would hear the odd sound coming from the walls — rustling leaves or the scrape of metal. All of them were so faint she chalked them up to her imagination, and there were no more strange shadow sightings along the walls. With the new decor and in broad daylight, the ghost stories surrounding Edenbridge seemed absurd.

She encountered August once in a while moving through the house. He was always tidying the furniture and loose articles scattered around, or reading and writing diligently in his study room. Their brief greetings in the hallways were cordial but brief.

Morning dawned with a golden sky and the sound of crickets chirping on the day of their departure. Leah was wide-awake the moment she opened her eyes. Apprehension stirred inside her, but she quashed her fears with the iron will she had begun mustering up since August proposed.

Her heart ached less than she expected, given she was leaving Carmel and her family behind. She had always thought, though she never told anyone, that she would grow old in Carmel with a respectable, simple gentleman. Leah loved stories and adventures, but traveling to far-flung places was never a thing she longed for, save perhaps for a passionate love. Her mind wandered to the wager Jessie made at the wedding, and she suddenly and severely doubted she would learn to give her whole heart to August Fox.

Leah jerked out of her reverie as a series of rapid knocks came on the front door downstairs. She heard it open a moment later, and Nyssa and Shay's high voices rang through the house.

Throwing on the loose-fitting dress she had laid aside for today, she raced down the stairwell and greeted her entire family and August by the front door. Mrs. Edwards was the first to throw her arms around Leah, and began weeping shamelessly. The rest of the Edwards crowded around them anxiously. Leah noticed August move away discreetly.

"Promise me you will write us often," she wailed.

"Yes, Mama."

Leah had sent word to her family immediately after August's news from Cariath. She simply wrote that his father needed him sooner than he expected. It felt strange leaving out the specifics. She preferred to be transparent, especially with Papa. Was she already learning to keep the secrets of her husband?

"We are moving out of the estate in a few weeks. Oh!" Mama turned to look at Mr. Edwards. "Did you give Mr. Fox and Leah the address of the cottage?"

"How could I forget, with you badgering me about the matter?" Papa winked at Leah once Mama turned her face away from him.

Nyssa seized Leah's arm. "I believe Mr. Langford is close to proposing — the good man did not bat an eyelash even when I told him we were losing the estate! We must visit one another when I'm married." She wrung her hands in excitement.

"You're all invited to visit, of course," Leah said earnestly. She was suddenly overcome with affection for her family and her voice caught in her throat. "I may grow lonely without your company." She attempted a faint smile.

Nyssa and Shay offered soft words of encouragement while Mrs. Edwards fussed over tying her dress and putting up her hair to make the long trip more comfortable. Papa was quiet, but his eyes shone with compassion and tenderness, and that brought Leah closest to tears.

As Mrs. Edwards fell into discussing the differences between balls in Cariath and Carmel with her two eldest daughters, Leah moved to embrace her father. His arms were thin but sure around her waist, and she laid her head on his chest. His steady heartbeat soothed her nerves and she closed her eyes, picturing herself a little girl again, curled up against him at home when she was downcast.

"When is the soonest you can visit?" Leah murmured after a long silence.

"It will need to be after we settle into the cottage. A month, at the least. Perhaps two."

Panic welled up in Leah's chest, making it hard to breathe. "That's so long!" she cried, though she had suspected as much.

Papa stroked her hair gently, and the calm brushing motion pacified her slightly. "I will do all I can, Leah."

"Or I could visit you," she exclaimed. "I could come sooner than you could to me."

"It would depend on August," he said quietly. "If you are both able, you know you are welcome with us at any time."

"I will come as soon as I can," Leah promised, ignoring his mention of August and slightly chagrined by it.

Papa either did not notice or chose not to press her on the matter. He held her gaze for a moment and beamed unexpectedly. "That may be the better course of action. Your mother and I are no longer young, and I don't know how much of the long trip we could bear, especially with those two girls talking until my ears fall off."

She laughed. "They would keep going even after that."

There was a lull in Mrs. Edwards and the girls' conversation. Leah turned and saw August return. She had nearly forgotten he had stepped out of the room once she appeared. She nodded at him and even smiled a little, grateful for his consideration of her and her family.

"I apologize for interrupting," he said, and looked to Leah. "I've put your bags into the carriage. We are ready to depart if you are."

Leah did not think she would ever come close to that, but she had spent the last few days gathering the strength to leave Carmel and her familiar life behind—and to do it without her resolve collapsing in front of her family and August.

She inhaled deeply. "I'm ready," she said, and forced herself to believe it.

August nodded and pulled open the oak-wood doors. The Edwards walked out, huddled together with Leah in the middle. At the end of the gravel pathway leading from the door to the road, the carriage was waiting. The horses whinnied softly, and one stamped the ground, a small cloud of dust rising around its hoof.

August had journeyed to Carmel alone on horseback, so he had to find a carriage the day before. Luckily, Mr. Langford offered him one along with a spare horse for—as August quoted—"a tour of Cariath and more Guardian stories when you return."

The weather was warm and nearby bluebirds sang a quiet melody. The sun beat down on Leah's neck and she felt sticky beads of sweat against her skin. She breathed in the crisp autumn air, which smelled of dry leaves and a hint of jasmine.

They said their farewells more quickly than Leah anticipated. It was almost awkward, since she had never learned to say goodbye to her family.

She came to her father last. He simply handed her an envelope. "This is from Jessie. She had a pressing engagement this morning so she could not come, but wanted this delivered to you."

Leah clutched the letter and simply dipped her head. "Take care, Papa."

"Be careful, my Leah." His voice was thick with emotion.

Leah blinked away tears that gathered at the corners of her eyes. She mustered a smile for all of her family and lifted her hand to wave at them feebly, not trusting her voice.

August had opened the carriage door and offered his hand to assist her up the steps. She quickly climbed in and watched her husband shake hands with the Edwards and bid them farewell before he swung himself up into the driver's seat behind the horses.

"Write us about the balls in Cariath!" Shay called.

"Write us if you find an eligible man for Shay," Nyssa yelled lightheartedly, earning a glare from her sister.

Leah could only nod and feign a roll of her eyes. She heard a whip crack and the carriage jerked slightly before it began moving. She stuck her face against the window and waved as her family shouted vigorous goodbyes. Soon, her breath fogged up the glass and their words grew indecipherable.

CHAPTER 11

The road was uneven and Leah jostled back and forth inside the carriage. She watched the passing scenery for a while, but it became a blur of trees and wide green fields. She lost track of time but could guess at the approximate hour based on the direction of sunlight. An hour or two into the trip, she remembered the letter from Jessie and pulled it out of her pocket to read.

It was shorter than she hoped, but warm and delightful nonetheless. Jessie wrote briefly about Mr. Whitefield and Laurel's upcoming nuptials and how Mrs. Lane was running around frantically like a headless chicken. She offered sweet words of encouragement and begged Leah to write her soon about Cariath and her developing relationship with August.

Leah folded the letter carefully back into the envelope. She felt a slight twinge in her chest as she thought of Jessie and the fond memories they made together. Friends, even dear ones, drifted in and out of life so effortlessly. Trying to hold on to them too tightly was like trying to grab a fistful of smoke. She would always love Jessie as a sister, but affection from afar was no substitute for the privilege of living nearby and regular meetings.

August said it was a full day's journey to Cariath. Leah pulled out the books from her bag. She was forced to only select some books to bring from the Edwards estate to Edenbridge—there was no way she could move an entire library—and she could take even fewer of those to Cariath. Among them, she brought *Arieh and the Guardians*, along with a few other historical tomes. She passed the hours reading and falling into and out of shallow sleep, the hoof-beats of the carriage horses blending with the strange sounds in her dream.

It was early evening when Leah awoke from a nap suddenly. The carriage had come to a halt. She sat up straight and peered out the window. It was turning dark, like an ink well slowly spilling across the skies. A few rebellious red and gold streaks still lined the edge of the horizon over the green plains. This was not Cariath, though. Leah strained her eyes forward and the rolling fields continued for as far as she could see.

The carriage door opened and August climbed inside. The front of his hair was stuck to his brow and sweat lined his forehead. He wiped it away with his sleeve.

"Are we resting?" Leah queried.

He nodded. "We're nearly there. The remainder of the journey is best made when night falls completely."

"Why?" She frowned.

"These roads are traveled by many. We don't want any followers attaching themselves to our trail."

A cold shiver crawled down Leah's backbone. "Are these parts unsafe?" She worked to keep her voice from wavering.

"The only danger is for those who bring it with them," August said, and his voice was hard. He looked like he was caught up in some distasteful memory. "Don't worry," he added, his expression softening. "I have traveled this way many times."

Leah nodded and did not press the issue. Instead, she reached for a basket behind her seat and pulled out two sandwiches wrapped in paper and a sealed flask of water. She handed a sandwich to him. "Dinner," she said.

They ate in silence and watched the darkness spread its blanket across the sky. Leah trembled a little as the wind howled like a hungry wolf across the plains. While scenic under the noonday sun, the landscape felt ominous under the cover of night.

"Are you feeling ill?" August's voice almost made her jump.

"No," she replied instantly and averted her eyes, not wanting him to see her fear.

He did not say anything and continued to eat his sandwich. She finally looked up at him again. His features were less clear without the full daylight, but he appeared thoughtful, seemingly untouched by the apprehension that had gripped her. She felt a wave of shame, though she told herself he was a man used to such travels.

"The darkness here makes me nervous," she finally admitted in a small voice.

August did not reply immediately but reached past her seat to pull out a thick wool blanket. He threw it around her shoulders. "Nothing bad will befall you here. I promise you that." His voice was unexpectedly kind.

She smiled faintly. "Thank you." Unsure of what to say, she added, "Most people never leave Carmel. I've only gone to Ephes twice."

"Count it a privilege to grow up in a sweet haven like that." His voice was soft, but some memory or thought lent a bitter edge to his tone. "Many are not so fortunate."

"I have no idea what to expect in your world," she said suddenly.

They looked at each other wordlessly, and Leah felt exposed as he studied her. Strangely, it did not prompt shame, but relief. Whatever he read in her face—vulnerability, fear, or bewilderment—she wanted him to know. She wanted him to bear the burden of understanding, without her admitting it aloud.

He either did not notice or did not wish to embarrass her. "I think Cariath will suit you better than Carmel."

"That's a bold claim—"

August was not finished. "Leah, I promised your father I would take care of you. You will have a good life."

She bit her lip and fell silent. *A good life.* It sounded safe and empty at the same time.

August crumpled up the paper after finishing his sandwich and climbed out of the carriage. Leah heard him rummaging through their belongings in the back. As he came around to the front, he stuck his head through the open door.

"There's a forest ahead of us. It's not the most agreeable sight at this hour and I would advise keeping your gaze inside."

Leah nodded and he closed the door firmly. As he swung into the driver's seat, she watched him through the window, and noticed a long sword hanging at his side.

~~~~~

Leah could not resist peering out at the forest when they passed through. A gust blew through the branches, making the place echo with a cacophony of ghostly sounds. The tangled branches spiraled skyward like menacing claws. They waved wildly and helplessly, almost as if they were demon-possessed, in the wind. She shuddered and drew August's blanket more tightly around her shoulders.

August. If Leah was frightened inside the walls of the carriage, how was he faring on the outside, as he drove relentlessly through the gloom with the breeze whipping in his face? She looked out through the front window. His back was to her on the driving seat, and he cracked the horsewhip every few seconds. *The horses must be terrified,* she thought. She could not see his expression, but he held himself upright, an undaunted black figure that could not be stopped by even the untamed terror of nature. A shadow of wonder mixed with fear crept over Leah — who *was* this man?

Unable to bear the dreadful fantasies her mind was beginning to spin about the black silhouettes outside, she closed her eyes, though pride kept her from covering her ears and cowering like a child.

She did not know how much time passed, but the wind's howl grew faint after a while, as if it were only a distant memory. Leah braved a glance outside and drew in a sharp breath.

The landscape had changed severely. Wide green plains rolled out like scrolls on both sides of the carriage. Stars freckled the night sky, and beneath the faint glow of moonlight, Leah could see small white daisies blooming in the tall grass. Ahead of them towered great brown mountains and a faint light glowed from beyond the peaks. The horses whinnied happily, and the hoofbeats grew steady and clapped soundly against the well-paved road.

Leah knocked on the front glass window. "Where are we?" she called loudly.

"Nearly home," he yelled over the sounds of hooves and carriage wheels. "The Bastion is just behind the mountains."

She stared in disbelief. "Will the carriage make it across?"

"There's a passageway between the mountains. We don't need to climb over."

Leah sat back in her seat, her mind uneasy. Her knuckles grew white as she unconsciously gripped her fingers into a tight-fisted ball. Again, she was helpless in the face of her confusion and trepidation. She thought of the wounded seagull she had once seen at the seashore with her family. It had a limp in one leg and when the waters sprang onto the sand, it fell, defenseless, into the waves. The ocean roar drowned out its sad cries.

She felt the same vulnerability now, about to be swallowed by the strange world August was from.

The carriage followed the pathway through a cleft between two mountains. Leah could not see much on either side, but the outline of a wide gate ahead slowly came into focus. They drew to a stop in front of it.

"Who goes there?" The voice was low and stern, and a dim light flickered behind the bars.

"Maor! Let me in, you blithering fool." August's gruff tone had a soft edge.

The gates flew open and a tall man emerged with a lantern in hand. He was about the same height as August, with shaggy hair and dark eyes. He wore a wide smile on his face. August leapt onto the ground gracefully and they threw their arms around one another roughly. The other man pounded him on the back soundly.

"Back from the dead, finally," the man named Maor said.

"You thought a jaunt to the seaside towns would kill me?" August withdrew from their embrace and laid a hand on his shoulder. "You would need to find a sturdier captain than that."

"I had full faith," Maor drawled, and Leah detected a faint accent that differed from August's. "Now, did you bring back any precious cargo?"

August walked to the side of the carriage and opened the door. "Leah, this is my good friend, Maor." He held out a hand to her and she stepped out. Her legs wobbled a little, and she was suddenly unused to feeling the ground beneath her feet.

Maor extended a hand and Leah took it. He stooped down and kissed her hand lightly before letting go. "Even without the light of day I can see August found a beautiful lady." He offered a roguish grin and she could not help but smile in return. She liked his lighthearted spirit immediately and felt a little more at ease.

"Pleasure to meet you," she replied, almost shyly.

"How did you know we would be arriving tonight?" August broke in.

"Your message reached us earlier today. Why else would I be waiting in dark and cold at this hour?" Maor growled, but there was no bite in his voice.

"You missed me, of course." August punched his arm, and the two men had a brief, friendly scuffle.

Leah looked at her husband in surprise. She had yet to see him so jocular, and was beginning to wonder if he was capable of lighthearted cheerfulness.

"Get in the carriage, both of you," Maor said, escorting them to the door. "I'll drive us in."

Once they were both seated comfortably, August facing forward and Leah backward, she looked hard into his eyes.

"You're a captain among the Guardians, then?"

He seemed uncomfortable under her scrutiny, and she wondered if it came from secrecy or humility. "We don't have a very strict hierarchy now. But I am one of the Marshals that leads the Guardians in Cariath."

Though she knew little of the title's significance, Leah sensed the weight of it. August had said the Guardians answered to the Marshals and Chief rather than an official governor from the crown. Anxiety grew in the pit of her stomach. She had expected the Fox family held high status and regard, but had not questioned what that entailed in Cariath's culture. She had figured August and Papa discussed it; that was part of the men's world, after all, but now she wondered what the implications would be for her.

"Is your father a Marshal too?"

August was silent for a moment.

"In a sense. He is the Chief of the White Tiger Guardians, and of the Marshals."

CHAPTER 12

En-doire, Island of Japha.
Month of Harvest: Third week, First-Day.

Even with only a last, desperate glimmer of sunlight streaking across the horizon, the air was still sticky and warm. Benedict hardly noticed the discomfort anymore after trudging across the Pharan. They completed the final leg of their journey into En-doire with a renewed burst of energy once he established their plan, eager to find the song and escape into a fairer climate. The temperature grew slightly more bearable as they reached the edge of the desert and the first cluster of settlements east of the Pharan. En-karah, En-haku, and En-maran were towns in the same region as En-doire, though they answered to Governor Rajan. Even years ago, Benedict recalled Marcum's ire that Black Tortoise Guardians began moving out of En-doire to the surrounding villages as they married and raised families. Unlike the closed-door culture of the Bastion, where Guardians rarely moved out, the traditions of the Tortoise Guardians spread into other towns, making them less of a novelty.

As they traveled, Gerard remarked that perhaps Nimrod sent them to En-doire so he could avoid the heat, choosing the more temperate Ebene for himself. He and Traven were more guarded over the last few days, but Benedict treated them as before, deciding to put the incident out of his mind.

Upon entering town, his men stripped their White Tiger emblems, clothing themselves in the commoners' attire they had packed. Their main disadvantage in disguise was skin color — people of En-doire were darker than men of Cariath, but he hoped their divide-and-conquer strategy would avoid suspicion. Their long trek through the Pharan Desert also bronzed most of the men, making the difference less conspicuous.

Benedict, Justin and Traven separated from the larger group, taking their own route to the Treasury, a large building of wood and stone. There was no pomp or frills attached and Traven had said it housed mostly old artifacts of En-doire and only occasionally served as a center for meetings among Guardian leaders. As they passed the main entrance, Benedict counted ten guards spread across the black-gilded gates.

"Will there be gates in the back?" Justin voiced Benedict's thoughts.

Traven shook his head. "Almost no one knows of the back entrance. I stumbled across it once by accident. But they usually have two or three guards there as a precaution."

Benedict caught sight of Wills and Gerard as they rounded the building, but as per their plan, neither party showed any signs of recognition. He led Justin and Traven on a slight detour into a grassy field nearby, but made sure to keep the other men in sight should they give the ready signal soon.

He spared a few glances at the surroundings, taking in the scenery. En-doire had a quiet beauty about it, with small homes and unpaved roads. In contrast to Pharan's desert wasteland, En-doire boasted a wide variety of greenery, from tall, leafy trees to shrubbery that sprouted all along the pathways they had taken into the heart of the town. It was like a natural oasis, similar in some sense to Cariath, a fertile land in the middle of a wilderness.

The last wisp of sunlight dropped out of the sky and the sliver of moon grew brighter against a blackening scroll. Benedict glanced back in the direction of the town hall. The number of people milling around had dwindled, and there were only a few stragglers in addition to the guards.

"They're ready," Justin murmured, but Benedict already saw Gerard's signal.

The three men walked swiftly toward the back of the structure. A rush of energy shot through Benedict, but his mind was in a calm, numb state. He was confident their strategy could succeed, but he never celebrated too early.

Meeker met them at the back entrance, the rusted door already held open by a twisted piece of bark on the ground. Benedict glanced at the hedges nearby—two uniformed guardsmen were conspicuously lying unconscious.

"Move them further into the bushes," Benedict ordered. "If another guard hears commotion, someone may come this way."

"Yes, sir." Meeker nodded. "Hound's group and Mert's are already inside."

"Any telltale noises?" Justin asked.

"Dead silence, mostly. It's a little eerie." Meeker had an uncomfortable look on his face.

Benedict felt cold in the pit of his stomach, but ignored it. "Move the guards out of sight," he repeated. "And close the door after us. If it comes to a fight, pull Wills and Gerard from around the corner."

Without waiting for a reply, Benedict ran through the open door, his right hand on his sword hilt. Justin and Traven followed close behind him. The lights had dimmed after visiting hours, making the large glass shelves against the walls cast ominous shadows on the hardwood floor.

"There," came Traven's voice. Benedict followed his line of vision to two more guards sprawled on the floor further down the hall.

Justin released a low whistle. "And they did that quietly—impressive."

"What would you expect of Hound?" Benedict retorted as they

sprinted toward the fallen guards. He did not have to like the man to acknowledge he was competent and deadly.

In silence, they followed the trail of unconscious guards through the hallway and up a stairwell. Hound and Mert's groups were thorough. There was not a single guard left in their path, and slowly, Benedict moved with more ease, tensing less at the shadows that fell across the floor. Without incident, they came to a large, oaken double door, where Mert was waiting for them.

"Hound and my men have drawn off the guards," he whispered, his breath a little short. Even in the darkness, Benedict saw the sweat on his face. "We cannot promise too much time."

"The Treasury," Traven murmured, laying his hand on the brass doorknob.

Justin cast a wary glance at Benedict. "Do you think we came through too easily?"

"Our men ensured that," Mert said, before Benedict could respond, an indignant look on his face.

"Yes, I know." Benedict raised his hand slightly to calm him. "Well done, all of you." He looked to Justin. "It doesn't matter. We need to get the song immediately."

While Mert stood guard at the door, the other three men forced open the heavy doors. Benedict blinked — there was far more light in the treasury room than any corridor they passed through so far. Candles lined the sill on the edge of the wall, their glow flickering against the dark shadows of the room. Large wardrobes and chests were scattered throughout the room, but otherwise, the floor and walls were plainly colored, with paint wearing off the edges. This part of the building was clearly not for display.

Traven and Justin were already standing beside a large, ivory-colored chest near the front of the room. Benedict hurried over and his breath caught in his throat as he saw the insignia on the corner — a tortoise overlaying a long sword. Without a word, they heaved it open. A cloud of dust flew off the corners.

It was empty. Benedict kicked the chest hard and sharp pain shot through his foot and up his leg. He swore under his breath and clenched his fists until his knuckles ached.

"Damn," he muttered, furious.

"Wait." Justin peered into the chest, where Traven's head and the upper half of his body had disappeared.

Traven pulled himself upright after a moment, a triumphant expression on his face. He held a long, thin sword in his hands. Benedict strode to his side, anger forgotten, and reached for the sword.

"Grip it lightly," Traven warned. "It's old."

Benedict blew the dust off the hilt and ran his fingers lightly over the metal blade. There were spots of rust, dark gold, but it was still smooth and the edge was dangerously sharp. A violet glint on the pommel of the sword caught his eye, and he ran his thumb over the amethyst nestled snugly at the top.

"What is this?" Justin asked urgently, his gaze straying to the doorway. There were loud footsteps, but they came from a distance and Mert had not stepped in to warn them.

"This," Benedict's gaze roamed over the sword again in wonder, stunned by the distinct design of the pommel, "this is Adair."

"The sword of Arieh," Traven gasped and his gaze rested on the pommel. "Most think it's only a legend."

Unperturbed, Justin looked at them both intently. "But it's not the song."

"There was nothing else in the chest?" Benedict turned to Traven.

The man did not flinch. "No, sir. Only the sword, and it was lodged on the side of the chest, so we nearly missed it."

Benedict swept his gaze across the room. At least a dozen nondescript containers lay scattered across the treasury. They could not afford to search through each chest, though if a written copy of the song existed, they were sure to have hidden it well. He thought hard, his heartbeat drumming against his ribcage.

Where would be the cleverest place to hide a written scroll? He blew out a loud breath. Perhaps it was not even in the building, if it was real at all. Benedict turned the sword over on his palm. He only recognized the weapon from a description in *Legends of Arieh*. But why hide Adair, a relic out of an ancient story, away in a rusted chest?

"Ben!"

He turned a hard glare on Justin. Only his family ever called him that.

His companion hardly noticed his ire. "There's an inscription on the blade."

Benedict turned the sword again slowly, watching as it glinted when the angle caught the light. Traven raced to grab a candle from the windowsill and held it over them. Small but visible print appeared, long lines engraved just above and below the center groove of the blade.

> *Between the turning of Light and Dark*
> *I walk in Eden's shadow-gray.*
> *Where men and gods, through ceaseless strife,*
> *chase winds of vengeance in vain.*
>
> *O dream in a dream, what is truth?*
> *that stands from age to age.*
> *Though mortal empires rise and fall,*
> *the eternal realm remains.*

"There's more on the other side," Traven said, his voice falling to an awed whisper.

As Benedict turned it over, Mert burst through the door, a wild look on his face. "We must leave."

Benedict handed Adair to Justin and turned to shut the chest. Without a word, the three men raced after Mert, out of the treasury room and down the stairwell they had come up. Justin asked Mert what happened, but Benedict was only half-listening, his heart thudding with the thrill of success. It suddenly occurred to him that perhaps Nimrod did not take this mission himself because he feared failure—feared he would not solve the riddle in time. Benedict smiled grimly to himself.

"...one of Hound's men," Mert was saying raggedly as they ran. "Reinforcements may arrive soon."

"What happened to one of the men?" Benedict interrupted.

Justin glanced at him strangely. "Mert said one of Hound's men went down. Their group was ambushed. Some guards caught wind that there were intruders and Hound played it too dangerously."

"We lost a man?" Benedict repeated, a sick feeling in his stomach.

"One man isn't terrible, sir," Mert put in. "This was a risky mission. If all the rest come out alive—and I see you found something in the treasury—this will be a rousing success."

Benedict shook his head and fell silent. He had wanted to come through the mission without a single casualty, and he had failed. Perhaps it was Hound's fault for throwing caution to the wind, but in the end, Benedict was the one in command. He had given Hound the authority to lead his group as he saw fit. There was a bitter taste in his mouth.

Meeker was still at the back entrance when they sprinted through the door. A look of relief spread across his features.

"Thank the gods," he breathed. "After Hound and his men came out, I thought the lot of you was left for dead."

"Then all our men are out of the hall?" Justin pressed.

Meeker nodded. "They're already making for our camp outside the town. Guardians will be swarming through En-doire once the word spreads. We need to hurry."

The five men loped through the outskirts of En-doire. Benedict's footfalls felt heavy, his mind still hooked on the thought of Hound's dead man, morbidly wondering who he was and how he met his death—and what his judgment would be after death: judgment for following the Oath-breakers.

When they arrived at the camp, a small fire was already lit and the men were spread around it, a taut silence among them. The stillness broke with loud cheers as Benedict and the other four men came into sight. Though they looked exhausted, the men rose to their feet and let out a few whistles.

"Welcomed like heroes," Meeker said dryly. "This is a first."

"Expect it to be a last, too," Benedict rejoined, but not without a touch of humor.

As they settled into the camp, men exchanged stories animatedly, boasting of their part in the mission. Spirits were high among most of the group, though Benedict watched Hound and his friends sulking in a secluded corner.

"You think he deserves a thrashing," Justin observed beside him.

"No," Benedict said quietly, his gaze fixed on Hound. The other man was sitting in a defeated posture, a stormy look of bitterness in his face. "He's already giving himself one. I can't blame him—I don't know what happened. All I know is we would not have the sword without him."

Though he was not looking at Justin, he could feel his friend's surprise. "That's a kind assessment." His tone was neutral. "You were upset over losing a man, but not because of Hound specifically."

"Forget it, Justin." Benedict voice had an edge. "Send a scout to Nimrod. Tell him we have the song."

Justin rose to his feet. He cast a glance at Hound, but his gaze returned to Benedict. "Wicked men always fear death."

"And good men don't?"

Benedict did not look up at him, but once again ran his hand along the smooth blade of Arieh's sword, which Justin had set down beside him. *Adair*. Here was the stuff legends were made on, and a shiver spiraled through his bones at the thought.

"I don't know." Justin offered him a weary smile. "When I find one, I'll ask him."

CHAPTER 13

Cariath, Island of Japha.
Month of Harvest: Third week, First-Day.

It was not a long drive from the gate to August's home, but Leah was dazed, drawn out of the continuum of time, as he spoke. Finally, she asked him to tell her of the Guardians, trying to piece a narrative together with the legends she read, and trying to grasp the world he had flung her into. His voice grew deep and rich as he began, as if the history enthralled even him as he retold the tales.

"The story of the origins of the Guardians is mostly lost. There was no written record in those times, only oral tales that were passed down. Much of our known history begins after the legend of Arieh, which you know already."

"Many think of the Guardians as puritans, or holding to old religious rituals," Leah recalled.

She glanced at her husband, and the stern image he cut before her. The sword that hung at his side earlier now lay casually at his feet. There was nothing ascetic or monk-like about him. If anything, he resembled a warrior figure from the old tales. Leah blushed for the frivolity her townspeople assigned to the Guardians.

But August did not scoff at her. "Time and isolation are earthquakes for world views."

"So what happened after Arieh?" She scoured her memory. "The Guardians were not all concentrated in one place."

"Correct. The Guardians broke into four major outposts. At Cariath, we are the White Tiger Guardians. To our south in Ebene is the Cobalt Dragons, and east across the river is Black Tortoise. The most reclusive of all is the Vermilion Falcon, hidden up in the Dammim Mountains. I can't remember when we last had contact with them."

The names and places reverberated in Leah's ears with an exotic aura, spinning through her mind in a heady rush. She knew of Ebene and the Dammim, but coupled with the Guardian outposts, they rang with the air of folklore.

"What do the names signify? White Tiger and Cobalt Dragon..." she trailed off, the words tasting foreign on her tongue.

"Legend says Arieh won four faerie generals to his side, once he entered the immortal realm." Anticipating her next query, he added, "Faeries appear in the mortal realm in the form of animals. Hence, the name of the four outposts, honoring Arieh's first followers."

"Legend," Leah repeated. She met his gaze. "Do you believe it?"

He raised his brow, a brief smile on his lips, perhaps recalling the same question he had put to her. "Arieh? I believe in his historicity, but I also think his tale has been embellished with myth."

"How do we know anything of Arieh's generals?"

"There were stories that Arieh would flit back into the mortal realm sometimes." He shrugged. "We do know faeries can still cross over, so it makes sense that he would too. He would not want to lose communication with his fellow Guardians. But if they happened, the occurrences were rare. Japha changed permanently after the Faerie Wars, when the mortal and immortal realms were sealed from one another. It was part of Arieh's bargain to spare his comrades."

She opened her mouth to ask another question, but they had come to a halt. Maor swung the side door open and held out a hand to Leah. She climbed out of the carriage with August close behind her.

"Welcome to Cariath Valley, Leah," Maor said regally.

She looked around, her eyes widening. The brown mountains she had seen earlier on the trip now surrounded them on every side, flattening out to form the circular basin they were in. Her attention turned to the small community they had arrived in front of. Large mansions of an off-white marble color rose out of the ground. They looked almost like castles, but more severe. Bright lights burned in many windows. On the perimeter of the valley and scattered throughout the basin were small camps, and they appeared to her as specks of light dotting the floor of Cariath.

"Those are camps of Guardians who protect the Valley," August explained. "And the Marshals of the Guardians live in these central manors, the Bastion. The non-Guardian settlements of Cariath are near the base of the mountains, extending up into the hills."

Before she could finish taking in the view, August was ushering her up the steps of one of the mansions. "You're shivering," he said. She had hardly noticed, but at his words she suddenly felt the rush of cold air.

August pulled a large key from the folds of his outer jacket and opened the door. Leah felt the warmth immediately. The three of them stepped inside to a well-lit, spacious hall. A hearth fire was burning and a few plates with fruit and cheese were still laid out on a wide, cherrywood table. The furnishings and walls were more modern than Leah expected, but there was an air of ancientness about the whole place she could not shake.

"Welcome to Fox Manor," August said.

Nimble footsteps approached from a distant hall. An older man with grey hair appeared and Leah was instantly struck by his resemblance to August. He looked to be in his fifties but still walked at a brisk pace with an upright posture.

"Father," August bowed solemnly. Leah looked at him oddly. He was jolly with Maor earlier, yet he appeared grave now.

"August! I thought it might be you." The elder Mr. Fox strode toward them with a spring in his step. A wide smile crossed his face as he clapped his son on the back. August only returned the embrace stiffly. "Maor, thank you for waiting for him," he continued, nodding in his direction. Maor bowed in return, but he appeared more at ease than August.

Mr. Fox turned to Leah. His eyes had the same keen quality as his son's, but Leah felt more comfortable under his stare than August's upon their first meeting. "So you are the new Mrs. Fox," he said, beaming. "Welcome to the family, and to Fox Manor. I'm Arthur Fox, though most just call me the Old Fox. They think I'm unaware." He winked and extended his hand, which Leah shook warmly, taking a liking to the kindly man. He waved them in the direction of the table. "Come, sit. I've left some food out."

"I should take my leave," Maor said. "I will allow you three to enjoy the evening." He looked to August. "You will be at the morning hunt tomorrow, right?"

August nodded and Arthur protested his leaving so soon. But after much insistence on Maor's part, the Foxes reluctantly saw him to the door.

"Remember, you and Stephen and Kirin must all be at the dinner tomorrow," Arthur called as Maor slipped into the darkness.

"Dinner?" August turned to his father.

Arthur waved his hand. "Just a small gathering I invited—the Marshals and your men. They want to welcome you and Leah. Come, put some food in those bellies. You've been on the road for a long time."

They sat at the table and ate in silence for a while. Caught up in the story of the Guardians, Leah had entirely forgotten her appetite. Her stomach growled as they sat down. The fruit was the freshest she had tasted in a while. Arthur brought out steaming bread rolls and she tried all kinds of cheeses as spreads. Before long, her hunger was slaked.

Beside her, August ate little, and she saw him picking at a wedge of cheese. He had hardly taken two bites out of an apple. His expression was somber still, and Leah wondered at his seeming discomfort.

"August wrote to me about you, Leah," Arthur said from across the table, his eyes twinkling slightly.

She cast a sidelong glance at her husband. "What did he say?"

"Oh, that you had a mind of your own. He liked that about you, said it stood out like a swollen thumb in your town."

Leah was surprised at his vivid and sharp opinion, unsure of whether to be pleased by the characterization or offended on behalf of Carmel.

"I must credit my upbringing," she replied. "Papa especially taught us to read widely and think critically."

"A good father," Arthur intoned. Learning forward a little, he said, "Has August told you much about Cariath?"

August jerked slightly beside her, but Leah pretended not to notice. "A little," she said carefully. "He was instructing me in Guardian history on our way over. Our time has been limited, though, so I expect to learn more in the days to come." She cast a meaningful look in August's direction.

The older Fox nodded vigorously and launched into retelling old legends. Leah listened closely, and Arthur's charisma and grandeur in storytelling held her attention. He was, from what she could see, as different from August as summertime glow from winter frost. An enigmatic smile lit his face and he waved his hands in elaborate gestures to convey his ideas.

Leah glanced at August in her peripheral view while Arthur rattled on with his tale. Her husband was eating slowly still, his head bent downward, and a disinterested look on his face. She tucked away the observation and decided to question him later.

"...and so, the torch passed on to me, and it will go to my sons after. The Foxes have a history of leadership among the Marshals," Arthur noted proudly.

"Sons?" Leah queried, catching the nuance just as she refocused on Arthur's words. She looked between the two men. "I didn't know you had any others."

A shadow seemed to fall across the dinner table. August's face darkened and his father appeared caught off guard. Apprehension seized Leah's heart and she suddenly wondered what other secrets this strange family kept.

"I have two sons," Arthur said quietly. "Benedict is August's younger brother."

"We don't mention him here anymore," August responded shortly and rose to his feet, casting a glare in his father's direction.

"Why?" Leah ventured, her eyes on her husband. She felt oddly brave.

He turned his dark eyes toward her and held her gaze. "Because," he began slowly, "he is an Oath-breaker."

"An Oath-breaker?" A cold shiver ran through her veins at the ominous term.

"He broke away from Guardian tradition," Arthur said.

A harsh laugh escaped August's lips. "That's a kind way to put it." He turned to Leah. "You know the history — the rogue Guardians who tried to penetrate the faerie realm? They were the first generation of Oath-breakers."

Astonishment and dismay broke over her like an icy wave.

"I'm sorry," she stammered, grasping for other words but finding none.

Arthur managed a kind smile that crinkled the corners of his eyes. "You deserve to know — you're family now."

You're family now. The words stunned Leah. It was nothing she did not know, but the impact of them would have bowled her over if she had been standing. What did that mean, to be a Fox and live in this place? She looked up at August, who was still standing erect, and felt a mixture of confusion and wonder and indignation. What had he brought her to?

"Sit down, son," Arthur was saying to August.

He remained standing. "Is there anything urgent we need to discuss about Cobalt Dragon and Ebene?"

"No, it can wait." Arthur ran a hand through his hair and sighed. "We can discuss it tomorrow."

August nodded stiffly. "I will turn in for the night, then. It was a long day."

Arthur sighed and a look of weariness crept across his face. Leah thought he suddenly looked much older than when he first greeted them, brisk and vibrant. "All right, then show Leah to your room so you can both rest."

Leah obediently got to her feet and followed August. She cast a wan smile in Arthur's direction. "Good night and thank you," she said on her way out. He returned the smile. August said nothing as he strode up the stairwell.

The upstairs living area was well furnished, and Leah suspected the Foxes remodeled it not long ago. It looked almost like a typical house in Carmel, and that was soothing to her.

August led her into a room on the far end of the long hallway. "This is my place," he finally said. "We do not have another room prepared, so if you don't mind…" He trailed off and met her eyes warily, almost as a prey awaits its predator's next movement.

Leah scanned the room quickly. It was more simply designed than the rest of the house, with just a bed, nightstand, and dresser. Each piece looked like a lonely island with wide spaces between them. The walls were a plain off-white, giving the room an austere ambience. The bed was larger than even Mr. and Mrs. Edwards', which would give Leah plenty of space, but that did not quell the unsettled feelings stirring in her stomach. He was still a stranger to her, and more than that, a man with constant secrets rising to the surface.

"That's fine," Leah replied weakly and shifted her shoulders.

He did not offer any comfort. August motioned at a door in the back of the room. "The bath is there. You are welcome to use anything you find. I will have your bags brought up in the morning, as long as you have something to sleep in."

She nodded numbly. "August," she called just as he turned to leave. His name felt alien on her tongue, but she was rewarded with a look of surprise from him. "I—" Leah paused, her words suddenly slipping like water through her grasp. "I *am* sorry. About your brother," she finally breathed.

The lines on August's face seemed to soften in the slightest. "I know," he said. Her ire was about to rise at his typical presumptuousness. "Thank you," he added, to her surprise—and by the expression he wore, perhaps his as well. "But it's in the past. I've left it behind me, and it's best kept there." There was a sudden edge to his voice.

"Is it?" Leah countered, though kindly. "He's still your brother—"

"I don't expect you to understand," August lowered his voice and his dark eyes looked nearly dangerous. "You may have silly, gossiping sisters, but you don't know the sting of betrayal. My brother is dead to me."

Leah shrank back a little but held her ground. "It doesn't sound like you've put it behind you," she challenged.

"What would you have me do?" he growled. "Beg for him to return? He has lost sense and wit."

"I don't know. But you haven't made peace with this."

August held her gaze for a long, hard moment before he spun around and stalked into the bathroom, closing the door behind him soundly. Leah let out a deep breath and sank onto the corner of the bed. A brief tremble went through her body, and she did not realize the tension that had built up within the last few minutes. Closing her eyes, she lay down on the soft covers and drifted off into an uneasy sleep.

CHAPTER 14

Leah awoke slowly, her brain still addled with the sweet drowsiness of sleep. Soft sunlight streamed through the crack between the window curtains, and she absently pulled the covers halfway over her face. After a few more moments of blissful oblivion, memories from the previous night hurtled into her mind and she jerked awake. Sitting up straight on the bed, her gaze darted around the room.

She was in August's bed—or *their* bed, she supposed, though that thought was too overwhelming—but he was gone. His side of the covers lay open. Her hand touched the cotton blanket that had slipped down to her waist. She remembered dozing off while August was in the bath. Her gaze drifted again to his side of the mattress and her spirits dampened as she recalled their last terse conversation.

With her mind fully alert, she stood up and stretched. Glancing around, she noticed her bags lying at the foot of the bed. Either Arthur or August must have hauled them up in the early hours of the morning. The Foxes did not appear to house any servants from what she had seen, and given her discussion on that subject with August, she was not surprised.

Leah padded downstairs and found the dining table lined with breakfast foods such as fruit, bread and juices. Did Arthur do all this himself? She felt a sudden sense of inadequacy.

As she picked a few pieces of watermelon out of the large glass bowl, hardy footsteps sounded on the staircase. Arthur poked his head into the dining hall.

"Good morning, Leah," he said cheerfully. "Help yourself to breakfast. August has gone to hunt some wild game with Maor and other men." He still wore loose-fitting sleep clothes and his graying hair stood upright at odd angles on his head. The sight of him was almost comical, and Leah nearly forgot he was a highly esteemed Marshal and warrior.

"Good morning," she responded. After a moment's hesitation, she blurted out, "I appreciate you doing all this, but you should let me help." She felt foolish and young as the words left her mouth.

Arthur only smiled warmly and put a hand on her shoulder. "I know everything now is new to you." He gave her a meaningful look. "Give yourself some time to adjust. And don't think of yourself as a guest here. You're home, and I hope you will see it as such in time."

"I want to do something, though," Leah protested, but her resolve weakened. A knot had formed in her throat at his kind words.

"Oh, you will. But for the time, allow an old man to dote some." He winked.

She smiled shyly. "Thank you, Mr. Fox."

"Arthur, please." He paused and caught her eye for a moment. "Or Father, over time, if you would like," he added softly. "Though, August tells me you are very fond of your own."

Papa entered Leah's mind and she had to blink rapidly to hold threatening tears at bay. She wondered if he was at home now, reading the paper with his glasses sliding down the bridge of his nose. She imagined the smell of Mama's buttered toast and her high voice scolding Papa for touching his food with ink-stained fingers. The image was so real in her mind, but the reality of it so distant that Leah felt a sharp ache in her chest.

She swallowed the knot in her throat. "I am," she said with more composure than she felt. "I'm surprised August said so. We didn't spend too much time all together."

"He's perceptive." Arthur chuckled before sobering. "Sometimes, too much."

"We had a difficult conversation last night," Leah said impulsively, surprised as the words escaped her mouth. She pulled out a chair from the table and sat. "About his brother."

He breathed out a sad sigh. "Well, I don't know how to advise you on that. We don't have that conversation at all."

"Were they close?"

"Yes, in a way," he mused. "They're very different, so they weren't the sort to talk much. They each had their own friends. But they trained for the Guardians together, rode knee to knee on everything from scouting trips to battles. That's enough to build a bond for fighting men, but above that, they're kin, too. You have sisters so you must know. In the world of warriors, that sharing of the same blood makes for even stronger ties."

Leah nodded. "My sisters and I are also very different. I don't always like their ways, but I love them." She grew quiet for a moment. "August said I don't know the sting of betrayal. I suppose that's true."

Arthur's eyes crinkled with empathy. "His words are often harder than his heart."

She offered him a grateful smile and they ate in quiet camaraderie. Leah's mind was still drawn to her home and family in Carmel and imagined them going about their daily activities.

"Could you tell me more about Cariath and the Guardians?" she asked, unable to quench her curiosity. "August only briefly told me of the four outposts."

"It's difficult to summarize." Arthur laughed. "Cariath itself has an entire history."

Leah felt the world she knew grow small in her mind. "All I knew was Carmel—the parks, the balls, the beaten roads. It seems like a cocoon now."

"Well, Cariath Valley has always been a great bastion of the Guardians.

Tradition says that White Tiger was the most influential of Arieh's followers. We were once central in communication among the four outposts, but time and tensions have stretched even those alliances thin. Before King Amir, we were also the ones who engaged most with the crown. Especially because Capitola is just a little outside the Cariath Mountains. White Tiger Marshals doubled as political representatives in the government for a long time." His expression became grave. "We trained up the most Guardians, sending them to Ebene and En-doire when their ranks grew small. Though Nimrod now leaves a black stain on our honor."

"Nimrod?" The name was unfamiliar, but rang with uncomfortable power in Leah's ears.

"He's the leader of those Guardians who broke away from us. The Oath-breakers. He was one of our most talented."

"I see." Leah nodded, and a quiet shudder went through her. So, that was who Benedict fell in with.

"The day is too bright to speak of such dark things," Arthur said. "If you would like, you are free to explore the valley. If you climb one of the small hills nearby, you will have a good view of the areas I mentioned to you. As long as you remain close to the Bastion, this is the safest place you will be."

"Thank you, Arthur."

He gave her another kind smile and reached for her plate before she could protest. "Go on, have a look around the area. Just come home for dinnertime. We will have a special celebration for your arrival." He was already moving into the kitchen with the dirty dishware.

~~~~~

Leah stepped into the cool breeze outside Fox Manor. Cariath Valley looked entirely different in the morning daylight. Lush green grass stretched from near the foot of the manor to the bottom of the mountains. Paved trails ran through the fields, and in the distance, the camps of Guardians looked like legions of small houses or pitched tents.

There were a few splotches of clouds in the sky, puffs of white against a vibrant blue. The sunlight glinted on the wet tips of grass and small flowers, reflecting sharp rays of light. She sucked in a deep breath and exhaled. The air felt fresher and cleaner than in Carmel, perhaps because she was in the middle of sprawling nature itself, with nothing to disturb the wild peacefulness here.

Leah meandered away from the Bastion and climbed a small hill. It did not provide a comprehensive view of the world beyond the mountains, but gave her a glimpse of the outer lands. She could see small white specks on shifting blue waters to the east, and gathered that was the Nathair River. She traced the outline of the river, but it wound up north beyond the reach of her sight.

She peeled off her outer cloak and placed it on the grass. Lying on the ground, Leah felt the uneven dirt prod gently against her back. Her mind drifted toward home again. She imagined Carmel going through the day's turning as it always did, with the bakery selling sticky cakes and women meeting in cafes for afternoon tea. The town would run without pause and would not notice her absence, no matter how sorely she longed for it. The realization pricked her heart and made her eyes water unexpectedly.

The Edwards and her friends would miss her, but they would continue with their lives as well. Papa must be occupied with planning the move into the cottage and the women could forget anything when an upcoming ball was announced. Leah wished there was something like that for her — something to relieve her of the brimming memories, if even momentarily. She wondered if the recollections that caused her heart to burn within her now would, slowly and with the passage of time, become nothing more than a gentle brush against her mind, leaving a faint trace of wistfulness and nostalgia. Leah closed her eyes and allowed the tears to run crooked trails down her face.

She lost track of the time passing, and drifted into a brief, light slumber as she lay there. Only when the wind grew stronger did she sit up and wrap the cloak tightly around her body.

Some time later, Leah heard quiet footsteps on the hillside behind her. Alarm rushed through her and shook the fogginess of sleep and soft memories from her mind. She scrambled to her feet and turned around.

A petite woman with light brown hair was about halfway up the hill. Their eyes met and the other woman offered a tentative smile.

"Hello. You must be Mrs. Fox. Word has been circulating in the Bastion that Marshal Fox returned last night."

The titles sounded odd in Leah's ears. "Yes. And you are?" she returned guardedly.

"I apologize; I did not intend to be rude. My name is Jenifer Norwich. My husband is a Marshal for the Guardians also." She spread her hands and appeared undeterred by Leah's aloofness. "I see you've found a good spot for quiet and solitude. I come here regularly myself."

The momentary fear that seized Leah faded. "I can leave if you would like some time alone," she said uncertainly.

Jenifer shook her head. "No, please. I would enjoy the company."

Leah nodded and with that, Jenifer continued up the hill. Her gait was rapid, and her garments were simple but neat. She sat down unreservedly on the grass and patted the space next to her, inviting Leah.

"Where are you from, Mrs. Fox?"

"Call me Leah. I'm from Carmel, one of the seaside towns." She cast a sidelong glance at her. "I don't know if you're familiar with it."

To her surprise, Jenifer simply laughed. It was a bright and clear sound, different from the high-pitched giggles of most women. "I'm from Ephes."

Leah started, but a pleasant thrill shot through her. "Oh! We were nearly neighbors."

"All of this," she gestured around them, "is quite a shock, I assume."

"It's not Cariath that is jarring." She wrestled for the right words. "It's —"

"The people?"

"Yes. The Guardians." Leah paused, smiling wryly. "And believe me, I read plenty of the legends. I was not entirely uninitiated."

Jenifer laughed, and they fell silent for a while. Leah found she did not grow uncomfortable as she often did around strangers. Instead, she felt a sense of solidarity wrap around her and Jenifer.

She glanced at the other woman in her peripheral vision. Jenifer had mousy brown hair pulled back in a loose braid. She was petite, not only in height, but her small eyes and nose also lent themselves to that impression. Leah would not call her beautiful — she was not gorgeous like Nyssa, with her pink cheeks and curls — but she was pretty. More than that, she seemed dignified, and not the least bit self-conscious. Leah envied that.

"Are you coming to the dinner tonight?" Leah said, breaking the silence.

"Yes, of course. No one misses the Old Fox's dinner parties. Though, sometimes I wonder if your husband wishes he could."

That piqued Leah's curiosity. "Why is that?"

"I thought I would ask you." Jenifer threw her an ironic glance. "I don't have the faintest idea. I just notice his expression sometimes."

"I wouldn't know either. August and I — we're not close." She felt a stab of shame in her chest as the words left her mouth and her face warmed.

Jenifer laid a hand on her shoulder. "That's the way with many of the Marshals. Rupert and I married nearly five years ago." Her expression grew thoughtful. "Sometimes I come into our room and still think I'm sharing a bed with a stranger."

"And you simply accept that." Leah looked at her incredulously.

"What other choice do I have?" Jenifer's voice hardened. "I was eighteen when he rode into Ephes and had the town alive with gossip. My father worked in a mill. There were no good prospects for my future. For the oddest reason, he wanted to marry me, and my family carted me off with him as quickly as possible."

"Did you like him at all?"

"I thought little of that until my stomach was filled. We didn't always have enough food at home." Jenifer's eyes met hers and Leah saw an iron will behind her brown pupils. "I suppose I learned to love him. He's a serious man, but he looks after me. I miss my family, but I was happy to leave Ephes behind. You learn to accept the hand you're dealt in life."

Leah was about to speak when the sound of approaching horse hooves interrupted them. She turned to see three men on horseback stop at the foot of the hill. The leader was August and one of the others was Maor. They were all fitted in loose hunting gear and breathing heavily. A small, furry creature sat in front of August, its damp hair a mix of brown and gold.

"Is that—a squirrel?" Leah asked without preamble, squinting to get a better view.

All the men and Jenifer chuckled. August said, "This is Kirin the Squirrel."

"Be prepared," Jenifer whispered behind her. "Kirin can—"

The squirrel leapt off the horse and gave a slight bow. Leah nearly recoiled in surprise. "Lady Fox, it's a pleasure," he shrilled in a high, but distinctly masculine voice.

"—talk," Jenifer finished.

"Oh!" Leah gasped before collecting herself. She got to her feet and dropped a slight bow in return. "Hello, Kirin. Please call me Leah."

Kirin glanced up at August, still on horseback, and Leah was not sure if they shared a secret smirk. There was an amused look on August's face. He proceeded to motion to the other man. "You know Maor already. This is Stephen." August nodded past her. "Good morning, Jenifer."

Greetings and courteous words were exchanged for the next few moments. Leah tried to pry her gaze away from Kirin, but her astonishment did not subside quickly.

"How was the hunt?" Jenifer asked. Leah observed the ease with which she conversed with the men.

"A few birds in the bag." Maor pointed at a sack slung over the side of his horse. "Nothing extravagant, but they should be delicious once the Old Fox throws them into his oven and works some magic."

"We're heading back home," August said. "If the two of you would like a quick ride over, we can take you."

Leah looked at Jenifer, who shook her head. "I can walk. I will stay out a little longer, anyway."

Leah's legs suddenly felt sore. "I'll come." She nodded at Jenifer. "It was good to talk. I will see you at the dinner, then."

As she clambered down the hill, the men began jesting. They quieted their voices, but as Leah drew closer, she heard Maor complaining lightheartedly to August.

"So now that you have a lady to take, I have to ride with the fur ball," he was saying, and Leah could only assume he meant Kirin.

"Oh, it's no better for me," Kirin returned in his shrill voice. "After every hunt, you stink to high heaven!"

"Kirin, ride with Stephen." August sighed, but there was a bright glimmer in his eye.

Maor cast both Kirin and Stephen a triumphant look as they were silenced. He gracefully hopped off his horse as Leah approached August and clasped his hands beside the horse's belly to offer her a boost. Leah gave him an appreciative smile.

"I apologize for the smell," Maor muttered under his breath to her.

Leah held in a laugh and shook her head. "No problem." She put her left foot in Maor's hands and pushed upward, swinging her right leg over the side of the horse. August reached a hand behind him to steady her.

"Impressive," Maor said and winked at her. "Have you ever mounted a horse before?"

"No," Leah breathed, as energy rushed through her. "But I liked that."

The men and Kirin chuckled as they turned toward the Bastion. August partially turned his head to glance at her. "Secure your arms tightly around my waist and hug the horse's body with your legs. Understood?"

"Yes, sir." Leah rolled her eyes upward but made sure to follow his directions.

August patted the horse on the side of the head, and without warning, it sprang into a gallop. Leah held in a shriek and squeezed until she was certain she was flattening him. She slowly loosened her death-grip as she adjusted to the horse's pace, its muscles contracting and expanding below her, and the air twisting into her eyes. Glancing behind her, she saw Stephen and Maor were close on their tail.

"Enjoying the ride?" August called over the rush of the wind.

"Yes, thanks for the warning," Leah called back. There was a moment of silence before she added, "Listen, last night, I didn't mean —"

"You make too many apologies. I'm unused to them, remember?"

To her pleasant surprise, Leah detected a trace of humor in his words. She figured that was his way of saying he had let it go, and it was not a barrier between them. *Though*, she thought ironically, *that does not mean there aren't any others.*

The horse slowed into a fast trot as the Bastion loomed large before them.

Leah leaned closer to August's ear. "Is Kirin faerie?"

His head dipped in acknowledgment. "He came to Cariath before I was born. My father rescued him during a fight with rogue faeries."

"You could have told me about him."

Staring at the back of his head, she could almost see a small grin form on his lips. "It didn't occur to me." She heard the lie in his voice. "And I thought we'd all enjoy your reaction."

Was he *teasing* her? Leah glowered with disbelief, then she was forced to bite back a smile.

CHAPTER 15

Pharan Desert, Island of Japha.
Month of Harvest: Third Week, Oath-Day.

The jeering and mockery of the men around him rattled in Benedict's head. He inched forward slowly, his legs heavy, and he was not sure if the pounding in his ears came from his footfalls or his heartbeat. People parted to the sides as he moved toward the center of the throng. There was a sick feeling in his gut and he swallowed hard to keep any bile from rising into his throat.

Nimrod stood in the middle of the mass, next to an older man who lay prostrate on the ground, his hands tied behind his back. Benedict's gaze went to his wrists, where spidery red lines marked the skin around the ropes that bound him. The prisoner lifted his head off the ground slightly, and they locked gazes. His face was caked with dirt and grime, but the dark eyes were familiar. Benedict felt like someone had dealt a sharp blow to his stomach.

"Benedict," Nimrod said, his tone both sickly sweet and derisive, "I suppose I should welcome you to your own family reunion."

There were a few snorts and laughs from the men behind him, but Benedict hardly heard them, the blood thrumming in his head. The other man's penetrating gaze had not left his face, and the world seemed to blur and narrow around him and Nimrod. Something deep inside Benedict ached terribly. He bit his tongue until warm liquid flooded the back of his mouth and he tasted the metallic flavor of blood.

"I'm afraid," Nimrod continued, "I will need to end the party early." He looked at Benedict, iron in his gaze. "Draw your sword."

The cold metal of the sword hilt startled him, and the sound of unsheathing it was uncommonly loud. It was heavy in his hands and he nearly staggered forward. Silence fell over the men, and he wondered if they could hear him think.

Time seemed to slow as he neared Nimrod and his prisoner. The former wore an expectant, impatient expression, tapping his black-booted foot. The latter had finally turned the direction of his gaze away from Benedict, resting the side of his face on the ground. Benedict paused as he came within spitting distance of the two men, his sword held awkwardly in front of him.

A cruel smile drew itself across Nimrod's face. "Fate has a sense of humor, after all," he muttered, more to himself. Raising his voice, he said, "It seems the Old Fox has provided an impeccable opportunity for his son to prove where his true allegiance lies." He lifted his foot off the ground casually and pressed it against the other man's back.

Nimrod stooped down, increasing the pressure of his foot against the spine. "At least, Benedict should be more merciful than me. Unless he is more of a monster than even I believed." He was whispering, but Benedict was close enough to hear.

Standing back up, Nimrod motioned for Benedict to come forward. Numbly, he stepped beside Arthur Fox's head and lifted his sword above his head. His father did not even lift his face to look at him again. Benedict paused for a moment, a quiver in his hands, and felt as if the world was holding its breath. Then, he brought his arms downward and thrust forward –

And ran it straight through Nimrod's chest.

He could not tell what happened in the next moments – there were shouts and chaos, and Nimrod shrieked as he toppled over, horror and hatred in his gaze.

Benedict stumbled backward and suddenly felt a sharp, almost unbearable pain in his side. Clutching at his abdomen with his hands, he glanced down to see a knife protruding from his waist and crimson coloring his garments fast. He sank to the ground, lightheaded, as his vision dimmed. Figures became shadowy outlines, and the vibrant hues around him darkened to shades of gray.

This was it – all his life amounted to was this moment: to die a traitor to both men to whom he had once swore allegiance. He was unready for death, but then, who ever was? Life was never taken away from man at a moment of his choosing. Benedict closed his eyes, feeling the sheer exhaustion and weariness of his body take hold until he hardly even felt the wound in his side.

"Benedict." The voice was weak but familiar, soothing.

He opened his eyes and strained his gaze in the direction of his father. He tried to open his mouth to respond, but his voice would not come, and his eyes widened as he saw another man running toward Arthur Fox from behind, a sword in his hands. Benedict tried to shout, and then get to his feet, but the pain in his side tore through his body and he collapsed.

"Benedict!" The sound echoed and grew distant.

"Benedict!"

He shot up straight like an arrow, his breath coming in gasps. Benedict's hand immediately reached for his sword. As his vision cleared and his surroundings came into focus, he found Justin kneeling beside him. The skies were a dusky gray. It was hardly morning and most of the men were still sprawled on the ground around their camp, fast asleep.

His breathing slowed and he lay back down, feeling the small rocks and dirt lumps beneath him prod at his back uncomfortably. He absently touched his waist—and felt a slight relief when he found no injury or blood.

"Same dream?" Justin inquired, all calm and collected.

This was becoming a familiar exercise between them. Benedict bit his lip in frustration. He prided himself on his independence and despised himself that he could not even conquer his nightmares. Justin had shaken him awake on many a morning before he could rouse the whole camp with his cries. While his friend was not one to gloat or lord over his shortcomings as Hound certainly would have, Benedict still privately hated that Justin had a glimpse into his weakness.

"Yes, almost," he muttered, his eyes closed.

"So you killed the Old Fox?" His tone was strikingly neutral, and

Benedict hated that too, wondering when Justin became so unreadable to him.

"It was a dream. I don't want to dredge it up into the waking world."

He did not open his eyes to observe Justin's expression, but his hard-edged words were met with silence. Benedict allowed his mind to drift to the day's plans. They had already sent a scout to Nimrod to report the success of the mission. The men spent the next day in informal training, setting up sword-fighting practice and wrestling matches. It was almost entertaining, but for the undercurrent of rivalry between Hound's men and Benedict's followers that dampened the otherwise lively spirit. Today would be another day like that, with no real agenda in place. Benedict could sense the men were growing restless, but he had promised to wait on this side of the Nathair until Nimrod sent word of his mission to Ebene.

Time was not in their favor. They had not cleaned up the Treasury in En-doire, given their hurried exit, and it would not be long before the Guardians realized the absence of Adair. Benedict decided they would move farther from En-doire each day, edging diagonally across the Pharan toward Whitewitch and the River.

"I remember when I used to have nightmares about my parents' deaths." Justin's musing cut into his thoughts suddenly, like a wrench thrown into turning wheels. "I was afraid of falling asleep."

Benedict opened his eyes and peered up at the other man, but Justin was staring out into the distance, a thoughtful look etched in his face. He rarely spoke of the past anymore, let alone his family, which was a subject untouched since their childhood days.

"You were young," he replied, with a hint of uncertainty over the proper mixture of sympathy and detachment under the current circumstances of their relationship. This was new territory, and he could not say he liked it. "I don't have the time to dwell on my dreams."

Justin simply shrugged, his gaze still cast far off. "I suppose there are enough worries in the land of the living."

They lapsed into another silence, but Benedict could not shake the uneasiness that settled over him. His dream was vivid in his mind again.

"It was the same dream, but a different ending." He did not think before the words left his mouth. "I killed Nimrod."

Benedict spoke in his usual volume, but it sounded uncommonly loud in his ears. He could not help but glance around him — most of the men were still asleep, though some were up and milling around the camp now. A hint of sunlight was breaking across the skies.

He detected a brief look of surprise across Justin's features, but it was quickly veiled by his usual dispassionate expression.

"That is different," was all he said.

"It was an impulse," Benedict continued, and at the same time, wondering why he did not put a pause to these thoughts spilling out, "In the split second where I could put my sword through either Nimrod or — through either of them, I just reacted."

"It was a dream." Justin repeated Benedict's earlier words back to him. He met his gaze. "You don't need to justify it to me."

Benedict felt a hot rush and his face warmed. "I wasn't justifying."

"Good." A barely visible smirk touched the corner of Justin's mouth. "Dream or not, Nimrod deserved it."

Benedict choked down a laugh rising in the back of his throat before he grew somber again. "Justin," he said, and paused, feeling a weight press on his mind. "You ought to return to Cariath."

"Your recommendation comes a little late," Justin replied dryly.

"You don't belong here."

They had grown up playing games and training in combat together, ever since Justin was orphaned, and the Guardians became the only family he knew. He was similar to August in some ways, and that drew Benedict to him. He was the unruffled, tranquil counterpart to Benedict's fiery and impulsive spirit. But unlike August, Justin judged and lectured him less for his recklessness, and instead, maintained a quiet loyalty to Benedict when many condemned his behavior.

A loyalty that led him even to severing ties with the men and duty to whom he had sworn oaths. *A senseless, blind loyalty.* It almost pained Benedict to think of the sacrifice Justin made to follow him to Nimrod. They spoke little of their true thoughts, but Justin never severed the friendship. Again, he differed from August, who Benedict knew would not forgive him.

Justin not only maintained their ties, but also walked the same dark road. Nimrod was a means to an end for Benedict, the consequences of which he would accept, but the Oath-breakers held nothing for Justin. Benedict wondered sometimes if his loyalty was to a shadow of the past, to a once close brotherhood they shared. But time and circumstances had frayed their connection, and he doubted there was much between them now but lingering old memories — a poor bond, he thought.

"And you are certain you do?" Justin's response cut through his musing.

"More than you, at least," he returned. "There is nothing for you here." *Only me.* The unspoken words played in Benedict's mind. But that would not — should not — be enough to hold Justin.

"There is only death for me in Cariath," he sighed. "You know what they do to Oath-breakers."

"You are hardly one."

Benedict kicked a loose stone by his foot and watched it sail through the air, the early sunlight catching it at different angles and glancing off its rough edges. It landed and tumbled ungracefully through the dirt.

His companion did not respond, as Benedict expected. He knew his words were futile. Justin might not be an Oath-breaker at heart. He, and even some of the Guardians, knew that, but the age-old judgment for Oath-breakers did not provide exception clauses or second chances. The thought produced a twinge in Benedict's chest, though he was unsure if he felt guilt, remorse, anger, or all of those emotions, twisted into one dreadful knot.

The silence they fell into this time seemed fraught with unspoken words. Perhaps things that had gone unspoken between them for years. But Benedict knew now was not the time to bring them to light. When Nimrod's quest ended, and if there was ever reconciliation between the sides – maybe then they would share honest words, if they both survived. But war rarely afforded such luxury.

"Look, to the west." Justin's voice was low and urgent.

Apprehension gripped Benedict. A lone figure was approaching their camp in the distance. He had a short, stocky build and the outline of a sword dangled by his side.

"Messenger from Nimrod?" Benedict murmured. He could not imagine who else would venture this far alone and on foot. His initial alarm began to wear off.

"Perhaps," Justin said, a note of wariness in his tone still.

Benedict rose to his feet, stretching his sore legs. "I will find out. Keep an eye on him, in the event that things go poorly."

The camp was more alive now with men eating breakfast, talking amongst themselves, or sparring casually. The sun had broken well over the horizon, and golden streaks slashed deep into the grey clouds, scattering them to unveil a bold cerulean palette. It would be another fair-weathered day, and Benedict could not help but feel his spirits lift.

He met the stranger on the outskirts of the camp. The other man was smaller than average, but his sturdy physique and facial hair gave him a sufficiently intimidating appearance. His countenance was familiar, though Benedict could not place it. As they drew near each other, the newcomer paused in his steps and bowed.

"Fox," he intoned in a gravelly voice. "Markus at your service. Nimrod sent me with a message."

At his introduction, brief recollections of seeing Markus among the men rose to mind.

"I am ready to hear it," Benedict replied swiftly. He was tired of pleasantries and banal talk, and that was one element of Guardian gatherings, particularly his father's overblown parties, he was pleased to be rid of.

Markus drew a compact scroll from inside the folds of his robes and handed it to Benedict, who felt suddenly alert again. He eyed Markus with a look of suspicion.

"He *wrote* me?" Benedict frowned, the downward turn of his mouth driving gashes in the sides of his face.

When the Guardians sent scouts, they nearly always memorized and delivered their messages verbally. It was a strategy Nimrod adopted for his men due to its sheer prudence. A written document could be lost, or fall into the wrong hands, but no one could extract the contents of the mind.

"He said it was for your eyes alone." Markus shrugged and appeared unperturbed. "I do not know what it says, but I guarded it with my life."

Such blind loyalty again. Benedict put the thought out of his head—now was not the time for philosophy. He turned the scroll over in his hand and found Nimrod's seal on it. That eased his mind slightly, so he broke it open and unfurled the parchment. Nimrod's handwriting was bold and sure, no frills. The message was brief.

I have what I came for. Waiting near E until I receive word of your success. Then, we go to the gate. Decided against going to Dammim.

It was sufficiently cryptic that if the message reached anyone else, it would make little sense. Benedict absorbed the implications of the concise note slowly.

Nimrod provided no indication of how he fared with the Cobalt Dragon Guardians in Ebene, but it did not matter. He recovered the lantern, or whatever form the Light took. Benedict calculated his message would reach Nimrod in a week's time, and that would drive him to action. If he did not want to go to Dammim and search out a potential fourth key among the Vermilion Falcon Guardians, he would want to move against Cariath immediately. Nimrod also suspected the mortal gate resided somewhere in the Bastion.

Benedict cursed to himself. He was convinced Vermilion Falcon had something they needed, even if they could not decipher the clue. Moreover, while Nimrod's breaking away put a dent in the Guardian host, the Bastion was still heavily secured, and not just by sheer force or geography. Not many knew of the Old Fox's gift, save perhaps the Marshals and Benedict. A few Guardians inherited rudimentary faerie abilities, and his father had honed his quietly. Nimrod surely knew nothing of it.

To sail into the heart of the Guardian stronghold without even an advantage of numbers was foolish.

"Sir."

Startled, Benedict looked down at Markus, having nearly forgotten his presence. "Yes?"

"The news seems grave, judging by your expression." Markus eyed him carefully. "Though, I do not mean to pry."

"Not grave, just…stimulating," Benedict replied. "Did Nimrod ask you to remain with me or return to him?"

"Nimrod advised I remain with you, unless you have word to send him."

Benedict quietly cursed Nimrod. Unless there were new circumstances he was unaware of—which seemed unlikely—they did not have the capacity to attack the Bastion. Nimrod was typically rational and coldly objective in his decision-making, while Benedict was the reckless one. He wondered if Nimrod was puffed up on their recent victories, and that had led him to make such a rash judgment. He was not one to seek counsel, and when Benedict offered any, it was often to no avail.

"I have sent a messenger to him already about our success. Go and refresh yourself," Benedict said, making an effort to pull himself back to reality. He pointed to Justin, who was eating with some of the other men now but watching Benedict and Markus discreetly. "That's my second-in-command. Go to him if you require anything."

Markus bowed. "Certainly. And yourself?"

"I'm going to take a short walk."

With that, the two men parted ways. Benedict wandered away from the camp. His thoughts turned again to his dream and the memory of it felt like ice pressed against his skin. He shivered. With the imminent battle between the Guardians and Oath-breakers, death's reality loomed too close for comfort. Most Guardians believed in gods who had power over the mortal and immortal realms. They were supposed to be good and just, showing no partiality between men and faeries, but opposing the wicked on either side. A number of Guardians believed they were serving the gods by protecting the mortal realm, and in the afterlife, they would find eternal rest after their lifetime of labor.

As far as religion went, Benedict thought it was sensible enough for those who didn't think too hard. Or who never felt the cruel blade of tragedy slash through their life.

If the gods were real, and if they were truly merciless to the wicked, Benedict knew he had no excuse. They would not look favorably on him, and who knew what punishment they would bring down on the head of an Oath-breaker in the afterlife? But if they were real, they were silent in the face of the faeries' crimes — and that silence was unforgivable.

On that thin but seemingly irrefutable logic, Benedict knew he gambled. *I damn them in life, and if they exist, they can damn me in death.*

Glancing up at the sky, he found the sun, luminous and unblinking, at the peak of its daily march across the heavens, making it nearly high noon. He retraced his steps and came back upon the camp, which was alive with boisterous conversation and sparring matches. The bright day must have lifted some of the men's spirits as well.

Justin met him near the outskirts of the gathering, so they were out of anyone else's earshot. He gave Benedict a curious look.

"What was Nimrod's message?"

"He wants to ride for the Bastion soon." Benedict observed the surprise that passed over Justin's face. "Maybe right after he receives our message."

"So quickly?" Justin frowned. "That seems imprudent. What about the Vermilion Falcon?"

"It *is* imprudent. I'm certainly not eager to ride headlong into a suicide mission."

"Did he say anything else?"

"He got the lantern from Ebene."

Justin nodded, unsurprised. "Markus said they lost ten men."

Benedict's chest contracted, first with a brief burst of pride that he did better, then with a surge of disgust. Perhaps he had nobler reasons for becoming an Oath-breaker, but would he end up a shadow of Nimrod?

"Will we meet him in Ebene?"

"We would need to cross the river and swing south, whereas Cariath is just due west." Benedict ran a quick mental calculation. "He should receive our message before we reach the edge of the Pharan. He might intercept our path."

As they made their way toward the center of the camp, Justin cast a sidelong glance at him. "What were you doing after speaking with Markus?"

"Nothing. Just thinking," he said vaguely.

"A dangerous activity."

Justin's words carried a lighthearted tone, but Benedict could only muster a small smirk for it. The effort at humor did little to lighten his subdued disposition.

CHAPTER 16

Cariath, Island of Japha.
Month of Harvest: Third week, Oath-Day.

The dinner party brought the spacious halls of Fox Manor alive with animated talk and laughter. What a contrast, Leah thought, to the quiet solitude of the previous night. It reminded her of August's housewarming party in Carmel. This time there were fewer attendees, but they made up for the difference with lively spirits.

Jenifer introduced Leah to her husband, Rupert, who was stern but courteous. The other Guardian Marshal was James Sky, a boisterous and outgoing man, and his wife Edina was sweet and quiet. Leah met Melina Landon, the widow of a Marshal who met his untimely death a little over a year ago. Her soft expression seemed to carry a trace of sorrow, and Jenifer privately commented that she had been deeply in love with her husband.

Leah learned that Maor, Stephen, and Kirin were directly under August's command and they were also his closest counselors. She noticed he was most comfortable around these three, and spent a majority of his time near them. He interacted little with the other Marshals or his father, and it was only with his men where Leah observed genuine mirth in him.

Besides a few brief conversations with Jenifer and the obligatory introductions, Leah stuck close to Arthur throughout the evening, helping him set the food and clearing the clutter. He protested vehemently at first, but Leah insisted. She enjoyed the simple tasks of serving and cleaning and found tranquility in the ease of them. Privately, she was relieved to escape from mingling and socializing.

When she found herself with little work left to do, Leah straightened the trays left out on the dining table to make herself look busy. Out of the corner of her eye, she saw Arthur motion for her to leave those alone and join the others, which he had finally done as well.

"Leah!"

She looked up to see Maor waving her over to join the men. A sense of relief flooded through her. At the least, she felt more comfortable around him and August's friends. They were cheerful and she enjoyed their casual jesting. The regal nature of some of the other Marshals intimidated her, and besides Jenifer, the other women did not seem eager to take the initiative in approaching her.

"Your husband has a problem," Maor began once she stepped into their circle. "The Old Fox is going to make him give a speech soon. And he will be a bore, as usual."

Kirin made a choking sound, and Leah glanced down at him, unsure if that was a laugh. He was curled up next to August on a stretch of cushions. Stephen was standing beside Maor, and he maintained a relatively grave look.

"Well," Leah looked back at Maor, "I fail to see how this is my concern."

Maor slapped August on the back. "What a wife you found! She is ready to stand by and watch you make a fool of yourself." Leah flushed and opened her mouth but Maor continued. "I like her more by the moment."

Her gaze strayed to August and their eyes met. She wondered if she imagined the glimmer of amusement that flashed in his dark pupils despite the somber look on his face.

"I told you before, my father forced me to give these superfluous speeches. I'm not good with words," August said.

That was as much of a request from him as she would get, Leah thought sardonically.

"I'm not good with people," she returned.

"What a pair you two make." Maor hooted. Kirin let out a shrill sound that sounded like a laugh this time and even Stephen's grimness melted into a wry smile. Before they could continue the conversation, the din slowly died down as Arthur was calling for attention. Leah noticed Maor give August a pointed look.

"Marshals, Guardians, and our dear families," Arthur began, "thank you for joining our celebration tonight. It is always a privilege to have such esteemed guests in the Fox home." His expression glowed, and for a moment, Leah could see him as a young man bursting with passion and charm. "As you know, we are here to welcome my son August home, and even more," he paused and threw an impish look Leah's way, "to celebrate his new wife, Leah." Polite applause rang from all corners of the room and some turned to give a nod of acknowledgment to August and Leah. "As is tradition," Arthur continued.

Leah was distracted by Maor's mumbling.

"Here it comes," he muttered.

"I will give August an opportunity to speak. After all, he is the rising lord of Fox Manor. I am just a doddering old man." Arthur smiled and motioned for August, who reluctantly moved to his side. "Son, I am sure our friends would like to hear of your journey and the story of how you and Leah came together in matrimony," he finished with a flourish.

"Arthur has such—" Leah searched for the right word, "style."

"I think he always hopes August will produce that same—as you put it, my lady—style," Kirin said in a quiet, gravelly voice.

"He asks for disappointment, then," Maor replied swiftly. "Ben was the one who took after the Old Fox in that way."

Leah looked at him in surprise, and her tongue was poised with a question, but August's voice stopped her.

"Cariath Valley was a welcome sight to my eyes as we rode in last night, and it is my pleasure to be among my brethren here. To be brief, I travelled to the seaside towns and spent time in Carmel, my wife's home." His gaze wandered over the guests until he found Leah. Her stomach lurched. "I met Leah at my housewarming party. She was one of the most sensible and steady women I've ever met, and I'm honored to bring her home as my bride." He dipped his head to indicate the end of his speech.

Applause rang over the hall again, and Arthur patted his son on his shoulder blade, though there was a small look of disappointment in his eyes. "Thank you, August. Everyone, please carry on with the merriment!"

"The Old Fox was hoping for something decidedly more romantic, I'm sure." Maor smirked and turned to Leah. "He married you for your sensibility. Really?"

August wove through the crowd toward them and seemed to catch the tail end of Maor's words. "I'm not an entertainer, Maor," he said tiredly.

"Arthur should have had Leah tell the story. The fine touch of a lady could do wonders."

"I believe my version would be equally, if not more, unflattering," she said, glancing at August.

Leah spent most of the remainder of the dinner party listening to August and his men recount old memories of scouting trips and battles: a few that involved rogue faeries breaking into the mortal realm, and more that dealt with militant cults who worshiped faeries and wanted to usher in their rule over the mortal realm. She had a difficult time picturing August and his fellow Guardians as warriors, riding headlong into fights with swords and spears. Squeezing her right hand into a fist, she recalled August's warm touch as he held her hand during the wedding ceremony, and as he helped her into the carriage outside Edenbridge. Her gaze strayed to his strong, callused fingers. How many spears had he thrown with that hand? How many men's lives had he ended? She shivered at the thought of such power.

"Has Coriander left for Ebene?" Stephen asked, after a lull in the conversation. "I didn't see him tonight."

Leah looked at her husband, remembering that skirmishes in the Ebene region was what prompted their swift return to Cariath. Was Nimrod the one stirring up trouble there?

August nodded. "He rode out with a few of his men earlier today." He furrowed his brow. "We spent a long time in council deliberating."

"Combat?" Stephen queried.

"Diplomatic, we hope. We didn't send enough men for a fight."

Leah caught Stephen and Maor exchanging a glance, but the context was mostly lost on her. "That's where the Cobalt Dragon Guardians are, right?" she ventured. "Does anyone else live in the Ebene?"

Her question seemed to break the grim atmosphere. "Plenty of nomadic groups," Maor said. "The culture in the grasslands is one of constant change. They don't have permanent settlements, but clusters of families move together through the land. They're hunters and gatherers by trade, and the resources in that region allow them to prosper in that way of life."

"So the Dragons are nomadic too?"

"More or less. They tend to be on the move, living in huts and tents." Maor smirked, perhaps seeing the expression on Leah's face. "Feeling thankful you didn't marry one of their Marshals?"

She flushed but did not deny it. The stability of Fox Manor and the Bastion did give her some comfort. She winced inwardly, imagining how she would adjust to life in Ebene.

"Well, let's hope none of their men are foolish enough to take a wife from the seaside towns," she countered.

The men chuckled, including August. The conversation remained light after that as they discussed further the differences between the White Tigers and Cobalt Dragons. Maor shared a story about one of his escapades in Ebene during Guardian training.

As she and August bade farewell to the guests as they retired for the evening, Leah was surprised when Melina Landon drew her aside before she reached the front door.

"Would you like to join me for tea sometime?" Melina asked softly.

Leah did not have a penchant for tea, but thought it would be rude to refuse outright. "If it's no inconvenience."

"Not at all." She smiled, and her face lit up prettily. "There are not many women around, so I'm glad you're here. My home is simple, but I love to have guests."

"I prefer simple." She liked Melina and found her gentleness sweet and unassuming. She did not have the resolute hardness of Jenifer, but a kindness that reminded Leah a little of Jessie, albeit quieter.

"I live just a few houses away. Your husband will know. You are welcome to call on me anytime."

"Thank you, Melina."

As Melina slipped out the door, August came by Leah's side. "You made a new friend."

"I hope so. She seems sweet."

"Alain thought the same. He said he married her before a line of suitors could unhinge her family's door."

Leah could hear the smile in August's voice and looked up at him. His eyes had a distant look in them. "What happened to him?"

A shadow passed over his face. "He died on a mission," he said bluntly. "I was there, but not when it happened. He was on night watch, and he and some men rode out from camp when they heard a disturbance. Thought it was a rogue faerie attack." He paused. "One of the men was Nimrod. He leads—"

"Yes, the Oath-breakers. Arthur told me."

August did not register any reaction to her interruption, still caught in the memory. "When they came back, Alain was dead and marred beyond recognition. Nimrod said they were ambushed." He sucked in a breath and seemed shaken back into reality. His eyes found Leah's. "I'm sorry. You didn't need to know."

Leah felt lightheaded. "You didn't believe him," she whispered, watching the storm twist and coil beneath his calm features.

"Nimrod?" His quiet tone sent ice through her blood. "He hated Alain. No one else came back with even a scratch. I was not a fool."

"Did you confront him?"

"I had no evidence. The men with him were either too loyal or too afraid to speak. I could not accuse another Guardian of such treachery without proof."

"Does Melina know?" It would be wiser to stop prying, but part of her was struck helpless with curiosity.

"I brought back his body and buried him. I simply told her he died valiantly, and he wished her to remember him as he was alive, not as a cold corpse." Raw pain was suddenly visible on August's face and his voice turned to steel. "But I will remember the corpse. Nimrod will answer for it."

For once, Leah felt undaunted by his hard words. "You were close to Alain," she observed quietly.

August did not respond, but she read the truth in his darkened eyes.

~~~~~

Leah was snatched out of her dreamless slumber like a fish pulled from the sea. Her eyes flew open as a shout cut across the room and she turned her head to see August flailing his arms beside her. Alarmed, she sat up and leaned closer to him. As far as she could tell, he was still asleep, caught in the throes of some nightmare. Hesitantly, she laid a hand on his shoulder and shook him.

His hand shot out and caught her wrist in a vise-like grip.

She gasped. "August," Leah whispered, trying to stay calm.

He slowly let go and turned to face her. Even in the shadows, she could see the corners of his eyes tinged with thin, crimson lines. He was breathing heavily through his mouth, almost panting. Clumps of his ginger hair were pasted onto his forehead, damp with sweat.

She watched him for a few moments in silence, allowing him to catch his breath, and wondered what terrible dreams plagued him to cause such distress. Was it his brother's betrayal? Or was it Alain, even other friends, who died beside him in battle? Leah suddenly felt very young and sheltered, having never lived close to death or war. Her nightmares normally involved awkward social gatherings or dancing with chatty, garlic-breathed men. Next to August, she felt as shallow as her sisters in their worst form.

"I didn't mean to wake you," August said finally. No apology, but Leah saw one in his face. "Was I yelling?"

"I heard you shout, and then you were flailing your arms."

"Bad dream."

"What happened?" Leah saw his puzzled expression. "In your dream," she clarified.

He lay back down on the bed, sliding his hands under his head on the pillow. Leah followed suit but lay on her side so she faced him, waiting for his response. August closed his eyes for a moment, but she was not fooled.

"It was Alain." His eyes remained shut. "I saw him murdered. The killer wore a black scarf about his face. After Alain was dead, the man tore the scarf away and I saw...him." There was a brief quiver in his voice, but otherwise, he betrayed little emotion.

Leah did not need to ask who the man was, and she fleetingly wondered if she was beginning to know August better than she thought.

"Do they come often? The dreams?" She wanted to express her sympathy, but the question tumbled out of her mouth first. It came with more ease. Leah had never been a good comforter and she felt helpless to console August.

"Often enough. It's the price a warrior pays. I have learned to control my thoughts during the waking hours, but we're helpless in sleep."

They fell silent for a while, but Leah was wide awake now and unsatisfied with the conclusion of the conversation. She searched for some words of kindness to share with him, but her mind was blank. Papa had a natural knack for tenderheartedness and Leah now wished she had a few doses of his talent.

But what could I even say? There was the warrior part of August, like an impregnable wall she was at a loss to breach. By all accounts, Leah was still a young girl, not even fully blossomed into womanhood yet, and completely ill-equipped to support a man of such stature and experience. Momentary despair clawed at her heart, but she quickly denied such despondency any hold over her.

"August?" she said softly.

"Yes."

Leah hesitated. Would it be unkind, or even wrong, to ask? "Was Benedict there? With Alain." She braced herself for a lash of fury.

But he appeared unmoved. "No." A long pause followed before he added, "He was not on the mission. But that does not excuse his other crimes."

"So he did not know what you suspected."

August turned on his side and met her with a fierce gaze. "He knew

110

enough. He knew what kind of man Nimrod was."

"Were they friends?"

He laughed, a harsh, grating sound. "He hated Nimrod. But he hated the faeries more."

Leah thought of the rogue faerie attacks August mentioned briefly. Even in the legends she read, she knew that peace between men and faeries was not undisturbed after Arieh. Many rejected his ways, and though the sealing of the immortal realm ended outright war, the enmity did not die. Time stitched some of the old scars, but just as the seal between worlds could fracture, allowing rogue faeries to slip through, wounds could be re-opened.

"Enough to follow a man like that?" She furrowed her brow. "Why?"

"It doesn't matter. There is no reason good enough to pardon him. Duty, honor, oaths. That's what runs in our blood." Pride mingled with pain in his words. "So, to betray our brethren or break an oath is a heinous deed."

"What happens if an Oath-breaker comes back? If he recognizes his wrongdoing and turns away from it?"

Leah thought of Benedict, her mysterious, traitorous brother-in-law. She wondered how he must feel now, having forsaken his kin and broken his pledge to the Guardians. Did he experience any remorse at such a cruel severing of blood ties and loyalty? In her gut, Leah could not imagine he walked away effortlessly, without any damage.

"He would be put on trial for his crimes, though for breaking faith with the Guardians, the sentence is death. There is no real coming back after you leave, Leah."

"Arieh extended mercy."

"I told you, I think his legend has been grossly embellished."

She fell silent, feeling the alien nature of August's world engulf her. His was a warrior's world, ruled by honor and fealty, bound up by blood. Her heart grew heavy as she thought of the wounds both sword and life had dealt him. No one in Carmel, seeing his gentleman's attire and demeanor, would guess the burdens he carried.

"And what about the gods the Guardians serve?"

"They've become like legends too, passed down through the generations. You'll find we all serve them in name, but that's not the same as real faith." He paused. "My mother was devout, but her culture was more religious than ours."

Curiosity tugged at Leah. August had never spoken of his mother before, but something in his voice prevented her from prying. "She wasn't from Cariath?" A safe, simple question.

He shook his head. "No. Father met her abroad."

When it became evident he would say no more, Leah said softly, "You know what I think? I've read about the Guardians' gods—supposedly good and just, wrathful toward evil. They are made in the image of the

Guardians, the upholders of all your morals and ideals. Easy to explain, until you suffer. They have no answer to *why* evil exists, or what cure there is. They have no answer to why a seemingly good man chooses the wrong path."

Something like understanding flickered through August's eyes, but his expression stayed steady, his gaze locked on hers. "Some might call you a heretic for those words."

"Would you?" she countered.

"I want to know what you think the answer is."

"I believe in one God, who is just and merciful. The gods of the Guardians are trapped in an endless cycle of punishing injustice, but there is no resolution to evil. I believe in a God who will one day restore all things and make final peace between men and the faerie-kind. Not through law, but through power that changes the soul. Look at Arieh—he didn't do what a Guardian should have. He laid down his own life as a substitute for war criminals. The power of that act is still reverberating through time."

As she spoke, Leah wondered if her words sounded naive to a man like August, who had seen darkness and death in a way that never touched her personally. But in the face of that reality, Leah felt her own convictions soar. Nothing but faith in her God could speak sufficiently into his pain.

"Reverberating, perhaps, but the evils of the past continue to repeat themselves," he replied, but his tone was not defensive or combative.

"History is a long, slow arc, but it bends toward justice," Leah said, quoting an old writer. "We haven't reached the end yet."

She swallowed her surprise as he reached for her hand, his wrapping loosely around hers. "I admire your faith, Leah. I wish I had it."

"You don't think it's a blind, untested faith?" She echoed her earlier doubts.

"Maybe. But, were it tested, I think it would still stand."

Unexpected warmth flooded through her. It was the kindest thing August had said to her—or, it was the first time she felt he really *saw* her, and found something inside her she wasn't even certain of.

"Thanks," she murmured.

August offered her a small smile. He turned away from her to lie on his back, though his fingers were still touching hers.

When Leah glanced over at him next, his eyes were closed and his breathing a steady, rhythmic pace. She relaxed her muscles against the mattress and allowed sleep to claim her also.

CHAPTER 17

The days passed like a blur to Leah. She fell into the routine of waking up late. August was usually long gone on his morning hunt with the men. He spent a number of afternoons in council meetings with his father and the other Marshals, so sometimes she would go without seeing him until dinnertime. The warm weather made for lazy days where she stretched out somewhere in Fox Manor or on the green plains outside to read her books or sketch the world around her. She had always loved to draw, though Mama considered it a useless preoccupation and afforded her no formal training in it.

As she adjusted to her new life, the desire to capture the world around her began to burn again. Leah contemplated sending her sketches home along with a letter describing her life among the Guardians. But something held her back, and she could not find the words to pen her family. Mama would be thrown into a terrible fright, and her sisters might not believe most of it—Oath-breakers, rogue faeries, Kirin. It would reek of absurdity. She did not know what Papa would say. Something strange nagged at Leah when she thought of him, but she could not identify it.

One bright afternoon, as she was pressed up against the cushions in the main hall of Fox Manor, Arthur stepped in to peer at her drawing. He indulged her pastime even more than Papa, sometimes sitting with her silently for hours, watching her sketch. At times, Leah wondered if he suffered from loneliness also, despite being surrounded by his son and the Marshals.

"You give the table a more flattering look than it deserves," he commented over his shoulder. She was illustrating the inside of Fox Manor, peopled with the Marshals and friends who frequented the Old Fox's dinner parties.

Leah allowed a slow smile, but did not take her eyes off her work. "I take liberties in art, since there is so little opportunity in reality."

He did not reply, so Leah continued drawing, her pen moving with liquid-like grace across the rough paper. There was a sureness in her hand when she sketched or painted, one she lacked in speech and actions, so she found a sanctuary in art. She was the master of her creation here.

She did not know how much time passed before Arthur spoke again. "Lila wanted that table terribly. I bought it to appease her."

Leah was startled and paused for a moment. Arthur had never spoken of his wife, and August had only made brief mention of her. Leah was wary to raise the subject herself, remembering how poorly that tactic had gone in the case of Benedict.

"What happened to her?"

"She was not an Oath-breaker," Arthur replied dryly, perhaps sensing Leah's guardedness. He grew somber. "She died a few years ago."

"Did you love her?" Leah bit her tongue hard, slapping herself mentally for allowing the words to slip out. "I mean—"

Arthur chuckled a little. "No, speak your mind."

Leah flushed, feeling her face warm. "Papa says curiosity will be my death."

"I imagine it will also color your life." Arthur laid a hand on Leah's shoulder. "I loved Lila," he said suddenly, and his gaze looked distant. "My family objected to the union, in fact, but I defied them and married her still. I was a brash and impulsive young man." He smiled ruefully, and Leah saw a hint of youthful playfulness as well as the sadness of long years etched in his expression.

"It seems the Guardians rarely marry for love," she said, working to keep any resentment out of her voice.

He stared at her for a moment, and strangely, she felt a small wave of guilt, wondering if he sensed a veiled accusation against August in her words.

"Leah, Guardian or not, there are few in this world who marry for love," he said softly.

"Well, that's a shame," she replied, more harshly than she intended.

"You are a romantic," he said, with a small smile, undeterred by her sharpness, "much like I was. August is different. He sees the world as it is, and not as he wishes it to be."

"I'm not naive about reality," Leah retorted.

"I didn't say you are. But there is a little dream, a little longing that flutters in here," and Arthur laid a hand on his chest, "that there will be a poetry to life and it will all come to good in the end."

Leah did not know what to say, but felt a slight wrench in her chest. Despite the short time they had known one another, Arthur had managed to take a figurative spear and cast it right into the heart of her. She felt a sense of discomfort, of bareness, as she was laid plainly before his eyes. Sometimes, she also realized August understood her more than she gave him credit for, though he spoke less of it.

"You know," Arthur continued slowly, "August was set to marry a lady from Cariath, months ago."

"What?" Leah stared at him.

"It wasn't love. August is next in line to be Chief. She's from Cariath, but not the Bastion, and her father is close to Amir's inner circle of advisors."

"A political marriage."

"I thought he would have gone through with it, but August has been...quite opaque for a long time. They only met twice, but not long before August set out for Carmel, he told me he decided against it."

"Were you in favor of it?"

"Not particularly." Arthur smiled ruefully. "August, unlike Benedict, spent his life being a dutiful Guardian at any cost. I told him if he carried that philosophy into marriage, he would be miserable. He isn't keen on my advice these days, so I don't know why he finally ended it." He paused, studying her for a long moment. "Imagine my surprise when he wrote to tell me of you."

Leah flushed. "I have even less to offer than her," she returned. "No status, no position—"

"There are better things than those, Leah. And however little he speaks of it, August knows that."

"He's not a romantic like you, though," she said lightly.

He chuckled. "No, he isn't."

"And Benedict?" Leah asked suddenly, recalling Maor's words during the dinner party. "Was he like you?"

Arthur was quiet for a moment. "Yes, he took after me in many ways." His tone was heavy. "That is the danger of romanticism, I suppose. When life and the world crush that spark of a dream, that ideal of goodness, it twists you terribly."

Leah thought of Alain and her gut felt hollow. What did Benedict experience to turn him away from his family and the Guardians to follow a man he once despised? She did not dare ask August.

"What happened?" she ventured.

"Lila died." Arthur did not meet her eyes, a taut moment before the hammer fell. "She was killed in a rogue faerie attack."

He hated Nimrod. But he hated the faeries more. The room stood still and silent, but his words threw Leah into a tailspin.

Either sensing her distress or lost in his own thoughts, Arthur continued, "In Cariath, the seal between the immortal realm and ours is strong, but the stitching is weak in some places. The Pharan, for instance. That's where it happened—but oh, how she fought." His voice cracked a little.

"You were there?"

"No. A small contingent traveled to En-doire. Two survived to tell the tale."

She shivered. The legends emphasized the cruelty of the faerie-kind, but it was always distant, trapped inside the covers of Papa's musty books. The haunted look in Arthur's eyes unleashed it into reality.

"So Benedict wanted revenge," she surmised.

"He fought long and hard to convince the Marshals to break our age-old treaty. He wanted to strike back at the faeries. But I could not support that."

"How? Can we enter the immortal realm?"

Arthur hesitated for a second, his gaze flitting around the room. "You know the four Guardian camps?" Leah nodded. "In Arieh's day, when the treaty was signed, the Guardians broke into four bases, each one taking a fragment of the secret to unlocking the faerie realm. If united, a mortal could find his way in."

Her mind reeled at the revelation.

"I've never heard that." Another thought occurred to her. "Then, you do recognize the truth of Arieh's legend."

He cocked his head. "I do. But I can't speak for everyone."

"Is that what Nimrod and the Oath-breakers are doing, then?" Leah sucked in a breath. "Trying to unlock the secret?"

"That's what we must assume. There was a skirmish in Ebene recently where Nimrod's men may have attacked to find the key kept by the Cobalt Dragon Guardians, which further confirms their intent. That's why I called August back early for an emergency council." He sighed. "Ben wanted me to rally the Guardian camps and attack the faeries together. But when I refused and Nimrod began to organize a mutiny among our ranks... I didn't think he would stoop to follow him." Arthur met her gaze with bald, unnerving sorrow. "Nimrod always lusted after power, but Ben—"

"He must have really loved his mother."

A long silence followed her words. Arthur simply bowed his head. Leah looked around the hall with renewed eyes. The ancient, weighty air of Fox Manor she had felt when she first stepped foot inside gave way to something different. Something more intimate, like a home that knew a family's joy and grief and legacy—a youthful romance, the miracles of birth, brotherly rivalry, a mother's cooking, the ghost of lost love...

"August was never so sympathetic about his motivation," Arthur said finally.

Leah considered her wayward brother-in-law, who probably thought a weak father and unfeeling brother spurned his anguish.

"He deals with pain differently."

"He buries it."

"And you?" Leah stared at him.

He did not shrink from her scrutiny. "I live with it." A sad smile flitted over his face. "In my time among the Guardians, I have always been able to protect the Bastion, to keep our home safe. But I couldn't do the same for my son."

Leah felt her throat tighten, unsure of what to say. She fell back on something Papa would tell her. "Well, love isn't safe. My father always said you can't really love if you won't risk the pain of loss."

Arthur nodded. "He's a wise man."

She broke her gaze away from his and turned to the window. The afternoon light was fast fading, and only the last rays of sunshine fell across the mountains and scattered into Cariath. Her head spun with a hundred strands of thought, and she looked with renewed wonder upon the world outside Fox Manor. There was an alien wildness to it, as of a completely foreign world, but it was not without a touch of familiarity. It stirred up a strange mixture of nostalgia and mystery within her.

"Does this feel far from home?" Arthur asked softly.

"Yes," she replied quietly, "and yet, no."

~~~~~

"This is the battle room," August said as he pushed open the scratched oak door. Leah thought briefly that the grazes in the wood looked like they came from a sharp blade.

She gaped as she stepped in. The room was attached to the very end of Fox Manor, and from the outside it looked deceptively small. Inside, it was as spacious as the main hall of the house. The walls curved to encircle the room, and bright lanterns hung from the high, vaulted ceiling. A large plank of hardwood sat a few steps above ground level in the center of the room, and Leah assumed it was the sparring ground August had spoken of.

Off to one side was a large, granite table with maps and drawings scattered across. Kirin the squirrel was perched on the end of the table and in his paws was a long document that draped onto the table and pooled at his feet. He set it aside nimbly as August and Leah entered the room.

"Leah," Kirin shrilled, dipping his head at her. He turned to August, and she thought he did the squirrel equivalent of a raised eyebrow. "You wish to be defeated soundly in the presence of your wife?"

"I don't believe that will occur," August replied smoothly.

Leah turned to him, an astonished look on her face. "You're going to duel with Kirin?" She wavered between wondering whether this would be comical or pitiful.

"You insult him with your doubt. He can hold his own — occasionally." A small smirk graced August's features, breaking his usual serious form.

Dressed in a black uniform with knee-high boots, his ginger hair was a stark contrast to his apparel. Leah was suddenly reminded of his stern handsomeness, something she had been acutely aware of the first moment she caught sight of him in the ballroom. There was no denying his dark but striking appearance.

"If you can't bear to see him lose," Kirin turned to Leah, "I would not fault you for leaving."

She rolled her eyes upward and moved to sit in the solitary chair beside the granite table. "Am I here to watch a fight with words or swords?" she shot at them. A smile twitched at the corners of her mouth.

"The lady has spoken," Kirin said solemnly. He leapt off the table with uncommon grace and removed the small sword from his side.

"Winner bags the other's birds from tomorrow's hunt." August stepped onto the sparring plank.

"Half the birds," Kirin corrected.

117

August grinned and showed his teeth, to Leah's surprise. It almost resembled the smile of a predator about to pounce on its prey, but for the lighthearted spark in his eye. "Afraid?" he inquired, and without warning, his sword flashed through the air.

Leah swallowed a gasp as light from the lanterns glinted off August's swift blade. Kirin was not unprepared, though, and the sound of metal against metal echoed through the room. To Leah, the match was one of the strangest sights she had ever seen. August was tall, even by human standards, and to meet Kirin's blade, he continually slashed downward while the squirrel was forced to simultaneously leap off the ground and fight to take the offensive.

The duel continued for longer than Leah expected, as she privately thought August would finish Kirin quickly. While the squirrel was small, he was nimble and quick, and even with an untrained eye she could see he was well-versed with a sword. They were almost evenly matched, but as the fight continued, August's size and stamina began wearing Kirin down.

August dropped to the floor and pulled his knees to his chest in a sudden tuck and rolled away from Kirin. The squirrel saw an opening and leaped forward, sword poised before him. At the last possible moment, August swept his sword up to push Kirin's aside, forcing the other off balance. He turned onto his knees, and as Kirin landed, pointed his sword at his rival's furry chest.

Kirin dropped his sword and panted. "That was a new move," he grunted.

"I need those, particularly against you." August returned his sword to the sheath at his side. "You fought well."

"I allowed you to beat me. Your lady is watching."

"Of course," August said, sounding unconvinced. He roughly wiped the sweat from his forehead with his sleeve and stepped off the sparring ground toward Leah.

Leah rose from her seat. "Impressive," she commented, keeping her tone neutral. "I imagine Nimrod should be afraid of men who fight like you two."

"He would if he was wise, but he is a foolish one," Kirin said in a huffy voice. He bowed to Leah. "We practice here every few days, with Maor and Stephen too. You are always welcome to join us."

"Thank you." She smiled, suppressing a laugh. Kirin's fur, soaked with sweat, stood up on end and he was trying unsuccessfully to smooth it.

"Would you like to take a walk?" August asked her suddenly, and for all his grace with a sword, he looked awkward now. "The evening air is cold and fresh."

"Certainly." Leah sensed some of his unease as they bade Kirin farewell and stepped outside. A melancholy feeling swept her up as she wondered if there would always be such a gulf between them. It was better when they were with August's men, who turned to jesting and teasing, but between the two of them, the uncomfortable silences were still often and long.

"How did Kirin come to Cariath?" She thought of the rogue faerie attacks and shivered, the conversation with Arthur still fresh in her mind.

"My father found him beyond the mountains on a scouting trip. He was gravely injured and we took him in."

"In battle? Did he come from the immortal realm?"

"I don't know the details. He was in a fight on the other side, yes, and the faeries cast him out into the mortal world. I was ten when he came to us, and he refused to speak about his past when he recovered. I've only learned a little over the years."

"Don't faeries have any special abilities in battle? Beyond fighting with weapons like men do?"

"Not in battle, at least in the mortal realm. Some do carry over special gifts, though. Kirin has the gift of dreams. It's rudimentary, but his dreams have usually proven true. I have always believed in him, at least." August glanced at her. "I suppose you can call that my brand of faith."

Leah dipped her head. "Well, it's something."

She imagined Kirin's small fur body lying bloody and helpless on the mountainside when Arthur found him. Her stomach twisted. He was not weak—she had just witnessed his prowess in dueling—and he treated her with touching, if a bit grandiose, chivalry.

"Why are some faeries so cruel, and some kind?"

August glanced at her sideways. "Why are some men?" he countered.

A breeze blew by them as they strolled away from Fox Manor. August led her on a trail that snaked through the grassy plains outside the Bastion like a thin scar. Leah noticed for the first time that the stars looked brighter here than they did in Carmel.

She bit her lip. "Was Benedict close to Kirin?"

"To a degree." He sounded matter-of-fact, and she relaxed. "Kirin became part of our family, but he was closer to me."

"Arthur told me... about your mother, what happened to her." Leah stumbled over the words. She stopped and turned to face him. "I'm sorry."

His face tightened and he said nothing.

Apprehensive, she continued, "He told me about the Guardian camps too, and how each guards a secret to the faerie realm. That's what the Oath-breakers are after."

August's eyes grew steely. "What else did he say?" His voice had a dangerous undertone.

"What's the matter? Is there anything *you* will tell me?"

"This is not knowledge to be thrown around. That the Oath-breakers even have a chance comes from careless chatter and rumors."

His words stung. "If you think I'm a fool or untrustworthy, you should not have married me."

"This has nothing to do with your character. I'm trying to protect you," he retorted, and a hint of anger threatened to snap his rigid exterior.

"You ought to trust your father's judgment at least."

August snorted unkindly. "My father raised a son who betrayed him and all that is good to join a mad man. You will forgive me if I don't always accept his judgments."

Shock overtook her indignation, as did the slow understanding of August's aloofness toward Arthur. "That's not fair," she spluttered.

"Let's go back," he said abruptly.

She stared at him for a moment. "August, this is your family. This is now *my* family. You can't close yourself off every time we talk about something that matters."

Leah turned around and stalked ahead of him toward the Bastion, leaving him to trail behind her in silence.

CHAPTER 18

Near the Nathair River, Island of Japha.
Month of Hope: First week, Toil-day.

"The men grow restless," Justin said.

Benedict cast an irritated glance at him. "I know. But there is no more word from Nimrod."

The two men were sitting near the banks of the Nathair River as dusk fell overhead. To the south, the hazy mist of Whitewitch created a gray, damp barrier. Behind them, their small camp of men was unusually quiet. They only lit campfires before daylight disappeared, to keep their presence inconspicuous. The sacrifice entailed bone-chilling nights but no one protested, at least, not directly to Benedict.

They decided to wait on this side of the Nathair to give Nimrod travel time, should he wish to meet them before going to Cariath. They had arrived at the river two days ago, and Benedict sent out small scouting parties in the evening to ensure their perimeter was secure and the Guardians were not close on their trail. It was unlikely they would be discovered, but the scouting trips provided the men an opportunity to feel useful. Benedict knew the value of morale—after all, how did the Oath-breakers form enough of a force to break from the Guardians if they were already satisfied?

"There were murmurings that scouts hoped to find Guardians abroad," Justin said, glancing at Benedict sideways. "Simply for the thrill."

A company of birds flew low over the water and small currents wrinkled across the quiet river. Benedict followed their trajectory as some of their beaks grazed the water before they swept upward and the steady flapping of wings was swallowed by the darkening skies.

Benedict's expression curled with distaste. "Sounds like Hound's ilk."

Before Justin could respond, they were interrupted by sudden shouts from the direction of the camp. Benedict leapt to his feet nimbly and sprinted away from the river, his hand resting on the hilt of his sword. He sensed Justin following close behind him. Anxiety pooled in the bottom of his stomach. Under the cover of darkness, there were no visual hints of what might be amiss as they raced back.

Mert and Traven met them first on the edge of the camp. Most of the other men were forming a scattered cluster a short distance away, still shouting and bustling.

"What's happening?" Benedict demanded, short on breath.

"Hound's scouting party just returned," Mert said swiftly. His gaze strayed to the growing huddle of men. "They brought prisoners."

Benedict and Justin exchanged a quick look before they hastened through the mass, pushing their way to the center. The men formed a loose circle around a small group consisting of Hound, a few of his close comrades, and five unfamiliar men, their hands bound behind their backs with thick cords.

For one sickening moment, the scene drew to Benedict's mind his recurring dream with Nimrod and the Old Fox, the circle of Oath-breakers surrounding them as Benedict was charged with the execution. He shook away the memory forcefully, focusing on the event at hand.

Hound circled the prisoners slowly, eyeing them like a predator did its prey. He gave little heed to the men around him until Benedict approached.

"A scouting party's first success," Hound announced triumphantly. He jutted his chin forward and stared straight at Benedict.

"Success?" Benedict echoed. "I consider it success when our scouts find no one." Hound's nostrils seemed to flare, but he pushed on. "Who are these men?" he asked, though he was fairly certain he knew.

Hound paused his pacing and positioned himself face-to-face with the nearest captive, their noses almost touching. The other man did not flinch and looked forward, unblinking. Benedict felt a grudging respect for him — Hound was much larger, and the perpetual cruelty etched in his face intimidated most.

"Answer him," Hound said. His tone was quiet but deadly.

"We are from En-doire," the man said coldly, after a moment's silence. "We are hunting the murderers and thieves who broke into our halls, and it seems we have found them."

"*We* found you, it seems." Hound bared his teeth in a feral smile.

"Do not think your actions will go unpunished," the other man retorted.

Hound paced around the group of prisoners again and he seemed to relish the attention he received as all eyes followed him. The rest of Benedict's company was silent but watching intently, as if this were a theater or drama playing out before them. Impatient and acutely uncomfortable with the direction of the situation, Benedict opened his mouth, but Hound was already speaking.

"Such bravery," he exclaimed, his words drenched in mockery. "Do you know how many have said such things to us? And yet, we are still free men." He spread his hands and finally looked to his comrades. A murmur of affirmation slithered through the gathering.

"Bondage to evil is no freedom," another prisoner spat. His words drew angry sounds from the men.

Hound was already moving toward him, his hand resting lightly on the top of his sword-hilt. His eyes glinted dangerously. To challenge Hound publicly was to put his pride at stake, and without any advantage in arms or political power, it was also to number the days left in a man's life.

"How long will you let him continue his game?"

Benedict's fists clenched, startled, as Justin's quiet voice came from close behind him. In the flurry of chaos, he forgot his friend was still nearby. The question stirred him from a momentary stupor.

He strode out to meet Hound, who was drawing his sword from his sheath slowly, to draw out the ring of metal on metal. His hard eyes bore into the unruly prisoner's face with a focused ferocity. Benedict's warrior instincts came alive as he quickly realized Hound would decapitate the man before he could reach him.

Abandoning further thought and calculation, Benedict barreled toward Hound and drew his own sword. He was a natural-born fighter, and though Hound held the advantage of size, Benedict was fast and precise.

Their blades crashed into each other in mid-air, only a breath away from the prisoner, who still stood staunchly in place.

Hound nearly dropped his sword, not for lack of strength, but out of sheer shock. Benedict recognized the expression on his face — that of a warrior shaken out of his tunnel vision. When he saw Benedict, a deep guttural growl came from his chest and his fingers clamped around his sword.

Benedict did not give ground, nor did he lower his own blade. He was not naïve enough to believe Hound would never attack him. *More likely he is looking for an opportunity*, he thought wryly.

The men around them were dead silent in the wake of their clash. A bird's sad cry cut loudly through the air. Benedict knew this was an opportunity to assert his authority over Hound's, to show his strength and keen strategy in a delicate situation. There were only moments, seconds, to consider his next move. He stood on a knife's edge.

"I don't kill in cold blood, Hound." For all his internal debate over the words to use, these came out with a touch of indifference.

Hound did not lower his blade either, pacing in small steps like a caged animal. He finally turned a venomous look upon Benedict. "No one asked you to," he nearly spat. "I was ready to do what you did not have the stomach for, and you had the nerve to interfere."

Murmurs broke the silence in the crowd around them. Benedict was tempted to glance around to gauge the reaction, whether his men were in accord with Hound or they disapproved of his defiance. He pushed his speculation aside and kept his focus on the other man — at the least, he *knew* what others would think if he let his guard down and Hound made a fool of him now.

"My stomach and nerves feel perfectly fine," he returned casually. "I am hesitant to say the same for your mind."

A short laugh sounded from somewhere behind him, and Hound

looked as if he were about to throw himself at Benedict. While they might match one another in physical combat, Benedict knew Hound could not counter his quick wit. He felt a wicked smirk crawling up his face. Benedict might have pushed the other man beyond what was necessary, and there might be consequences, but for the moment, he allowed himself the unholy satisfaction of seeing Hound's pride stripped before his comrades.

Hound finally dropped his sword to his side, but stepped forward until he was inches from Benedict's face. His breath was hot and putrid.

"Don't think you can humiliate me so easily and walk away unscathed."

"Don't pretend you would not have thrust a dagger through my back before, if given the chance." Benedict dropped his voice to a dangerous and low tone so no one but Hound could discern his words.

"Oh, I don't pretend," Hound whispered cruelly, baring his teeth.

But he took a step back, and Benedict saw he had mind enough to realize he could not win this battle. Benedict held higher authority in their ranks, and if it came to a break in their company of men, only a small minority would follow Hound. He would know that, though he would also look ever more fiercely for a way to take vengeance and nurse his wounded pride.

Benedict swept his gaze across the circle of men around them. Dusk had turned the sky a deep shade of indigo, and while it was hard to distinguish their expressions, it was easy enough to see all eyes were trained upon Hound, Benedict, and the prisoners. It was the most excitement they had seen since the raid on En-doire, a thought that aggravated Benedict. He did not take some of the most skilled Oath-breakers on a mission to simply sit idly by, watching a political game play out.

He raised his voice so all the men could hear. "I do not kill in cold blood," he said, repeating his earlier words. "These men did not meet us on the battlefield, so I choose to spare them. Lives are costly, and I do not believe in extinguishing them needlessly."

There was some rustling from the mass of people around him, and he caught a few furtive glances exchanged. He knew this would not be the speech or ideology of Nimrod.

A momentary hesitation forced him to pause — was this a tactical error? If he condoned Hound's murder of the prisoners, would he acquire greater respect? Benedict found Justin's face in the first ring of the circle around him. He was not exchanging glances with anyone or casting unconvinced looks at Benedict. Rather, he wore the same unreadable expression that had become so familiar in recent times; Benedict could identify it even in the dark. Somehow, it was enough to bolster his conviction and continue.

"We will hold them captive until we must move. And," he glanced at Hound, who stood sullenly nearby, "we owe a debt to Hound and his scouts for finding them."

He waved his hand to dismiss the men, and the crowd slowly thinned as people wandered off to their camps. There was some muted chatter, but for the most part, an eerie silence hung over the company. Out of the corner of his eye, Benedict saw Justin did not move far from him, and some of his other more loyal men—Traven, Wills, and Gerard—also kept near Justin.

Hound did not move from his place, and Benedict guessed the others were wary that he might still strike. For a moment, the idea of his men watching his back, not out of duty or for personal gain, but simply for camaraderie's sake, warmed him. With a slight pang, he briefly wondered if they too, like Justin, still belonged with the Guardians.

He shook the thoughts away and focused on Hound. If they worried for Benedict's safety, it was unnecessary. He could read Hound, just as he read Nimrod months ago when he demanded leadership among the Oath-breakers. Hound was a reckless man, not afraid to torment or kill. But he was not fearless, or adroit. He would not have the gall to wager against Benedict in a game of strategy. And to literally or figuratively plunge a dagger in Benedict's back now—they both knew that would be a losing gamble.

Hound finally stalked past Benedict, pausing only for a moment in front of him. He stared straight ahead, so Benedict could only look at his profile and the blood-rimmed edges of his left eye. His sword lowered, he felt his body painfully exposed, but resisted the urge to bring the blade up. He refused to give Hound the pleasure of seeing any weakness.

"I see mercy is no longer your exception," Hound said softly but coldly, almost like a snake's whisper. Benedict followed as his gaze drifted for a moment to Traven.

"This is not mercy." Benedict tried to clad his words in steel.

The other man continued as if he had not spoken. "You are not even weakened by mercy." He finally turned his face and looked fully at Benedict. "You are marked by it."

Before Benedict could reply, Hound strode off into the camp. He followed him with his eyes, watching as the black outline of his figure fell away into the night. Hound's words felt like poison worming its way through his bloodstream.

You are marked by it. He would not describe even his father or August in such a way. The Guardians had their own brand of mercy where forgiveness among friends could be praised as generosity of spirit, but chiefly, the men were known for their gravity and high sense of justice. Beyond a certain point, mercy was not counted a virtue but a flaw. The Oath-breakers thought the Guardians were too soft, so to imagine he might be even weaker twisted Benedict's gut.

He slapped the troubling thoughts away as Justin, Traven, Wills and Gerard drew near. Justin glanced over him swiftly, and apprehension seized him for a moment, as he feared his contemplations were written plainly across his face.

But Justin simply gestured at something behind him. "What shall we do with them?"

Benedict turned around and the sight of the En-doire men jolted him back to the task at hand.

"Move them to the center of the camp. Gather some spare blankets for their use. We will have an alternating guard rotation throughout the night to watch them." He issued the orders calmly and rapidly. Falling into the role of a military leader came easily.

Wills, Gerard, and Traven moved away to escort the prisoners into the camp, but Justin lingered behind. Benedict cast a sideways glance at him, wary of an onslaught of probing questions or commentary. But Justin merely stared off into the distant darkness for a long while before speaking.

"He will not forget it, you know."

"Certainly not." The words sounded confident, even to Benedict's own ears. "An enemy always has the quality of a long memory."

But now, with the adrenaline of challenging Hound gone and the long, black stretch of nighttime ahead, the knowledge no longer tasted of the same victory as it did earlier.

"You called Nimrod's decision to charge into the Valley a suicide mission." Justin turned to face him, his dark eyes gleaming. "Sometimes I think you are on one of your own."

Benedict did not respond but watched his men lead the En-doire hostages away. They did not struggle against their guards, perhaps knowing it would come to no fruition. But the one who had defied Hound twisted his head around, his eyes searching for something. His gaze rested on Benedict's face, and his mouth tightened into a sharp line. After a few moments, he broke the gaze.

It was not a puzzled look, nor even a suspicious one. It was a hard look of condemnation, telling Benedict they did not owe him nor were they grateful for him sparing their lives. *Just like the White Tiger Guardians,* Benedict thought. Past a point, mercy was a foreign concept. They would not accept his, and if he ever fell into their hands, they surely would show none. There would be no debts between them.

"I'm going to look around the river," Benedict said abruptly. "En-doire may have sent more men."

"I'll come with you," Justin replied, which was what Benedict expected.

He would prefer going alone, but after the night's events, numbness pierced to his bones and he was too tired to object. The two men moved silently away from the camp, Justin walking a few feet behind Benedict.

Before long, the rhythmic sound of water washing up against the shore came within range. They walked along the edge of dry ground and Benedict took in the darkened scene before him. The Nathair River wound northward into the night. To the east, a faint flickering came from En-doire, a bright orange glinting against the cobalt skies. And the stars — they looked especially bright that night, like some greater light from beyond the cover of the worlds was pricking through.

The land was quiet but for the lapping water and a few brief but violent drafts that blew through the open air.

"I'm tired," Benedict said finally, and his voice sounded strange after the long silence. He was glad Justin was behind him, unable to see his face.

"Of living?" Justin finished.

"This is hardly living." His words felt heavy, like a weight around his neck. "The world's — gone gray to me."

"Since you joined the Oath-breakers, or since your mother died?"

Anger and resentment coiled in Benedict's gut. *How dare he?* He nearly whirled around to face Justin but stopped himself. He did not want to meet his companion's shrewd gaze.

Justin spoke again. "Revenge will not give you peace."

"And doing nothing will? Like my brother?" Benedict spat. "After mother, after Alain even…"

"I don't mean he's right."

"I'm not looking for peace." His fury subsided, and a bitter, hollow feeling came over him. "I don't want to philosophize, Justin. I don't want to justify myself. I know I'm not a good man, and I can't be a Guardian. But I can't be like Nimrod either."

"You will never be."

Benedict felt a chill press against his spine. He stopped walking and heard Justin's footfalls cease behind him too. Turning around, he looked his friend full in the face.

"And why are you here? With the Oath-breakers?" he asked hoarsely. His stomach tightened and he feared he already knew the answer.

"You are my brother, Benedict." He held his gaze steadily. "But I can't justify myself either."

Benedict stared at the other man, feeling the words sink into him like deep, sharp claws. His blood brother disavowed him for his convictions, while his friend did the opposite. But there was no comfort in that — for a moment, he hated Justin's loyalty more than August's repudiation.

"I never asked," was all Benedict could muster. He suddenly felt spent; all the vigor in him bled dry.

"Because you are not Nimrod."

"But — why?" Tired of keeping up pretenses, he stared at Justin in bewilderment. "You cling to Guardian morality nearly as much as my brother!" His voice dropped. "Hound mocks you for being my lap dog, but that was never true."

"There is nothing to understand," Justin said, and a touch of hardness undergirded his tone, reminding Benedict he was still deeply private and, in many ways, impenetrable. "Perhaps I can be a fool, too," he added, more lightly.

By silent consent, they were retracing their steps back toward the camp. The darkness had deepened, and without any campfires to guide their direction, mere familiarity and instinct made them sure-footed.

Benedict drew in a long, cold breath. "Then, if the gods do judge us at the end of this, I hope they will judge you as a fool and not a criminal."

CHAPTER 19

Cariath, Island of Japha.
Month of Hope: First week, Fire-day.

Leah knocked on the pale yellow door quickly before clutching her hands over the small basket she held. She shivered a little, drawing the heavy cloak more tightly across her shoulders. Mornings in the Bastion were chilly at best, and even as the sun splashed against the rooftops, it did little to warm the air.

The door creaked open and Melina Landon's bright face peered at her. Her hair was tied back loosely and she wore a dark blue bathrobe and a kind smile.

Sudden embarrassment warmed Leah's face. At least in Carmel, it was far too early an hour to call on anyone, particularly unannounced. She felt absurd standing there in the cold, holding a hastily thrown together basket of fruit from Arthur's stock, and staring into the face of a woman who was nearly a stranger. A quick appraisal of her actions only increased her mortification, and she had half a mind to turn on her heel and flee.

"Good morning, Leah." Melina spoke before she could move.

Now she was trapped. Leah sighed inwardly and resigned herself to the situation her impulsive actions brought about.

"Hello, Melina. I was—taking a morning stroll, and I know you said I could come by for tea at any time. Not that I'm here for tea at this hour. Your house was along the way and I thought to stop for a greeting, and we have far too many fruits at Fox Manor." Leah rushed through the words, while simultaneously scolding herself for the incoherent babble.

Melina either did not notice or glossed over her nonsensical jabbering. "Come in. I'm glad you could come."

Warmth rushed at her as Leah stepped through the doorway. Melina's home was much more modest in size and grandeur than Fox Manor, but she was instantly drawn to it. A fire burned in the living room fireplace. The chairs, tables, and dining furnishings were complimentary shades of beige and turquoise. The walls were a light yellow, a shade that matched the door, and they lit up as the sunlight streamed lazily through the windows.

The delicious smell of warm butter and toast floated from the kitchen. Leah set down her basket on the dining table and pulled up a chair at Melina's insistence that she make herself comfortable. The other woman disappeared into the kitchen momentarily before reemerging with three large plates balanced on her arms.

"Oh, let me help you." Leah quickly rose to relieve her.

"Sit, Leah, please. I can manage." Melina expertly slid the plates brimming with eggs, toast, cheese and fruit onto the table. She smiled brightly. "You came just in time to join me."

Leah only felt a wave of guilt. "I'm terribly sorry for intruding like this, without even sending a note in advance."

"You certainly are not intruding," Melina returned, with the first hint of indignation Leah heard from her. "When I say I enjoy company, I'm not simply being polite." The twinkle in her eye softened her words.

"Thank you," Leah said, awkward but grateful.

"I usually say grace before meals," Melina said, "if you don't mind joining me in that."

Melina offered a short but sweet prayer, and they began eating in a comfortable silence. The food tasted as wonderful as it smelled and the buttered toast, which was not a staple at Fox Manor, brought Leah back to the Edwards' estate in Carmel, where Mama always piled the bread and butter high in the mornings, knowing that Papa would demolish them in record time.

"I hear you are from the seaside towns," Melina said, her voice soft.

"Yes. Carmel."

"I'm from Ephes, same as Jenifer. I moved here when I married Alain." She smiled.

The mention of Alain reminded Leah of his terrible and untimely death, and the black look in August's eyes when he recalled the event. Her own trials suddenly appeared trifling in comparison.

"I'm sorry," Leah said, "about Alain. August told me." Her condolence sounded hollow and useless, and she wished she knew how to express it with more feeling.

Melina did not seem to mind, but cast a grateful glance her way. "August was very good to me in the time that followed. He came to see me almost daily at first, and even offered to put me up at Fox Manor if I was too lonely or if this place," she motioned to the walls around her, "stirred up too many memories."

Leah only nodded, helpless, unsure of what to say. She thought her heart might have warmed more to August at Melina's words if they had not argued the previous night.

"Those two were close," Melina was saying, "so I think he felt a duty to me, to see that I was looked after."

"You loved Alain."

Leah did not ask, merely stated. She could hear it in Melina's voice, which was peaceful but sad when she spoke of him. There was a distant look in her eyes, as if she were lost in a fantasy world where he still lived. She felt a slight wrench in her chest. Was it simply out of sympathy, or was it also a pang of disappointment in thinking she would never know such a love? She swatted the nagging thought away.

Melina did not answer, only smiled at Leah, who saw sorrow mingled with joy etched in her expression.

"It seems unfair," Leah plowed on, "that where love is rare among the Marshals' marriages, a true instance of it is snatched away."

"Life isn't fair." She did not seem bitter saying it. "Sometimes, that is a mercy." Melina's eyes cleared, her cheeks rosy. "I am not unfortunate in the least, either. I would choose the love Alain and I shared, however brief, over a lifetime of anything less."

There was a fire and conviction that seared her words, though her voice was quiet. She suddenly seemed much less fragile than upon first impression.

"That is what I would choose too," Leah said softly, "if given such a choice."

"You have one," Melina said, earnestness coloring her tone. "August is one of the best men I know. Alain always said he was at once a gentleman and warrior, and he was honorable in both."

"I think you see more of his goodness than his faults." She could not help her wry tone.

"He's human, Leah. We all are born flawed." Her words were gentle, where they might otherwise have sounded condescending.

"Yes, of course…" she began, but Melina was not finished.

"Alain was not the sort of man I dreamed of marrying. He was too bent on the rules and grave for my taste — perhaps a little like August. But I found he had a heart of gold and even some hidden pockets of humor. But I had to learn to love him."

"I *have* been trying," Leah burst out, unable to contain herself. "I have tried to love him in action and word, even if my feelings rebel. But then, last night —" She broke off abruptly and blinked hard to hold threatening tears at bay, feeling deeply ashamed of her weakness.

Melina handed her a handkerchief and reached across the table to take her hand. She squeezed it and wordlessly waited for Leah to continue. She wiped at her eyes roughly and sucked in a long breath.

"I should not burden you with this, Melina. We are hardly acquaintances yet and I have surely overstayed my welcome."

"Nonsense," Melina gave her a hard but not unkind look. Softening, she added, "Our husbands were like brothers. You come here, and you are family. Please, burden me — as you call it — with all you have." She winked.

Leah felt a wild rush of gratitude and smiled, a little tearfully still. Melina's warm words dulled the foreignness of Cariath in her mind.

"August is all secrets. His mother, his brother…" She trailed off. "Arthur is all he has left, and he scorns him."

"He has you, too."

"I'm just a girl to be coddled, in his eyes."

"Are you?" Melina challenged. Something glinted in her eye. "I would think he'd choose someone weaker for that."

Her mind turned to Arthur's revelation. "Did you know he nearly married another woman? From Cariath?"

"Yes. Lady Arinda." Melina paused. "It's not widely known."

"Arthur told me. Did you know her?"

"Not particularly. But I didn't think they were well-suited. She may have brought the Guardians back into standing with the crown, but I didn't want a political marriage for August. Arinda may have status, but she lacks the strength he needs in a wife."

"I don't think he did too well in either category, in the end," Leah said dryly.

"I disagree."

She waved off her comment. "The goodness you see in him—I don't deny it's there. But he has another side I don't understand. He gets stoic and cold…" She felt traitorous, but the words spilled out anyway. "I can almost understand why his brother turned away."

Melina took her confession in stride, looking neither surprised nor horrified. "Who will understand him then, if not you?"

"What?" Leah started.

"None of us are easy to love. Maybe you sympathize with Benedict because you are more like him." She raised a hand to quiet Leah's forthcoming protest. "August lost the same mother. He lost Alain. And he's lost his brother." Sorrow colored her gaze. "It's hard to be a good man after all that. But he is."

"That's exactly why I don't know what to do. His experience is beyond me." She felt guilty and helpless.

"You are his wife, not counselor or fellow warrior. He has men to advise him and fight alongside him. Just love him."

Just love him.

Leah sighed deeply, trying to expel the restless anxiety and resentment that gripped her. She nodded.

They fell into silence, each lost in their own thoughts. After a while, Leah glanced across the dining table. She had hardly taken more than a few bites out of her toast, and the food was still piled high on plates in the center, forgotten in the midst of their conversation.

"Let me help you clear the table," Leah said, shaking herself out of her reverie, "and then I should head home and finally leave you in peace." She smiled a little at that last part.

Melina protested at first, but Leah was insistent. They stored the food away in the kitchen and scrubbed the dishes clean, all the while making casual but comfortable conversation about their lives and childhoods. It was approaching noontime when Melina saw Leah to the door.

Leah, though usually not affectionate, grasped Melina's hands. "Thank you."

"I'm glad you came to Cariath." Melina beamed.

The two women embraced, and Melina extracted a promise from Leah to visit again soon. When Leah stepped outside, the striking sunrays momentarily blinded her. Lifting her hand above her eyes as a cover, she hurried home, feeling brighter than she had in days.

~~~~~

As Leah approached Fox Manor, she saw two men on horseback coming from the opposite direction but heading for the same destination as her. As they drew closer, she narrowed her eyes to bring them into clearer focus. Their faces looked unfamiliar and they were dressed in dark green and brown uniforms, while the Guardians in Cariath wore white and black stripes.

A wave of anxiety washed over her but quickly passed. The Valley, particularly the Bastion, was heavily guarded. Arthur had also hinted that more than just men protected their home. Certainly there was no way a hostile force could come through so quietly, let alone only two men.

They had already dismounted from their horses as Leah came to the front of Fox Manor. They were talking quietly to one another and there was a stern air about them.

Gathering her courage, Leah strode toward them. One of the men noticed her first and drew his companion's attention to her as well.

"Hello," Leah said, trying to sound confident, but her greeting seemed woefully childish in her ears. "Are you from Cariath?" she asked politely, a little more pleased with how that came out of her mouth.

The two men glanced at each other. "We ride from En-doire," one said. "I am Guardian Lawrence and this is Lee. We have urgent business with the Marshals, particularly Fox."

Leah felt a brief sense of alarm. August had said their contact with En-doire had grown limited in recent times, so to send scouts all the way to Cariath must indicate something severe.

"What business is this?" she asked quickly, forgetting her earlier nervousness.

The men looked at one another again. "I am afraid we cannot say, my lady," Lee replied. "It is information that concerns the Marshals and Fox alone."

"I am a Fox," Leah countered.

She could not help enjoying the look of surprise that dawned on both men's faces.

"Forgive us then, since communication between the White Tiger and Black Tortoise Guardians has been rare for some time. We did not know." Lee offered a small bow to her.

"Regardless, our message is for August Fox," Lawrence rejoined, clearly less patient than his companion. "So however you relate to the family, I daresay we will wait for him, or for a meeting of the Marshals."

Tired of the back-and-forth and having lost interest in demonstrating her propriety, Leah simply returned, "I am August's wife. If it concerns him, it ought to concern me."

"Well," Lawrence said slowly, as he seemed to absorb the new information, "then I regret to inform you that the Black Tortoise Guardians are bringing a charge against him for murder and theft."

CHAPTER 20

The tension in the air was palpable, but despite the grimness on the men's faces, Leah could not help the thrill of wonder that enveloped her. For the men at the table, she suspected the immediate concerns of Black Tortoise's accusations gripped them. Yet she felt time would weave these events into the fabric of legend.

They were gathered at the granite table inside the Foxes' battle room where Leah had watched August and Kirin's duel. It was a small group — Lawrence and Lee, Arthur, August, and the other Marshals, Rupert Norwich and James Sky. They were called on short notice, not long after Leah finished her conversation with the foreign Guardians. She had asked Arthur for permission to join the meeting, and she thought he acquiesced only because he had too much weighing on him to make the effort to deny her.

She sat between him and August, with Rupert and James to the other side of her husband and Lawrence and Lee to the other side of Arthur. She noted a flicker of surprise in August's eyes when she walked in with his father, but he did not comment.

Arthur first broke the silence. "I think we all know the intent of this meeting," he began without preamble, and his face looked drawn and tired. "The Marshals welcome Guardians Lawrence and Lee from En-doire."

"Thank you, sir." Lee nodded in the Old Fox's direction.

"That will depend upon the content of their message," James muttered under his breath.

Leah overheard his words, and given the small space they were in, thought everyone else did too. He must have caught wind of their accusations against August.

Arthur turned a pointed look on James, who simply raised his shoulders, looking impatient and unapologetic. Leah recalled him being boisterous and lively at the dinner party — his hot-headed demeanor did not surprise her. The newcomers either did not catch the subtext or pretended not to notice.

"They have brought some grave news with them," Arthur continued. He nodded at the two messengers.

Lee looked to Lawrence — and Leah suspected the latter was senior in rank — to speak. "Nearly a week before we rode from En-doire, we suffered a grievous assault on our treasury. The attackers were thorough and competent, and our guards were unable to sound any alarms in time. Reinforcements arrived too late. Many of the guards were dead or unconscious, and the perpetrators had already vanished with one of our prized possessions."

"I'm sorry to hear that," Arthur said sincerely, though a troubled look registered on his face.

Lawrence acknowledged him with a quick glance and bow of his head. "There has not been such an attack in En-doire in a very long time. We were woefully unprepared."

"We began to send scouting parties out," Lee said, picking up the narrative. "A few crossed the river to question those stationed at Guardian dock posts. At one of the southern docks, we received word that a Guardian entourage crossed straight into Whitewitch more than two fortnights ago, in the month of Thunder." He paused, hesitating, and did not look up to meet anyone's eyes. "It was led by August Fox."

James slapped the table and snorted loudly. "I would check your sources, brother. August was away by the seaside towns then."

August laid a hand on James' shoulder and shook his head briefly. "Allow the man to finish, James," he said quietly. Leah was surprised both by his demure tone, and that he did not quickly come to his own defense.

"Furthermore," James was not deterred, "what senselessness would prevail upon August to cross the river down south into Whitewitch of all places, when there is a northern dock?"

"Marshal Sky," Arthur intoned, and though he looked weary, iron laced his words. James glanced at him and quieted.

Lawrence raised his hands when the clamor died. "I am simply reporting our findings. The evidence is not certain, so Marshal Fox can clear his name."

James sputtered indignantly beside August. Leah stole a look in his direction and found him shaking his head vigorously, his hands clenched together, appearing to exert all his willpower not to burst out in speech again. The effort made his face redden, and with his rounder features, it looked almost tomato-like. Despite the gravity of the situation, she bit her lip to contain a smile. On his other side, Rupert Norwich sat still as a stone, wearing an expressionless mask.

Leah returned her attention to the discussion, and found all eyes were turned to August now. She looked over at him and found him staring at the edge of the table, his eyes dark and unreadable. Her stomach tightened briefly, and she wondered if it was out of anxiety for him.

"What do you know about the Fox family?" August asked, turning his gaze on Lawrence and Lee.

The two men appeared taken aback and glanced at each other. "Apart from your high station in Guardians ranks, little," Lawrence said. His eyes drifted to Leah. "We did not even know you had a wife."

"I married very recently," August replied, unruffled, though he did not look at Leah. "Tell me what you do know, then, about my family. It should not take long if that knowledge is limited."

There was a silence around the table and Leah furrowed her brow, wondering where he was going with this line of questioning.

"I was raised in the Guardian ranks in En-doire," Lee finally broke the stillness, "and I knew the Fox family was famous for its rare shade of ginger hair." He looked almost embarrassed. "There is very little else —"

"You have a brother," Lawrence broke in. He nodded to Arthur. "Arthur Fox had two sons, I recall."

"Do you know what became of my brother?"

They both shook their heads, and the truth began to dawn on Leah. The scouting party that crossed on the southern dock, led by a supposed August Fox... A shiver crawled down her spine. What did that mean about the men who attacked the treasury?

"We assumed he was still in Cariath with you," Lawrence said.

James snorted again, unable to contain himself. "Do you know who Nimrod is?" he asked acidly.

"Why, yes, of course." Lee was beginning to look flustered.

James simply raised an eyebrow and fell silent, as if he thought that was enough of a hint for them to grasp the whole truth. August did not speak either, appearing deep in thought. Neither of the men from En-doire seemed to have made the connection, though, and they were looking from face to face expectantly. Leah could not help but squirm a little in her seat, as the silence grew uncomfortable.

"His brother is with Nimrod." Rupert spoke for the first time.

Shock fell across Lawrence and Lee's expressions. The rest of the men at the table appeared stoic.

"It is no fault of the Black Tortoise they do not know," Arthur said. "We have guarded that knowledge for the sake of morale."

And pride? Leah thought, as she cast a sidelong glance at her husband. He did not react visibly to either Rupert's or his father's words.

"Then," Lee mused, "the party that crossed the river down south was likely led by Benedict Fox, impersonating Marshal Fox." He glanced at Lawrence, who grimaced.

"He could fool the guards, if they never met you," he conceded.

"What did they take?" August broke in abruptly.

Startled, Lawrence stared at him for a moment before speaking. "From our treasury?" He hesitated, chewing on his lower lip while his gaze skimmed across the table. "An old sword."

"Was it significant?" August pressed, and Leah sensed a vein of edginess breaking through his stern and serene demeanor.

"It was Adair," Lee replied, earning a scowl from Lawrence.

Leah's breath caught in her throat. August glanced sideways at her. *The sword of Arieh*, she thought. For a brief moment, she violently missed Papa, and wished she could share these events with him.

Here was history writing itself and she was tangled up in its cobwebs, most likely in far over her head.

As she drew her attention back to the meeting, she found Arthur and the Marshals looking at each other with alarm. Her chest constricted.

"If there is nothing else to your message," Arthur said, looking at Lawrence and Lee, "we would kindly ask you to step outside as we have things to deliberate. Perhaps one of the men here can show you around the Bastion..." He looked to August.

"Maor and Stephen are outside. They will take you to the guest quarters," August replied.

As the door to the battle room closed behind them, James blew out a heavy breath. "Wasn't that pleasant?" he grunted.

"Perhaps it would have been if you demonstrated a wit more respect and self-restraint," Arthur returned, his tone sure but not unkind. Leah thought she saw the slightest twinkle of amusement in his eye.

"I mean no disrespect," Rupert interjected, and Leah was surprised to hear from him again, almost forgetting he was in the room, "but Lady Fox is not a Marshal. These conversations always take place in the highest confidence."

Leah rose from her seat. "I understand."

To her surprise, August held his hand out behind her, preventing her from leaving. "She can stay. These matters concern her closely." Leah could not read his expression as his face was turned toward Rupert.

"These matters concern all people," Rupert returned, and there was the slightest sign of ardor in his voice. "But none of us brings our wives into these meetings."

"It's not because she's my wife," August said quietly. "She knows about the keys. She also knows the legends of Arieh well. I want her insight."

Leah worked hard to suppress her disbelief. He held her at arm's length from family secrets, yet he wanted her input on events far beyond her?

August turned to face Leah and shifted his gaze to her chair. She obeyed the silent request and reluctantly took her seat again, assuming his words held enough authority that she did not need to leave. His eyes did not betray any emotion, and he returned his attention to the men, his posture upright and proper, once she was situated.

"Fine." Rupert turned from her, perhaps deciding it was not worth contending his point. "Do we think Adair has greater significance than they revealed?"

"Those two may not know themselves," James muttered.

"Isn't the sword of Arieh significant enough?" Leah asked.

All eyes turned to her. She felt surprised as well. The question came naturally. The men appeared caught off guard to hear her voice. She could not blame them—she was not a Marshal, not even a Guardian. She was absurdly out of place, a girl from Carmel, sitting in a warrior's forum.

"They think it's Black Tortoise's key to the immortal realm," Arthur said quietly.

Leah's jaw nearly dropped open, and only a fleeting sense of decorum secured it in place. "The sword of Arieh is the key?" For a moment, her reticence in the presence of the Marshals wore off.

"We do not know," Rupert said, and he cast a meaningful look at August. Leah wondered if it was more intended for her, as she had derailed the discussion. "It's supposed to be a song... but its manifestation is unknown to all but a few of their leaders."

It made no sense to her how a sword or a song could be a key to the faerie realm, but she kept silent this time.

"It must be," August murmured, tapping his knuckles sharply against the granite, his brow furrowed and head bowed. "Nimrod would not attack them simply to collect old relics."

"Damnation," James breathed.

"Please, James." Arthur gave him a hard look, before his gaze slid to Leah.

"My apologies, milady."

She bit back a smile. "I know 'fiddlesticks' and 'dragons' are too weak for most ill news we receive." At their bewildered expressions, she added, "Those are the profanities of polite society in Carmel."

Arthur broke into a fleeting smile, and James let out a guffaw.

"Good woman!" He winked at her, and then cast an approving look toward August. His amusement dimmed quickly though, as he returned to the topic at hand. "So, Nimrod has gone after Cobalt Dragon and Black Tortoise now. He's fearfully close to the immortal world."

"He has not come after us yet. And I doubt he can break the Vermilion riddle," Rupert said. "Even we have no idea."

August nodded. "But that is a thin thread to hang our hope on."

"I think it's high time we rally the Guardians. Coriander is already in Ebene. We should send a contingency to En-doire, and even the Dammim, if we want to reach the Vermilion Falcons." James looked around the table. "We can't turn a blind eye."

"Our cross-camp alliances are weak, if not absent," Rupert murmured. "You saw how Lawrence and Lee were."

"Yes," August said, and he looked up. "But there is too much at stake. I will go to En-doire. I don't think we have the time to send anyone to the Dammim, though."

James and Rupert's gazes shifted to Arthur, but he remained silent and his expression revealed little. Leah felt a small pang inside her and she wondered at it. Just as she was growing used to Cariath, the world around her began shifting again. Could it be some small part of her was loath for

August to leave?

"I don't think you should be the one to go," said James slowly. For a moment his teeth gnawed his lower lip, and his forehead creased. "They think you're a traitor."

"All the more reason," August returned. "I will go with Lawrence and Lee and I will clear my name directly with Marcum."

The name caused a quiet stir. "Oh, that man makes it even worse." James looked to the Old Fox, as if seeking support. "You know what he thinks of you."

"If Adair was really taken, he needs to look past old grievances. We are united in urgency." He spoke quietly, but Leah could already tell he would not be dissuaded.

"I agree with August, though I fear the Black Tortoise will not see it the same way." Rupert sighed, his tone grave. He looked to the head of the table. "What is your thought on the matter?"

All eyes turned to Arthur. His hands were clasped together loosely, his elbows on the edge of the table. He glanced down the side of the table at each of them. When his gaze came to Leah, she was struck by how exhausted he looked, hardly a trace of the briskness and energy she vividly recalled from their first meeting. It was as if he were a dry sponge, all the vigor squeezed out of his being. She felt a painful tug inside her chest.

"I think it is necessary that we reestablish these alliances." Arthur sighed and glanced at his son. "And if August wants to go, he has my blessing."

August gave a small nod to him. Leah looked between the two of them. She was not certain if she imagined the coldness between them had lessened from when she first arrived, or if they simply ensured that they were all cordiality during such gatherings. *It is,* she mused, *taxing enough without dragging personal family matters into the equation.*

"Then it's settled. I will put together a small force, perhaps one or two dozen men, and we will set out as soon as things are in order." August looked at the others.

Rupert dipped his head in acknowledgment and James grunted his approval.

"What have we heard from Coriander?" August asked.

"The last scout he sent back said the Dragons were still skeptical of our intentions. Nimrod was a former White Tiger." Arthur sighed. "He couldn't confirm yet if their key was stolen—they were reluctant to share any information. I didn't think the Dragons would be quite so hardened toward us. Tortoise, yes, but not them."

"Coriander will get on their good side. He's our best diplomat," Rupert said.

"More than I am," James chimed in.

"Low standard," the Old Fox returned. They shared a quick laugh.

"Well, I think that adjourns this meeting."

"There's no time to waste," James rumbled. "While August is gone, the rest of us can draw out a battle strategy. Gods forbid it should come to that, though. But if Ebene and En-doire have both been attacked..."

"Gods forbid many things come to pass," Rupert said solemnly. He rose from his seat. "We'll meet again soon."

As he stepped out of the battle room, James also stood to leave. He slapped August on the back on his way. "You're walking into a thorny mess, going east." He grinned unexpectedly, showing a line of crooked teeth. "I would be anxious if you were anyone else."

August allowed for a small smile. "Your confidence reassures." His expression hardened. "This is beyond the personal and political. We are speaking of too many lives in the balance. This is what we are made to fight for."

In his stern face — jaw line set and eyes penetrating — and commanding speech, Leah saw an outline of the great men of fable and legend. Something inside her stirred. Whether it was awe, or inspiration, or something else, she could not say.

"I know," James said assuredly. As he slipped out the door, he called back, "Do a good job and don't leave the mess to us, August."

"Mess is a bit of an understatement here," Leah murmured, after James was gone. Arthur gave her a sympathetic glance, but August did not react.

"I should ready the men and prepare for the journey." He stood abruptly, gave a brief nod to Arthur and Leah, and followed the other Marshals in disappearing out the door.

"I know that was overwhelming." Arthur raised his hands helplessly and looked at her with an apology in his eyes once they were alone. The battle room suddenly felt cold and austere.

She tried to muster a brave face. "Don't worry about me."

He smiled at her, though something like sadness crinkled the corners of his eyes. "Shall we?" He rose from his seat, and Leah followed him out of the battle room and into Fox Manor silently, her heart heavy as if the weight of the mortal realm was hooked beneath it.

CHAPTER 21

"When do you leave?"

Leah watched August stiffen slightly. She stood a distance behind him in the old barn near Fox Manor, where he was feeding his horse. His back was to her, and she was quiet, so only the sound of her voice echoing off the walls alerted him to her presence. Leah had debated between opening with the question she asked and the question of why he was doing a servant's job, and decided on the one she actually cared to know the answer to.

"Noon tomorrow, if possible. Maor and Stephen are readying the men." His reply was short and smooth, covering his surprise at her appearance.

Her stomach plummeted a little. "They must be efficient," she said, ensuring her voice was neutral.

"Desperation will motivate that." August did not turn to face her still.

"Is that where we are now?"

"Better to act swiftly before the situation is beyond saving."

He was stroking the horse's mane roughly, but Leah thought she saw some gentleness in the way his fingers moved through its wild hair. Something tugged inside her chest—so perhaps he had a tender way about him, when he was not putting on a warrior's arms or a diplomat's face. Or the awkward, stilted facade he seemed to wear around her still.

"What's his name? Or her?" Leah realized she did not know, though it was the same horse she rode behind August on the day of the Fox's dinner party.

"Her. Simi."

"Does it mean anything?"

She had not moved any closer to him, but thought he stiffened again, this time more visibly.

"My brother named her when we were young. There is no meaning." He shrugged and tightened the straps around Simi in a swift, hard motion, but not too forcefully. "It's too late to have her answer to another name."

Leah sighed inwardly, her spirits further dampened. Even a seemingly innocent question could stir up bitter memories in this place. The shadow of Benedict hung like a pall over August and everything around him.

"August—" she began finally, stepping closer.

"I don't want to hear about my brother." His voice was quiet with weariness, but firm.

She bit back a sharp retort. "I'm not here to discuss him. This is about the other night...I'm tired of your secrets. I know I'm a sheltered girl to you, but you married me. I don't need to be coddled." Leah felt awkward as the words tumbled out, but she forced herself to plow forward before she lost her nerve. "I went to see Melina. You should thank her for how much faith she has in you." She let out a breath. "So, I'm here. I want to help, but you need to let me."

At last, August turned away from Simi and rose from his bent position to face her at full height. His eyes were dark, but she could not read the emotions in his face. He simply met her gaze steadily, and she was certain that where he was impenetrable, she was an open book to him.

"You misunderstand. I don't keep secrets because I think you're weak or untrustworthy."

"Would you have ever told me you had a brother if Arthur didn't say so?"

"You said you weren't here to discuss him." A hint of jest played in his voice.

Ire stirred inside her. "It's one example of many. I haven't written a letter home because God knows what I can say to my family. My father-in-law leads the Guardians who, by the way, are not just some harmless religious devotees? My brother-in-law joined a murderer who is trying to rain havoc upon us?"

"What would you say of your husband?" He did not take his gaze off her.

Leah looked back at him steadily. "Perhaps that I don't really know him still."

His eyes softened in the slightest. "Leah, I have seen the catastrophe Guardian secrets have caused, from the first Oath-breakers to today. I didn't want you to become entangled in them."

"But they are not the stuff of distant legends. They are secrets that have wreaked disaster in your family. In *my* family. I was already entangled."

"I know." He paused. "I should have done better."

She could hear the regret in his voice. She blew out a long breath, and with it went some remnants of bitterness toward August. Leah recalled her confession to Melina, that she could almost understand why Benedict walked away. Shame welled up inside her, but she could never admit that aloud to her husband.

"You know everything now," he said. "Even what happens in council meetings."

"And that the Black Tortoise Guardian leader is no admirer of yours?"

August's face darkened. "A story for another time. An old grudge he holds."

"I will never get to the bottom of who you are," Leah murmured. "But you don't need to tell me that now. If there is anything you can tell me—"

"Yes?"

"I don't even know why you married me." She looked at him boldly.

"The real reason."

A light flush rose to his face, and his gaze fell to roaming the barn floor. "I thought that was obvious."

"Well, it's not." She paused. "You could have married Lady Arinda."

If August was surprised she knew, he hid it well. "It seems I can't keep a secret from you, even if I wanted to." His tone was dry, not accusatory.

"August, you picked a woman without title, wealth, or position over someone who had all of it. I'm not saying you're shallow, but I can't imagine why you'd say the reason is obvious."

He looked up at her again, this time resolutely. "Yes, I could have married Arinda. And you said I could have married your sister, or any other woman in Carmel, too. Perhaps you were right. But I did not want them."

Now it was Leah's turn to glance away. Her face warmed, and she did not trust her voice to speak. After a long pause, it was August who spoke again.

"Well," he said abruptly, "I must see that the men are ready for the road tomorrow."

He turned to Simi and rubbed her neck vigorously as if to say goodbye before sweeping past Leah, sending straw and hay flying behind him.

"August," she called after him.

He was nearly at the old barn door when he stopped, looking back at her with a hesitant guardedness.

"Could I come? To En-doire, with you and your men." She rushed on, seeing the stunned expression on his face. "I don't want to sit and wait here uselessly. I know a few things about tending injuries, mending cloth...things you may need along the way."

"It's too dangerous," he responded immediately. "A woman never travels with a company of Guardians, particularly when battle is imminent."

"A woman also never sits in on council meetings."

He frowned. "Cheek wins no favors at sword-point."

"You said this would be a diplomacy mission, not a fighting one. Besides, Carmel is no safer than here if the Oath-breakers find the keys. Here can be no safer than En-doire if Nimrod is successful."

"The Bastion is still the safest place right now. You know my father and I have our challenges, but I trust him to protect Cariath Valley. No one, not even Nimrod, can outmaneuver him here. And — if he told you about my mother, you know she was killed out in the Pharan." He paused, and she thought the memory swept through his eyes like a storm, but passed just as quickly. "Why do you wish to come?" He was looking at her now with undisguised bewilderment.

Leah opened her mouth to respond, then closed it again, pausing to reconsider. The idea had seized her all of a sudden. Though her nature was cautious, impulsiveness would rear its head at the most startling times. She was unsure if August's implicit expression of affection emboldened her, but the request fell from her mouth before she could properly consider her motives.

"I know I have no reason you would be unable to counter." She shrugged helplessly. "You know I love the legends of Arieh. The desire for adventure and seeing the world beyond these walls runs in my blood. I want to come. That's all."

She squirmed as August's dark eyes rested on her. She could almost sense the way he heard her defense, as weak and naive.

"Father would disapprove."

Leah waited for the remainder of his argument, but he fell silent. There was something different in his tone—a reluctance mixed with grudging regard, if she was not mistaken. A glimmer of hope sparked.

"And since when do you concern yourself with his approval?" she rejoined, her spirits buoyed.

"Leah—"

"You told him yourself I am unlike other women from Carmel. If you truly do, well, like that," she flushed, but pressed on, "do not tease me with a taste of this world and then leave me to rot behind closed doors."

He did not reply but locked his gaze onto hers. Her hair a windblown mess, cheeks pink from the cold, she returned his stare levelly, feeling a stubborn resolve harden within her. When he finally glanced away and sighed, Leah allowed a quiet smile to crawl across her face.

~~~~~

August and his company totaled only a dozen men, not including Leah. They decided to travel as lightly as possible, since it was unlikely there would be many Oath-breakers in their path, if any. They could move quickly and discreetly in smaller numbers. Maor, Stephen and Kirin were all a part of the group, and some of Leah's apprehension dissipated as she caught sight of their familiar faces. Maor threw her a casual salute and wink as he passed her.

There was little fanfare for their send-off. It was nearly high noon, and the sun was bright but the air chilly. The men had rounded up their horses on the grassy fields near Fox Manor, saddling up their belongings. For Leah, choosing the clothes to bring was a trying matter. She was not caught up in fancy dresses and the latest fashions, but August said she could only bring so much as would fit in a middle-sized knapsack. That was a hardship for any middle-class woman of Carmel, given they would be on the road for at least a fortnight. She ended up borrowing some of Lila's old clothes from Arthur, given her sore lack of appropriate attire.

Arthur offered almost no resistance to her joining August, which was a pleasant surprise. August broke the news to his father initially, and when he came across Leah later, she thought there was a strange twinkle in his eye.

"Leah!"

She turned to see Jenifer and Melina crossing the field toward her. They hurried over, their breaths coalescing into mist before them. Leah greeted them with genuine pleasure. Her heart warmed to think she had made good enough friends of the women for them to come and see her off.

Jenifer reached her first. "I would come with you if I could." Her eyes glowed. "Rupert would never allow for it."

"I'm not sure he likes me too much," Leah said, half in jest.

"Leah," Melina exclaimed. She threw her arms around her neck, and Leah returned her embrace heartily.

"Thank you," Leah whispered, knowing the other woman would understand.

The women spoke of inconsequential things as they waited for the men to be ready to leave. Jenifer talked animatedly about the landmarks Leah would encounter along the way—the winding, endless Nathair River, the old witch fire camps near En-doire, and more. Melina, more soft-spoken, simply listened. Leah felt a tremor of excitement rush through her as she thought of the adventures ahead, ones that might be carved into the history books one day. Or, perhaps like Arieh, her stories would entwine with myth and legend.

After some time, August approached the women. He dipped his head in acknowledgement of Jenifer and Melina before turning to Leah. "We are ready."

The women embraced her again and offered their well wishes before she followed August into the midst of his company. The scent of horse sweat and hair stung her senses and she wrinkled her nose. Leah's stomach twisted a little. This was no longer cozy Carmel, and soon she would not even have the growing familiarity of Fox Manor and the Bastion surrounding her. It would only be wild, open land, the warrior-like men she rode with, and the one she learned to call husband.

The realization hauled up a mixture of emotions within her—a bittersweet nostalgia for home, a thrilling yet terrifying anticipation, and a strange but not entirely painful sort of loneliness.

Maor lifted her onto Simi behind August as all the other men mounted their steeds. The muttering of men around them mixed in with the horses' whinnies and stamping, but the fields grew quiet as Arthur stepped forward to address them.

"This is not one of my dinner parties, so I will spare you the elaborate speech." Some of the men laughed, and Leah smiled at the unexpected humor. "You know the gravity of this mission, for you know the gravity of all we do as Guardians. There is little I can offer you in advice or aid."

His gaze moved slowly across the men. When his eyes came to Leah, she suddenly felt shy.

"So I will simply say, may your steeds be swift, your swords be sharp, and your gods be true."

The crisp sound of metal against metal rang in Leah's ears. All the men, including August in front of her, drew their swords and thrust them upward in a silent salute. Sun rays bounced off smooth silver, and Leah was forced to glance away to protect her eyes from the sharp light.

When the swords were sheathed again, August wordlessly coaxed Simi into a slow trot as they turned away from the Bastion and eastward to the Cariath Mountains. Leah heard the sound of horse hooves stamping the ground behind them as the rest of the men followed.

CHAPTER 22

Near the Nathair River, Island of Japha.
Month of Hope: First week, Star-Day.

Benedict and his men continued to trace a path north beside the river, their restlessness growing since Hound captured the En-doire scouts. He decided against sailing west for fear of missing Nimrod, but his frustration grew as time passed. Each day posed a greater risk that the Black Tortoise Guardians would discover them.

Craving solitude, Benedict kept a distance from the others. He certainly did not want to confront their prisoners, who were straggling in the back with their designated guards. Hound made even more of an effort to avoid him, and the tension was thick and palpable among their small party.

His last revealing conversation with Justin made his friend's company a burden too. The Old Fox had taken Justin in, raised him alongside his sons, and gave him a purpose. Justin had done the unforgivable, and Benedict felt the blame resting upon his shoulders. In a conflict of contrasts, he almost appreciated August's stalwart rejection of him. His brother would never come for him, whether to redeem his ideology or save his soul, let alone join him. It was a strange, bitter relief.

Something on the water glinted, drawing Benedict's gaze. He heard a shout behind him.

"Someone's coming from the Nathair!"

Nimrod. Benedict felt ambivalent about his arrival. It was another move on the chess board, another step toward unlocking the immortal realm.

But as a small sailboat came into focus, he realized it wasn't Nimrod. They all stopped along the shore to watch the waters carry the vessel toward them. A lone figure stood at the helm.

"Is it another messenger?" Traven appeared beside him.

"No." The man wore a voluminous red robe that blew wildly in the wind. Underneath, wide shoulder pads and armor covered his frame. The outfit appeared foreign, unlike anything Benedict had seen in Japha.

"Blades ready," Benedict murmured down the line of men. His fingers played at his sword hilt. "We don't know who else might be aboard."

Uneasy muttering and metal rustled around him.

When the ship was close enough to shore, it became evident the man was in a bad state. He seemed half-emaciated, staggering under the weight of his attire, and his robe was torn in various places. Benedict did not allow his guard to fall—this could be an actor, with an ambush ready below deck.

"Who are you?" His voice mingled with the sloshing of the water.

The bedraggled stranger did not respond. He dropped the anchor and shakily clambered off onto land.

Benedict moved to stand between him and the rest of his men. "Who are you?" he repeated. "And are there others?"

The man stared back at him. His cheekbones were sunken, but there was a startling clarity in his dark eyes.

"I come in peace. And I am alone." His thick accent betrayed his foreignness, but Benedict could not place it.

"Where are you from?"

Benedict started when Justin tapped him from behind. Silently, he pointed at the man's upper left breastplate.

A faded, but nonetheless distinct, falcon perched on the armor.

He drew a sharp breath. "You're from the Dammim. You're Vermilion Falcon."

"My name is Hansuke Ren." His gaze shifted past Benedict, surveying the men crowded behind him. "You do not need your weapons. I have none myself." He flung his robe back—there was not a sword in sight, unless he hid it well.

"I never knew a Guardian to walk around defenseless," Benedict countered.

Hansuke refocused on him, and an unreadable smile touched his lips. "I never said I was defenseless."

A shiver went down Benedict's spine. He exchanged a quick glance with Justin, who was also studying the newcomer. The Vermilion Falcon had been shrouded in mystery for ages. There were no reported encounters with Falcon Guardians for at least four or five generations, and any explorers who ventured to scale the Dammim never returned. Whatever culture or traditions the Falcons maintained were utterly unknown to the other Guardian camps.

"I have not asked you the same question," Hansuke said. "Who are you?"

"My name is Benedict. We are with the White Tiger Guardians." He did not even hesitate.

Pleasure dawned on the other man's face. "I have been searching for other Guardians since I left the Dammim."

"Will you tell us your story?"

When he acquiesced, Benedict had the guards move the En-doire prisoners out of the sight. The rest of his party gathered around Hansuke. Hound still appeared sullen, muttering about all Guardians being their enemies. Most of the other men ignored him, though, as an excited undercurrent swept through them. Every Guardian knew the history and rampant speculation that surrounded the Vermilion Falcon.

They offered Hansuke leftover game and dried berries. When he had eaten and seemed satisfied, a look of serenity settled in his gaze.

"He's monk-like," Traven whispered.

"What's there to do up in the mountain besides meditating?" Mert returned.

"I have never left the Dammim in my life," Hansuke began, and they all grew quiet. "None of the Falcons in my generation have. I have always looked at our land from above. I feel like I have planted my feet on the earth for the first time. We do not commonly refer to ourselves as Guardians anymore," he said, as he looked to Benedict, "though I understand why you called me that. Our people are all descended from the first Guardians who came into the mountains."

"But you know the legend of Arieh?" Benedict asked.

"The legend?" Hansuke stared at him. "Do the other Guardians no longer believe it?"

A rustle went through the camp. Benedict did not break his gaze from the newcomer, sensing an opportunity. "We believe it."

"We do, too. The Vermilion Falcon hold to a strong identity in our roots. We are taught from an early age of the battle between faerie and men, and that our purpose was to guard the keys to the immortal realm. The Guardians are woven into the fabric that stands between the worlds."

"And you believe the faeries are good angels that need protection from mortals?" Hound's voice rose from the back, his mockery evident.

Fury stirred in Benedict's chest.

Hansuke appeared unmoved. "No. The faerie-kind are known for their cruelty. But we are all named for the Guardians on the other side, who followed Arieh and protect the mortal realm — like the Vermilion Falcon. We are not alone in our efforts."

That silenced Hound but provoked a nagging suspicion within Benedict.

"What efforts have you made in the Dammim? And why have you left now?"

"We secluded ourselves to protect our secret of the immortal realm. But after all these years, my people are dying out because our population is small. There are no other settlements in the Dammim beside the Falcons. Our council decided to send out men to discover what is happening in the wider world, and if the time has come to change our practices to fulfill our calling."

"Seemed a long time coming," Mert muttered under his breath.

Benedict glanced around. For the most part, the men's gazes were now directed at him instead of Hansuke, visibly wondering what his next move would be. He knew his late-night brush with Hound and the En-doire prisoners led to whispered gossip, even if he was not privy to it.

Now, he felt a hum of anticipation and curiosity drum the air. What would the unpredictable Benedict Fox do next?

"Your arrival is timely," he said finally. "The Guardian Marshals seek to reunite the keys. We did not know if we would ever reach the Vermilion Falcon."

Hansuke fixed his penetrating gaze on Benedict, who braced himself to hold it. "Why? That is a dangerous decision."

"We have lived in a forced peace for generations by separating the faerie-kind from men. Our leaders believe sufficient time has passed for wounds to heal, and for us to seek true reconciliation with the immortal realm. Japha was once unique in our world as the nexus of the mortal and immortal realms. We have lost too much in giving that up — now, we're nothing more than another nation ruled by squabbling politics. King Amir's government practically ignores the existence of the faerie-kind."

"So, the truth of our origins becomes a myth," Hansuke murmured. "And the Guardians are no longer needed."

"To most people in Japha, we are nothing more than a religious sect, devoted to old legends." Benedict reached for Adair and unsheathed it. "This is the sword of Arieh, with the song inscribed on the blade." He handed it to Hansuke, who accepted it with wide-eyed reverence. "It comes from the Black Tortoise Guardians. We of the White Tiger camp hide the Mortal Gate. My father is Marshal Fox, and he gave me the task of gathering the keys together. The gods smile upon our meeting today."

"There is also the Light," Hansuke said hoarsely, his attention still turned on the sword. "*To enter Faerie's blessed demesne / four secrets must be found: / the land unbound by time and space / opens only to the one who knows / the Light, the Song, and Mortal Gate.*"

A few others had joined in his recitation near the end, and Benedict felt an unwanted chill slide down his spine.

"One of my fellow Guardians is retrieving that from Cobalt Dragon." Benedict leaned in, knowing this moment was crucial. "What can you tell us of the Falcon's key?"

Hansuke looked at him with his mysterious smile again. "But isn't it clear? Your men know the saying."

"But it says there are four secrets, yet only names three. What is the fourth?"

"Ours is not the fourth secret. It is the first." He paused, and a thick silence hung in the air. "The land unbound by time and space," he said, raising an eyebrow, and then continuing with emphasis, "opens *only to the one who knows.*"

"Opens only to the one who knows," Benedict repeated, and felt a veil slowly being lifted. "Only to the one who knows..."

"A person," Justin said, just as clarity dawned on Benedict. "The last key is a person."

CHAPTER 23

Outside Cariath Valley, Island of Japha.
Month of Hope: First week, Rest-Day.

Leah forced herself to swallow the last of the dry carrots. They left a slightly bitter aftertaste against her tongue, which she tried to dispel with a mouthful of cold water. She watched as the men around her devoured their dinners voraciously and felt a fleeting sense of shame. The Edwards were not the wealthiest in Carmel, but they were never in want and Mama was a decent hand in the kitchen. Fox Manor also lacked nothing in its supply of fresh bread, fruits, and meat from the men's daily hunts.

A full day had not even passed since they set out from the Bastion, and Leah was already painfully aware of her spoiled nature. Her legs ached from dangling in the same position on horseback for the larger part of the afternoon, though she was not required to do anything but sit obediently behind August and not fall off. Her stomach felt uncomfortable after their last meal. The men had shot a few birds — their marksmanship with bow and arrows dangerously precise — and pooled vegetables from their packs, roasting them all together over a small fire. There was no seasoning of any sort, and for the first time, Leah realized the natural taste of duck was appalling.

August had finished his dinner quickly, and he was hunched near the campfire with Stephen, a crinkled map thrown out before them. Not far off, Kirin was initiating a mock duel with two other men, Jasper and Wren. Leah had met them briefly during their journey. They were both stocky, jovial men. Kirin was little more than knee-high beside them, but the comical scene was offset by Leah's memory of the small squirrel inside the battle room with August. He could hold his own ground.

As Leah cleared the rest of her food from the makeshift wooden platter, Maor slid onto the ground beside her, his platter still half-full.

"A feast fit for the gods," he commented, a smirk sliding across his face. The crooked smile suited him well, Leah thought, complimenting his rounded features and the spray of brown hair across his forehead.

"Your gods have rather poor taste," she countered.

He laughed easily, and Leah felt her mood lighten. The sound drew August's gaze, and she offered her husband a small smile as his gaze came to her. He nodded briefly in return, but his expression looked drawn, almost wary. Beside her, Maor threw a spontaneous salute at him.

"That's right. August mentioned you're quite the heretic when it comes to religion."

She raised a brow. "Is that what he said?"

"Well, not in those words. I extrapolated." He grinned. "I know most people who come from the seaside towns or villages around Japha believe in the one God. It's endorsed by our monarch, so why argue with the crown?" His voice was light, though tinged with slight mockery.

"I don't believe in God because of the government's endorsement," she returned, allowing some heat into her words. "Why, do you think my God is too weak for warriors?"

"The God of mercy," Maor mused. "A nice invention by sheltered villagers. I don't think he's seen what some men are capable of." Maor cocked his head and looked at Leah, a glint of challenge in his eye. "What say you?"

"I don't think your gods have seen what *all* men are capable of. Our hearts condemn us all. Your gods of unflinching justice? A nice invention of the self-righteous who failed to do much self-examination."

Rather than appear put off, he pursed his lips and looked at her thoughtfully. "Quite the evangelist. The Guardian gods better beware."

"If they can't hold their own, it's time you gave them up." She took a bite out of her vegetables and could not stop herself from grimacing. He saw her expression and laughed.

"Not all of us eat from the Old Fox's kitchen every day," Maor said, after swallowing a particularly large slab of duck meat.

"I know. My mother was a capable cook as well," Leah admitted.

Maor shook his head and registered a look of mock seriousness. "I wonder at August's judgment, bringing a pristine lady on such a venture. He must be in the throes of love."

Leah nearly choked. "You don't know August if that's what you think," she rejoined.

He grinned at her, his teeth peering out behind his lip. Leah could not help but chuckle. Maor did not have the regal, stern presence of August or the same sort of well-defined features, but he was merry and handsome in an offbeat manner, with his head of shaggy hair and casual confidence.

The sort of brother I would have liked to have, Leah thought. Someone easy to trade jokes with, less sensitive and demanding than her sisters. Or any well-to-do woman of Carmel, for that matter.

"Believe me," Maor was saying, as she returned her attention to him, "August may not be the expressive kind, but he would not have married you without seeing…something."

She brushed it off with a shrug. "He needed to marry. It was more a practical than romantic decision." August's half-confession the other day pricked her thoughts, and for a moment, her words felt dishonest.

Maor simply raised his eyebrow, a skeptical look written on his face. They fell into silence as he consumed the rest of his meal while Leah stared off into the distance. The wind was whistling past them, though the tall trees nearby provided some shelter. Late in the afternoon, August had halted the company halfway between the Cariath Mountains and the river to make camp by a small forest.

Her gaze wandered to August. He was still sitting with Stephen, tracing something along the map and speaking. His voice was inaudible to her with the distance, but she could see the sureness of his hand on the map, the unwavering gaze he nailed on his companion, the steady movement of his mouth as he spoke.

"What do you mean by something?" she asked abruptly. Maor glanced at her in surprise. "You said he would not have married me without seeing something."

His normally flippant expression grew solemn, and he suddenly looked older, more mature. He stared at her for a moment, as if searching her face for the words. Leah flushed slightly.

"Something worthwhile," he said finally. "Something worth having for a lifetime."

"Oh," was all she could think to say.

You said I could have married your sister, or any other woman in Carmel. And you were right. But I did not want them. August's words from earlier were still wrapped around her mind, but she did not quite know what to do with them. He was likely far too proud to echo those sentiments again, and she was far too embarrassed to touch upon the matter.

Maor interrupted her thoughts. "But don't tell him I said so. He will have my head." The seriousness in his air was gone, replaced once again by his jocularity.

"That would be unsightly," Leah said mockingly. "I shall keep your secret."

"Has August taught you any defensive maneuvers?" Maor asked suddenly. He gestured at the darkness enclosing them. "We are, after all, in unprotected land."

Her skin tingled at the thought. "No, though they would be little use. I'm a woman from Carmel," she said, as if that were sufficient explanation.

"Does that make you incapable or unwilling?"

"In theory, both, but I can't say I'm entirely unwilling." A hesitant smile crawled across her face. "I would have tried archery as sport, had my mother not opposed me so vehemently."

"Well, she is no longer here to object." Maor sprang to his feet and offered a hand to Leah, who pulled herself upright and brushed the small twigs and leaves from the bottom of her cloak.

"If she were *here*," Leah paused, imagining the upheaval that would follow in such a scenario, "she would be fainting, not objecting."

He laughed again, a throaty chuckle, as she followed him a distance away from the campfire and other men. Leah's spirits felt higher than they had all day. She could not recall the last time she simply laughed with someone, no dark history or distressing situations to cloud the mood between them. It felt like all the conversation and thought of late revolved around the Oath-breakers, or some other deceit and treachery.

They pushed through tangled shrubbery and stepped into a small clearing. It was suddenly brighter since there was no canopy of tree leaves above them and the stars shone clearly. Leah peered behind them, in the direction they came from. The flickering flames from the campfire were still visible, but the colossal trees overshadowed the men and their voices were inaudible.

Maor flung his pack onto the ground, sending a bed of leaves flying. He unrolled it and picked up his bow, nocking an arrow in a few deft movements.

Before Leah could even blink, the brief, sharp sound of wood splintering reached her ears. Maor's bow was empty, and she swung her gaze to the tree directly in front of him — his arrow was lodged firmly in the center of it.

"You don't need to impress me," she said, trying to maintain an even tone.

"Certainly not," he replied, a glimmer in his eye. "I should have done that weeks ago."

Leah shook her head. "I don't know how August stands you," she muttered.

"He needs someone of good humor to balance his ardent somberness." Maor grinned and nodded to her. "That's why you will be good for him. Someone needs to have a laugh at his expense every once in a while."

"I fear my supposed good humor mostly places me at odds with him," she sighed.

He waved her lament away with a toss of his free hand. "Men are like fine wine. They will improve with time."

She stared at him for a moment. "That's an absurd analogy."

Maor ignored her last comment, though she thought a smile twitched at the corner of his mouth. Instead, he was nocking another arrow onto his bow.

"Watch carefully," he instructed.

His motions were far slower this time, for Leah's sake. She observed as he pulled the bowstring back with three fingers and leveled his arm to align with the arrow. Aside from the look of concentration on his face, holding position seemed effortless to him. The release was simple — his fingers uncurled from the bowstring and with a *twang* the arrow sailed into the air. She followed its trajectory with her eyes as it landed a hairsbreadth away from the previous one.

He handed her his bow and a single arrow and gestured at the target tree. "Use my arrows as a guide for aim."

The bow was lighter in her hands than she expected, but stretching the bowstring with arrow into position felt awkward. "Am I holding it properly?" She turned her head to peer around her arm at Maor.

"Bring your elbow higher," he said, as he came to her side and moved it into position. "And your hand ought to stretch back to the edge of your mouth."

Her first shot twisted far off to the left, missing the tree entirely. But Maor was a patient and effective teacher, perceiving her main weakness was in the grip, causing the bow to shift at the moment of release. As Leah focused on tightening her hold on the bow, she began to find her mark. After firing a dozen or so, she surrounded Maor's initial two arrows with a throng of her own.

Leah's arms were quivering slightly, but it was a delightful ache. She wiped the sweat from her brow as they retrieved the arrows, twisting them out of the bark wood.

"You learn quickly," Maor said, a note of admiration in his voice. She saw him smirk as he pulled an arrow out. "Perhaps if En-doire denies us aid, your services will be needed." His tone was half-jesting, but she could not quite distinguish the other half.

Scoffing lightly, she said, "You give me so little confidence. To think, our world in danger of darkness, and its fate may fall into the hands of one woman. I don't know how the Guardians have fared all these years."

"Well, these are desperate times. Else I doubt men like me would make the ranks." He wore a roguish look and Leah could not help but laugh out loud.

As they collected the last of the arrows, Leah heard heavy boots pressing against dry leaves. Her breath stole away and a sudden fear seized her. Her hands clamped down hard on the weapons and she spared a quick glance at Maor. He had moved closer to her, an arrow held beside his ear, lodged in the crook of his fingers. His previously impish expression was replaced with one of rapt concentration.

"Leah?"

It was August's voice, and her chest unclenched as the outline of his figure moved out from the shadows. Next to her, Maor also relaxed, and they strode briskly toward him.

August, however, sported a stern gaze, his mouth tight-lipped and drawn. "If you were any louder, I imagine the Oath-breakers across the river could hear the commotion." He did not speak harshly, but there was an iron-like quality to his words.

"We weren't that loud—" Leah protested, but Maor cut her off.

"They are welcome to come—we will end their troublemaking before they ever reach the Bastion."

Maor was as flippant as August was severe and Leah winced inwardly as her husband's eyes darkened. It was a similar expression to the one she witnessed when she first confronted him about Benedict.

"I am not disposed to your sense of humor now, Maor." His tone did not change but Leah thought she could hear an edge of bitterness bleed through.

Maor bowed his head. "My apologies," he replied formally. There was no trace of jocularity in his voice this time.

Leah frowned at August, but he either did not notice or chose to ignore her. An awkward silence fell over them for a few moments, as Maor appeared contrite while August continued to stand austerely before them. A sense of indignation welled up inside her and she scowled at her husband.

"Is it a crime to joke?" she blurted out. "You can't command other people's moods according to your own."

"Please, don't concern yourself—" Maor began, glancing at her, but August interrupted.

"I know how to handle my men." He gave her a hard stare. "Your presence here is already against my better judgment. Do not further my regret."

"Oh, so you will lord that over me now?" Leah exclaimed. "It's as if I'm always your mistake, beginning with your decision to marry me!"

She did not wait for a reply, but she briefly caught the look of pain that cracked August's grave veneer and the astonishment on Maor's face before she whirled away and sprinted out of the clearing into the thick of the forest.

The path appeared similar to the one she followed with Maor earlier, but there was no sight of August's men. The campfire was visible from the clearing they were in, but in her hurry to escape, Leah did not determine the proper direction before hastening away. She was breathing heavily and loose strands of hair pasted themselves against the side of her face. The thought of not having a proper bath for days to come only disheartened her further, and she sank to the ground against a thick trunk.

The idea of being lost in a dark forest would normally frighten her more, but Leah was already too exhausted to dwell on that. Surely, August and his men would come searching for her when they discovered her absence. A cold draft wafted through the trees and she shivered, the heat and sweat from her archery exercise wearing off fast.

She did not know how much time passed in her solitude, but it was enough to make her curse her pride and swift tongue. August had spoken sternly, but not unkindly, until she provoked him. Guilt hovered over her like a cloud as she recalled the severity of his present trials: He was on a race against time to call for aid from men who thought him a traitor. All the while, his brother was working against him in the trenches of the Oath-breakers.

And who is shouldering these burdens with him? Leah thought bitterly. *Who would, if not I?*

In light of his hardships, her resentment toward him began blowing away. Rather than providing any comfort or aid, she goaded him and made him look a fool in front of Maor. This time it was not difficult to forgive, but to accept that she was the one who would require his pardon.

"Leah."

She did not even hear him approach. Leah lifted her head and met his solemn gaze. August stared at her for a moment before unclasping the brooch of his cloak and throwing it around her shoulders. He sat down beside her.

She pulled his cloak tightly around her arms. It still carried a tinge of warmth. "Thank you," she murmured, finding her throat and mouth dry.

They remained silent for some time, listening only to the sounds of the forest. The trees rustled beneath the breezes that swept through and an occasional cricket-like noise echoed, stirring a quiet ache in Leah's heart. They reminded her of the crickets chirping in the bushes on late summer nights in Carmel.

"Maor says you have excellent aim." August's voice was soft, nuanced with the same uncertainty she often found when he spoke to her. It was mystifying, given his commanding aura in all other arenas of his life.

"He's too kind." She was equally hesitant.

August released a long breath. "I'm sorry," he began haltingly, "I've been unfair with you."

Surprise and shame simultaneously fell over her. Surprise, because it was the first direct apology she had ever heard him issue, and shame, because she did not think he owed her one.

Leah could not resist a small jab. "You are quite out of your element here, aren't you?"

"I'm unused to apologies," he reminded her, a slight edge entering his tone.

A small smile crept across her face before the solemnity of the circumstances overtook her again. "No, I should apologize. I've been insensitive and childish while you are caught up in such weighty issues." The words came in a sudden rush, and she was glad for the cover of night, which hid her reddening cheeks.

It was his turn to appear startled. "You're too severe with yourself. You have borne your circumstances with uncommon grace."

"Uncommon grace?" Leah cried in bewilderment. "I accused you of wrongfully marrying me before Maor!"

"Ah," he exhaled, as if he was only now remembering. "But you are not the childish one. I spoke out of jealousy."

She looked him fully in the face, but he cast his gaze downward. "*Jealousy?*" she repeated, unable to grasp his meaning altogether. "You envied Maor?" Her voice lifted in incredulity.

"Is it so unreasonable to believe?" he returned.

"Why—yes."

August still did not meet her gaze. "I thought it was clear to you."

"No!" She stared at him in disbelief, her mind scrambling to make sense of the matter. "I—I don't know what to say."

He was silent for a moment before simply saying, "I have never heard you laugh as you did with him. At least, not since you left your family."

"But…" She sputtered for words, still stunned by his revelation. "You know jesting is his native language. The men were all laughing with him earlier this day. It doesn't mean anything more."

"You vanished from the camp with him alone," August replied, but his tone was more weary than sharp.

"He's one of your closest friends and an honorable man," Leah retorted, a defensive temper rising within her. "He offered to teach me archery, which I have always wished to learn, and I did not think you could ever afford the time or desire to accommodate me." Her eyes bore into his. "Tell me, what part of my reasoning was inequitable?"

"None." He heaved a sigh. "That is why I have apologized to Maor, and I am apologizing to you."

His words, though still bearing the underlying firmness of his general speech, were contrite. Leah grew embarrassed as she recalled just moments ago, she was set on refusing his apology and pleading for his pardon. She closed her eyes and prayed briefly for a gentle and humble spirit, and tried to turn the world to see it through his eyes.

"I ought to have told you where I was going with him," she said finally. "But I feared you were too busy with more important things to think of me."

"And there is my fault. I should not act in a way to give you any such idea."

Leah risked a small smile. "You're awfully obliging tonight."

He did not reply and his expression was difficult to read. The events of the day began to sink more deeply into Leah's mind now and she could not rid herself of her earlier disbelief over August's revelation. Did he care for her more than he let on? She thought of his words in the barn that implied affection, Arthur's inscrutable but somehow knowing smile when he learned Leah would join the En-doire expedition, and now his jealous sentiments. When and how did he grow so attached to her? *Certainly not as a result of our ill-fated first encounter at his party in Carmel,* she thought wryly.

But there was little else along the way of their acquaintance and then marriage where she could have won his heart. She did not have enough charm or style, and he did not have enough leisure to think of giving his heart away, even to his wife. At least, that was what Leah conjectured.

"August," she began, when he did not speak. He turned to her, and something tugged in her chest at the sight of his tired eyes. "Please don't think of it again. I think of Maor as the brother I wish I had, an antidote to my gossiping sisters and someone to challenge my wit in banter." She paused for emphasis. "Nothing more."

He nodded slowly. "I do not doubt you — or him — and I'm glad you have found such a friend."

She glanced at him, hesitating for a moment before adding, "It's not true that I have left my family." At his confused look, she said, "You said you have never heard me laugh like that since I left my family. *You* are my family. God has joined us together as one."

She recalled Papa's words to her before their wedding. *You will know far more of him than anyone in time. The two shall become one, as the husband cleaves to his wife.* That time felt an eternity away from now.

An expression of surprise and mild pleasure gleamed on his face. "So it is God who joined us together?" There was a teasing note to his tone.

Leah laughed — perhaps not with the same boisterousness as earlier in the night with Maor, but it was genuine mirth nonetheless.

"Certainly," she replied, coating her words in friendly mockery. "I never would have chosen you myself."

It was the first smile she saw break across his face that day. Her spirits soared like a bird winging for blue skies.

"Clever," he muttered. August stood up and brushed the leaves and twigs from his breeches. "Come, let's return to the camp."

She took his proffered hand, warm and strong, and he pulled her to her feet.

CHAPTER 24

"Have you traveled to the northern end of the Nathair River?" Leah looked to August and a light breeze blew the hair from her face.

He shook his head, his arms pressed against the railing of the ship they had boarded four days ago. "Guardians don't have the luxury of being explorers. At the northern tip, the river runs into the Swift Sea."

"You've never left Japha, then?"

"No. Benedict was the one who always wanted to sail out, see other nations. But Japha was a wide enough world for me." August glanced at her. "What about you?"

"Carmel was enough for me." She laughed lightly. "Books took me to faraway places, but I never imagined leaving home. I didn't believe I had the stomach for it."

"Oh, but you do," August said, before turning to look over the railing again.

They lapsed into silence. It was a five-day journey across the river aboard the *Meadowlark,* and the first four had passed uneventfully. Leah and August had passed the first hour of the day on the deck watching the sun flare into the sky and talking of the mortal and immortal realms. Her curiosity came to life again as they finally found a moment's peace, and she was hounding August with all the unanswered questions that had sprung up over the time she was living in the Bastion. The ship was quiet, as some of the men took the time to sleep and others lounged about various parts of the vessel.

He was patient, though never verbose, in answering her queries. Since their reconciliation in the forest, he had been more attentive to her in small ways: pointing out landmarks as they journeyed from the forest to the river shore the morning after, digging out a spare shawl to shield her from the chill, and now satisfying her inquisitiveness during the river crossing.

"There is one established Gate between the worlds, the one we agreed to lock away for good," August said, in response to Leah's most pressing interest in unlocking the immortal realm.

"What are the keys that each Guardian camp guards?" Leah paused. "If you can tell me."

"There is an ancient poem that names them. Even the Oath-breakers know it now, so I see no reason I can't tell you."

"Glad I meet that low standard," she murmured, but he seemed too lost in thought to hear her barb.

"To enter Faerie's blessed demesne / four secrets must be found: / the land

unbound by time and space / opens only to the one who knows / the Light, the Song, and Mortal Gate."

Leah turned the phrases over in her mind.

"What's the fourth secret?"

August smiled grimly. "I don't know. It's protected by the Vermilion Falcon in the remote Dammim Mountains. Nimrod should have a fine time uncovering that one."

"So the Black Tortoise guard the Song." She thought back to the council meeting at the Bastion. "We and the other Guardian camp each guards the Light and the Mortal Gate. And the Song, the Light, and the unknown key somehow unlock the Gate." She glanced at August inquiringly.

He sighed, but not unkindly. "You are dangerously sharp."

Leah bit back a smirk, though her mind swirled with unanswered questions. "So none of you know what you really guard," she said, "yet you dedicate your life to it."

"We are dedicated to an ideal, and a pact between our worlds. It is safer if no one person holds all the knowledge."

"Then," she added suddenly, as a thought occurred to her, "the Oath-breakers do not know how to use the keys even if they gather them all."

August nodded, an expression of grim satisfaction spreading across his face. "That is where our ignorance is an advantage. No living Guardian knows, so there is no way for them to steal that knowledge."

Leah's mind wandered into speculations of how the keys and gate worked. It was a frustrating endeavor, as it was hard to shake the traditional image of large doors and brass keys fitted to them.

Footsteps came from behind, and she turned to find Maor and Stephen coming toward them. The sun was at their backs, shadowing their faces and forcing her to squint.

"Morning, lovebirds," Maor crowed.

Leah's cheeks warmed and she could not muster the courage to look at her husband. She still felt a twinge of anxiety in Maor's presence, knowing what August had thought of them together, even if it was only a fleeting consideration. And Maor knew it too, since August had confessed to him before seeking Leah out, but he seemed perfectly at ease.

"Good morning Maor, Stephen," August replied, dipping his head in acknowledgment. There was no noticeable change in his demeanor either.

"We've been trapped onboard for days when we're usually out hunting at this time," Maor sighed. "We felt an itch to do something to occupy our time. Most of the men simply want to rest."

"*You* felt an itch to do something," Stephen corrected. "I had the misfortune of being found awake by you."

"But it appears our path has only run into a couples' haven here," Maor continued, ignoring his companion, "so I fear fate frowns upon us."

His histrionic flair tugged a small smile out of Leah and she caught a brief twinkle of amusement in August's eye. A tendril of pain skated through her knuckles, and she noticed they were pale from gripping the ship's railing. She loosened her grasp as her unease slipped away.

"You are welcome to join us," August said, "though I don't know if we will match your high standards for entertainment."

Maor scoffed mockingly. "You certainly will not do."

To Leah's surprise, August turned to her. "It may be that you know some worthy pastimes for these men to engage in."

"Oh, the gods save us," Stephen muttered. "I have played one too many village games in the past." He cast an apologetic look at Leah, though he could not disguise his sourness entirely.

She simply laughed. "I have no interest in most of those either."

"Then, there is hope," Maor said, and he winked at her.

Leah shook her head and rolled her eyes upward before an idea struck her. "We could play a round of True Tales, Tall Tales."

A look of confusion fell across all three men. August raised an eyebrow, an almost wary expression on his face. "The name suggests the game is mere gossip, cleverly disguised."

"The sort women play over afternoon tea," Maor quipped.

"It is not," she protested, indignant. "My father taught us the game. Our family would spend hours indulging in True Tales, Tall Tales on cold winter nights." Though the memories still pricked her heart, the ache lessened. "It was an Edwards family tradition."

"What are the rules?" Stephen asked, the resignation on his face as clear as the noonday sun.

"The game is simple. We take our turns asking questions, and each of us responds with one true tale, one tall tale. The others endeavor to determine which was the truth and which the lie. You gain a point for each individual you are able to deceive."

Maor rubbed his hands together. "Ah, deception and trickery. I wonder who shall prevail at this sport."

"Nimrod would," Stephen muttered.

A hush fell over them for a moment, and Leah wondered if that was a joke that slipped too far out of August's line of propriety. But Maor laughed and gave Stephen a friendly thump on the arm. Leah grinned, and August eventually allowed for a smile as well.

"Fine, let's play," August said. He glanced at Leah, his expression stern and regal as always, but there was a hint of softness in his eyes. "Perhaps it will touch you with the warmth of home."

The trembling sensation in her stomach—the same one she experienced in the barn—stirred up again. "Thank you." She tried to ignore the feeling and a smirk curled up the side of her face. "Though, I imagine this game will take on a vastly different flavor with you three than with my family."

Her prediction proved true as the four of them sat on the *Meadowlark*'s deck, trading questions as the morning sun splashed across the ship and light breezes whipped around them. To Leah's surprise, August turned out to be the best of the three men, tricking them with subtle tactics since they knew his life and stories too well. Maor and Stephen were less able to deceive him, and Leah was a discerning guesser, even though she knew little of their history. She held the upper hand throughout the game, given her distinct advantage of having a past all of them knew little about.

They danced around common topics such as favorite foods, childhood friendships, and hoaxes pulled. She learned that Maor privately despised eggs, but stomached them out of courtesy to the Old Fox, who specialized in fashioning all sorts of egg delicacies at dinner parties. Stephen, who seemed the embodiment of austerity — with a touch of sarcasm — once conned August into attending a glitzy ball, insisting it was a Guardian gathering.

As for August, Leah gleaned little additional knowledge of him. She was unsure if it was due to his guarded answers or the fact that she already knew him more than she thought.

"What is your deepest regret?" Maor asked with flourish.

"One, that I agreed to participate in this game, and two, that I did not marry that colonel's daughter in Ephes before Merriman stole her." Stephen went from a wry tone to a growl in one breath.

Maor put on a mockingly thoughtful look. "Well, I knew you fancied her, but you have been such a poor sport so far I'm inclined to think your first statement is the truth." He looked to August and Leah. "What do the romance experts say?"

"I am not one, and I say the second statement is true," August sighed.

"Second," Leah agreed. "His voice reached an entirely different pitch when it came to this woman."

Stephen scowled. "A point for August and Leah."

"And what is yours, Leah?" Maor swept his gaze over to her, a wicked gleam in his eye. "Marrying a man to whom the gods gave a rock in place of a heart?"

She laughed. "I have none. All of my life is composed of divine Providence, even the sorrows."

"That unshakable faith." Maor nodded, winking at her.

"That theology is a sure balm for life's troubles," Stephen muttered.

"Stephen," August said, his voice deepening, and Leah was surprised to hear the note of warning. Then he added, grudging acceptance in his tone, "There's something to be said for such an effective balm." He cast a quick look at Leah and her spirits soared a little.

"What is your answer, August?" Stephen looked to him.

August glanced again at his wife, an indecipherable expression falling over his features. "Unlike Leah, I have many to choose to from," he said, his

166

tone carefully neutral.

Before he could continue, a flurry of footsteps resounded on the deck. Wren jogged toward them, the sunlight throwing the sweat droplets on his tawny skin into sharp relief. He was panting lightly, and a thrill of alarm raced through Leah. She glanced at the other three men, and their faces were taut and anxious.

August was on his feet in one graceful movement. "What is it?"

"No cause for immediate alarm, sir," Wren said. He gave a nod of acknowledgement to each of them briefly. "Kirin and I were at the head of the ship on lookout. We are coming within view of shore and there appears to be a small campsite near the river."

"Oath-breakers," Maor cursed beneath his breath, which drew Wren's gaze.

"Perhaps. Or it may be men from En-doire. We can't say for certain."

Even with the blue skies and smooth, warm wood beneath her feet, Leah felt a sudden chill descend over her. Would Nimrod be among them? She pictured a cold, pale man with a devilish face. Though he did not know her, the idea of being within throwing distance of him paralyzed her bones.

"Maor, convene the men," August said. His earlier, more relaxed demeanor faded instantly into his usual stern bearing. "Wren will take Stephen and me to see the campsite before we meet and determine a route after docking." He glanced at Leah and a silhouette of worry entered his eyes. Was her fear so visible? She colored. "Leah," he began, before pausing, and turning to the men again. "I will take her to our cabin inside first. Meet me on the lookout."

Without a word, the men hurried away to their duties. Leah felt August's hand press lightly against the middle of her back. "Come," was all he said, firm but more kindly than the tone he used with the others.

She allowed him to lead her into the covered portion of the ship. The *Meadowlark* was larger than it appeared from the outside, with a stairwell in the back that led to a series of small cabins below deck. The doors to each were plain and unadorned, the entire floor and walls painted with a simple beige-wood color.

August pushed open their cabin door. The bed was neatly tidied since they were docking later that day. The warmth of the small room comforted her—it was simple, but had become a familiar refuge over the last few nights. A round window was opposite to the door, and she could see the waters churning casually outside. Leah sank onto the corner of the bed, hearing the springs creak under her.

She thought he would leave immediately to attend to the men, but he stood silently in the doorway, watching her.

Leah could not help herself. "Is Nimrod with them?" she asked, trembling.

His eyebrows drew together, and his mouth set itself into a grim line.

Something akin to understanding also dawned across his face. "I don't know." There was a fervid look in his eyes that came and went in a flash. "But if he is, I swear to you, he will not lay a hand upon you."

His intensity sent a tremor through her. "Arthur said he was one of the most talented Guardians," she murmured.

A rigid silence hung between them for a moment before the slightest smile twitched across August's face. "You worry I can't defeat him."

"Can you?" She hated the fear mingled with strained hope she heard in her voice.

"I faced him in single combat in the battle room for many practices. I know how he fights."

"And you would win? As you did with Kirin last time?"

August's expression was still tight, but she caught the brief hesitation that fluttered across his face before it was quashed again with his sternness. Her heart clenched. "A swordsman's skill will only go so far," he said, "and I have greater incentive to crush him." His tone was low and certain.

"Greater incentive than controlling the immortal realm?" Leah forgot her fear in a rush of skepticism.

His hands tightened into white-knuckled fists at his side. "He desires power. But that man has robbed me of greater things."

His gaze fixed on her for another second before he turned and stalked away, the tail of his cloak blowing up lightly behind him. He left the door ajar, and Leah sat on the bed numbly, listening to his sharp footsteps fade.

"Vengeance," she whispered into the air, and her voice sounded hollow and strange.

CHAPTER 25

Nathair Riverbank, Island of Japha.
Month of Hope: Second Week, Water-Day.

August fetched Leah from her cabin after they docked at port. The last flares of the day's sunlight splashed over them as they disembarked. She watched as dock workers bustled around, securing other ships and carrying gangplanks around the station. The commotion and normalcy of it warmed her.

Sheltering aboard for a final night, particularly in a guarded post, seemed far more appealing to Leah than hard ground and open air. But the men were tired of being ship-bound, and the horses were particularly restless.

"You'd rather sleep out in the cold?" she asked Maor. The *Meadowlark* had been a welcome change from the open forest.

"We aren't all pampered ladies," he returned lightly. "If you don't have cabin fever, your husband does, and if he doesn't, your horse certainly does."

She refrained from pointing out that cabin fever was a better alternative to an encounter with Oath-breakers. But August was also eager to put his feet on land, and she did not want to quarrel. He proposed they ride south a bit so they could stretch their legs and put more distance between them and the campsite Wren and Kirin spied out.

"Shouldn't we tell the dock guards about it?" Lawrence asked.

"We don't have anything to report," August said. "They could be anyone. Making camp by the river isn't a crime." His voice was tighter than usual.

Leah doubted he believed that, after their tense conversation in the cabin. Whether they were Oath-breakers or not, the specter of Nimrod and Benedict loomed over them. But Lawrence did not push the subject, and they saddled up to ride down the riverbank. She felt a pang leaving behind the safety of the ship and the comforting flurry of activity at the dock post.

That evening on shore, Leah shivered and drew her cloak more tightly across her shoulders. The air was noticeably colder in the open moorlands than in the valley, and the nighttime breeze stung her skin with a frosty bite. They did not light a campfire for fear of attracting attention, particularly with the open and flat landscape stretching before them. But Leah could not shake the thought of Nimrod entirely, and her unease only grew as twilight cast its veil over the skies.

She found August's steady presence calming to an extent, but he was also preoccupied. Very few subjects were brought up in general that evening—the men prepared their dinner and ate quietly, as if a somber mood had come over them all. Even Maor was more subdued.

When dusk fell, Leah was unable to sleep, tossing and turning as her back ached against the hard ground. Spending a night outdoors in the wild was inconceivable to a proper woman from Carmel, and as much as Leah wished to prove herself a capable exception, she found her skin bruised and muscles sore. Then, with uncomfortably vivid thoughts of Nimrod lacing her imagination, slumber eluded her.

Leah ensured August was completely unconscious before she rose from beside him. Wren and Stephen were on guard at the edge of their small camp, and the two men looked questioningly at her.

"Is there any shrubbery around?" she whispered. "I need to, you know…" She trailed off, her face warming in a blush. Even after traveling with August's company of men for over a week, the propriety of Carmel's polite society characterized her more than the culture of warriors on the road.

Stephen looked uncomfortable, but Wren pointed at a hedge near the water, unembarrassed. "Go around the back."

After relieving herself, Leah meandered further downriver, sucking in the fresh air. There was something soothing about the rhythm of the water beside her and occasional cricket chirps. A lonely thrill surged through her as she looked at the yawning skies and land sweeping around her without another waking soul in sight. The security and warmth of home were far gone and the wide world beckoned all around her. Panic welled up in the pit of her stomach, but Leah quieted it quickly. She was not the same woman who had left Carmel. The reality of the Guardians and immortal realm struck a deeper sense of gravity—and steadiness—into her being.

The faint tap of footsteps stopped Leah in her tracks. She froze, whipping her head around, but the darkness obscured her vision. She could still see their camp behind her, but she had put a fair distance between them. She also spotted the ship dock on the other side of her, twinkling with a faint light. It was even farther away. Ice spread through her veins.

She listened hard for more sounds, her thoughts spinning. *Could it be Nimrod, from the camp of Oath-breakers they spotted earlier? But weren't they much farther off…?* Her palms felt cold and moist. If she fled back toward August and the men, she risked alerting whoever was nearby to her presence immediately. Even at a cursory glance, she knew she was at a disadvantage—she was standing exposed beside the river, while the surrounding hedges and upward sloping banks could easily hide another person.

Her breath hitched in her throat, and she turned silently on her booted heel. Her blood beat in her ears like a war drum. Every cricket chirp or bird call set her skin tingling as she listened for any telltale signs indicating their awareness of her presence. She stood on the balls of her feet and pointed herself in the direction of the dock, hardly allowing herself to breathe or think.

Something behind the hedges rustled, and she was certain it was not the wind.

If it's an enemy, there's no reasonable escape. The realization cut through her panic with blunt clarity.

"Who's there?" she whispered, steeling herself for the worst.

A long silence persisted.

"We could ask you the same."

The answer came in an equally low whisper, but it nearly knocked her over. The unmistakable sound of an unsheathing sword followed.

Numb acceptance spread through her and momentarily swept away her distress. She considered the possibilities methodically — she could flee, but they would certainly overtake and overpower her; she could cry for help, but they would capture her before August and his men could reach her; or she could simply meet them on her own volition. She forced away the plaguing thought that she might be walking straight into Nimrod.

Oh, help me, God. Leah drew in a deep and shaky breath.

"You could at least show yourself," she returned, injecting some defiance into her words. "Since you can clearly see me."

Two shadowy figures emerged from behind the shrubbery. They were far enough that she could not make out their features clearly, though one of them beckoned her to approach.

"There. Now, your turn. Who are you?" The voice belonged to the man who had spoken first. Not knowing what else to do, Leah moved toward them. The nighttime veil still obscured her vision, but the outline of their features slowly came into focus.

"My name is Leah," she said, her voice steadier than she expected.

She came closer and could see the men glancing between her and each other with undisguised amazement.

"Are you from En-doire?"

The other man spoke for the first time. He had fair-colored hair and a kinder face than Leah imagined of any Oath-breaker. She felt a glimmer of hope. Perhaps they were from the Black Tortoise Guardians, or simply travelers through the land.

Her gaze shifted to his companion and her heart leapt into her throat. His ginger hair, high cheekbones and jutted chin nearly bowled her over with their violent familiarity. She shuddered and closed her eyes for a moment to steady herself as anxiety, shock, and even a thrill of anticipation pounded through her.

Gradually, the emotions coalesced and settled into one of dread. She was facing two Oath-breakers, and it did not matter if one looked outwardly kind and the other was family. They were with Nimrod in cause and spirit. If she betrayed her identity or August's mission, all would come to naught — they had come to the precipice of inciting war with the faerie-kind. The significance of this moment dropped its weight on Leah mercilessly.

"I am not." She finally found the words, as she realized they were still awaiting her response.

The ginger-haired man — Benedict Fox, she was almost certain — moved out from behind the hedge and circled her slowly and deliberately, his hand resting on his sword hilt. Leah followed him with her gaze as he prowled around her.

"You will give a full account of who you are and why you are here," he said quietly, though there was a clear warning in his voice, "or you will learn these are not simply playthings." He tapped his sword.

"You don't need to threaten a lady," the other man said quietly.

"A lady would not be wandering in these lands at night for no cause," Benedict returned. He continued to circle.

He means to intimidate me. The thought sparked Leah's ire and she forgot some of her fear. "And are you lord of these lands, that you can demand to know anything of me?" Her voice shook a little, but it was strengthened by the hint of mockery that played at the edges of her words.

She watched as Benedict glanced at his comrade, a flicker of amusement in his eyes. "She has some fire in her."

The smirk he wore looked almost identical to August's. A pang shot through Leah as her mind turned to her husband and regret churned inside her. She should have returned to camp immediately.

Benedict returned his attention to her. "Are you certain I am not?" He moved closer to her.

"I know who you are," she sighed, tiring of his game already.

He cocked his head to the side, running a critical eye over her face. He had a piercing gaze like his brother's, but it did not daunt Leah, who was inured to August's scrutiny by now. She cared even less what his traitorous brother made of her, and the thought stirred up sudden courage.

"You think we are Oath-breakers," he surmised. He glanced at the other man, who nodded some unspoken agreement. "Then, you are from En-doire. Perhaps one of your missing scouts is someone dear to you, so you have come searching." He scoffed a little, but there was a faint light in his eyes. "Foolish, but you have spirit, particularly for a woman."

"If only you knew," Leah muttered beneath her breath, feeling the irony of his words. Gathering her wits, she said more loudly, "What missing scouts?"

"The scouts your leaders sent to look for us," Benedict said. He furrowed his brow. "They can thank me for sparing their lives."

A cold shiver pricked the back of her neck. Before she could think up a response, Benedict's companion spoke.

"I don't think she is here for the scouts." He was looking at her intently, and though his eyes did not drill into her the way Benedict's did, there was something about their quality that told her not to underestimate his insight.

"What?" Benedict swung his gaze sharply toward him.

"She doesn't know what you are speaking of." He paused and his jaw line tightened. "She is too pale to be from the Black Tortoise. And her accent..."

"...is from the seaside towns." Benedict spun to face her. "I ought to have noticed immediately."

"The lord of these lands is not so capable then, is he?" Leah clung desperately to her inspired bravado, but it was quickly disappearing beneath the dire circumstances. She was caught like a mouse in a trap.

"I will only ask you once more." The light in his eye glinted dangerously as he stalked toward her. "Are you here with the Guardians who crossed the river? There's no need to play innocent. I know that ship, and we spotted it well before it docked. So, Leah, who are you?"

She fought the urge to shrink before him, and it took all her wits and willpower to keep her feet firmly planted on the grounded. Whispering a wordless prayer for help and fortitude, she drew in a long breath.

"Perhaps that is a question to ask yourself," Leah murmured. She hesitated a moment, then added, "Benedict."

The astonishment that broke across his face made Leah feel a rush of satisfaction. He might be an Oath-breaker, a hardened warrior, but she held the higher ground in some respect still. That ground was quickly crumbling, however, and her brief sense of gratification fell away as a dark scowl cut across Benedict's features. His gaze slid over her and she flushed at the wrath rising in his eyes.

He took a deliberate step toward her, but his companion was immediately beside him, laying a hand on his shoulder. Benedict flung it off angrily.

"No," the other man said quietly. Leah felt the weight in his tone, and Benedict must have too, as he paused for a moment.

"I am your commander here, Justin," Benedict growled, a note of contempt in his tone.

Justin appeared stoic, unmoved. "And I am your advisor." His gaze flickered to Leah. "Tread carefully."

"What, do you think she is a witch from those old legends?" He shook his head mockingly.

"She's here with the Guardians, Benedict. They docked a few hours ago. She's from Cariath."

Leah did not dare to look in the direction of August and their camp. It was possible Benedict and Justin had not spotted its location in the dark, though they were dangerously close. She willed herself not to give it away.

A tense silence fell over them as Benedict stared hard at Leah. It was almost as if she were looking at August, though Benedict's eyes possessed a greater fervor and unhidden antagonism. But there were moments — when the veil of his zeal and anger slipped away — Leah glimpsed a lost quality in his dark pupils, like a young boy stranded in a maze. It was the same look she caught on August when his commanding aura dropped, like in the barn with Simi, or when she shook him out of his nightmare about Alain. A sad pang pierced her deep in the chest and softened the edges of her fear.

He could not be much older than her; perhaps they were the same age even. But he was adrift in the world, his feet set on a dark path. And she was suddenly struck by how similar he was to his brother. Benedict forsook the integrity August held so closely for licentiousness and power. August lived by law and honor but allowed a quiet bitterness to slowly consume him. Both clung to their ways as the means to freedom, but were unknowingly fettered by their own ideals. Compassion for both men suddenly gripped Leah's heart.

"You have a wise friend," she said to Benedict, her tone calm. A small smile even played at the edge of her mouth. "That is fortunate, given the men you have fallen in with."

Benedict and Justin both regarded her with surprise, though she did not know if it was due to her serenity or her unlikely smidgen of humor.

He cannot be entirely evil, without hope. It could be a naïve thought and stupid gamble, but Leah ignored the voice of caution. She had thrown caution to the wind when she left August and the camp — or when she begged to join the mission — or when she married him in the first place. It was too late for timid steps and passivity. She would leap on instinct and leave the rest to Providence.

"I am Leah." She repeated her earlier words. "Leah Fox…August's wife."

The amazement she witnessed earlier when she identified Benedict was hardly anything compared to the undisguised shock on the men's faces. Justin's expression quickly fell out of her main line of sight, though, as she focused on Benedict. A spectrum of emotions stormed through his eyes, but one gripped her attention most — pain. He was not immune when it came to his brother.

Leah did not know what to anticipate in his response. How did a man react to news such as that? Was it grief, seeing someone close to his estranged brother standing before him, without warning? Did it reopen old wounds? Or was it simply a reminder of their feud, stirring up nothing but fury and hatred?

Warrior instincts or a hardened heart allowed Benedict to recollect himself more swiftly than she would expect.

"If you would tell me that outright, my brother did not choose a woman of much wisdom." He spoke lightly, scoffing, the veil of zeal and anger cloaking his expression again.

"I will not dispute that," Leah returned. "I am not wise in the ways of the world or men. But I don't think you are as cruel as you wish me to believe."

Disdain and anger flared in his face. "Then you are even more naïve than you appear." He looked to Justin. "We will bring her back to the camp."

No! The cry ripped silently through Leah. Flailing images of a black-clad man holding a knife over her and leering faces lit by harsh firelight flashed in her mind's eye.

"No." Justin echoed her thought in a low, serene tone.

"You are quick to give your opinion tonight, though I have not asked for it."

Benedict did not meet Justin's gaze, but examined his blade with casual indifference before sheathing it at his side. He crossed his arms at his chest and glanced between Leah and Justin. His dark pupils grew stormy, like a tempest brewing beneath a thin surface. His companion appeared unfazed, stepping closer to Benedict and placing a wider berth between Leah and the two men.

"What do you think men like Hound will do when you bring a woman back?" Justin said quietly, though Leah could still make out the words. "And your brother's wife, no less."

"No less? That is what makes her leverage in this war."

Cold dread and desolation fell over Leah. The way he said those words—so unfeelingly—turned her stomach into knots. She was wrong to chide August for thinking harshly of his brother. A veneer of tears caught on her eyelashes, but she blinked them away rapidly. Leah already felt enough like a simpleton for her belief in Benedict's redemption, her wandering away from the camp after dark... she could not give in to whimpering like a child too.

Indignant resolve began to harden in her bones. She ignored her wobbling knees and the mocking doubts that tried to sour her determination.

"...is what makes her family," Justin was saying, as she returned her focus to the conversation. His tone was sad, and Leah briefly wondered what a seemingly decent man was doing among the Oath-breakers.

"Listen."

Her voice shook a little, but it was otherwise firm and clear, cutting through their words and drawing the men's attention. Benedict wore an irritated expression, while Justin's face registered a blend of curiosity and mild surprise. Leah sucked in a deep breath.

"Listen," she repeated. "I am tired of being used as a chess piece in your battles. I will not be traded, bargained with, or used as leverage. You will let me walk away from here, or I will scream until I can't and August and all his men will be upon you before you can draw your swords."

Leah's blood thrummed in her ears and her whole body trembled with adrenaline and fear.

Benedict's stare bored into hers for a long, silent moment. Numbed by her sudden speech and trepidation over the consequences, she could not help but return his gaze, unblinking. A thin smile etched the corner of his mouth.

"He certainly did not choose you for your mind," he said softly, though she detected a dangerous undercurrent pulsing beneath his words, "and I have seen prettier women in the seaside towns." He paused, running his gaze down the length of her. For all the gravity of the circumstance, Leah still flushed at his words. He did not look at her in a scandalous manner, but as a soldier assessing its prey with a calculated eye.

"But perhaps he liked your bravado."

His words unwittingly threw Leah's thoughts back to the ball at Edenbridge in Carmel, with all its bright, blooming dresses and chandeliers. Her pointed words to August that night rang in her ears again along with Maor's musing. *He would not have married you without seeing...something. Something worthwhile.* The idea almost prompted a laugh, but it died in her throat as reality poured over her again.

"Perhaps he did," she murmured, and fell silent.

"What you failed to consider," Benedict continued, his fingers playing at the hilt of his sword, "is that I can kill you. So I would not advise screaming for help."

This time, Leah allowed herself to smile a little, despite the anxiety coursing through her blood. "I am not screaming for help, but to alert the Guardians to the camp of Oath-breakers rotting in the land." She stopped to catch her breath and lower her tone. "What you failed to consider is that not all men are like you. We don't all fear death."

"That is a lie," Benedict hissed, but there was enough uncertainty in his voice that Leah could not determine if he was attempting to convince himself or her.

The metallic ring of his unsheathing sword echoed loudly in Leah's ears, drowning out the night sounds of the lapping river waves and bird calls. She spared a glance at Justin, but he did not move and wore an impenetrable expression. In his quiet, indirect way, he had protected her from Benedict's mood swings and impulses since their encounter on the shore. Had she persuaded him that she could hold her own with Benedict now? The frightened, sheltered girl within her wished she had not.

"Now you choose to fall silent?" Benedict did not remove his gaze from Leah, but they both knew his words were for Justin.

"Let her go." His quiet answer felt like it came from a distance. "You are gambling against a woman with nothing to lose."

They continued to lock gazes and Leah determined that she would not be the first to look away. Her heart still pounded against her ribcage, but she drew desperately on her favorite Guardian stories and Papa's tales for courage—if she was to die tonight, she would leave this world bravely.

A muffled cry broke the silence. Benedict spun around and Leah watched as a silent figure appeared behind Justin, who was now out cold on the ground.

"Hansuke!" Benedict brought his sword up into a defensive position, but the other man was already upon him, though he held no weapon in hand.

Leah stumbled back as the two warriors grappled with each other. The newcomer was thin and wiry, and she could not make out much of his features as he wrestled with Benedict. Even through a fog of shock, she marveled at how his nimble, weaponless attack was ruthless. He seemed to anticipate where Benedict would strike and weave out of the way. He cut through his defenses until they were hand-to-hand, elbow-to-elbow.

Something in Benedict's style reminded her of August, but his skill seemed unmatched to his opponent.

She heard a soft *crunch* as the other man thrust his elbow down into Benedict's leg. He shouted, but was cut off with a hard knock to his head.

"No," Leah said numbly, as she watched the other man loosen Benedict's sword from his grasp. "Please."

He turned to face her. His dark eyes were sharp, though his cheekbones were sunken.

"You seek mercy for a man who threatened you."

"It's complicated."

He removed the sword from Benedict anyway but moved away from his unconscious form. "I was not going to kill him. This did not belong to him."

"Who are you?" Leah asked.

"My name is Hansuke Ren." He stepped toward her, and she felt a shiver go down her spine. "I am from the Vermilion Falcon. These men," he gestured at Benedict and Justin, "masqueraded as Guardians to me, but Falcons are not easily deceived."

"Vermilion Falcon!" Her mind raced. "You... you didn't tell them your key, did you? How to access the immortal realm?"

Hansuke stared at her for a long, disconcerting moment. "I did. But they do not know how to find it."

Fatigue and shock threatened to overtake her, and Leah swayed on her feet. Hansuke offered his arm, and she grasped it to steady herself. Her gaze fell on the sword he took from Benedict. A violet gem glittered on the pommel. She inhaled sharply.

"You recognize this?" He was watching her.

"I think so. It was stolen from the Black Tortoise Guardians." She thought back to Lee's admission in Cariath, coupled with the descriptions of Adair from Papa's books. She smothered her anxiety and met Hansuke's gaze. "How did you know it wasn't Benedict's?"

"Falcons are not easily deceived," he repeated. "We have a gift for seeing. He did not handle the sword as if it belonged to him."

"Will you come with me?" she asked. "I am with the real Guardians, from Cariath. We need to hurry."

He nodded silently, and she led the way back toward their camp, the fog closing behind them.

CHAPTER 26

August and his men were wide-awake and battle-ready as Leah and Hansuke staggered into the camp. Though Wren and Stephen were first alerted by the commotion from the shore — mostly the shouts and scuffles when Hansuke jumped Benedict and Justin — the noise was loud enough to awaken everyone.

"Who are you?" Stephen held Hansuke at swordpoint, his stern figure tall and intimidating. The others clustered around.

"No, wait." Leah held up her hands. "He helped me. He's Vermilion Falcon."

A pregnant pause dominated before multiple voices spoke up. Even in the darkness, she saw a spectrum of expressions, ranging from disbelief to wonder. She sought out August's face. He stood beside Stephen, who had lowered his sword. While most the men were staring at Hansuke, August's eyes were fixed on her, a ghostly look behind them.

She moved away from Hansuke toward him.

"August—"

He removed his cloak and wrapped it around her, even though sweat gleamed on her face, strands of hair stuck to her forehead. The adrenaline of the last hour felt like fire in her veins still, though the nighttime chill was beginning to creep under her skin again.

"No," he said quietly, "you don't need to explain. Lie down and rest. I'll talk to him."

"I have to tell you—" she began, protesting, but he held up a hand.

"No, Leah. You're in shock." He took her hand and led her back to her makeshift sleeping place, her blankets crumpled on the ground. "Let me meet with the men, and I'll come talk to you after you rest."

Feeling the fight leave her, she lay down. But as he turned to go, she said, "You wouldn't coddle your warriors this way."

August met her gaze. "You're not one of my warriors. You're my wife."

Leah closed her eyes as he walked away, listening to the audible snatches of conversation around her. She thought of Benedict and Justin, unconscious at the shore, and the events of the past hour replayed in her mind.

At some point, exhaustion must have overtaken her, because the next thing Leah knew, she was snapping awake from a shallow sleep. It was still dark out.

She sat up straight, feeling her legs and back protest against the swift motion. The men were scattered around with their horses, conversing in low tones. Many had their bags packed and saddled. August was tending Simi nearby, and deep in conversation with Hansuke.

She noticed August's gaze flutter over toward her, deep lines etched in his face. When he noticed she was awake, their eyes met, and apprehension welled up inside her. She did not have a warrior's unflappable disposition, and he could read people unusually well. Leah suppressed the alarm that raced through her. What had Hansuke already told him?

August said something to Hansuke before approaching Leah alone. He held out a makeshift wood platter with berries and dry meat to her.

"What did he say?" she asked quietly.

"He said you were by the river when you met him. He left the Dammim in search of other Guardians, but he crossed paths with Oath-breakers instead. They saw our ship earlier, and were spying on us." August stared at her. "You should have come straight back to the camp."

Leah could tell he was trying to soften the tone of rebuke, but it glanced off of her easily. She looked back at him, bewildered.

"That's all he said?"

August was silent for a long moment. "He said he met my brother."

Of course. Even as Leah stared at her husband, his face obscured by the darkness, the resemblance became stark. When she first saw Benedict, she saw undeniable traces of August in him—now, she could see traces of Benedict in August.

"Yes. I did too." Unsure of what to say, she added, "Did he show you the sword?"

"What sword?" his voice sharpened.

Leah caught Hansuke's attention as he was stroking Simi's mane behind them. She motioned for him to come over.

When Hansuke came near, she said, "Do you have the sword?"

He handed it to August wordlessly. Her husband sucked in a sharp breath and she found him staring at the violet gem on the pommel, his severe expression looking as if it was carved in stone. When his eyes found hers, they were dark with bewilderment and anger.

"Do you know what this is?" he asked in a low, dangerous voice, and Leah shivered. His similarity to Benedict was suddenly striking.

"I have an idea," she replied weakly.

"You took this off one of the Oath-breaker spies? Where did you find it?"

She gave a helpless shrug. "Benedict had it," she mumbled, and then the entire story tumbled out, unrefined and awkward.

There was no time for Leah to consider how to paint the events to lessen the impact on August—if that was even possible—so the words just fell out as she relived the awful yet exhilarating evening. She did omit certain parts, such as overhearing Benedict call her leverage, and his comment about August appreciating her bravado. It was still less than an hour ago, but it seemed so distant, even dream-like, that Leah felt the need to glance at the sword repeatedly to persuade herself of its reality.

Though she would cast her gaze away occasionally out of embarrassment, she was acutely mindful of August's countenance. He hardly flinched when she first mentioned Benedict appearing out of the fog, and his expression remained unchanging throughout most of her report. When Leah recounted her threat to scream, though, there was a flicker in his eye but still he did not interrupt.

A prolonged silence followed Leah's retelling. She was tempted to fidget in place, dreading yet undeniably curious what August would say.

"Well," he breathed. "You have me at a loss for words."

Leah bit her lip until it hurt. "Are you upset?"

He stared at her for a moment. "My traitorous brother nearly killed my wife. Should I be upset?" There was a rigid flatness in his voice, cut through only by an edge of cynicism.

It was unclear whether he was angered more by Benedict's actions or Leah wandering from camp in the first place. She did not know how to respond, and simply shifted her gaze between the ground and his drawn face. Hansuke stood by, listening to the entire story in silence.

August finally heaved a sigh and rose to his feet without another word.

"Wait," Leah called out, even though she had nothing left to say.

He met her eyes and she thought there was a glint of empathy in his dark pupils. "There is no time to discuss our feelings," he said firmly but not harshly. "You said Benedict thought you were searching for the En-doire scouts, which means they are held captive, if they are still alive." He looked at Hansuke, who nodded.

"I discovered they had prisoners. I spoke to one. That was when my suspicions were confirmed that your brother was not a true Guardian."

Something in August's eyes flinched. Even Leah felt the sting of those words, spoken unabashedly by an outside observer.

He made to leave, but paused only to look again at Hansuke. "Thank you, for protecting Leah. I am in your debt."

The newcomer gave a slight bow. "No debts. We are Guardians. That is what we do."

August dipped his head in acknowledgement before glancing at her again. "We can talk more later."

"Wait," Leah said again, a sudden thought occurring to her. "What about Benedict and Justin? They were unconscious down by the river."

"Leave them," August said automatically. "We don't have time for a confrontation. We have the sword, and we need to make haste."

Leah glanced at Hansuke, but he did not react. She wondered if August was so quick to decide because he truly wanted to save the prisoners and make for En-doire, or because he was unprepared for a confrontation with his brother. What good would it do? They could fight to the death, or

August could bring Benedict in to face Guardian justice. Leah felt her chest clench. Perhaps it was better to leave him on the riverbank — far better for God than August to be the arbiter of Benedict's fate.

"Right." She nodded numbly, and allowed him to walk away, with Hansuke trailing behind. He called Maor, Stephen and Kirin to join him at a distance from the other men. Leah felt a blast of frustration. August had not reacted terribly to her confession; in fact, he almost entirely veiled his reaction. That, she suspected, was why she felt so unsettled. He did not curse or fall into a rage, but she was unsure what feelings he harbored beneath his calm façade. Yet, she was more irritated with herself. Without a word, he knew her desire was to work through the knotty emotions last night's events stirred up in them. August was able to put that aside for action first — and he was right. Men's lives were at stake.

Her appetite lost, Leah picked at the food August handed to her and watched as her husband and his advisors spoke animatedly. They broke their huddle sooner than she expected, and all the camp regrouped at August's signal.

"Time is short, so I will be brief." He glanced around at the men and Leah, his gaze passing over her as he did everyone else. "We have reason to believe the Oath-breakers captured some En-doire scouts in the desert. Stephen will lead a small group to find and free them. They are probably at the camp we spotted earlier. Wren, you will join him, and Lawrence and Lee, you may be helpful in recognizing the scouts."

The two men from En-doire nodded anxiously. The company exchanged uneasy glances at August's news.

"The rest of us will make for En-doire," he continued. "I would like us to arrive by the following nightfall." Some surprised murmurs interrupted August. "It is achievable on horseback, though we will need to be swift."

Leah groaned inwardly. She was already sore from bouncing on Simi behind August. Even when they traveled at a slower pace, spending long hours of the day on horseback wore down her legs and back. But she was determined to swallow the pain without complaints — there was too much hanging in the balance, and she had already caused August enough headaches on this trip.

He gestured at the newcomer beside him. "This is Hansuke. You know he comes to us from the Vermilion Falcon in the Dammim." The men were casting furtive glances at him, but August continued without pause. "I know you will have plenty of questions for him, but speed is of utmost importance now. He has agreed to accompany us to En-doire."

With that, the men all returned to their belongings and horses to prepare for the journey. Leah watched as Stephen, Wren, Lawrence and Lee rode off with an abrupt farewell before she hurried to join August and stuff her blankets into the knapsack. He was silent as he adjusted the saddle on Simi's back.

"I'm sorry, August," she said in a small voice.

He turned to face her, the lines on his face softened. "You don't owe me any apology."

"I didn't mean it as one."

As the terror of last night faded, the thought of Benedict mostly left an ache in her chest. *Your brother was not a true Guardian.* She would never know the fullness of August's burden, but she understood it a little better now.

He seemed to grasp her meaning, and briefly touched her shoulder.

~~~~~

Morning to midday passed like a long, tiresome blur. For most of it, Leah jostled uncomfortably behind August on horseback. They were riding more hastily than before, though she suspected August still maintained a relatively reasonable pace for her sake—she had watched him ride back with his men from morning hunts in the Bastion, and their breakneck speeds made the company's current hustle look like upper-class women riding in the park. With Stephen's small party gone, there were only eight men left, and Leah was sure they were capable of greater swiftness, if not for her.

August did not make any mention of accommodating her, and the men were simply following his lead. Still, the thought stirred up self-reproach and remorse as Leah recalled the lives hanging precariously in the balance.

In spite of her aching limbs, she swallowed all complaints and grumblings. Instead, she determined to look for ways to make herself useful.

They estimated it was a little after noon when August finally called for a halt and short break. The men pestered Hansuke with questions for a while, which he obliged, but then they fell silent as weariness took over. It was a hot day, and the sun felt molten against their skin. The heat rising from the rocky, desert ground broke through their boots and warmed the soles of their feet. As they dismounted, the men poured water liberally over their heads for relief.

Their food supply was running dangerously low, but if they reached En-doire by nightfall, it would be of little consequence. Though she was famished, Leah tried to accept her meager portions gratefully and quietly whispered a prayer of thanksgiving.

As August was busy tending to Simi again, she joined Maor and Kirin as they ate.

Before she properly situated herself on the ground beside them, Maor began without preamble, "Are you sure you're from Carmel?" His tone was laced with exasperation and skepticism.

His question confused Leah, but she felt oddly defensive. "Who do I strike you as?" she returned.

"Show the lady some common courtesy," Kirin sniffed, chiming in simultaneously.

Maor snorted. "It was not an insult. I'm honestly bewildered."

Realization dawned over her. "Oh." Leah glanced down at her portions and picked at the food. "August told you what happened last night." The fight drained from her, and she simply flushed with embarrassment.

"Ignore Maor." Kirin waved his paw dismissively and straightened. The fur on his small back rippled slightly. "I salute your courage."

Leah smiled ruefully at him. "You mean my idiocy."

"Ay ay," Maor chortled.

She scowled at him, but there was no real vigor behind her glare. They fell silent for a while, munching on their paltry meal, each pondering their own thoughts. Leah observed the rest of the men around them. They sat in pairs or trios scattered nearby, most in quiet and somber moods. August was still off on his own with Simi, and Leah was unsure if he was brooding over the course of events or strategizing. Knowing him, it was most likely the latter.

Though they spoke little during the morning leg of the journey, Leah felt reassured by the passing moment of kinship they shared earlier. Whatever his thoughts were, he did not seem bitter over her unruly actions.

Watching him pace beside Simi, his dark eyebrows slanted inward in thought, she heaved a quiet sigh. Though she was growing accustomed to August's ways, much of his experiences and trials were beyond her. She could not know his heart, not truly, unless he revealed it to her.

"What does August think of my encounter with Ben?" Leah blurted out abruptly. She glanced between Maor and Kirin.

Maor gave her a puzzled look. "What did he say when you told him?"

"He said—he was at a loss for words."

"Then he probably did not know what to think," Maor said pragmatically.

Leah shook her head, dissatisfied. "But what *will* he think? What is he thinking now?" She shrugged helplessly, sensing her line of questioning bordered on nonsensical, but she was anxious to gather some insight. "He tells me nothing."

"Because there is no time," Kirin said gently, and there was a surprisingly wise look in his eyes. "There is a war coming, Leah."

Chastised, she bit her lip. "I know."

"I think," Maor began slowly, "he still does not know what to think. You see his struggles as too great for you to grasp, but you should not assume he has it all sorted out." He paused, glancing in August's direction. "Life may have burned his youth away too soon, but he's still young. He doesn't know everything."

She stared at Maor, simultaneously startled by his eloquent depth and moved by his understanding.

"And," he added, almost as an afterthought, "he loved Benedict."

184

The past tense did not escape Leah, but she chose not to comment. "How does he reconcile that with the wickedness of his ways?" she murmured, more to herself.

"I think he wonders too, though he will not say."

"August has more than disowned him in name," Leah said, remembering his forceful conviction the night she learned of Benedict's existence. *My brother is dead to me.* They were not the words of an uncertain man.

"The heart is not so simple," Kirin remarked quietly.

Leah's gaze flickered to the squirrel, unsure of how to respond. She still did not know what to make of him, or how he processed human complexities. Maor did not say anything either. Kirin did not appear to notice their reticence and, his back hunched slightly and gaze cast downward, he continued speaking.

"The Faerie world is ruthless, but loyalty runs deep in our tribes. I think that is why I felt at home among the Guardians. I grew alongside August and Benedict. Sometimes the ways of men are foreign to me, but I knew their brotherhood well. It was an unspoken one, silent but strong." Kirin finally looked up at Leah and Maor, his eyes moving between the two of them. "When you have two vines that grow entwined, and you tear one out in a violent haste, you will rob some part of the other vine too."

"So," Leah murmured slowly, processing his words, "you think August is torn in loyalty between his principles and his love for Benedict."

Kirin lifted a small shoulder. "He would deny it. But I do not think his devotion to his brother was so easily dissolved."

"He said Benedict was dead to him," Leah said, and the weight of the words hit her like a tower of bricks.

"Because a dead brother is better than a treacherous one," Maor injected.

They fell silent after that, and Leah felt her head ache along with the rest of her body as she tried to untangle the Fox brothers. How did she wind up in such a disheartening quandary? Her mind wandered to her sisters, safely nestled in their cottage by now. Their worst dilemmas probably consisted of deciding which suitor to dine with and which balls to attend. To her surprise, thoughts of her family had grown fewer and farther between as time wore on. It was bittersweet, but she was privately glad they were spared the knowledge of her adventures.

She closed her eyes briefly, feeling exhaustion deep in her bones. *August Fox.* It seemed like years ago when he arrived in Carmel, lighting a fuse to the gossip and giddiness of every single woman in town. *Hardly any of them would survive two days as his wife.* The thought almost brought a wry smile to Leah's face. Except Jessie — she would take it all in stride, and likely do far better than Leah.

Oh, Jessie. She felt a twinge in her chest as she thought wistfully of her friend. She missed her vivacity and humor. *Japha could use some of that now.*

Leah thought of her wager at the wedding. Was she learning to love August? It was not the fire and romance she always imagined, but in a slow and quiet way, he was filling up her world a little bit more with each passing day. Was that love? Or loyalty? Or were the two concepts also like Kirin's vines—entwined and a part of each other?

Maor interrupted her thoughts. "August is signaling us to get ready."

She glanced around. The men were dusting off their cloaks and boots, preparing to mount their steeds again. August was already on Simi, who was trotting in small circles restlessly, stamping her hooves.

Maor sprang to his feet lightly and offered Leah a hand.

"Thank you," she nodded to him and Kirin, "for sharing with me."

Some of his characteristic humor glinted in Maor's eye. "We do not envy you. You married a complicated man."

"What an understatement," she muttered, fighting the smile that twitched at the corner of her mouth.

CHAPTER 27

Nathair Riverbank, Island of Japha.
Month of Hope: Second week, Star-Day.

Benedict jerked awake, his head throbbing. Dawn was breaking, the sunlight rubbing against his dry eyelids. He bolted upright and the world spun. Justin sat beside him, laying a hand on his shoulder.

They were back at their camp. Some of the men were already up, but they paid little attention to him. The events of the night flashed through his mind and Benedict massaged his forehead.

"What happened?" he demanded.

"I think it was Hansuke," Justin said. An ugly maroon bruise colored his temple. "I woke up by the riverbank a few hours ago and brought you back."

"A few hours?" Benedict grimaced. How could he have been out cold for so long? And how had Justin managed to drag both of them all the way back to camp while he was injured himself?

"You took a worse beating than me."

As Justin spoke, Benedict bit his lip to keep from crying out. He bent his knee backward and a splintering pain shot up his leg.

He cursed. "I think it's fractured, at least."

"Try not to move so much. I'll find some cloth to bandage it."

"Once you do, we need to leave. We need to cross the Nathair."

Justin paused, staring at him. "You can hardly walk on that."

"It doesn't matter," Benedict said through clenched teeth. "You know what will happen. Hansuke will go to August, and the Guardians will come hunting us. I'm surprised they didn't come for us at the riverbank."

His friend did not respond, but nodded and left to find supplies. Benedict closed his eyes as images of Leah's thin, trembling form went through his mind. While an undercurrent of fragility pointed to her sheltered upbringing, there was an enigmatic sense of conviction about her — the way she spoke, and the way she held his gaze when even soldiers could not. To imagine August married threw him off kilter, and he had not regained his poise before Hansuke ambushed them.

Even in this godforsaken desert, his brother found a way to haunt him.

When Justin returned with loose strips of cloth, Benedict wrapped them around his upper leg tightly. He stood up and tested his weight on it.

"This will do. Gather the men."

"What will you tell them?" Justin cocked his head.

"The truth." As they formed a loose circle in the camp, Benedict strode forward, trying to conceal his limp. Lifting his voice, he said, "We need to move. A contingent of Guardians from Cariath crossed the river yesterday, likely heading to En-doire." A rustle went through the group. "We will go to the north dock and meet Nimrod's company on the other side of the Nathair."

The men exchanged startled and uneasy glances at the mention of Guardians. Momentary anxiety crept under Benedict's skin. The Oath-breakers, with all their boldness in breaking away from tradition, lived in the shadow of their history as Guardians. Would they have the stomach to kill and burn their old home and comrades? Would *he*? Benedict could not shake the images of the Old Fox groveling before Nimrod, or Leah's piercing eyes.

"What happened to you two?" Hound piped up, gesturing at Justin's bruised temple and Benedict's leg. His voice suggested no real concern.

"Hansuke did not want to befriend us," he returned dryly. "But he served some purpose. We will not pursue him."

"What about the Vermilion riddle? He gave us nothing to go on," Mert said.

To Benedict's surprise, Justin spoke. "He told us their key is a person. We already know more than any Guardian outside the Dammim has for ages."

The men grew silent after that, perhaps considering the weight of his words.

"If there's nothing else, prepare to break camp," Benedict said. As the men dissipated, he turned to Justin. "Thanks."

His friend shrugged. "It's true." He paused. "Did you notice what Hansuke took, though?"

"Adair." Benedict had realized it moments after he awoke. "I have the song memorized. I'm sure you do, too."

Justin nodded. "You know whose hands it will end up in."

He scoffed a little. "If I know August, he will simply deliver it straight back to Marcum. And find himself in a pretty bind explaining how he acquired it."

~~~~~

The north dock was only lightly guarded. Benedict estimated less than two dozen men prowling the harbor as his company approached. He kept a vigilant eye out for August's Guardians, but their camp seemed to have disbanded and moved inland, which was what Benedict suspected. August was clearly on a mission to En-doire, and even if Leah gave him a full recounting of what happened, he doubted his brother would take a detour to confront him now. He would only press on harder to win Marcum's allegiance for the coming storm.

As the contact between Cariath and En-doire cooled over the years, fewer men sailed across the river. The Old Fox used to tell stories of the days when bustling ships came and went frequently, and Guardians would rotate their posts between the valley and east of the river to garner knowledge of the terrain and variations in culture.

Since Benedict came of age to be considered a full-fledged Guardian, he recalled few visitors from En-doire. The marriage between the Old Fox and Lila — a daughter of a prominent En-doire Marshal — placed a strain on relationships between the two strongholds.

If August planned to rally the men of En-doire to fight alongside the White Tiger Guardians, he would face hardy resistance.

"Your trick at the southwest dock will not suffice here," Justin commented, as they came to a halt near the shoreline.

"We will need to take the dock by force," Benedict said pragmatically.

"That would be Hound's specialty."

He grimaced at the mention of Hound. Since their fateful clash over the En-doire prisoners, he had sulked quietly, licking his wounds and keeping a guarded distance. Benedict was not tricked into thinking he had silenced Hound's opposition. A stab to a wild animal would only subdue it for a time; then, it would come back with roaring strength and retribution.

Hound was not ambushing Benedict yet, though. He remained silent even when Benedict left a stock of their food supply and water with the En-doire prisoners, who they bound to trees before leaving. Benedict caught wind of others grumbling about their likely escape and endangering the Oath-breakers. He ignored them — chances were, the prisoners would survive and report to their leaders, but he and his men would be long gone.

Benedict gestured for the men to form a tight huddle around him. It was hard to travel unseen near the Nathair, but the men were well trained in moving silently. With the arrival of August's men on this side of the river recently, Benedict surmised the Guardian uniforms his men still wore would allay any immediate misgivings.

"We will need to take the dock by force," Benedict repeated in a low but clear tone. "I estimate no more than thirty men, so nearly two of us for each of them. Break into pairs and spread out quietly behind the harbor; at my signal, we move."

He glanced around, catching the eye of as many men as he could. Most were nodding affirmatively. "Do not kill unless you have no alternative," he added. Hound's face came into view, but he only stared back at Benedict blankly.

"No alternative?" One of Hound's men raised a bushy eyebrow and stared at Benedict, doubt in his dark eyes.

"Unless your life is threatened," Benedict amended. He returned the gaze unflinchingly. "I trust that should generally not be the case for skilled warriors such as yourselves."

"Which ship are we taking?" Traven asked.

Benedict craned his neck to scan the harbor. He had not planned that far in advance yet, assuming they would have time once the dock guards were unconscious, but Traven's inquiry reminded him that was not always a safe wager. There were at least ten middle-sized vessels lined up against the dock that would suit his company. He mentally weighed the benefits of each craft's location and condition.

"The *Meadowlark* is here." Justin cut into his silent consideration.

He spotted the ship drifting near the end of the harbor. It stirred up a muted nostalgia in Benedict's gut, which he quickly stifled.

"The *Meadowlark* it is," he said mechanically. His familiarity with the vessel would give them a distinct advantage.

As the men scattered across the back of the harbor, Benedict cast a sidelong glance at Justin beside him. "August would not forgive you for that."

The other man only shrugged. "I think I crossed that line long ago."

They fell silent as they jogged to the center of the back harbor and waited as the rest of the company spread itself in a line on both sides of them. Benedict perused the docking area again — fortunately, the workers were spread thinly across the shoreline, which would expedite their formation strategy.

As Justin gave the signal, the Oath-breakers leapt from their places and flew upon the unsuspecting guards. A few shouts rose from the victims, but Benedict's company silenced them quickly. The entire fight lasted mere minutes. As the men congregated around the edge of the shoreline, Benedict swept his gaze over the harbor, which was strewn with unconscious bodies. The sight twisted his stomach a little, but he ignored the bitter sensation. Hound's accusation of his merciful bent still rang uncomfortably in his ears.

He led the group rapidly toward the *Meadowlark*. It was August's favorite craft, and while the Guardians in Cariath shared in common ownership of the vessels, they respectfully left this one to the elder Fox.

"I gave August Adair. He should think nothing of his ship."

Justin simply shrugged. "If the thought comforts you."

Vexed, he returned, "It's a trade in his favor."

Benedict marched off to the helm of the ship and barked orders for the men to hurry their actions as they loosed the *Meadowlark* from the dock. As much as he hated to admit it, the course of recent incidents unsettled him. From Benedict's heightened feud with Hound to their encounter with Hansuke — not to even mention Leah — the trajectory of events was quickly gaining wind and rushing into a climax.

And the consequences of any outcome would be staggering. If Nimrod triumphed, the immortal realm would be open and vulnerable, inciting a potential war. If, however, the Oath-breakers failed, the survivors among them would be tried and likely executed for their crimes. Justin, Wills, Gerard, and Traven... men he still counted as comrades in more than name.

He thought of Justin standing at the gallows, a noose around his neck, wearing his usual serene, indecipherable expression. It was sickening.

"Sir."

He spun around and snapped his attention to the lone man behind him. Traven looked at him, and quickly dropped his gaze to the deck.

"Traven," he acknowledged, working to maintain an even tone.

"Are you feeling unwell?" Actual concern gleamed in his dark eyes.

"Why did you follow Nimrod, join the Oath-breakers?" Benedict asked abruptly. He noted the surprise and confusion in Traven's face, and turned to pacing the deck slowly.

There was a long pause before Traven spoke. "My father nearly worshiped the Guardians for the ideals they embraced—strength, honor, justice—but he could never join the ranks because of his crippled leg. He decided I would fulfill his dream." He blew out a long breath, his brow furrowing. "I was an outcast with the Guardians. I was not strong physically and did not have the charisma to win many friends. You and your brother were always held up as the models of the Guardian ideal."

"I think that was only my brother," Benedict scoffed, but his tone was light. The corners of Traven's mouth tipped upward a little, and he felt a brief moment of kinship.

"To the small men like me, you were portrayed as a dynamic pair. He was stern and regal in bearing, but you were winsome and bold." Traven's contemplative expression morphed into curiosity. "I have no great love of Nimrod, but his path was my only way out. I never understood why you chose to follow after him too."

Mixed emotions churned beneath Benedict's breastbone. "Is that what all the men wonder?"

"I don't know, but I think he is a lesser man than you."

The quiet conviction and sincerity in the way Traven spoke presented a jarring contrast with Benedict's first vivid memory of him, at Hound's mercy in the marshes at Whitewitch.

"Well, no one can fault him for lacking vision," Benedict muttered, suddenly uncomfortable.

Traven smiled half-heartedly in return. There was a lingering moment of despondency between them before he straightened and took on a look of formality.

"I came to tell you there is an issue on the dock. Some of the men are recovering and may sound the alarm."

Benedict cursed and sprang toward the railing, dragging his injured leg behind him. Two of the men on the dock were already on their feet, examining their unconscious comrades and shouting to one another. One of the men turned in their direction and waved his hands wildly at the *Meadowlark*. His eye caught Benedict's for a fleeting moment and he yelled something to the other man, pointing to his own hair.

"He recognizes you," Traven said from behind.

"Or he thinks he does."

Benedict broke into a sprint to the lower deck, with Traven close on his heels. He snapped a few orders for the men to hurry, though the vessel was already pulling farther from shore. Leaning against the rail, he waved until the two Guardians returned their attention to him.

"The White Tigers send their regards," Benedict called, shouting to make himself heard above the men's voices and the noise of the boat's hull thudding against the water. "This is the reward for En-doire's disloyalty."

The men on the dock wore bewildered and indignant expressions. As the *Meadowlark* accelerated away, they turned to their unconscious companions again.

"So, you were able to make use of the same ruse again." Justin was beside him again.

"That was quick thinking, sir," Traven noted.

Benedict turned to face them. "My brother shall have a political disaster welcoming him into En-doire."

CHAPTER 28

Pharan Desert, Island of Japha.
Month of Hope: Second week, Star-Day.

Despite the hard saddle beneath her and the wind rushing against her face, Leah nearly dozed off numerous times behind August. The rhythm of the hoofbeats around her and the fading sunlight made her drowsy. With her hands clasped loosely around August's waist, she drifted in and out of shallow unconsciousness and the afternoon hours passed by in a dreamlike haze.

The scenery between the Nathair River and En-doire was mostly desert-like, a sharp contrast to the lush greenery of Cariath. In the heat of the day, the land was a dusky red shade that stretched to the rim of the horizon. A trail of dust rose in their wake, stamped up by the horses. A tingle went up Leah's spine when she learned this was the Pharan Desert, where Lila died in a rogue faerie attack.

"How close are we?" she asked, sometime in the late afternoon.

A pause followed as August glanced at the sky. "We can reach town by dinnertime." Grim satisfaction clipped his words.

"Mm," she mumbled languidly. "If their feasts are even half of Arthur's, I will forget all my sorrows." She felt the muscles in his back stiffen slightly. "Should I expect less?" she asked lightly, though a shot of anxiety ran through her.

"Do not count on much of a warm welcome." August's voice was tight.

Leah hesitated for a moment before venturing, "Because of Benedict?" She glanced at the additional sword now hanging off the side of Simi's saddle.

"There's more than that."

He fell silent and urged Simi into a swifter gallop. The men around them followed suit effortlessly and Leah blinked against the sudden bloom of dust that swirled into her face. She sighed inwardly, but conceded that August did not want to explain further.

She tightened her grip around her husband as they cantered over craggier ground, the unevenness shaking her from side to side. Though she was not easily dizzied, vertigo swept over her and for once she was glad their meals that day were so scant.

Though August's thin layer of clothing was damp with sweat, he still smelled faintly of fresh soap and linen, despite the long days and lack of a proper shower. As Leah spent most of the days pressed against him on horseback or sleeping beside him in open land, she grew increasingly comfortable with their physical closeness, even though most of it was out of practicality and decidedly unromantic. It was almost as if they were comrades, rather than husband and wife, and the idea of it perplexed her. On the one hand, it was notable given her initial distaste of him, but it made her melancholy as well.

As evening drew its covers over the sky, Leah caught sight of large trees and buildings in the distance. They were much more modest than the Bastion's grand and towering edifices. The men stirred in their saddles, echoing her relief and gladness aloud.

August pulled to a sharp halt, and the men circled their horses around him.

"You rode well, all of you," August commended them, though his tone was solemn. "We will reach En-doire soon, so a word of caution — we do not know how they will greet us, but under no circumstance shall we provoke them." He paused for effect. "We need their allegiance."

The men nodded, wearing serious expressions. Leah felt a tremble in her stomach as she sensed the importance of the next few hours.

"Perhaps we should wait for Stephen to recover the captives," Maor said, a shadow of concern hovering in his dark eyes. "Lawrence and Lee can vouch for our good will."

August only shook his head. "We don't have time."

Maor wore a troubled look but did not protest further. The rest of the men were silent too, and without further word, August spun Simi in En-doire's direction and coaxed her into a swift trot.

Leah was wide-awake and alert now as she took in the gradual transformation of the landscape. The desert receded and they entered into settlements boasting foliage and vibrant life. August pointed out a few neighboring towns, like En-karah, as they passed through. The outskirts of the towns were quiet, where small homes were interspersed across large open spaces. The houses grew more dense as they ventured deeper into the towns.

As they made inroads into En-doire itself, she caught sight of people milling around. Most of them featured darker complexions than the residents of Cariath, making the White Tigers distinctive in appearance.

Though August's party was small, they drew gazes from all around. It was not uncommon to see men on horseback, so Leah wondered if they could identify their origins as Cariath. Though August and most of his men were wearing plain clothes, some had their white and black-striped Guardian uniforms draped visibly across their saddles. Or it could be some recognized August, with his signature head of ginger hair, or they were simply gawking at Kirin, who was riding in front of Maor.

Or it could be me, Leah thought wryly. Since when did women ride with warriors? Whatever it was that garnered attention, they were surely a strange sight to behold.

August guided Simi unwaveringly through the well-paved paths of En-doire as the rest of his men fell in line behind him. Leah did not ask if he remembered the town from his previous visits or if he studied the maps to ensure he knew the roads. Either way, she recognized his good judgment in this regard. They did not need to inquire for directions, which would only draw more notice and emphasize that they were foreigners.

The town hall was unexceptional in size, but Leah recognized it for the stately design. While much of the Bastion's architecture was grandiose, En-doire's town hall resembled the old forts of warrior tribes, which Papa would describe in his tales of the Guardians.

Word traveled quickly, or security was simply high after the Oath-breakers' recent breach. A contingent of uniformed guards lined up before the town hall halted their movement. At August's signal, his men dismounted. Leah clambered off Simi — not too gracefully, but at least she was capable of descending without aid now. As August swung himself off after her in a fluid motion, his hand brushed over hers purposefully and she drew her gaze up to his in surprise.

He stared back at her for a moment, his face taut. "Be brave," he murmured, and then looked away.

Before Leah could grasp his meaning, he was striding out to meet the En-doire guards. The rest of his men led their horses in behind him, and Leah found herself walking between Jasper and Maor, who was guiding his own horse and Simi. She spared a glance at their surroundings, and realized they garnered a growing audience, straining to see what would unfold.

The line of guards parted way as an older man stepped out from their midst. He wore a regal brown and green robe, and his gray shoulder-length hair was twisted in a tight braid. August bowed his head as they met in the middle.

"Marcum," he greeted.

"August." The other man's voice was heavy and coarse, and he spoke with a rough accent. He did not bow.

"May harmony and wisdom plant deep roots in your soil."

A thin smile touched Marcum's lips, though Leah thought it held an edge of cruelty. "Your mother taught you well."

It was a strange comment to Leah's ears, and August did not seem to acknowledge it. "I do not know what rumors have reached your ears, Marcum, but I am here in peace, seeking to forge our alliance anew."

Marcum raised a bushy eyebrow, his expression unchanged. "I have heard some troubling news."

August turned his head briefly and Jasper moved to untie the sword on Simi's saddle. Leah's breath caught in her throat as he brought it forward and offered it to Marcum. The other man took the blade and hardly flinched.

"As a token of our goodwill, we recovered your stolen treasure,"

August said.

"How did you know it was stolen?" Marcum countered, his steely eyes fixed on Leah's husband.

"Two men from En-doire, Lawrence and Lee, traveled to Cariath to inform us of the tale. A party of my men returned with them to seek your aid in combating the Oath-breakers."

At the mention of Oath-breakers, whispering and rustling broke out from the spectators around them. Leah glanced to either side of her and observed the uneasy expressions people wore. While some appeared caught in low, heated conversations, most were still absorbed by the dialogue between Marcum and August.

"Yet, I do not see Lawrence and Lee with you."

Leah nudged Maor's arm beside her, and his eyes slanted in her direction. "He is as obstinate as August," she muttered beneath her breath.

The edge of Maor's mouth curled slightly, but it was a grim smirk. "But his heart is not half as good."

"Quite a judgment," she mumbled.

Her hands grew damp and cold with worry. *Be brave.* What did August anticipate would happen in En-doire? Offhandedly, it occurred to Leah that his gesture—brushing her hand, wishing her courage—was almost tender. They had exchanged few words since her revelation about Benedict. She felt a stir of frustration until she remembered they were hanging in a precarious balance. She did not fully understand what possible danger they were in.

August was speaking as Leah returned to the interchange between the two men. "Your scouts are missing. Lawrence and Lee accompanied two of my men to search out the land while we rode here first." He paused. "We cannot afford to waste time." Leah heard the subtle challenge in his voice.

"I am not in the habit of wasting time," Marcum intoned.

His gaze shifted away from August to scan the small row of his men behind him, resting a moment longer on Leah and something behind her. She guessed it was Hansuke, who remained silent and watchful. Still, Marcum wore an impenetrable expression. He lifted his hand to summon two of the guards behind him. They placed themselves squarely on either side of August.

"When Lawrence and Lee return with my scouts, we can listen to your tale of woe again," he said severely.

Ignoring the guards beside him, August stepped forward to close the space between him and Marcum. The other man did not move, though the guards seized August's shoulders in alarm.

"If you think I robbed you, then accuse me. Unless you are afraid to."

Leah's breath hitched in her throat as she numbly watched the scene unfold. August's tone was dangerous and daring, and she briefly recalled his warning to not provoke the Black Tortoise. Even she could see he was treading a perilous line.

But Marcum appeared unaffected. "Afraid? Boy, you are the one begging me for aid." Disdain brimmed in his voice. "My men saw you pilfer the town hall and leave the guards for dead. You have a brazen nerve to come in the guise of friendship and demand an alliance."

"It was Benedict," August said flatly, and Leah heard a mixture of cold disregard and thinly veiled anguish bleed into his words.

"You would lay this on your little brother?"

"He fell in with Nimrod months ago. We guarded that knowledge."

Marcum cocked his head, but his countenance remained the same. "I remember you two running around here once as children. How you protected that boy so." He shook his head. "What would your mother say, August?"

August recoiled visibly, and Leah realized her fists were clenched so tightly her nails dug red marks into her skin. Her face flushed hot with indignation and resentment, and she felt an unholy urge to rush at Marcum and give him a hard blow to the face.

"What a devil," she breathed.

"Quite a judgment," Maor returned lightly, though his face was drawn and haggard.

"Take him inside," Marcum was saying, motioning at the town hall. The guards beside August prodded him forward warily, but he followed them without resistance.

"Put the rest of his men in the cells."

The remaining guards circled Leah, Maor, the rest of the men and their horses. Leah's gaze continued to follow August. He did not give a backward glance, even as he was about to disappear into the town hall. A reckless impulse surged in her, and she suddenly had half a mind to dash after him—and if she could not reach him, at least give Marcum the blow he dearly deserved.

She felt a hand encircle her wrist tightly. Maor looked at her seriously. "No."

"How did you—" She faltered.

"August warned me. And I figured. My conception of Carmel and the seaside towns is falling apart. What happened to soft, plump women, filled with cakes and gossip?"

His attempt at jesting was feeble, but Leah tried to smile. "Just as we have made you into myths, so you have made us."

Around them, the crowd was dispersing and many were engaged in animated chatter. Leah dully thought the events of the evening had provided enough gossip to last for weeks.

Half the guards led their horses away, while the other half motioned for August's party to follow them. Leah's legs felt heavy as she trudged along with the men.

But Kirin appeared beside her, knee-high, and tapped her with his paw. "Do not underestimate August."

"Kirin is right." Maor placed a reassuring hand on Leah's back. "He may surprise you yet."

Leah laughed weakly. "He always does."

She whispered a wordless prayer as they walked down the dimly lit roads of En-doire, strengthening her resolve. *Be brave.* She would not fail August on this one.

~~~~~~~

En-doire's prison was dank and cold. Leah was grateful they hustled all of their party into a large cell. She could not imagine sitting alone in one of these. Maor remained close by her side, and she caught him stealing furtive glances at her. She wondered if August privately instructed him to look after her, or if it was his natural instinct. Regardless, his steady presence was a salve to her troubled spirit.

Most of the men sprawled across the floor, perhaps trying to catch some sleep, but rustling gave away their restlessness. Maor tried to engage her in hushed conversation, but her mind was elsewhere and they fell silent as well.

Leah continually replayed August's exchange with Marcum, the scene vivid in her mind. August's sure, strong words and Marcum's cold tone still rang in her ears. A gnawing thought grew in her mind.

"Why does Marcum hate August?" she asked suddenly, breaking the quiet lull. A few men stirred from their places.

"He thinks he's the traitor who stole the sword," someone called out, but Leah could not distinguish whom the voice belonged to.

"No, but that would prompt outrage." Leah shook her head. "There was something else — an edge of old bitterness — when he spoke. I'm not sure how to describe it."

"Ah," Maor said, sitting beside her. "You have keen eyes and ears."

She turned to face him. "So, there is a story behind it?"

He chuckled grimly. "There is a story behind every feud and rivalry. And — well, I think every story circles home to the same things."

"August said before that Marcum did not like him."

"Marcum doesn't like any of the Foxes. Save, perhaps, Lila. She was from En-doire originally."

Realization dawned on her. "He loved Lila. But she chose Arthur."

Jasper chuckled from the corner. "This is the danger of women. They see too clearly."

"Yes," Maor confirmed. "Cariath and En-doire were still on good terms, but their marriage soured family relations. Lila's father wanted her to marry Marcum instead. But Lila still brought August and Ben to En-doire often when they were young. She was the bridge. After her death, connections grew colder between our two camps."

"Stars, what kind of a family did I marry into?" Leah murmured, her head swimming.

"Surely, you do not come from a simple family either." Hansuke spoke up for the first time. Some of the others stirred at hearing his voice.

What a strange statement. She found his eyes in the dark. "Trust me, we are simpler than the Foxes. So, what are we going to do?" she asked, changing the subject abruptly. Anxiety coursed through her as she thought of August. "Does August think he can talk any sense into Marcum?"

"We could engineer a breakout." Kirin glanced at Hansuke. "I heard you defeated Benedict and Justin single-handedly without a weapon. Do you have other tricks?"

The Falcon Guardian returned a somber look. "A warrior is not made by his weapons. I would not call what we do *tricks*."

Kirin huffed, but before he could give a response, Maor cut him off. "We will wait for Stephen to come back with the scouts. We hope. We don't need to make things worse." He glanced around, his gaze settling on Leah. "I suggest you all try to sleep a little. There's not much we can do."

No one spoke after that. Maor and Jasper bundled their robes together and handed them to Leah to use as a cushion.

Accepting it gratefully, she lay down, and a wave of drowsiness overtook her.

"Will August be all right?" she murmured.

She heard Maor give an affirmative. Another disconnected thought entered her mind.

"Maor, who is Justin?"

A long silence followed, and she thought he had fallen asleep.

But his quiet answer came eventually.

"He's a fool."

CHAPTER 29

Without windows in their cell, Leah could not tell when it was daybreak. The same dark walls met her gaze when she awoke. Her muscles felt stiff, the stone floor cold and hard against her back.

Maor sat nearby, carrying on a hushed conversation with Jasper. He glanced her way every so often and offered a faint smile when she caught his gaze.

"Did you sleep?"

Leah pulled herself upright. She was the last one to rise. "Better than I expected, inside a prison. But then, I never expected to end up inside a prison."

"None of us would," Jasper piped. "Except Maor."

A few of the men chuckled and Leah managed a short laugh. Her chest clenched as the events of the previous day rushed back into her mind. Where was August now? What would Marcum do to him? What would become of them all? She noticed Hansuke, Kirin and a few others glance her way, so she tried to disguise her anxiety.

Maor seemed to guess some of her thoughts. "Marcum is a bit of a beast, but he's not without honor. He won't hurt August."

Her response caught in her throat. Mortified, she felt a sudden urge to cry. She did not know if it was out of concern for August, herself, exhaustion, or a culmination of recent events. Leah swallowed her words and just nodded, hoping Maor would grasp her appreciation.

Thankfully, Kirin rescued her from embarrassment as he spoke up. "Yes, but every moment Marcum delays, the Oath-breakers grow closer to achieving their goal."

The men went into a discussion of Nimrod's possible tactics and plans, which allowed Leah to collect herself. Only Hansuke remained quiet, though she could tell he was paying attention to the conversation.

Kirin, however, broke off from the group and hopped to Leah's side.

"Did August tell you that his father rescued me after I was cast out of the immortal realm?" he asked quietly.

She looked down at him in surprise. "Yes. He did."

"Among the faerie-kind, that means I owe him a life debt. I include his family in that—Arthur saved me from death, but they gave me a life. As long as I have breath, I would not let anything happen to August."

Tears stung the back of Leah's eyes, but she blinked them away. Brotherhood and sacrifice shone brightly behind the Guardians' hard-edged justice and pride. She felt the urge to ruffle Kirin's fur out of affection but resisted, unsure if that would be an affront to his dignity.

"He would not let anything happen to you either." Kirin was still looking at her with his dark-orbed eyes. "I had a dream about you, Leah. Before August brought you back to the Bastion."

"What?" A shiver went through her. She remembered how August said Kirin had the gift of dreams.

"I didn't know who you were then. But I told August there was a woman in the seaside towns whose fate was linked with his. He needed to protect her, at any cost."

"But—how did you know it was me? How did *he* know?"

"Neither of us knew. I'm not a prophet, and my dreams are more like shadowy outlines, a vague glimpse into the future. All I told August was that she would be someone who would change him, and he her. I didn't even consider that he might marry her. That was all him—improvising, or whatever you might call it." Kirin paused, fluffing the fur around his ears. "All I can say is, as I've gotten to know you, you color in the outlines well."

Leah closed her eyes, turning over this new piece of information. August had said he trusted in Kirin's dreams. Did he go to Carmel with the express purpose of finding this mystery woman? And could it possibly be her?

"Did you tell him before he planned his trip?" she asked quietly.

Kirin did not seem surprised by her question. "No. He was going already. I told him the night before. Leah, I only tell you because I know you are a woman of faith. Some may call it fate or coincidence that brought you together, and you might call it divine Providence. You can trust your God if you would like, and I tell you, you can trust your husband." He flashed what looked like a smirk to her. "He might believe me, but he didn't marry you just because a squirrel had a dream."

She put her hand on Kirin's back, feeling the soft fur tickle her palm. "Thank you."

He dipped his head in acknowledgment and left to talk with Maor and Jasper.

The day passed in a haze, and she marked the time by when the guards delivered meals. She imagined prison food to be stale bread and dirty water, but they received fresh rolls, cut vegetables, and venison. The meat was warm and well-sauced.

"We are still fellow Guardians," Maor said, by way of explanation as they ate. "Not common criminals."

Her thoughts drifted to Papa, Mama, Nyssa and Shay throughout the day, imagining them nestled in a new cottage. It had been less than two months since she left home, but Carmel felt like a distant world now, a past life that was slipping through her fingers.

Nyssa might be engaged to Mr. Langford by now. Had Jessie or Shay met any eligible gentlemen? Laurel Lane and Mr. Whitefield should be married already. She wondered what Papa had done with their collection of Guardian tales. Leah felt a rush of affection for the people at home, followed by an ache for the life she was missing.

But her mind kept returning to August, replaying yesterday's events in an endless cycle. How he brushed her hand, how he faced Marcum boldly, and how the other man spoke of Benedict. *What would your mother say?* Leah felt his words graze her like a sharp knife, and she wondered how deeply they cut August.

Where was he now? She imagined him in chains, or alone in a cell, and it hurt her.

It must have been nearly dusk when the doors clattered open. Leah expected it was dinnertime, but no platter came through. Instead, Lawrence, Lee, and Stephen appeared. Their faces were ruddy from exertion and hair damp with sweat, but they appeared grimly satisfied.

The men leapt to their feet. Maor rushed to clap Stephen on the shoulder.

"You made it! I thought we were in for a few more nights here, eating Marcum's cooking and imagining Nimrod traipsing through the immortal realm."

Lawrence and Lee wore embarrassed expressions. Stephen rolled his eyes upward, but smirked. "Ye of little faith. There was a reason August sent me to find the scouts instead of you."

"Where is August?" Leah asked, coming beside Maor.

"He's with Marcum," Lawrence chimed in. "We recovered the En-doire scouts and vouched for August's story. They are preparing a feast for us all tonight."

"Ah, so now Marcum wants to be friends," Maor said beneath his breath.

"After what he did yesterday?" Leah muttered darkly.

He grinned again. "Play nice, Mrs. Fox. It's all politics." In a quieter tone that only she could hear, he added, "Though I heartily approve of your grudge."

~~~~~

Despite a sour first impression of En-doire and the Black Tortoise Guardians, Leah admitted they could throw a magnificent party.

After allowing all the Tiger Guardians and Leah to take hot baths, they gathered in an outdoor arena lined with long cherrywood tables. Strings of lanterns hung overhead, set against the darkening skies. The liberal spread of food rivaled the Old Fox's in variety and decadence.

Over a dozen Tortoise Guardians milled around. A few wore bandages and looked weather-beaten, but they were all conversing energetically. Leah assumed some were the captured scouts just returned home. August's men were beginning to mingle with them, and she hid a smile as she watched Kirin race down the benches, his fur still wet from a washing.

Leah felt terribly out of place when she arrived. They had given her a maid to guide her to the baths and lead her back out, but she entered the feast alone.

August, who stood near Marcum, saw her and immediately came to her. They stood facing each other, and for a moment, all the old awkwardness between them resurfaced. His expression was unreadable, and Leah did not know what to say, conscious of her arms hanging limply at her side.

Then, without thinking, she closed the gap between them, putting her hands on his shoulders and leaned against his chest.

He stiffened for a brief second before his body relaxed and he wrapped his arms around her. Warmth flooded through her. They had shared a chaste kiss at the wedding and she had been pressed against him for hours on horseback, but August had never really held her. Not like this.

It felt like a silent promise, a fierce assurance of his protection.

"Are you hurt?" she asked quietly.

He loosened his grip and stepped back slightly, turning his head to look at her. "No. I daresay Marcum treated me better than the rest of you. I was in a guest chamber, just with guards outside."

Leah let out a breath. "Good."

His expression softened. "You didn't need to worry about me." He hesitated, then reached up to brush a strand of hair out of her face. "I'm sorry for what I've put you through. But Maor told me he'd never seen a stronger woman."

"I think you're getting better at apologies." She grinned wanly. He returned the smile, and she was relieved to see it was genuine. "Maor probably thinks I'm insane."

"How could I not?"

Maor and Stephen were coming toward them, just within earshot.

Crossing his arms, Maor looked at August. "I didn't tell you yet that she would have made a run at Marcum if I didn't stop her. Imagine what *that* would have done to Tiger-Tortoise relations for another generation."

Stephen and August both stared at her, taken aback.

Leah flushed. "Good thing you stopped me," she mumbled.

"Almost wish I hadn't," he quipped in reply.

They were interrupted by a drum roll. The Guardians fell silent, and Marcum stood on top of a dais, commanding their attention.

"We welcome August Fox and the White Tiger Guardians to En-doire and thank you for recovering our scouts." Some of the Tortoise Guardians clapped. "In celebration, I would like to commence this feast in honor of our guests, our Guardians who have come home safely, and a renewed friendship with Cariath." Marcum lifted a goblet in salute. "Let us eat!"

A cheer went up, and Leah noticed that the number of people in the arena had increased. More women were milling around with children, likely the families of the returned Tortoise Guardians.

"See, he's not horrible," Maor said.

August gave him a stern look. "I'm going to introduce Leah to him later."

"Don't hit him too hard," Maor whispered, so only she could hear. She stifled a laugh.

They filled up their platters with steaming potatoes, meat, and hearty soups. It was the best meal Leah had eaten since leaving Cariath, and she relished each bite.

She sat at a table with August, Maor, Stephen, Kirin, Hansuke, Jasper, and a few Tortoise families. August seemed lighthearted in conversation with his men, so she quietly hoped the sting of Marcum's words yesterday had worn off.

As nighttime descended like an inky scroll with bright stars across the sky, they lit bonfires around the arena. A band of musicians played and Leah watched them in fascination. Their instruments were unfamiliar, but the music touched something deep inside her.

"En-doire's musical tradition has no equal," Kirin noted. A few of the Tiger Guardians shot him hard looks, but Leah noticed that no one disagreed.

She glanced at August. "Did your mother play music, then?" she asked softly.

He glanced at her before his gaze drifted off. "She would sing."

Leah suddenly realized she never heard music in Cariath. It was common in Carmel at balls and weddings, and even her sisters played piano at home. But August's home was barren in melody. She imagined the years when Lila would sing, a lone voice filling Fox Manor with a beautiful foreign sound, planting roots from En-doire inside her sons.

Well into the evening, Marcum stood up for another announcement. The music died down.

"Let us drink to our friendship!" He raised his goblet and gestured vaguely towards Leah and August's table. "Our friends in Cariath are fighting for Japha against those Oath-breakers." His voice was clear, but his words slurred slightly. "Black Tortoise will not sit aside! Arthur — August," he corrected, "I will give you a contingent of my men to command. Take the battle to those fiends!" He wobbled slightly and sat down to raucous applause. The music picked up again.

"Had a bit too much wine, I think," Jasper said with a smirk. He raised his glass, and everyone at their table did the same. "But mission accomplished. Here's to taking the battle to those fiends!"

They laughed and drank. Leah swallowed a mouthful of red wine, feeling a heady rush.

She felt Hansuke's gaze on her. He had been quiet through most of the meal, and she squirmed in discomfort under his scrutiny. Nothing malevolent, but given how they met and his quiet intensity, Leah was still not used to his presence.

But he was only trying to get her attention. "Listen," he said.

She looked at him, confused, until she realized the music had changed. It was a slow, hypnotic melody now, and a chorus of voices sang.

Between the turning of Light and Dark
I walk in Eden's shadow-gray.
Where men and gods, through ceaseless strife,
chase winds of vengeance in vain.

O dream in a dream, what is truth?
that stands from age to age.
Though mortal empires rise and fall,
the eternal realm remains.

Something stirred inside her. It sounded so familiar... Leah looked at Hansuke again.

"The words on the blade," he said, and the pieces fell into place. She drew in a sharp breath.

Before the passing of the Night
I feel the worlds groaning in place.
Will the songbirds herald hope,
and sing a verse of dawning Day?

O legend of legends, what is truth?
that guides the seeker's way.
Teach me to be pure in heart
and open the immortal gate.

Some of the others seemed caught up in the music, but the significance was lost on them. As it drew to an end, Leah turned to grip August's arm.

"Those lyrics," she began, but broke off at a warning glance from him. She read the comprehension in his eyes.

"I know," he murmured.

August leaned across the table toward Hansuke, so only he and Leah could hear him. "I need to ask you. What is the key from Vermilion Falcon?"

Leah held her breath as she watched Hansuke, who looked back at them both unblinking.

Finally, he leaned forward too. "The heir of Arieh."

CHAPTER 30

West of the Nathair River, Island of Japha.
Month of Hope: Third week, Fire-Day.

When they reached the west side of the Nathair River and docked, it did not take long for Benedict's scouts to catch scent of Nimrod's party. When the Oath-breakers first left Cariath, they designed a system of obscure markings to identify their trails to one another.

The reunion between the two groups was lackluster. They met deep in the forest bordering the Nathair, the high leafy canopy sheltering them from the midday heat. While a few men greeted each other with enthusiasm, many eyed others with some suspicion. A large portion of Nimrod's men were blindly loyal to him, and they did not disguise their scorn toward Benedict, especially after he was named second-in-command. Hound was one of the few in Benedict's party who fell into that group, and he quickly slipped in with Nimrod's followers.

Justin, Traven, Gerard, and a few others stuck close to Benedict's side. The remainder of the men were more aloof. Perhaps some had their own vendetta against the faerie-kind, or they simply despised the Old Fox's leadership.

Nimrod strode forward to meet them. A silver cloth draped over something in his hand, and Benedict had a good idea what was underneath.

"Did you collect yours?" Nimrod asked without preamble.

"Good day to you too," he returned smoothly. "Yes, I have it."

Nimrod flung the cover off to reveal a small lantern, the sides inked with dragon patterns. The other men hovering around them strained for a good view of it.

"I lost ten men for this in Ebene." There was no real remorse in his voice, and his tone stung Benedict. Disgust coursed through him.

"I lost one," he said quietly. "And that should not have happened."

"Where is it?" Nimrod brushed off his last statement as if he had not even said it.

Benedict tapped his temple. "Here. It's a song."

The other man narrowed his eyes. "Do not play games with me, Fox."

While the others were milling around and engaged in their own conversations, the chatter lessened as they sensed the tension. Benedict saw Justin and Gerard out of the corner of his eye. They were in clear earshot but appeared to busy themselves with reorganizing their packs.

"*The land unbound by time and space / opens only to the one who knows / the*

Light, the Song and Mortal Gate," Benedict quoted. "It's a song. What would you like, for me to deliver it on a piece of paper to you?"

He knew his flippant irreverence would anger Nimrod, but a reckless spirit seized him, similar to the first evening when he asked to be second-in-command. One way or another, they were nearing the end. Benedict took in Nimrod's black-clad, stern figure. Even in Cariath, he intimidated other Guardians. But in light of the cataclysmic events they were moving toward, he was almost an insignificant pawn, masquerading as a leader.

"Where did you find it?"

Benedict had hardly bothered to rehearse the story, but it came out naturally. "It was graven on an old relic in the Tortoise Treasury. A few of my men memorized it to be safe." It was not, strictly, a lie. While someone like Hound could color in the tale further, he did not think Nimrod would care for the details.

"We also encountered a Vermilion Falcon Guardian," he continued. "He told us what the last key was."

He gambled right. Even Nimrod's unreadable facade broke with this revelation, his thoughts moving off of the song entirely.

"What?"

"His name was Hansuke. He was sent from the Dammim to investigate the current state of Guardian affairs. We convinced him long enough that the Guardians were seeking to reunite the keys, but the Falcons have some sorcery of their own. I think he saw through the deception and escaped."

"And the key?"

"It's a person." Benedict allowed the words to sink in, and he could see Nimrod reciting the clue mentally, a light turning on in his mind. "But we do not know who."

He saw more of Nimrod's men gathering around, now unabashedly listening in. Benedict gave a quick recounting to all of them about how they crossed paths with Hansuke, up through his escape and their capture of the *Meadowlark*. The story drew a few sharp exclamations from even the stoic Oath-breakers. Of course, he left out the details of how he escaped and their entire encounter with Leah, which only Justin was privy to.

Nimrod was also listening intently. "So, August has gone to En-doire too, if the *Meadowlark* was there," he surmised. "Likely with some of his best men. Now is the time to move on the Bastion."

Benedict stared at him. "Did you hear what I said about the Vermilion riddle? We don't know who the key is."

"We were ready to go without it. You know the Mortal Gate is in Cariath, right?" He raised a brow. "In Fox Manor?"

"It's a guess," Benedict said tightly. "I have no more confirmation than you do."

"We have built our entire mission upon risks and guesses, yet we are closer to opening the Faerie realm than any mortal in ages." A dark gleam entered his eye. "As long as you swear you have the song, we ride."

"I'm not a liar, Nimrod."

A taut silence stretched between them and the conversations nearby ceased.

"I can't say I am confident about that. But I trust your lust for vengeance is still hot." Nimrod raised an eyebrow.

Benedict did not flinch, but his gut coiled. Unwanted images of his mother, Fox Manor, and his first dark night with the Oath-breakers flashed through his mind. He recalled Nimrod's words when he boldly asked for the position of second-in-command. *It is a hot and bloody motive that is hard to exhaust.*

"Prove to me you have the song," Nimrod said, when Benedict did not reply.

He glanced around and motioned for Traven to come forward. A fearful look swept over the man's face, but he obeyed.

"Traven is from En-doire originally," Benedict said, "and he can put the words to song." He nodded to his companion, offering a tight smile of encouragement.

Nimrod turned his attention to Traven, who drew in a shaky breath.

Between the turning of Light and Dark
I walk in Eden's shadow-gray.
Where men and gods, through ceaseless strife,
chase winds of vengeance in vain.

O dream in a dream, what is truth
that stands from age to age?
Though mortal empires rise and fall,
the eternal realm remains.

Traven was not a particularly talented singer, but Benedict felt the melody reach deep into his being with a strange and disconcerting power. It almost *vibrated* through the woods and trees, as if the song plucked on the soul-strings of the earth itself.

A few of the men around him looked distant, carried away by the music, though Nimrod's expression remained the same.

"There is more, if you would like to hear it," Traven said quietly, after a pause.

Nimrod returned his attention to Benedict. "That will do."

"You really want to go to Cariath now?" Benedict asked, though he knew it was a useless question.

"It is time for our old friends and the faerie-kind to fear us." Nimrod glanced around and raised his voice. "Gather your things, we prepare to complete our mission."

~~~~~

Nimrod and his men brought all the horses they managed to capture from the Guardians. Benedict settled comfortably into the saddle of one, realizing how sore his feet were from weeks of traveling on foot. He had always loved horseback riding, yet coaxing his unfamiliar steed to follow his guidance made him wish he still had Simi.

Justin rode beside him in silence for a good measure of the time. Gerard was behind him, cracking a morbid joke about death and destruction once in a while to Traven, who did not seem to appreciate his sense of humor.

Hound had sidled up to ride with Nimrod near the front of the pack. He kept up a constant stream of speech, which the others could not hear, but Nimrod appeared disinterested. *Hard to blame him for that,* Benedict thought dryly. Hound was a faithful lapdog and a deadly warrior, but lacking intellectual acuity. He was useful to Nimrod, but nowhere near an equal to their leader.

By nightfall, the Cariath Mountains came into sight. A brilliant sunset scraped the horizon with crimson and orange hues, igniting an old ache inside Benedict's chest.

"Nothing quite like that view," Gerard commented from behind them.

Justin glanced over at Benedict. "Are you ready for this?" he said in a low voice.

"Which part?" he retorted. *Seeing the Old Fox, plundering his old home, or potentially unlocking the immortal realm to a madman?*

"I heard Nimrod earlier. What he said about trusting your lust for vengeance."

"He calls it vengeance. Maybe it's just justice. Justice that no other hand is willing to deal out." Benedict stared at his friend. "Guardians are peacekeepers. But who will repay the faerie for their crimes against us?"

"You are playing God, Benedict."

The words emerged from Justin not as a warning, but resigned commentary. They had come too far.

"Because God is silent," he said, soft yet cutting.

"And if Nimrod enters the immortal realm? Is that worth the price?"

"You think Nimrod can seize control in the faerie world? They are immortals, not weaklings. He will be dead before he claims a single slave."

Justin did not look away, his expression ever unreadable. "And you?"

"I haven't made plans for a long life ahead," he said dryly, dispensing some of Gerard's dark humor. Benedict paused, then dropped his gaze. "I would wish otherwise for you, though."

They fell silent again after that, watching the skies dip into mahogany as dusk descended.

CHAPTER 31

They threaded through Cariath Valley and reached the edge of the Bastion without meeting any resistance. Benedict felt uneasy. Disguised in their White Tiger colors, they had split into small groups of two or three and followed different paths through the valley. They had the advantage of surprise, and most of their men knew Cariath like the back of their hands. But the Old Fox never left their home defenseless. His father was an expert with clever snares, and more than that, he had a connection with the Bastion, a sixth sense for the land that extended to the edges of their home. Benedict knew each of the Guardian camps had some innate protection or power, woven into it by the faerie-kind. A few could tap into it, like the Old Fox, who had always known if danger was impending in the Bastion. Benedict's stomach knotted a little. He felt certain they could not have come this far undetected.

Not all of them had crossed the mountains. Nimrod had left three dozen men to scout the foothills beyond Cariath. Nimrod, Benedict and about two dozen of them came in. Their small troupe was not equipped to fight through the full strength of the White Tiger Guardians. They needed to infiltrate quietly.

The day was bright as they crossed into the Bastion. Benedict rode beside Justin in silence. He wore an oversized hood that covered his face. He and Nimrod were the most recognizable, especially as they entered more familiar territory.

"Someone must have been alerted to our presence," Justin said.

Benedict shrugged, though his companion was not looking at him. "Maybe. Or we've done better than expected. We hit the Tortoise Treasury successfully, and we actually know this place."

"Your father is far better than Marcum."

He did not reply to this. Besides him, Benedict knew Justin would be least convinced that they could outsmart the Old Fox. Justin was one of the few who knew of his father's gift.

Since they entered Cariath, he felt cold and distant. The memories his old home evoked seemed to belong to another person. They were part of him, yet emotionally disconnected. Benedict could not risk allowing them to touch him.

They met Nimrod, Hound, Gerard, Traven and a few others deep inside the Bastion, not far from Fox Manor. By now, Benedict agreed with Justin—it was impossible they came this far without arousing any suspicion.

211

Nimrod, however, seemed flushed with pride. "I was ready to fight. A disappointing defense from the Old Fox."

"Don't boast yet," Benedict warned.

Nimrod ignored him. "I've spread the others around the Bastion to keep watch. I say five of us go search out the Gate."

"Fine. I want Justin, Traven, and Gerard."

"You're not in charge, Fox."

"Justin has searched for the Gate with me before, so after me, he's most familiar with the manor. Traven knows the song. Gerard is one of our best fighters." Benedict kept his tone neutral and light.

"Fine." Nimrod glared but conceded. "These three and Hound." Hound stirred proudly.

"You don't need to come yourself then."

Their leader laughed grimly. "Good joke, Fox." He swept the silver lantern from Ebene out in front of him. "I have one of the keys."

Benedict shrugged. "If you insist. We should go."

Nimrod instructed the others to disperse nearby and stand ready should anything go wrong. *So much could go wrong.*

The six of them filed through a secret backdoor to Fox Manor, hidden in the hedges. Benedict stifled a twinge at the betrayal. The Old Fox would not tell even the other Marshals of that entrance—it was a secret that belonged to the family. Outside of the Foxes, only Justin and Alain had known of it.

It felt defiled now, with Nimrod and Hound coming in. But Benedict shook off the thought. He had already done far worse than divulge a family secret.

"We've searched most the floors already," he muttered, "and never found anything."

"But you didn't have this."

Nimrod handed the lantern to Hound while he struck a match. Even though it was well-lit inside, Benedict flinched at the conspicuous brightness of the flame.

The silver edges glowed orange with heat, and shadows danced across the dragon imprints on the outside as the fire flickered. They watched it closely, holding their breaths, waiting for some magic to take hold.

But it burned like any other lantern, and in the middle of the day, it was next to useless. Nimrod cursed.

"It might not do anything until we're in the right place," Gerard said, eyeing him carefully.

"Keep it lit as we walk through the halls," Justin suggested.

"Is the Old Fox home?" Hound asked. He wore a hungry look and Benedict felt a spark of hatred.

"Even if he is, there are six of us." Nimrod seemed unconcerned. "Show us the way, Fox."

As Benedict led them down the halls, familiar walls rose up around them. Most of them were bare, unadorned by decoration or artwork, but he felt like they had accusing eyes burrowed inside. *How dare you come back after what you've done? How dare you bring* them?

Beside him, Justin's face was unreadable as ever. He had spent many of his early years in this home too, treated like a son by the Old Fox and Lila. Was his conscience cutting into him?

The Manor seemed empty. They pressed against the walls as they went down the hallways, occasionally knocking against them for hollow sounds. He heard Traven humming the Song to himself nervously, perhaps afraid he would forget it in their moment of need.

Nimrod and Hound were both restless with frustration. They had traversed the common area, dining hall, and bedrooms. Benedict avoided entering his own, choosing to search his brother's instead. It was as austere as always, though a few dresses in the closet suggested a woman lived there too.

"There's nothing," Nimrod growled, rattling the lantern. Hound glowered at Benedict, as if this were his fault.

"Is there anywhere we've missed?" Traven spoke up nervously.

Benedict avoided Justin's gaze. Only he knew his old suspicion... yet they had never uncovered anything. He felt reluctant to say it aloud. Though he had brought Nimrod this far, something inside him struggled against giving away this last insight.

"There's one more room," he finally said. "We haven't searched the battle room yet."

The battle room was at the far end of the Manor, and he always felt there was something eerie about the place. August used it often for practice, and Justin never found anything off-putting about it, but Benedict avoided the area when he could.

He led them down the long corridor until they arrived at the old, scratched door. He gave it a heave with his shoulder and it popped open. They stepped inside.

The Old Fox looked up, his eyes finding Benedict first.

"Hello, Ben," he said quietly.

His chest clenched and the men behind him drew in sharp breaths. His father was standing behind the granite table, papers spread across it. Benedict's gaze darted around the circular room, but the Old Fox was alone.

Nimrod recovered first and moved in front of Benedict. "You know what we're here for."

Arthur Fox was unperturbed, straightening the papers on the table. His gaze moved past Nimrod and scoured the faces of the other men.

"Do I? Do you even know what all of your men are here for?"

"We're here for the Mortal Gate," Nimrod ground out. "We have the keys."

The Old Fox ignored him. "I know you were dissatisfied with the Guardian life, unhappy under my leadership." He drew himself up and met Nimrod's gaze with a steel look of his own. "But you have not quite learned critical lessons of leadership, have you, Nimrod?"

"I'm not here for your lectures, Fox."

"You want the Mortal Gate. You want what's beyond that." His words, cold and certain, sent a shiver through Benedict. "Yet you don't even know what's behind you."

Nimrod's hand went to his sword hilt. "I don't need your riddles either."

"Do your men actually support you? Are they after your same ends?" Arthur's gaze skimmed over them again. "Justin could have warned you I never leave the Cariath Mountains unwatched, even if you don't see my men. I don't think Gerard ever actually *liked* you." His tone went wry, and then grew serious. "And Benedict could have told you that only those I allow to step foot inside Fox Manor can even enter the estate. There is deep power embedded in Guardian strongholds you cannot understand, Nimrod—you, who found this life boring and unworthy. You are out of your depth hunting the immortal realm. And your men could have warned you." He paused. "Or, maybe they did warn you, and you were too arrogant to listen."

His words were clad in iron, hammering in Benedict's ears with strength and resolve. Something inside him stirred — *this* was the father he hero-worshipped in his boyhood. A man who could cut as deeply with his words as with his blade, and who could also turn those words effortlessly into breathtaking stories for his sons, sweet nothings for his wife, and raucous speeches for his parties.

Bitterness washed over him. Where had this resolve been when his mother was murdered?

He sensed Justin, Traven and Gerard go still behind him, but how they were affected he could not tell. Nimrod and Hound, however, were trembling with rage.

"We can lay this place to waste," Nimrod breathed, "and your words will be worthless. Unheard echoes in this room."

The sound of metal rang. Hound was advancing toward Arthur, who still did not move.

"I can finish him, Nimrod," he said.

"Stop." Nimrod turned to Benedict. "You do it."

Hound sheathed his sword and turned to Benedict, a feral grin on his face. He was savoring this moment.

Benedict could not look at Justin or the Old Fox, his mind spinning with his recurring dream. *I could be a prophet.* His arms felt limp and his hands cold.

He had thought of this scenario, of course. And he knew, no matter what happened, he could never kill his own father. If Nimrod did not know it, all the other men did. They had seen him barrel in front of Hound that night, throwing himself in front of his blade to stop the murder of En-doire scouts. Strangers. How could he lift a hand against his own flesh and blood?

But his dream replayed mercilessly, and the horror of it paralyzed him.

"You can't ask him to do that," he heard Traven say, and Benedict felt a touch of gratitude. It was a small thing, but brave for him.

Nimrod ignored him. "You swore me fealty, Fox."

Half-recovering himself, Benedict stared back at him. "Not like this."

The other man's eyes glittered darkly, but Benedict felt his mind and strength returning. What else could he lose? Nimrod could demote him — he almost laughed at that. As if anyone cared at this point.

Hound wore a look of triumph. "Then he's mine."

Many things happened at once. Benedict stared at him, still dazed and bewildered by his statement, before Hound pulled out his sword fully and charged toward the Old Fox. Nimrod did not even look at his lieutenant, his gaze still fixed on Benedict, who felt rooted to the ground. The air rushed around him as Justin dropped to the smooth hardwood floor and slid himself after Hound, angling toward his legs.

They collided, and Hound rolled onto the granite table, roaring with rage and sending a sheath of papers flying. Justin was on his feet immediately, and their blades met.

Hound was all fury and metal, but Justin was a skilled swordsman, parrying every stroke. No one else entered the fray. Gerard and Traven seemed unsure of what to do, and Nimrod looked as if he were calculating his next move.

The Old Fox still did not move from his position behind the table. "My Marshals knew when you were at the border of Cariath, and August is bringing reinforcements."

Nimrod turned his attention back to him. "We are not here for you, or Cariath." He held up the silver lantern. "We are here for something far more."

A grim smile touched Arthur's face. "I know what you're here for. The Guardians are charged to protect the realms, and you are going counter to all we stand for. You did not think we were good enough to stay with. Now you will find out what we are made of."

A knife, straight and steady, flew past Arthur's ear, missing him by a hairsbreadth.

To his credit, he hardly flinched. But Hound and Justin froze, looking over to Benedict, who still stood with his hand outstretched, an imprint of the knife's handle pressed into his skin.

"Enough," he said quietly, his eyes finally meeting his father's. "Tell us where the Gate is. You're right, I'm not here for Nimrod's agenda. I'm here to do what you could not — I'll avenge Mother."

215

CHAPTER 32

Nathair River, Island of Japha.
Month of Hope: Fourth week, Fire-Day.

Leah leaned over the prow of their ship, the *Voyager*, as the western bank of the Nathair River came into view. Her heartbeat quickened as she imagined what awaited them once they docked. Benedict and his men already had at least a week's time on them, and if they were ready for open battle, she could only imagine unhappy endings. While she had wavered between despair and hope that there was some goodness in him, the scales tipped in favor of the former when they found the *Meadowlark* stolen. The Tortoise Guardians had to convince the dock workers that Benedict did not represent Cariath, and the White Tiger Guardians were not the enemy.

The entire episode sent August into a dark mood. Maor explained his well-known affinity for the ship, and the theft as a rather low blow from Benedict.

"It's not exactly the worst thing he's done," Leah had said, though she guessed each jab pressed harder on August as they neared the inevitable confrontation.

When they had taken leave of En-doire after the feast, Marcum sent them off with two dozen of his men, including Lawrence and Lee. Leah was still reeling from Hansuke's revelation. *The heir of Arieh.* That verified Arieh was an actual, living figure, and he had children. None of the tales she read ever hinted at that. From August's reaction, she surmised he never heard such a theory either. There were too many people around them that night, so Hansuke did not share more. She wondered if August uncovered further information later, but she had not asked him yet. She kept to herself, poring over a book on Guardian legends she found aboard the ship and doodling sketches of the Pharan Desert, En-doire, and other scenes from their journey. August had spent most of their time on water closeted away, planning with his men. She was often asleep by the time he would come into the cabin each night.

As they neared the western bank, one of the Tortoise Guardians joined her at the prow. Few of them had spoken to her during the trip. August said En-doire was much more patriarchal and traditional than Cariath, and they did not know what to make of a woman traveling with warriors. Maor simply said they were intimidated by her because of her husband. Regardless, she did not mind — she had never enjoyed socializing.

"Lady Fox," he greeted. "I don't think I've had the pleasure yet. I'm

Hiram."

Leah remembered him from the feast, and as one of the leaders who vouched for August at the eastern dock. She smiled. "Call me Leah, please."

He inclined his head. "I learned I have you to thank for saving our lives."

She started, glancing at him. "What?" Then she saw the angry red welts on his wrist, peeking from his sleeves. Her gaze shot back to his face. "You were one of the captured scouts," she surmised.

"I led that expedition," he said ruefully.

"Well, it was Stephen, Lawrence and Lee who found you. I didn't do anything."

She felt the truth in that statement resonate painfully inside her. *What had she done on their journey but cause trouble for August?*

"They never would have come searching if you didn't alert them." He raised a brow, meeting her gaze. "I spoke to Hansuke—you would have been the most exciting person to meet, but an actual Falcon trumped August's wife, unfortunately—and he gave me the full story."

Leah looked over the deck, seeing Hansuke perched against the side of the ship, a solitary figure. Her thoughts flitted to that awful night by the shore with Benedict.

She smiled ruefully this time. "Maybe I would have been the more interesting of us two if you all knew August married a mad woman."

"Bravery is usually momentary madness." He smirked, half-jesting and half-genuine, some of his formal Guardian aura falling away.

"You don't need to spare my feelings," she said with a small laugh, "but thank you."

They fell silent for a while, staring at the long river snaking around them. The sun warmed Leah's face and back. Drowsiness washed over her.

Hiram did not leave, and she felt him glance at her every so often. Even in a half-conscious state, she realized he wanted to say something besides thanking her for her role in the scouts' rescue.

She caught his eye and he flinched ever-so-slightly.

"I can't help but ask," he said finally, looking down at the railing. "What happened to Benedict Fox?"

Her chest tightened. "Why are you asking me?" She worked to keep her tone neutral and followed his gaze to August.

"I can't ask your husband." He paused. "I knew of August and Benedict growing up. Not personally, but they visited En-doire often with their mother. They seemed...very close."

How you protected that boy so. What would your mother say? Leah heard Marcum's sly and distasteful words again.

"It's not my place to say," she replied, but not unkindly. "I never knew Benedict. I only met him that night by the river."

Hiram nodded, and she could tell he would not pry. But Leah did not fault his curiosity. She imagined his shock when the Oath-breakers took him captive and he found the familiar ginger-haired man among them. A man who was supposed to be a Guardian. A man who was once good and noble.

"What was he like?" she asked quietly. "When he captured your men."

He did not respond at once, and she wondered if he would not answer her either.

But he did speak, and his reply was not what she expected.

"He saved my life, actually."

Leah's eyes widened, turning to stare at him full on.

"One of his men caught our party and brought us in. He was raving, the bloodthirsty sort. I said something rude to him and he was ready to kill me—then Fox stepped in."

"Momentary madness on your part?" she asked absently, as her mind swam with a mental image of Hiram and Benedict.

"Something of the sort. Fox met the man blade-to-blade to stop him. Then gave a little speech on not killing in cold blood." His face was grim as he remembered.

"Did you say something to him after? To Benedict?"

A bitter laugh choked up his throat. "Like a thank you?" he said caustically. Seeing Leah's expression, he softened. "I had nothing to say to Benedict Fox. I was ready to die there. I did not need a twisted man's mercy."

"But—"

"I've heard you're new to Cariath and the Guardian ways, Leah. There is no redemption for an Oath-breaker." His words were hard and final.

Leah shrank away slightly, taken aback but not entirely shocked by the change in his demeanor. When Hiram began his story, she thought he had asked about Benedict because he noted the conflict in her brother-in-law.

But it didn't matter to Hiram that Benedict spared his life. It would count for nothing if they ever met again. That was the iron resolve of a Guardian.

Leah imagined that resolve inside August coexisting with his love for his brother. Eventually, one would burn the other out.

Around midday the *Voyager* pulled into dock on the other side of the Nathair. As they unloaded, she caught up with August, who was strapping a pack of supplies onto Simi's back. He gave her a small smile, but his mind seemed elsewhere.

"I saw you talking to Hiram," he noted.

"Yes." She hesitated, not wanting to bring up the content of their conversation. "I didn't realize he was one of the captured scouts," was all she said.

August nodded.

Leah dropped her voice to a whisper. "Did you learn anything else from Hansuke?" she asked urgently. "About the heir?" She had been waiting for a chance to question him, but they had spoken about little of consequence aboard the ship.

He stiffened, taking a long moment to reply. "Nothing notable," he said finally.

Frustrated, she could tell he was keeping something from her, but she restrained herself from nagging.

As all the men and Leah made ready to ride through the forest again, a shout cut through the trees. Leah was already seated behind August, and she froze and gripped his arm. His hand immediately went to his sword hilt.

"August Fox? *August Fox!*" the shout, once faint, grew louder.

The men rustled, glancing at each other, their hands sliding weapons into place. She saw Maor off to their side, nocking an arrow to his bow. In front of him, Kirin unsheathed his sword.

"Who goes there?" August demanded, his voice piercing in return.

Finally, a weather-beaten man emerged from behind a large trunk, wearing the black and white colors of the White Tiger Guardians.

"Thank God," he mumbled, near collapse. "Marshal Fox, the Oath-breakers are inside Cariath."

CHAPTER 33

A grim cloud of determination hung around August as they galloped through the open terrain. Though he seemed in control, and the White Tiger messenger said Cariath was prepared for Nimrod, Leah's stomach knotted.

She imagined the Oath-breakers burning through the Bastion. She thought of Melina and Jenifer and Arthur. And Benedict—would he really follow Nimrod to the bitter end? He had called her naive, but some small part of her could not believe it.

"Should we send for more reinforcements?" Lawrence called to August over the rushing wind.

Once the messenger delivered the news, they had wasted no time in racing through the forest. While August's men were shaken, the Black Tortoise Guardians seemed to be in greater shock, plunged into the reality of the Oath-breakers' actions.

"No time," he returned. "And we don't need it. Nimrod will not be trying to take Cariath by force."

August had resumed his stern Guardian mantle. He led them at breakneck speed and the others followed. Leah did not know what to say to him, and even Maor rode in silence beside them.

She spared a glance to her side, the wind sweeping into her eyes. Maor and Kirin were closest to them, their horse a length behind Simi. Lawrence, Hiram, and Hansuke rode to their far right. The Tortoise Guardians wore varying expressions of anxiety, while Hansuke maintained an unperturbed demeanor. Jasper, Stephen, Wren, and Lee were close on their tails, and the remaining Tiger and Tortoise Guardians trailed behind them.

They were a formidable party, maybe even the stuff of legends, and Leah briefly marveled that she rode among them. That she was married to the greatest of them.

The Cariath Mountains were drawing near. She felt August pulling on Simi's reigns slowly as they approached, and drew to a complete stop near the foothills. The horses trotted for a bit, their manes glistening with sweat as they stamped up whirls of dust.

August pulled around so he faced the others. "Stephen, I want you to lead a contingent to the Bastion. Find my father and the other Marshals."

Some of the men stirred, confusion crossing their faces. Stephen, however, nodded without question.

"Take all the Tortoise Guardians," August continued, scanning the faces before him, "and all my men except Maor, Kirin and Jasper."

Hiram was staring at him. "Where are you going?"

"The rest of us have another dire mission."

"Other than protecting Cariath? Your home?" Lee chimed in, shocked and partly indignant.

Leah could not blame him—she was as bewildered at August's instructions as the rest of them.

August met Lee's gaze evenly. "I am going to the Mortal Gate."

A sudden thick silence fell. Leah's breath caught in her throat, and though she tried to keep it quiet, she was sure August noticed. From the look on even the Tiger Guardians' faces, she could see most were stunned by his statement.

She faintly heard Wren mutter, "Thought the Gate was inside Fox Manor."

"Well," Hiram said after a long moment, "that seems even more critical. You need more men."

"I am taking Maor, Kirin, Jasper, Hansuke and Leah. I don't expect to meet an army." He paused. "I cannot take your men, Hiram," he said bluntly, perhaps interpreting the other man's hint. "This key belongs to the White Tiger Guardians."

"Yet you would bring a Vermilion Falcon," Lawrence challenged.

"He has something we need," August replied tightly.

"Marcum sent you to help where we needed," Maor cut in impatiently. "You can help us defend Cariath or return to En-doire."

"If this is the gratitude we receive—" Lawrence began, but August held up his hand.

"We are indebted to you for your help," he said quietly, and turned a stern look on Maor. "The Guardian alliances were once as solid as woven cords, but they have faltered over the years. We have a chance now to renew those bonds. My father always said we were the real fabric and shield for the mortal realm, but we are only strong if we are together. Believe me, Lawrence—all of you—I am not making a political power play. I want to defend Japha, and I cannot do it alone."

No one spoke. Lawrence seemed to shrink in resignation, and even Maor looked a little shamefaced. Leah could tell his words were not just for the Tortoise Guardians, but for all of them. A reminder of what they were facing, and an example of humility that quietly demanded the other men lay down their pride too.

She felt a swell of pride on his behalf. He might not have Arthur's flair, but his conviction could command a legion's loyalty. *This is why men will follow him. This is why Nimrod will lose.*

"We will do as you say and go to Cariath," Hiram said finally. "We stand together as Guardians."

"Thank you." August inclined his head. Though he did not show it, Leah felt him let out a breath. "Godspeed."

Leah watched as the Tiger and Tortoise men rode off, Stephen leading the way. Maor, Kirin, Jasper and Hansuke watched beside them as the large party grew small in the distance. Then, they turned to look at August expectantly.

"So Captain, where *are* we going?" Maor asked, his tone hushed even though no one else was around to hear them.

"The Mortal Gate. I was telling the truth." August met their gazes. "Just follow me."

They set off again. It felt strange to only hear a few sets of hoofbeats behind them now, and Leah sent up a silent prayer for Stephen and Hiram and the others.

August swung around the outskirts of the Cariath Mountains. The terrain was new to Leah. Grasslands, some dry and some green, extended across the landscape. Simi's sinewy muscles pulsed beneath them as they rode hard, the sun warm on their backs. The rushing wind made it too hard to speak, so Leah was forced to keep her growing list of questions quiet.

Where was the Mortal Gate? She assumed the Marshals of White Tiger knew, but no one else in their party seemed privy to that information, not even Maor. Though her tenure in Cariath was short, she was not surprised by Wren's guess that it was inside Fox Manor.

And had Nimrod discovered its location? Benedict had found Adair, and she could only assume he had the key from Cobalt Dragon, which led him finally to go back to Cariath. At least Hansuke said he did not know the Vermilion riddle...

Which led to her other burning curiosity—who was the heir of Arieh?

Another forest lay ahead of them. Leah craned her neck slightly to see if August would veer away, but he seemed to be making straight for the woods.

"Are we going through there?" Jasper's dubious voice came faintly from behind.

August's only answer was to continue their gallop in the same direction, at the same speed.

"Please tell me we won't be killed by wood faeries if the Mortal Gate is in that thicket," Maor called.

Finally, August urged Simi to slow down, which she did with little prompting. Leah imagined she was even more tired carrying two people on this entire journey, and she patted the horse's side in apology.

She could not fault the men's hesitation as they entered the forest. It was different from the one by the Nathair, which was all sturdy redwoods and high canopies. This place had none of those. Spindly trees stretched out in all directions while branches and dry leaves littered the ground. It was unkempt, with no clear trails. The horses had to tread carefully, and she could easily imagine getting lost inside.

Though their pace slowed, August did not falter. He knew the way. Leah felt some of her apprehension fade, but nevertheless she gripped

August's waist more tightly.

As they went deeper into the woods, something familiar tickled the back of her mind. Almost as if she had seen this place before. But it was impossible, if even Maor, Kirin and Jasper did not seem to recognize their surroundings, following tightly on Simi's heels.

Except — there had been a forest that night.

She let out a soft gasp, which only August heard. Distracted, he twisted his head around to glance at her, sudden concern in his eyes.

"Leah?"

"I've been here. When we came from Carmel that first night."

He turned back to face forward. "Yes. I'm surprised you recognize it." She could almost imagine the small smile that touched his lips. "I thought you wouldn't have dared to look outside the carriage."

A rush of defiance shot through her before she felt mollified by his flattery. That night came back vividly to her now. The eerie forest, the howling wind, and the silhouette of August at the front of the carriage, upright and fearless.

"I'm not that much of a coward," she muttered.

"No, you're quite the opposite, I've learned. What I'm not sure of is whether my world changed you, or simply unshackled you."

She did not have an answer to that.

After some time, she spoke again. "Are you going to tell us where we're going?"

She felt him sigh. "There's no reason to hide it. You'll be there soon." He paused. "Wren was not wrong when he, like many other Tiger Guardians, thought the Mortal Gate was in Fox Manor."

"What?" Leah stared at his back, wishing she could see his face. "Then why aren't we going there? You said —"

"Not that Fox Manor."

His interjection bewildered her for a moment before the awful truth broke over her like ice-cold water.

"Damnation, August."

"I never thought I'd hear you curse."

"Fox Manor — *in Carmel*? As in, Edenbridge?"

"I didn't purchase it because I really needed a second home, much less a vacation home," he said wryly. "We've been watching over it quietly for years, and given the situation with the Oath-breakers, we thought it might be best to formally buy it. We couldn't leave a place like that as public property of the crown forever."

"There were always rumors," Leah murmured, still in shock, "that the place was haunted. I guess the stories really do come from somewhere, don't they?"

"Probably. But it's also a normal house, if you don't know any better. I doubt the previous owners ever discovered anything uncanny. You lived there for a bit too," he reminded her, which stunned her all over again.

"Stars, I had no idea." Now Leah remembered the strange shadows on the wall and the whispered sounds she woke up to in Edenbridge—now, they no longer seemed like the product of an overactive imagination.

In a haze, her thoughts turned to her hometown, and a greater fear gripped her. "Nimrod doesn't know, does he?" she asked urgently. "Carmel," she struggled to get the words out, "would be in danger."

She thought August's hands tightened on the reins. "He shouldn't. But I don't know what's happened in Cariath since we left."

Leah probed for the unspoken implications in his words. How could Nimrod know? The only way would be if one of the Marshals betrayed the secret...no, they would die before doing that. But what kind of power did Nimrod have? What kind of bribery or blackmail?

"Can we go faster?" she pressed.

August picked up the pace a little. "Leah, I won't let anything happen."

It felt like forever when they exited the forest—she heard the men behind them breathe sighs of relief. Rolling fields stretched before them, and the horses fell into a quick gallop again.

They rode across open terrain for a few more hours, stopping only for brief breaks so the horses would not be worn out completely. Well after dusk, Carmel came into view from a distance, and she felt a sharp throb inside her chest. She had been reeling over the revelation of Fox Manor and the Mortal Gate and worrying over Nimrod and her town, so she did not spare much thought for the obvious fact that she would see Carmel soon.

She would be home.

August brought them to a halt at the edge of the town, and they all dismounted.

"This is Carmel," he said abruptly and without fanfare. Leah saw the tired circles beneath his eyes.

She felt Maor, Kirin and Jasper's gazes go to her, while Hansuke continued to watch August. He probably did not know the significance of the place.

August rushed through the same explanation he gave her, revealing that Edenbridge in Carmel contained the Mortal Gate, hence why they were here. The others were all surprised, but the truth did not strike them hard like it did with Leah, who felt the personal impact hit her between the eyes.

"We'll leave the horses here and enter on foot," August said. "We don't need to draw attention."

The familiar sights and sounds swirled around Leah but hardly touched her. Her heart was pounding the whole time, encased in a hard shell of anxiety, where other feelings could not penetrate. She briefly wondered if they would encounter someone she knew, or if she was even recognizable now. It felt odd to think her appearance remained much the same when so much else had changed.

The roads leading up to Fox Manor were relatively quiet as they wove through. They had the advantage of entering after dark, so the roads were mostly empty. Leah watched the other Guardians looking around curiously, having never been to one of the seaside towns. On another day, she might have excitedly pointed out landmarks or shared stories of Carmel, but she could not muster up the heart for it.

August pulled out the key when they arrived at Edenbridge. She wondered if he carried it with him all this time, and if that meant he knew he'd end up here somehow before going back to Cariath —

She was too tired to follow the train of thought through.

It was quiet when they stepped inside. The familiar common area was just as they left it. Leah remembered the elegant decorations from the night of the party, which transformed into simple furniture pieces when she moved in.

"Charming," Maor said, wandering toward the kitchen.

Kirin bounded after him, while Jasper and Hansuke moved toward the stairwell.

"So, what now?" Jasper looked down at August.

"We wait here, and hope no one else shows up. My father will send word when he can about Cariath."

"August," Jasper said again, his voice tightening.

August and Leah both looked up at the stairwell. Her blood ran cold. Jasper and Hansuke stood frozen as a man clad in black appeared out of the shadows from the second floor.

"Your father sends his greetings. I saw him recently," the man said.

Leah felt her husband go still, whether from shock or fury, she could not tell. His hand immediately went to his sword hilt.

"Nimrod."

"Hello, August."

Maor and Kirin emerged from the kitchen and came to their side, reaching for their weapons too.

Nimrod looked at them with disdain. "You didn't need to bring an army. Unless you find me that hard to fight."

"I know you're not alone," August growled.

"And we're hardly an army," Maor muttered.

"I'm not, but I've learned it's not always numbers that wins wars." He bared his teeth in a cold smile. "Oh August, your whole family is a bit predictable, and I've always known how to play you."

He flicked his hand, and Benedict, Justin, and a mousy-looking man stepped up behind him. August's gaze locked on Benedict, but Leah saw the others. She reached for August's arm, her hand going to her mouth.

Another, cruel-looking man appeared behind Justin, guiding her Papa and holding a knife to his throat.

CHAPTER 34

"It's a full house now," Nimrod commented, his gaze drifting from his men and Papa down to August and Leah.

Paralyzed with dread, words froze in her throat.

Beside her, August appeared livid. "You are a snake, Nimrod, to stoop so low."

For a moment, his voice snapped Leah's attention away from Papa. She had seen August stern with his men, aloof toward his father, indignant with her, and coldly threatening toward Marcum. But she felt something different from him this time, like a barely chained dragon twisted inside him, ready to burst out. A dragon that fed on his pain and kept silent score of Nimrod's personal offenses—Alain, Benedict, and now her.

For a moment, she believed he would do anything to crush Nimrod, and she was more frightened of him than anyone else in the room.

Nimrod cocked his head. "For such a devoted Guardian, you take things very personally."

August turned his hot-iron gaze on Benedict, who looked away quickly. Justin, however, regarded them with a somber look.

Leah found Papa's eyes. Those familiar, kind eyes. He looked helpless but not afraid. She finally found her voice. "Let him go."

Nimrod looked at her and she forced herself to hold his gaze. "Oh, I'm not in the business of unnecessary killing. Your husband left him the spare key to this place, and he happened to be in the library when we arrived. I have no quarrel with him, as long as you give me what I want."

"You think we will bargain with you?" Maor growled, but August held up his hand.

"What do you want?"

"I know the Mortal Gate is here." Nimrod raised an eyebrow. "The Old Fox would have died rather than tell me—" August stiffened and Leah's breath caught in her throat—"but some of your Marshal friends burst in and gave away the knowledge to spare his life." He leaned over the stairwell railing. "Now, are you the sort to gamble with another's life?"

The man holding Papa tightened his grip and flicked the knife around his fingers.

"You have all the keys," August said. "What else do you want?"

Nimrod looked at Benedict, who spoke for the first time after a long pause.

"We don't have the Vermilion riddle."

"And conveniently," Nimrod added, "you brought along just the right

227

man." He looked at Hansuke.

Leah watched as August and Hansuke looked at each other, unable to discern what unsaid things were passing between them, if anything. Her husband wore a dark, grim look of determination, while Hansuke was unreadable as always. He seemed to wait for August to decide on his next move.

Awful realization crashed over Leah. *Could it be...?*

"It's you," she breathed, staring at August, who turned to look at her.

The heir of Arieh. The Fox family was one of the oldest Guardian families, held in high prestige. She stared at him, waiting for a reaction. His expression did not change, and she saw his gaze flicker to Hansuke, a question in his eyes.

August didn't know either. It felt strange that she could read that in his face, but that moment of uncertainty was not hesitation over whether to reveal himself. He was trying to confirm if she was right.

So at some point, he had begun suspecting it too.

"No," Hansuke said. He glanced around the room, before his gaze landed on Leah. "It's you."

She blinked, uncomprehending. "What?"

"The Vermilion Falcon have the gift of second sight. We can identify the heir of Arieh." His gaze did not move from her. "I knew from the moment by the river, though you did not."

If not for the deadly situation they were in, Leah would have laughed aloud. Was Hansuke a fool or an imposter from the Falcon Guardians?

Nimrod seemed to have similar thoughts. "The girl?" he scoffed, with scorn and disbelief. "Is he mad?" He turned to Benedict.

August and Benedict did not brush off the ridiculous claim. They were both staring at her with undisguised astonishment, as if accepting Hansuke's statement as plausible. In the periphery, she noticed Maor and Jasper were also gaping at her, bewildered. Kirin, however, did not appear surprised.

"You bear the bloodline," Hansuke said calmly, as if he were merely reporting the weather. He nodded up the stairs at Papa. "He does too."

A brief silence held.

"No—what—impossible," she spluttered.

But slowly—very slowly—Leah saw glimmers of possibility. Papa had many Guardian legends and manuscripts, which were otherwise unseen around Carmel. She had always felt a deep kinship with the stories. And her adventures with August and the Guardians seemed to unleash a latent passion inside her. She remembered Arthur asking her if Cariath felt far from home, but the truth was, Cariath felt *like* home.

In a way, she belonged with the Guardians more than she did in the sheltered bubble of Carmel.

And there was Kirin's dream. Vague and shadowy, but as he said, she colored in the outlines well.

She looked at her husband. August did not dismiss Hansuke's claim outright. It was almost as if something clicked into place and finally made sense.

"You didn't know—did you?"

August stared. "Heavens, no." He had dropped his hand away from his sword hilt, his fingers clenched tight by his side. The shock still had not worn off his expression, but she saw anguish and fear begin to grow there. She could guess why.

She looked up at Papa. Her father, who would share in this revelation with her more than anyone else. He did not seem surprised.

"Did *you* know?" Leah choked, unable to fathom the thought.

By now, Nimrod seemed to falter in his rejection of Hansuke's claim. Everyone was staring at Papa, wondering, waiting.

"I didn't think it mattered," Papa said, and it startled Leah to hear his voice again after all this time. "My grandfather told me, and if I ever did tell anyone, Leah, it would have been you." His voice turned to pleading. "You were always different, and I thought it was some greater design when August came asking for your hand, like you were made for that world that was lost to us. I didn't know we would end up here."

She closed her eyes, reeling from his words. She felt August's hand on her shoulder, and Jasper cursed quietly beside her.

"Well," Nimrod said, "it seems like fate worked out perfectly in our favor. Hound, release him."

The cruel-looking man stared at Nimrod, puzzled, but let go of Papa. Nimrod stepped in front of him, pulling a silver lantern out.

"You will open the Gate for us."

Papa stared at him. "I don't know how."

"*To enter Faerie's blessed demesne / four secrets must be found: the land unbound by time and space / opens only to the one who knows / the Light, the Song, and Mortal Gate*," Nimrod recited. "You simply need to light the lantern and sing the song."

"I don't know the song."

"Traven can teach you." Nimrod flicked a finger at the mousy-looking man who stood behind Justin.

"And why do you think," Papa said, his eyes flaring, "that I would do anything for you?"

Leah could not bear to see what would happen next.

"I know the song," she interrupted, before Nimrod could do anything.

Everyone turned to her. She did not allow herself to look at August or Papa.

Nimrod spread his hands. "By all means, come join us."

To her surprise, neither August nor any of his men tried to stop her as she slowly ascended the stairs, feeling like lead weighed down her ankles.

A shiver went down her spine as she reached the top, where Nimrod, Benedict, Justin, Traven, Hound and Papa stood in a cluster.

Nimrod placed the lantern in her hands, and she felt the weight of silver and cool metal on her damp palms. She looked up to meet Papa's gaze. Fierce concern burned in his eyes. He was uncowed by the enemies standing around them, and in that moment, she believed Hansuke completely. He was not a doting old man who only knew Guardian stories to tell bedtime tales. Some crimson fervor and legend ran in his veins.

Courage and recklessness stirred inside her.

The man called Hound struck a match and lit the lantern, and they all looked at her expectantly.

She spoke to Nimrod, unafraid this time. "You underestimate us, if you think we will bow to your power-hungry whims."

She knew she would pay a price for her insolence, but her heart was ironclad in that instant. It felt good — right — to deal him a taunting blow.

Leah saw the flash of a blade and a commotion at the bottom of the stairs. "No!" August shouted, his voice cutting loudly through the air. She braced herself for terrible pain, but Hound did not go after her.

He had his blade back on Papa's neck. The sharp edge cut just slightly into his skin.

Her boldness vanished like smoke, and her hands shook, gripping the lantern. Her eyes flashed toward Benedict for a second, and Nimrod caught that.

He let out a sharp laugh. "You look to the wrong man for mercy." He stared at her. "Do not test me again."

"You think I will let you slaughter countless faerie and restart a war?" Her voice quivered.

Nimrod glanced from her to Papa. "Oh, I think people will do many senseless things to save someone they love."

"Don't, Leah," Papa whispered, flinching.

"You can sing the song," August said tightly at the same time.

"Point proven," Nimrod murmured.

Leah knew she would do it. In spite of the consequences, she would do it to save Papa. She hated her frailty, her lack of nobility, her inability to sacrifice. She spared a look at August. And he, a Guardian Marshal, would let her — had given her permission. Because he wanted to save her.

We all have a weakness in our armor. She closed her eyes and pushed the thoughts away. She went back to Marcum's feast in En-doire.

The words spilled through her mind again, and she sang.

Between the turning of Light and Dark
I walk in Eden's shadow-gray.
Where men and gods, through ceaseless strife,
chase winds of vengeance in vain.

O dream in a dream, what is truth?
that stands from age to age.
Though mortal empires rise and fall,
the eternal realm remains.

She heard the gasps around her and opened her eyes.

The lantern flame was burning brighter, but even more than that, patterns appeared on the walls around them. Some looked like maps, some like images of a great battle. She faintly thought she saw a white tiger and cobalt dragon take shape near the ceiling above them.

Before the passing of the Night
I feel the worlds groaning in place.
Will the songbirds herald hope,
and sing a verse of dawning Day?

O legend of legends, what is truth?
that guides the seeker's way.
Teach me to be pure in heart
and open the immortal gate.

Everything around her spun and her vision blurred. Papa reached for her, but he seemed far away, like everyone else.

And she felt like she was falling…

Falling…

Falling…

CHAPTER 35

She plummeted, a bird in a nosedive, but the sensation slowly faded without any hard landing. In fact, as her vision cleared, Leah realized she had not gone anywhere. She still stood at the top of the stairs in Edenbridge, but Nimrod, his men, Papa, and August had all vanished.

The patterns on the wall remained, and they were *moving*. She stared, enthralled, as large eagles beat their wings and tigers and lions charged over canyon ridges. There were images of battles, and also of merriment: men and animals gathered around campfires, toasting with drinks.

"This was Japha, before the Faerie Wars."

She whipped around to find a man ascending the stairs. He wore a plain robe and a single sword hung at his side. His face was ordinary by any measure, though he had an ageless look in his eyes.

He looked nothing like the depictions she had seen in Papa's books, but she knew him anyway.

"Arieh."

He smiled. "Hello, Leah. I assume you have some questions."

Leah almost laughed. "Why don't we start with: Am I mad? Or am I dead?"

Arieh sat down on a stair ledge, and she did the same. To her surprise, the floor was solid underneath her, and the texture felt like it did in Edenbridge—which she assumed she was still inside. But it did not explain where Arieh came from or where everyone else disappeared to. Anxiety for Papa, August, and his men shot through her.

"Neither," he said. "You are on the cusp between the mortal and immortal realms. This is the Mortal Gate." He raised his hands and motioned around the room.

"But—"

"Think of the mortal and faerie world as two sides of a plane." She shrank back, alarmed for a moment, as he pulled his sword out. But he simply balanced it flat on his fingers. "Your world sits here." He swept a hand over the top side of the blade. "The faerie world is like another dimension, running in parallel to yours." He moved his hand below the blade. "You are still in Edenbridge. You have simply slipped to the other side of the plane."

Arieh turned his blade over to the other side.

Leah stared at the silver weapon in his hand. "Then why," she said, mentally struggling, "is the Mortal Gate here? If our worlds run in parallel everywhere?"

"There are places where the seal between our worlds—our two sides of the plane—are weak. Hence you have heard of rogue faerie attacks." Sorrow dimmed his eyes. "Before, the mortal and immortal realm flowed effortlessly into each other on Japha. We were an island unlike any other, where faeries and men dwelt alongside each other. After the Faerie Wars, the Mortal Gate was one designated location where we allowed a portal between our worlds to open, provided one had the keys."

"One of the keys was your heir," she said quietly.

He smiled again, sadly. "I left a family behind when I entered Faerie. Vermilion Falcon thought only someone in my bloodline should be able to reopen the Gate."

Leah thought of all the stories she had read. Arieh had always been presented as a great warrior, not a husband or father. She wondered how much of what she knew was truth and how much was myth.

"What happened to you? Back—then," she stuttered.

A long silence prevailed, and she wondered if he would answer her.

"The names of the first Oath-breakers have been blacked out from Guardian records and legends," he said finally. "But I will remember them. Micah was always a better man than me. He was stronger, nobler, destined to be a leader. Then something inside him became twisted. I never really knew what it was." He met Leah's gaze, and she was unnerved to see the haunted look he wore now. "He was my brother, though not by blood. But sometimes a friend is even closer."

A hollow pit opened in her stomach. How long had it been? He must have spent centuries in Faerie, seen otherworldly wonders, and still his wound felt fresh.

"I wasn't selfless when I gave myself up in place of the traitors. I couldn't bear the thought of Micah shut in some faerie prison forever. I was a fool, not a hero. I left my wife and child behind, and left the rest of the Guardians to deal with the devastation."

"Did you know they would make you one of them? A faerie?"

"No, and I had no interest in living for some cause on the other side either. I spent a long time wandering aimlessly through Faerie. Those were the days I met them—White Tiger, Vermilion Falcon, Cobalt Dragon, and Black Tortoise, as you know them. They befriended me and sought to teach me their ways. I found I had things to teach them too.

"The faerie way is fair but unforgiving. All justice, no mercy. They thought I was weak to give myself up for Oath-breakers. You might find a similar attitude among the Guardians."

She nodded. "That's a familiar refrain."

"I saw the same mind grow among the Guardians. I watched, from the other side, as they put all the Oath-breakers to death. I believe their actions deserved it, but some were repentant... but they were never even heard, never believed."

234

Leah did not have the heart to ask him if Micah was one of the penitent ones.

"And it was then that I thought Micah's betrayal could either harden or soften me. It's strange that I learned compassion in Faerie, where it was a foreign concept. But I believe there is something deep in each of us—mortal and faerie—that sees the beauty in mercy."

"So you became known as a protector of mortals," she surmised.

"It's a title of condescension to many. But after all this time, you find you care less what others think of you." He smiled wryly.

"Do you get tired of fighting?"

She thought of the rogue faeries, and knew his battle still went on. She saw the scratches on his blade and its razor-sharp edge. The immortal realm was not an idyllic place either.

"Do you?" he countered. "Before the world is made new again, there will always be Oath-breakers and traitors. But it is a worthy fight."

"Do you believe the world will be renewed?" Leah paused. "That's not the Guardian theology."

"It's because of all I've seen that I believe. We weren't designed to be broken, Leah. Men and Faeries, we're all God's creatures, and I believe He will set things right again. A day is coming when sorrow will be a distant memory." For the first time, a faint light danced in his eyes, hinting at a reservoir of hope behind the battle scars he bore. "No, it is not Guardian theology, which solidified after the first Oath-breakers. The gods were made in the image of man, designed to keep mortals in check. The true God can't be tamed by what men want. He is renewing hearts, and He will renew all things one day."

Tears stung Leah's eyes. For a moment, the reality of Nimrod, Papa, and the rest of them faded, and she felt her heart soar at Arieh's words. For a moment, she felt the weight of his presence and unexpected faith, and the sensation was like a rising ocean tide, ringing with power inside of her.

"I believe that too. But so few do."

"Fight on, Leah. Few do here as well, but I haven't given up. I'll labor as long as He calls me to."

She nodded. "Maybe that's why you were destined for the world of Faerie."

He inclined his head. "Maybe."

It was odd, Leah thought, how he was so *ordinary*. Perhaps not ordinary as the typical Carmel gentleman went, but ordinary in the way August had become to her. A man—a great one in many ways—but still human. Stories had placed him on a pedestal, painted him in gold and glory, and forgot his brokenness.

"I'm afraid August sees compassion as weakness," she confessed. "And that Benedict will break him." She didn't explain further, but assumed he knew their stories.

Arieh held her gaze. "Maybe that's why you were destined to be his family."

She allowed a small smile at that.

"Nimrod can't come through the Gate, can he?" she asked, already suspecting she knew the answer.

"Not unless you bring him willingly."

"And the others?"

Arieh pointed at something behind her, and she turned to look. August, Benedict, and Papa all stood by the banister. Leah gasped.

"How did they—?"

"They are also heirs. Part of the bloodline, or brought into the family."

"Papa? August?" she said tentatively. They looked at her, but no one replied. "Were you here the whole time?"

"*Time…*" Arieh said. "Remember, you have entered the land unbound by time and space." He smiled enigmatically. "Things do not work as you are used to."

Her mind spun. Had they heard her whole conversation with Arieh? Or were they each having their own, because time did not move in a linear fashion? Before she could formulate a question, Arieh spoke again.

"It is time for you to go back, though."

"Wait! I don't know what to do," Leah pleaded, remembering their dire situation with Nimrod.

"You will, Leah." He paused. "I'm not anyone special. I can't tell you what to do. It is your family there, and I just pray you will have wisdom to act rightly." Their eyes met once more, and his gaze was as penetrating as August's had been that first night in the ballroom. "This is goodbye for now."

The falling sensation kicked in her stomach again, but for a flicker before that, she thought she saw an image of a man beside a tiger, falcon, dragon and tortoise, walking through the forest and laughing.

CHAPTER 36

The men materialized around Leah in the same positions she had left them. The silver lantern was still in her hands, though the flame was faltering.

"What's happening?" Nimrod demanded, one hand gripping his sword hilt.

Leah glanced at the walls. The images and patterns were fading away now, and simultaneously, the silver cooled against her palms.

Hound still held Papa, his blade pressed against him. She felt a flash of hatred toward him, but then thought of Arieh and Micah. Who had this man been once? What turned him into an Oath-breaker? Her anger did not subside, but softened in the slightest.

At the bottom of the stairwell, August, Maor, Kirin, Hansuke and Jasper were crowded around the banister. She could tell from August's tense figure that he was ready to spring up the steps.

Benedict had not moved from his position either, but Leah thought his eyes looked glazed. What had happened in those last moments with Arieh?

"The images just formed and faded," Hound muttered, his gaze darting around the house.

"Were we here the whole time?" Leah ventured.

Nimrod's attention snapped to her, his eyes narrowing. "What whole time?"

She caught the glimmer of recognition in Benedict's face, and quickly looked at Papa and August. Their eyes widened slightly, as if they understood something too.

No time had passed. To Nimrod, Justin, and the rest of the men, nothing had happened except for the patterns that filled the walls when Leah finished singing. But for her—for her family—an entire episode with Arieh had occurred. *Am I mad?* The question echoed in her mind again. She really might have thought so, if not for the comprehension in the others' faces that seemed to validate her experience.

She sucked in a breath and tried to calm her nerves. Nimrod would not be able to get through the Gate. All his grand efforts, and it amounted to nothing. There were some things daring and ambition could not achieve, and all his striving seemed foolish now.

He could not get through. But she had to protect her family. A slip of Hound's fingers, a moment of fury on his part, and Papa would be gone. Leah cast a fearful look down at August.

His gaze probed her for a moment, and she tried to make him

understand silently.

"Leah," August said finally, "tell us what happened."

His words were soft but urgent, and she knew he was trying to achieve something. The thought brought some measure of comfort.

"I was falling for—I don't know, minutes. I ended up in Edenbridge still, but everyone else was gone." She spoke rapidly, hearing the nerves in her voice. She knew it was critical she sound genuine to Nimrod. "The images on the wall were moving. And then he was there."

"Who?" Nimrod demanded.

"Arieh. We talked and—"

"Did he say how you could open the Mortal Gate?" August interrupted. She stared at him, and saw him take a small step up the stairs. No one else noticed.

"I need you to help me," she said, beginning to understand. She extended her arms, holding the lantern. "If I have another Guardian..."

"Lies," Nimrod hissed. "You saw *Arieh*?"

Leah felt her heart sink, but then Benedict spoke.

"I saw him too."

Nimrod whipped around to stare at him. "I don't need more of your games, Fox. I'm done with you when this is over."

In the moment his back turned, August leaped to the top of the stairwell and tackled Nimrod to the ground. Leah stumbled out of the way, her gaze still fixed on Hound and Papa. Kirin suddenly appeared on the railing beside them, jumping onto Hound's sword arm and pulling it away.

Chaos broke out. Papa rolled out of Hound's grip, and Leah ducked and rushed to his side, dragging him away from the fray.

Kirin was now all over Hound, who roared and slashed at the squirrel. Maor, Jasper and Hansuke also reached the top of the stairs.

"Get him out of the house!" Maor shouted to Leah, and he dropped his bow and arrows over the ledge to the first floor.

She helped Papa to his feet and they raced blindly down the stairs, where she picked up Maor's spare weapon.

But Leah could not bear to leave. She looked at her father. "You go," she said urgently.

He gripped her hand. "No."

They looked up as blades flashed, glints of light sparking on metal. Nimrod had recovered impossibly fast, and he was now blade-to-blade with August, dueling fiercely and dangerously close to the ledge.

"Stop them!" Nimrod yelled. "Kill them all!"

Jasper joined Kirin in his fight against Hound, while Maor engaged Justin. The latter defended himself skillfully, but Leah thought he never went on the offensive, never aimed for a fatal blow.

She searched for Benedict in the brawl. Hansuke, who still had no sword, was wrestling him with arms and fists.

Her heart was in her throat as she watched, one hand gripping Papa's tightly, the other Maor's bow.

August was pushing Nimrod closer to the railing, and Leah might have seen it coming before he did. She pushed Papa toward the kitchen just as Nimrod swept his legs over the banister and jumped.

She forced Papa behind the island counter as she nocked an arrow with shaking hands.

Nimrod was in the doorway, his sword upright, a wicked glint in his eye. He knew right when August was behind him, and the two men were trading blows again. Leah felt her pulse stop when August caught Nimrod's blade on his, a hairsbreadth away from his chest.

August cursed, and she saw a light sheen of red color Nimrod's blade. August's left sleeve was torn, where Nimrod's blade found its first mark.

It looked like a mere graze, but Nimrod grinned, encouraged.

Outside, she heard a shout and *crunch* interrupt the sounds of clashing metal. She prayed none of their men were hurt.

"Stop!" Benedict shouted. "Maor, he's not even an Oath-breaker!"

Who, Justin? Leah felt torn between her curiosity and fear of what was happening upstairs and her even greater concern for August in front of her.

Another sickening crunch, and Benedict roared. *"How dare you!"*

Her blood ran cold. Would Maor really kill like that?

But it was not Maor who replied. "You said, he's not one of us, Fox." It was Hound's voice.

Footfalls pounded on the stairs and she knew they were approaching. Papa gripped her shoulder from behind, and her gaze remained riveted on August and Nimrod.

Nimrod was slowly gaining ground, backing August against the wall, though both their blades were still flashing furiously.

Before she could think about it, Leah had lifted the bow in her hands and pulled the arrow back.

Could she really do this? Could she aim to kill, even Nimrod? Her fingers trembled.

"August, watch out!" Jasper's warning rang from around the corner.

At the last second, Leah turned her arrow downwards and let it fly.

It pierced Nimrod's upper thigh, sinking deep because of the close range from which she fired. He let out a guttural yowl of pain, staggering back. August paused for a moment, looking stunned as well, his gaze skating over to Leah. She held the empty bow in her shaking hands.

Before August could press his advantage, Benedict rounded the corner and tackled Nimrod to the ground with a battle cry. He no longer held his sword, but gripped Nimrod's chest between his knees, pummeling him with bare fists.

"We got Hound!" Maor shouted, still out of sight to Leah, and she heard growling and scuffling.

But her eyes were caught on Benedict, beating Nimrod into oblivion, while Leah's arrow still protruded from his side. A pool of blood began to form beside him.

"You...will not...hurt...anyone else."

Benedict's eyes, full of wrath, were fixated on the man beneath him.

Leah felt sick and dizzy watching. She glanced at August, who was also frozen over the scene on the ground, breathing heavily.

"Ben," August said. No response. "Ben," he repeated with more force, his voice finally breaking through his brother's dark haze. "Stop."

To her surprise, he listened. His whole body sagged, and he rolled off of Nimrod, who was bloody and unconscious.

Hansuke and Kirin came around to the kitchen, their gazes roaming over the scene—Nimrod unconscious, Benedict lying on the ground with his eyes closed and face wet, August leaning against the wall, and Papa and Leah behind the counter, the bow in her hand clattering to the ground.

Kirin, his fur matted with sweat, finally looked up at August. "We have Hound and Traven tied up. Justin is...I'm not sure." He broke off, his gaze going to Benedict.

"Well done," August said, closing his eyes.

"What should we do?" Kirin asked.

August looked down at Nimrod and Benedict. "Tie them up. Clean the house. We'll go back to Cariath immediately."

Kirin, Hansuke and the others set about following his orders while August came to Leah and Papa. She gripped his hands and immediately looked at his left sleeve.

"We should bandage that."

He brushed it off. "It's a scratch." He looked to Papa. "I'm sorry for the terrible ordeal. I take full responsibility."

Papa stepped around Leah. "Nonsense. I never told either of you what I knew of our family history." He hung his head. "August, you saved us today."

"Your daughter did a good bit herself." He looked at Leah. "I need to return to Cariath. Do you want to stay here for now with your family? I'll come for you once I get things in order."

She looked over his shoulder at Benedict. Jasper was binding his wrists and he did not resist. She thought of the Micah-shaped wound Arieh still bore. "Getting things in order" felt like such stoic words, ones that failed to wrap their arms around the upheaval that was ahead.

When she looked at Papa, he nodded at her.

"No, August." She gave him a tired smile. "I'll go with you. You are my family."

CHAPTER 37

Cariath Valley, Island of Japha.
Month of Healing: First week, Star-Day.

Benedict awoke with a dull headache and sunlight struggling through his eyelids. He kicked his leg and heard a chain rattle.

He was in his old room in Fox Manor—Fox Manor at Cariath. He bolted upright in spite of his aching muscles. Metal clanged and pressed against his ankle. His leg was chained to the post of his bed.

He had drifted in and out of a hazy consciousness the past few days—or however much time had passed. He recalled the dull clap of horse hooves and rattling of chains around his hands as they traveled back to Cariath. Faces and voices blurred around him—August, Leah, and Nimrod, bloody and beaten. Benedict felt numb to it all, allowing sleep to claim him whenever possible on the journey.

Now, the events leading up to Edenbridge rushed through his mind with awful fury. The moment he flung that knife at his father with an empty threat, startling clarity dawned upon him: the Old Fox had outmaneuvered Nimrod. From his stirring speech to James and Rupert's staged desperation, offering to trade the location of the Mortal Gate for Arthur's life, he had prepared for this scenario thoroughly. Benedict was hardly surprised when August appeared in Carmel so quickly.

It was almost ironic. The Oath-breakers thought they could defeat the Guardians because they came from them. But the White Tiger Marshals proved it was the opposite.

Puffed up in his pride, Nimrod stepped into their trap, like prey caught in a spider's web. He overestimated the weakness of affection among the Guardian leaders. Benedict knew there was not a chance the Old Fox, James or Rupert would sell such a secret to save one another.

They gave it away willingly. And Benedict could surmise from there that Edenbridge was not defenseless.

The worst part was, when he grasped their cunning stroke, he felt a swell of pride for his father. Bold, brash, traitorous Nimrod never really had a chance against the legendary Arthur Fox.

His bedroom door opened and the Old Fox stepped inside. They regarded each other for a long moment until Benedict broke the gaze.

"Don't give me a trial. I'll accept the sentence."

Arthur Fox just raised an eyebrow. "Because you think it's deserved, or because you no longer want to live anyway?"

"Does it matter?"

"It matters to me."

Mixed emotions churned through Benedict. He could hardly think of what happened in Carmel without the dam inside him threatening to burst.

"I deserve it," he whispered, in a fierce but hushed voice. "I deserve whatever judgment you want to render, but Justin did not. Have you noticed? It's always the undeserving who get dealt the worst hand."

He could not shut out the image of Hound standing over Justin's slumped body.

"I hate him." Benedict closed his eyes, realizing he was not even thinking of Hound. "I hate him for whatever idiotic reason made him follow me and Nimrod. In all the last few months, I didn't take a single life. I was almost cut in half by Hound when I stopped him from killing those Tortoise Guardians. I stopped him from abandoning Traven in Whitewitch. *I couldn't do it.* Hound said I was weaker than a Guardian." His eyes flew open again, and he knew he wore a wild expression as the words tumbled out, half-coherent. "I knew you played Nimrod when James and Rupert gave him the Gate location, because I knew you would have sacrificed each other in a heartbeat to protect what you had to. I'm not like that. Hound was right about me. He said I'm *marked* by mercy."

He drew in a ragged, shuddering breath. "And for all that, in the end, Justin's death is on me. If only—if only he hated me like August did. I would have been spared this."

A long silence followed. Benedict did not want to look at his father. Would he see disgust? Pity?

Shame filled Arthur's voice when he spoke.

"Astute as ever, Ben. Except on the last part. Justin's death is on me."

Startled, Benedict stared at him.

"After Lila died and I saw you growing more and more frustrated that I refused to organize an offensive against Faerie, I was afraid you would do something rash. I asked for Justin's help."

"He...was your *spy?*"

"Briefly. Only long enough to warn me of rumblings that Nimrod might lead a revolt. And that you might be tempted to follow."

Benedict did not know what to think, or feel. He remembered those as the last days he honestly confided in Justin—in anyone—about his struggle: was it worth riding on a despicable man's shoulders for a chance to strike a blow at Faerie? His father's revelation now tainted those memories with the bitter flavor of betrayal. Had Justin listened as a friend or a spy? But he knew he would be a hypocrite to judge. Benedict himself was an arch-traitor to the Guardians and his family.

But to think Justin had not been by his side purely out of friendship and brotherhood... it struck a painful chord inside him, even though he knew it was contradictory. He had just wished, fervently and genuinely, that Justin had abandoned him, followed in August's footsteps.

He couldn't be angry at him simultaneously for both those reasons.

The recollection of his broken body drained away all his anger, leaving only exhaustion and the thousand-ton weight of guilt.

"So you weren't caught off guard when I left," Benedict said dully. "And you had an inside man within Nimrod's ranks."

"No. He wasn't giving me information anymore after Nimrod broke away. There was no way to really deliver messages." Arthur sighed. "We had one conversation before it happened. I asked if he would go with you, if you followed Nimrod. I didn't ask him to feed me information. I just asked if he would protect you."

"You *sent* him with me? As a mission?"

"It wasn't a mission. No other Guardian knew. It was a personal request, from a father."

Benedict's mind raced. "You mean, you asked him to be an Oath-breaker, off the record, for my sake. Knowing what it would cost. You knew Justin was straight as an arrow, just like August, and you backed him into this corner."

"It wasn't a demand. He wanted to do this. He swore he would never truly be loyal to Nimrod, but he would go to protect you."

"I didn't need protection! If anything, I had to protect him from everyone who distrusted him!"

The words felt hollow as he said them. In the end, he had failed at that.

"Not physical protection. Protect your humanity, your conscience. If he could."

"And sear his own in the process," Benedict spat.

Arthur's eyes crinkled with sorrow and weariness. "Probably. And that's on me. I think Justin loved you as a brother, in his quiet and unassuming way. He would have done anything to save you. But he was also a good man, one who would always be faithful to the Guardian values. Perhaps in a strange sense, I gave him a way to do both — tacit permission to follow you, without wholeheartedly betraying the Guardians." He held up his hands as Benedict opened his mouth. "It's not an excuse, Benedict. I should never have asked him, and if I even suspected he would do this on his own initiative, I should have stopped him. That would be the right course of action. That would have been the Guardian way."

"Then — why?" Though he had a faint inkling of the answer.

"I have a weakness too. Perhaps similar to yours. Yes, I would have died rather than give away information to Nimrod unwillingly. But could I give up my son?"

The question hung in the air, and Benedict feared it would haunt him for a long time, just as his mother's ghost did.

"I suppose it doesn't matter now. We've reached this point, and you have to put me on trial."

Benedict did not have the capacity to say more. He was half-reeling from Arthur's words, and from a detached perspective, thought he would be outraged with his father and Justin if he were anyone else. But he saw clearly enough: there was no point to blame either of them ultimately. He was the one who backed them into a corner, the one who forced their hands.

Again, if only they had been more like August.

"What happened here?" Benedict asked, with just a thin spark of curiosity, as Arthur rose to leave.

"There was a very short fight in the Bastion. Nimrod sent a sizeable number in after you left, but our defenses held and August sent most his men and Tortoise Guardians to assist. Those who surrendered are in the dungeon, along with Nimrod, Hound and Traven, who were with you. It's all over now. August and Leah are here now too, helping to put things back in order."

He thought of Gerard, Wills, Mert, and the other Oath-breakers he knew, those he considered comrades, maybe friends. He felt a pang and wondered if they survived.

"Why am I not in the dungeon too?"

His father was at the door now, poised to leave. But he gave him one more long look. "August asked that you stay here. There was another point you were wrong on earlier — your brother never hated you."

~~~~~

That evening, August came to see him.

It began as a painful and awkward encounter. While he knew the Old Fox would fill the empty silences, August was a master at prolonging them. That had never been a problem for Benedict, who was quick to throw out a quip and shatter the tension.

But what did he have to say now? August stood frozen in the doorway, staring at him.

"If you have a rebuke, August —" he began tiredly.

"What would be the point?" His brother cut him off, not harshly, but in a tired manner. "Words and time can't make things right again."

"No, they can't." Benedict paused. "You should have just thrown me in the dungeon too."

August finally stepped inside, pulling up a plush chair and sinking into it. A sliver of fast-fading sunlight from the window slashed across his face.

"Would you have done it?" August asked.

"What?"

"Everything."

He seemed unwilling or unable to elaborate, but Benedict knew what he was asking. This was one point of similarity between them. Where Arthur Fox learned to leave the past behind, neither of his sons could unshackle themselves from it. *Would you have, what if, if only…* they sought desperate answers to those useless questions.

"Opened the immortal realm, yes. Let Nimrod seize it if he even was able, no. Murdered for gain, no." He met his brother's gaze evenly. "Does it matter?"

"No. Not to most people."

But to you? He did not say it aloud.

"What happened to you, when Leah opened the Gate?" August said suddenly. "Did Arieh speak to you?"

That memory had dimmed in light of the following events — the frenzied fight in Fox Manor, Justin, the black hate he felt toward Nimrod and Hound, the long journey back to Cariath. Even something as monumental as stepping foot into Faerie and meeting a Guardian legend nearly fell out of his mind.

In another time, he might have been bursting to speak of it. It still held a tinge of wonder, but Benedict felt a gray veil drawn over all things.

"He told me about the faeries who were responsible for Mother," he said bluntly. August went still in his seat, his gaze locked on Benedict. "They were punished and imprisoned. I demanded to see them. To make them pay for their crimes. He said they were already doing that."

Did he see a flicker of empathy in August's face? Or was it just the ghost of the same pain he felt?

"He said, you think there is no justice because you cannot see it," he continued. "Justice can be done even if my need for vengeance is unfulfilled."

"Did you believe him?"

"Yes." August looked surprised, before Benedict added, "In theory. In a lesson book. But she was my mother." His tone sparked with feeling for the first time.

"She was my mother too."

August did not look at him when he spoke, but Benedict allowed the tentative moment of kinship to form and fade in silence.

"Arieh asked me, if I could come in and deal my own justice to those faeries, what then? What would come next? He said, well, what you said earlier — words and time can't make things right again. Even justice dealt can't undo time. It can't blot out the past."

A moment passed before August replied. "I think you always knew that."

Benedict did not want to think of it anymore. "And what did Arieh say to you?"

"He told me about a friend he had. He went down the wrong path, did some terrible deeds. In the end, he was sorry for them. But no one cared for his repentance, and he found no forgiveness among men."

Was this even a true story, or an allegorical lesson? Benedict would need to be blind to not see the parallels.

"So what happened to him?"

"He was sentenced to death." The smallest, bitter smile pulled at the corner of his lips. "In this case, it was justice done that left Arieh with a scar."

Dusk had descended entirely now, covering Benedict's room in shadows. For a moment, they both looked out at the Bastion—the green fields and towering edifices he had once called home, and the Cariath Mountains that were dark mounds against the mahogany skies.

August stood up and switched on a light, turning the window from a viewport to a mirror reflection.

"I need to go." He paused awkwardly, as if unsure what to say next. "When is the trial?"

Taken aback, August's gaze flickered to Benedict. "In a few days."

As with Justin, Benedict felt a swath of unspoken words hang heavy between them. But when he thought of what to say aloud, he came up empty.

Finally, just as August was halfway out the door, Benedict said, "I like Leah. You married up." He paused. "I don't mean just because of her bloodline."

His brother turned briefly and inclined his head, a small smile on his face. "I know."

CHAPTER 38

Cariath Valley, Island of Japha.
Month of Healing: Second week, Fire-Day

Leah stepped into the rotunda alone. She had never visited this part of the Bastion, where, according to August, they held Guardian knighting ceremonies, trials, weddings, and funerals. She marveled at the structure of the ancient edifice and the history made inside its walls. Meticulous paintings spiraled up the sides that reached to its dome-shaped covering.

Was Micah tried and sentenced in here, centuries ago?

Arthur, August, James and Rupert—the Marshals—sat on a raised platform on the floor of the rotunda, while the Oath-breakers sat below them. She did not see any chains around their hands or feet, but a line of guards stood nearby. Craning her neck, Leah identified Benedict, Nimrod and Hound. About two dozen others crowded around them.

Seats ringed the floor, rising to forty or fifty rows high. Guardians and residents of Cariath streamed in as Leah arrived, and about half the room was filled. She recognized a section filled with delegates from Amir's government, distinguished by their royal purple attire. August mentioned they still attended formal trials and ceremonies in the Bastion when it concerned them, and given the damage done to the Nathair docks and its officers, they wanted to ensure reparations were made. Leah briefly wondered if Lady Arinda was among them. Her gaze scanned across the rotunda. She caught sight of Melina and Jenifer across the room, and the women gave her a wave. She acknowledged them with a smile, but she had no desire to join them.

Since the flurry of revelations and events at Carmel, Leah felt like a marked woman. Her mind could not grasp that she was the heir of Arieh, or even that she was August Fox's wife. It was almost as if she were watching another woman's life unfold intimately before her eyes, but it was not *her*. It could not be her. She was waiting for Papa or Mama to shake her awake from this dream, and she would find herself back in their old estate, the last few months nothing but a figment of her imagination.

Her gaze went to the first row. A number of the Tortoise Guardians filled the seats—Lawrence, Lee and Hiram. Behind them, Hansuke sat alone. She made her way down the steps and took the chair beside him.

"Leah," he greeted her solemnly.

The men in front of them turned around and nodded to her too.

"We heard you faced Nimrod bravely," Hiram said. "You must know it's not often women join dangerous expeditions like these. We salute your courage."

"August and his men did most of the work," she protested. "But thank you. And thank you for coming to defend Cariath." It felt odd thanking them for that, but it seemed the proper response, given her status as a lady in the Fox family.

Hiram inclined his head. "An honor. We are ready to stand with you today to see justice done."

A quiet shiver went down her spine. *Justice. What* would *happen today?*

When Arthur Fox rose to his feet, silence fell. The Old Fox was robed in black, his expression regal but tired. Leah had seen little of him since their return to Cariath, but when she did, she noticed dark circles beneath his eyes and weariness in his step.

"We are gathered for the trial of these men." He swept a hand across the floor of the rotunda. "They have broken faith with the Guardian tradition and devoted themselves to all we stand against. Today, we strive to see justice done. God help us."

Arthur went on to explain the proceedings. He would give an opening statement. Then, a select few of the White Tiger Guardians who were closely engaged in the battle against the Oath-breakers would be allowed to speak. Leah saw them sitting in the first row opposite her. Maor, Stephen and Kirin were among them. All of them, even Maor, looked somber.

Finally, they would open the floor to statements from anyone else in attendance. The Marshals would render a judgment at the end of the trial.

"That's four men holding a lot of power," Leah murmured.

Hansuke glanced at her. "For the Vermilion Falcon, we have one judge for a trial."

"What if he's wrong?"

He shrugged. "What is wrong? The verdict, or how you might weigh punishment and mercy? Why is your vision of justice better than another? Our Guardians were given the gift of second sight, so we are able to see beyond the surface. Then, we simply need to appoint a man of integrity."

"Second sight," she repeated. "That's how you knew who I was, right?"

He nodded, but before they could continue their conversation, Arthur was speaking again.

"As many of you know, this trial is deeply personal for me. I cannot help asking, where did I fail as Chief of the White Tiger Guardians, that another generation of Oath-breakers would rise up during my time? Yes, it is in these dark times that legends are made. I think of Arieh, who made his mark on our history during the first uprising. He was a great warrior, but he is remembered more for his great sacrifice. What will our future generations remember us for?" He paused, and his voice echoed briefly. "Much of that depends upon what we do here today.

"I would be remiss not to mention that the question that haunts me even more is not my failings as Chief. My son, Benedict Fox, is among the accused." His gaze went to the Oath-breakers, where Leah could only assume he found Benedict. "I ask, where did I fail as a father? I have thought about this in the long stretches of the night. Not only since we captured these men, but ever since Benedict walked away. I admit, I am complicit. I think of all the ways I might have been a better father, a better man, a better mourner in the aftermath of my beloved Lila's death. I fell short. Could I have changed the course of many things by being better? I will never know. For the damage that has been done and the ripples caused, I am deeply sorry."

Arthur looked back up and swept his gaze around the rotunda. Leah's heart ached at the intensity and pain in his face.

"But today, I am not the one on trial. One day, we will all stand trial before a greater judge for the lives we led. Today, we will do our best to deal out justice to these before us. They each are men, dignified with life and spirit, and even more, they once served honorably among the Guardians. They each have a story, some that are sympathetic, for why they broke faith with us. But we understand, as upright men and as White Tiger Guardians, that victim-hood and tragedies do not excuse a man's crimes, which is what we will judge today."

When Arthur sat down, Leah glanced around the rotunda. The silence held, but it was not a drowsy one. Though his exhaustion was apparent, Arthur commanded the attention of the room. Many were nodding quietly, and she sensed a general sentiment of approval and respect.

She felt a swell of pride for her father-in-law. Lila's death and then Benedict's betrayal were daggers to his heart. To stand and judge his son now before Cariath — she imagined it was thrusting that blade in deeper.

"August said Oath-breakers are always sentenced to death," she whispered to Hansuke.

"Do you think they deserve better?"

His tone was not challenging or defensive, merely curious.

"They may not. But some of them may do good with a second chance. Who knows what we lose when we end their lives?" Leah did not know why she felt more comfortable talking with him about this, but she did not want the Tortoise Guardians to overhear.

"Fair point. But we have lost incomparably more in the lives they have taken."

She could not argue with that.

The other White Tiger Guardians stepped onto the platform to speak in turns. Most gave testimony of their experience with the Oath-breakers, incriminating them for their ruthlessness and disloyalty. Coriander spoke of what happened when he went to the Cobalt Dragon Guardians, who had their lantern stolen by Nimrod. The bloodshed seemed much greater than what happened when Benedict plundered En-doire. Stephen spoke briefly of the quick but violent fight in the Bastion, where Nimrod's men were trying to capture Fox Manor. He paid tribute to the Guardian lives lost in the defense.

Maor and Kirin both spoke of their encounter with Nimrod in Carmel, although neither of them named the town nor Edenbridge. They spoke of Nimrod holding a hostage to deter them, though they did not identify him as Leah's father. She was grateful for the anonymity.

"Does Arthur Fox know you are the heir of Arieh?" Hansuke asked quietly.

"No. We haven't told anyone. Perhaps later." *Or never.*

Leah held her breath as August stood to speak. He would be the last one before they opened the floor to any in attendance.

"My father spoke of how personal this trial is to him." He glanced over at Arthur. "I echo that. For a long time, I hated the Oath-breakers, particularly Nimrod. He lusted after power, and in his ceaseless striving to achieve that, he trampled over many lives. He took—much from me. I blamed my brother for following him, but I transferred all my fury onto Nimrod. I looked forward to the day I would face him and end it."

She stared at him, stunned at the depth of emotion he conveyed in front of so many. A flicker of surprise seemed to cross James and Rupert's faces too.

Leah thought of Alain, but knew August would not mention him. Melina was present in the audience, and even if she wasn't, she knew that was a private, silent mark August counted against Nimrod.

"We have ended it, in a sense," August continued. "And I learned a few things along the way. Not every Oath-breaker sought after Nimrod's power. Some followed him because they did not find a home among the Guardians. Some followed him because they did not respect our leadership. I hope we can remember this, not to pardon them or excuse us, but move us to grow as Guardians. Some sought vengeance against the faerie-kind, many of whom have committed their own inexcusable crimes." He paused, looking into the throng of Oath-breakers. Leah was certain he sought his brother rather than Nimrod. "I was humbled to look in the mirror and realize I sought my own vengeance. I would never break faith with the Guardians, but there was a monster inside that threatened to overwhelm me. I am grateful to those close to me who challenged me or simply lived in a way that shed light on my life and thinking. I acknowledge my wife, Leah, especially."

So much for anonymity. Leah felt hundreds of eyes turn toward her, but she kept her gaze on August.

"Let us remember we are all prone to fall. Let us not spend so much time vilifying the demons around us that we do not defeat the ones within."

She drew in a deep breath when he finished, his words ringing in her ears. Since returning from Carmel, she had had little opportunity to speak with August. The Guardians were putting things back into order after the battle in the Bastion, preparing for the trial, and the Marshals were locked up in long conferences with other leaders, including Hansuke and the Tortoise Guardians.

August only mentioned to her in passing that he went to see Benedict, and they hardly spoke of what happened in Carmel.

As she listened to his speech, though, she realized he was not the same man who coldly said that his brother was dead to him. Whether that change had come gradually over the months of their marriage, or in the hectic last few days, she did not know.

"We will open the floor now to any of you who have a testimony or statement to share," Arthur said.

Leah was not surprised when Hiram stood up and spoke of the Tortoise scouts' captivity with Nimrod and his men. This time, he did not mention that Benedict spared his life.

Hansuke glanced over at her. "You should speak."

Startled, she looked at him. "Why?"

"You have seen this struggle from beginning to end. You have an opinion, and one that likely differs from many here. Why let those words die?"

She recalled Arieh's words. *Maybe that's why you were destined to be his family.*

Before she could change her mind, she stood. A rustle of surprise went through the rotunda. A fleeting look of disapproval flashed over Rupert's face, but oddly, that lightened her mood. He thought of her as a simple girl from Carmel who tried to insert herself into a man's world.

And he was right. She was not speaking on her authority as Arieh's heir—only a handful of people knew that now—nor her status as August Fox's wife. She was simply Leah from Carmel: the girl who sparked August's interest, in whom Melina and Maor saw strength, and who played some small part in shaping the man her husband was becoming.

"August spoke eloquently of vengeance. When Arthur told me that was what Benedict was chasing, I ached with him. He hated because he loved his mother fiercely, and she was taken away. I wish I had the honor of knowing Lila." Leah took a deep breath. She could not tell if Benedict was looking at her, but she kept her gaze anchored on August. "Benedict, I wish someone told you revenge would only empty you. It leaves you with nothing. There are other ways to mourn and honor her memory. Vengeance won't bring back the dead or turn back time. I hope you will remember that today, Guardians, as you mete out judgment. This was a personal war for you, where brothers went out from among you. I hope you will remember the best of what you stand for. So I urge you to serve justice as well as you can, for the virtue of justice and not for revenge."

When Leah took her seat again, she refused the temptation of scanning the rotunda and gauging the reaction. She only looked to a few: August's eyes crinkled with admiration and – perhaps – affection, Arthur smiled more broadly with pride, Maor put his hands together in miming applause, and Melina nodded vigorously at her with appreciation.

"Well spoken," Hansuke whispered.

Hiram turned around. "You have unconventional views." He paused. "Yet great understanding. You remind me of Lila."

Her throat tightened. "That's an honor."

Leah's limbs still trembled with adrenaline as the floor closed. No one volunteered to speak after her, so her words would be the last voice of the trial before they made a judgment. She felt acutely conscious of all the ways her speech was lacking, despite the approval from those around her.

No one moved from their seats during the Marshals' deliberation. The four men huddled together in deep discussion, while a dull hum of chatter filled the rotunda.

Hardly an hour passed when they declared the verdict ready.

A sweeping hush fell over everyone as Arthur stood. Leah scrutinized him urgently in the seconds before he spoke – did he wear the face of a man about to drop the hammer on his own son? But he was every bit the ironclad Guardian, his expression resolved and regal.

"Thank you, citizens of Cariath, for coming today and supporting our way of justice. It has been a dark time, and I am blessed to stand with such good men and women. And thank you especially to those who spoke today, for sharing your experience and insight." His gaze alighted on Leah for a moment. "I will be quick to read the verdict. Nimrod and Hound, this council sentences you to death for your crimes, which include threatening the safety of the mortal realm, the taking of innocent lives, and utter lack of remorse for your actions."

A rising tide of voices broke the stillness, and Leah could hear the shock around her.

"I thought this was expected," she whispered to Hansuke.

"Well, they singled Nimrod and Hound out. That seems unusual."

Arthur continued, disregarding the reactions. "For all other Oath-breakers here, this council sentences you to a life in chains. You will be detained for your complicity in Nimrod's effort and breaking faith with the Guardians. You are each deemed responsible for your own crimes. But we give you life in order to give you a window of opportunity: perhaps a change of heart, a change of your ways, and we will give you small means of serving the Guardians again." He paused. "This is not freedom for you, or weakness from us. You earned this punishment, but let us remember this day that Guardians value life, and we will not take it lightly."

Leah sank into her seat, stunned. Arthur's final words were drowned in the multitude of voices that filled the building – some excited, some indignant. Even though it was her first Guardian trial, Leah could understand the groundbreaking nature of the Marshals' decision. This would be a day marked in the history books for its significance. Whether future generations would judge the verdict right or wrong, only time could tell.

As people began filtering out of the rows, Hansuke remained seated beside her. He glanced over. "In your mind, was justice done?"

She grasped for the right thoughts. "I don't know," she said honestly. "Yes, I think they dealt consequences to those deserving them. But whether the sentences were right...who can say? I feel that we are all inadequate in judgment, colored by our biases and experiences, and limited in our wisdom." She looked to the floor of the rotunda. "But I believe they did the best they could, with integrity, and I admire that."

Hansuke nodded. "Who can truly judge a man's heart?"

"Who can?" she echoed quietly.

As the room emptied, Leah watched the Marshals below them. The guards had led the Oath-breakers away already, and the four Marshals were rising from their chairs. As James and Rupert walked out, August put a hand on Arthur's shoulder. His father turned, a flicker of surprise in his face, and they looked at each for a long moment.

August inclined his head, and a weary smile touched Arthur's lips.

CHAPTER 39

Carmel, Island of Japha.
Month of Healing: Fourth week, Rest-Day

A thin layer of snow covered the ground as Leah peered out the window. She felt exceptionally warm inside, with the fireplace roaring and chandelier lit. Guests were beginning to fill the empty spaces in the living room and dining areas, their colorful attire flattered by the lighting.

As much as she feigned groaning to August about hosting a lavish party the day after returning to Carmel, she appreciated the rush of people around her, even the snatches of gossip and superficial chatter she overheard. She had felt reluctant to return to Edenbridge, its long halls and spacious rooms, with its last memory of horror and bloodshed. Filling the home with familiar faces and celebration covered those scars—perhaps even began to heal them.

It was strange, though, how so many continued on with their lives, unaware of how close their world came to the brink of war.

"Welcome home, Leah!"

"Our girls are dying to hear all about Cariath!"

"The chicken is scrumptious!"

A few guests floated by, calling greetings to her as they moved from room to room. She smiled kindly and allowed them to continue on their way, content to observe more than engage in actual conversation.

She lost August in the flurry of activity, unsure if he was entertaining visitors upstairs in the ballroom. Unlike her first party at Edenbridge, Leah felt obligated to act as the lady of the house, greeting newcomers and ensuring the tables were well-stocked with food.

"Leah!"

Her heart leaped as her father, mother, and Shay entered. Forgetting propriety for a minute, she raced to meet them and threw her arms around Papa and Shay, with Mama enfolded in the middle. She felt Papa's strong arm clasp her back. Mama was mumbling something excitedly, her voice muffled against them.

Nyssa came in right behind them on Mr. Langford's arm. She broke through the fray and embraced Leah.

"I'm engaged," she whispered, her breath tickling Leah's ear.

"Oh!" Leah pulled back and gripped her arms. "Congratulations!" Her smile widened as she drank in the sight of all of them. Cloaked in heavy jackets dotted with snow, they looked unchanged. Something ached inside her chest.

The chaos of recent events and revelations had overtaken her mind, muting thoughts of her family. But seeing them in front of her — touching them — reawakened her to how much she missed them. A wave of guilt mixed with longing and joy assailed her. Beset with party preparation duties upon returning to Carmel, Leah was unable to see them privately first. But she knew August was doing this for her — to make Edenbridge feel like home again, and not a cosmic battleground.

Leah blinked back tears. "Tell me everything," she said, ushering them further inside.

"We want to hear about Cariath!" Shay protested. "It's been so long. Your stories must be more exciting."

"You tell me first," Leah insisted. "Trust me, your most boring stories will be delightful to me."

She caught Papa's eye for a moment. Of them all, he knew the most of what she had experienced — and even that was a limited knowledge. His gaze swept over the staircase and dining area and Leah felt a pang. Would he be troubled by his last memory of this place?

He seemed to read her thoughts, giving her a quiet smile to reassure her.

"We're settled into the cottage," Papa said. "It's smaller, but quaint. We have tried to make it home. You and August will visit us there tomorrow, right?"

"Of course."

"I actually quite like it," Mama admitted, though she threw a warning glance at her husband. "Don't think of gloating. It's simply less space we have to maintain and clean. And we will have more room soon, when Nyssa gets married."

"Is the date set?" Leah turned to Nyssa and Mr. Langford.

"We want you to be there," her sister exclaimed. "We will plan it for a time you can come."

Leah felt the tears threatening again. "Whenever you decide, I will make sure I attend."

"It has been all routine in Carmel lately," Mama said. "Really, the last big event was Laurel's wedding, but that was not as exciting news as your marriage. Since you sent out invitations for another party, this has been the talk of the town. August Fox is back! What is Cariath really like? How does Leah like it? How will this party compare to his first one?" She imitated different pitches of tone. "You know how it goes here."

"Yes, the rumor mill of Carmel," Leah said dryly, but with a touch of fondness.

Shay tapped her foot impatiently. "So, what *is* Cariath like?"

She had prepared for this question — and variations of it — to hit her multiple times. But she could never settle on a good response.

What was Cariath like?

Leah thought of the towering edifices in the Bastion. The way the sunset scraped the top of the Cariath Mountains each evening, its last rays striking across the sky like a whip. She thought of August and Arthur. They hosted their own lavish feasts at Fox Manor, an ancient place haunted with both grief and joy. She thought of the White Tiger Guardians – their nobility, their rigidity, their honor and their flaws. She thought of her friends – Maor, Kirin, Stephen, Melina, Jenifer – and the loss of those she never knew, but whose presence lived on in others – Lila, Alain.

Overwhelmed, she pulled out of her thoughts, and realized they were still waiting in expectant silence.

"Why don't you come visit me there?"

Shay's eyes grew round, and excitement colored Nyssa's features. Her father and mother looked at each other for a moment, before they both nodded.

"We haven't been on a trip in a long time," Mama said. "I am terribly curious to see it."

"I can't do it justice by explaining, so you might as well come." Leah smiled. "I like it there, though. It feels like home. At least, as much as home can be without all of you."

Papa touched her arm. "We won't be jealous." A twinkle entered his eye.

"And what's it like, being married to August Fox?" Nyssa queried.

"Being married to August is – an adventure."

"You need to tell us stories!" Shay pressed.

Leah had led them into the dining area, where other guests were crowding around the spread of food. Baked chicken, ham, roasted vegetables, potatoes and desserts covered the long cherrywood table. *It is almost on par with the Old Fox's feasts,* she thought.

"Oh, I have plenty of stories to tell you." Leah laughed as she spoke. "We'll be home for at least a week. How much time do you have?"

She caught sight of August entering the room with Mr. Whitefield, Laurel's husband. Mama waved them over and they exchanged avid greetings all around. August stood behind Leah, placing his hands on her shoulders. Nyssa raised her eyebrow at Leah, who flushed slightly.

"Thank you for taking care of our daughter," Papa murmured, and Leah knew that only August would understand the full substance of his meaning.

Leah felt a light squeeze on her shoulders. "She takes care of me, too."

"I invited them to Cariath sometime." Leah turned to look at August. "What do you think?"

"My father was insisting I invite you all. We would love to host you anytime."

Mrs. Edwards put her hands together. "Lovely. Leah thinks highly of

Cariath, which I tell you, is no easy achievement. I hope she hasn't proved too much for you to handle, August." She cast her gaze between the couple.

Leah crossed her arms. "Mama—"

"Oh, she is a handful." She could hear the grin in August's voice before his usual solemnity set in. "In truth, she is far better than I deserve. Thank you for trusting her to me."

Mama smiled indulgently and Nyssa winked at Leah.

"Please, help yourselves and eat," August said, interrupting the moment. He gestured at the line of dishes. "You must be hungry." He glanced at Leah. "Someone is looking for you in the ballroom."

"Oh!" Leah left her family with large plates, and they fell into mingling with others. She followed August upstairs.

"Who is it?"

A small smile tugged at his lips. "You shall see."

As soon as she reached the top step, Jessie nearly bowled her over. "Leah!" The two women embraced tightly and August moved aside.

"Jessie, I never saw you enter!" Leah exclaimed. She pulled back to look at her friend. Jessie's cheeks were ruddy—probably from exuberant dancing—and she wore an elegant emerald dress. "You look amazing."

"Me? Nah," she protested. Her eyes searched Leah's face. "You look wonderful, though."

"You don't need to be polite with me," Leah muttered.

She had worn a silky maroon dress that emphasized her dark eyes, and while she received compliments throughout the evening, she knew she fell below the mark of beauty in Carmel. Leah was never stunning, but neither was she plain—yet the last few months had roughened her. Her hands and feet bore blisters, her skin was no longer soft and supple, and her frame was bonier than before.

Jessie waved her hand. "I don't mean you look like you've been living inside a beauty parlor. But you look like you've *lived*." Her eyes glowed. "You look like you've been on the inside of a great story."

Leah squeezed her friend's arm, reminded of how much she appreciated Jessie's view of the world.

"Is that your way of saying I look awful?" She feigned indignation.

"Who cares how you look? You already snatched the best-looking gentleman around." Jessie shot a look at August, who was now out of earshot.

"You're insufferable."

"I expect you to tell me everything." She fixed her with a stern gaze. "How long are you staying?"

"A week. And I will. Actually, I will do something even better." Leah paused for effect. "Come visit me in Cariath? You can come with my family when they go."

Jessie's mouth dropped open. "Yes. Of course. A thousand times." She smirked. "Are there any potential suitors there, or did you take the best one?"

"I took the best one, but I might be able to find you a satisfactory gentleman." Leah thought of Maor and suppressed a grin.

"You have someone in mind!"

"Come visit me and find out."

Before Jessie could press her further, August reappeared beside them. "Do you two want to dance?" He looked at Jessie. "The gentlemen far outnumber the ladies inside right now."

"Happy to oblige," she returned. "I'll go choose one, and leave you and your beloved alone."

Leah glared at her, but Jessie was already skipping off to the ballroom.

August met her eyes and smiled, a light flush on his face. "May I have this dance?" He extended his hand.

Feeling shy all of a sudden, she took it wordlessly. The fluttering, giddy spell in her stomach, absent for so long, rose inside her. For a moment, she tasted the fairytale inside this strange story. August Fox was not the man she had dreamed of. Romance was not the fiery passion she once imagined, but a slow burn, leaving an irrevocable mark in her soul. He was hers, and she, his. Somewhere between the altar and Cariath and Endoire, their hearts had twined together.

His fingers closed around hers and he led her inside the ballroom. A familiar waltz began playing, and August guided her onto the floor, moving past other couples.

"Is this piece—"

"The one we first danced to, yes," August supplied. "Good ear."

Leah laughed, her self-consciousness vanishing. "That was a disaster."

He raised an eyebrow. "I didn't think so." He sent her into a gentle spin before pulling her back.

They danced in silence for a while, and Leah could not help but notice that he held her closer, his grip more sure, yet also tender. As the music slowed and they simply swayed in place, she closed her eyes and leaned her forehead against his chest.

August's chin rested on top of her head. "Are you all right?" he asked quietly.

"I'm still not sure some days if everything was a dream, starting with you coming to Carmel."

Their last few days in Cariath were filled with feasts, sending off the Tortoise Guardians and Hansuke, who invited them to visit the Dammim. Even some government delegates from Capitola attended the festivities, hinting at King Amir's desire for stronger ties between the crown and the Guardians. They were joyous affairs, though the shadow of the Oathbreakers still hung over the Bastion.

With Arthur's insistence, August and Leah immediately followed that with plans to return to Carmel, see her family, and spend some quiet time away from the bustle of the Guardians.

In the midst of these events, they spoke more of inconsequential things, like what dishes to prepare for the party and who to invite. These were the easy topics, resting above a deep and difficult well of other subjects — the consequences of the trial, Benedict, the Oath-breakers, Arieh.

But Leah felt at peace. She knew they would broach these conversations in time, when August was ready, and when she was ready.

"Do you wish it was? A dream," he clarified.

"No." Unlike a multitude of other questions, this one had an easy answer. "If it was, I wouldn't have you."

His hands were warm against her back. "You don't think I'm more trouble than I'm worth?" August joked weakly, and she heard the catch in his voice.

Leah lifted her head to look at him. "I'll take your troubles if you'll take mine."

His arms tightened around her. "Always."

As they danced, Leah's gaze skimmed the edges of the ballroom. She thought she saw a shadow flicker on the far wall — a tall man, a lone figure, with his cloak billowing behind him. He vanished as swiftly as he appeared.

It might have been no more than a trick of the light, but Leah lifted her hand from August's shoulder in a brief wave of acknowledgment.

"Do you think it was me?" Leah asked, after a moment. "In Kirin's dream of you?"

She had not spoken of it to August yet. In the aftermath of the battle with the Oath-breakers, it felt almost irrelevant. She was the heir of Arieh. What woman would better fit his vision?

August stepped back slightly so he could meet her eyes. "I didn't marry you because of that, you know."

"That's what Kirin said." She paused. "And I know that."

"I wasn't sure until Hansuke revealed who you were. When he did — well, I don't know why I didn't see it all along."

"Maybe because I was nobody," she returned dryly.

"That I never believed. No, when I first met you, I couldn't know. You could say I gambled on it. But I wanted it to be you."

Leah wondered if she heard a hint of bashfulness in his usually confident voice.

"You took a leap of faith," she corrected.

"One of my best decisions."

A smile crept across her face. "Someone asked me what it's like to be married to August Fox. I wonder," she mused, "what it *will* be like, without war, desperate missions, prisons..."

"You'll find out, I hope." He chuckled, before growing serious again. "I pray that I don't disappoint you."

"You won't." Leah paused, a mischievous twinkle in her eye. "Love is blind, right?"

In retaliation, August dropped her in a surprise dip on the last long note of the waltz. Leah bit back a squeal. She swatted at him as he pulled her upright, joining her laughter to his.

END

About the Author

Dana Li is a software product manager by day, and a novelist by night. She holds an MS in management science and engineering from Stanford University and a BS in computer science from USC, but she's always been better at writing stories than code. Her writing misadventures began with a dozen now-deleted Star Wars fanfiction tales. She loves good fantasy/sci-fi, classy cuisines, and roller coasters (but not all at once). Dana currently lives in the San Francisco Bay Area, and *The Vermilion Riddle* is her first novel.

Follow Dana and find out more about her work at: *www.penandfire.com*.